DRAKON

A NOVEL

A.M. TUOMALA

CANDLEMARK & GLEAM
2016

First edition published 2016

Copyright @ 2016 by A. M. Tuomala

All rights reserved.
Except as permitted under the U.S. Copyright act of 1976,
no part of this book may be reproduced, distributed or transmitted
in any form or by any means, or stored in a database or retrieval system,
without the prior written permission of the editor and publisher.

Please respect the authors' rights: don't pirate.

This is a work of fiction. Names, characters, places and incidents either
are the product of the author's imagination or are used fictitiously.
Any resemblance to actual events, locales or persons,
living or dead, is entirely coincidental.

For information, please address
Candlemark & Gleam LLC,
38 Rice Street #2, Cambridge, MA 02140
eloi@candlemarkandgleam.com

Library of Congress Cataloguing-in-Publication Data
In Progress

ISBN: 978-1-936460-69-4
eISBN: 978-1-936460-41-0

Cover art by Alan Caum
Glyph design by A. M. Tuomala

Composition by Athena Andreadis
Typeface: Crimson Text
Header font: Typo Gothic HPLHS
Drop caps: Grimswade

Editors: Athena Andreadis, Kate Sullivan,
and AnnaLinden Weller

Proofreader: Christopher Pipinou

www.candlemarkandgleam.com

For Kylee, who gave me the dream;
for Pip, who showed me the Intrepid;
and for Waverly, who never let me falter.

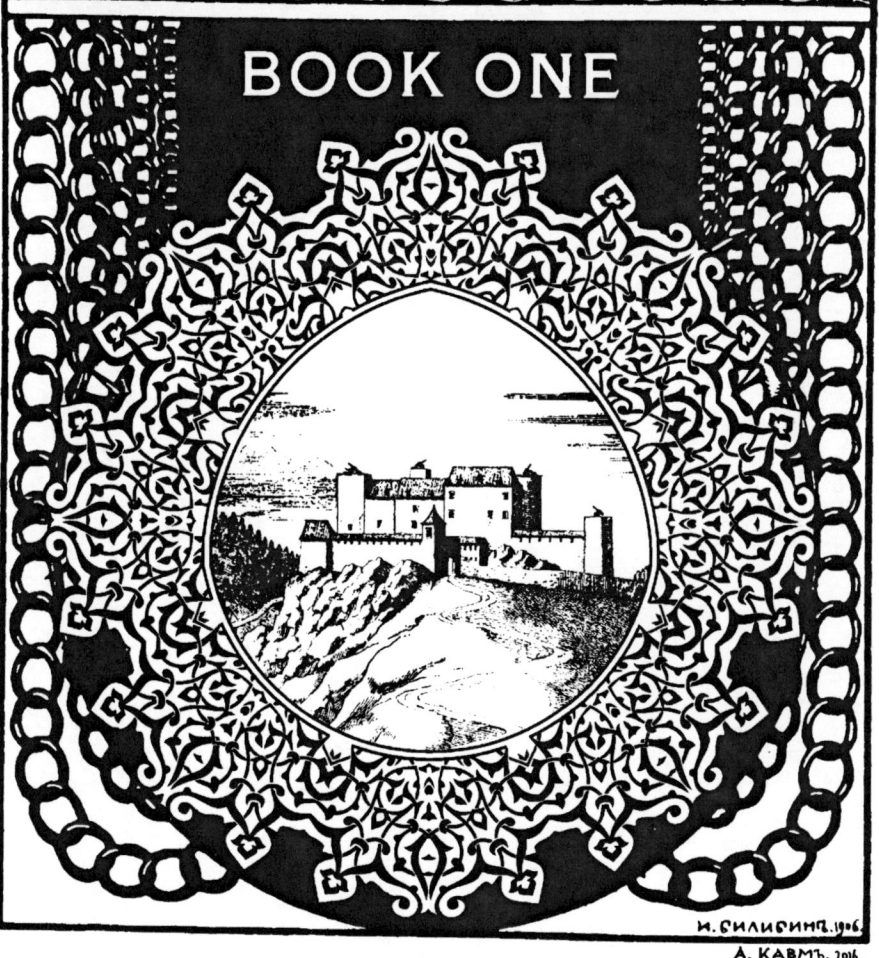

DRAKON

BOOK ONE

PROLOGUE

By noon, the cold had grown so deep that Elizaveta was forced to give up her spyglass. The heat of her body was fogging up the eyepiece, and no amount of wiping could get it to stay clear. Not that it would do much good in any case, since the clouds lay so thickly across the sky that she couldn't find the sun through them, but it wasn't the Tarasov way to let incapacity stand in the way of work. Her father had manned the gunnery turrets whilst drunk, enraged, and plagued with the gout, and he'd take it very poorly if Liza let a bit of a chill stand in her way.

The cloudy days were the worst, although the clear days were colder. On a truly clear day, with her spyglass, Liza could see all the way to Turkey. Even on a hazy day, she could still make out the sinuous shapes of the dragons against the sky.

She took a swig of vodka—poor stuff, but it warmed her belly—and wiped the back of her mouth with a gloved hand. "The clouds are too thick," she muttered, passing her father the bottle. "If there were a dozen up there, we'd have no way of knowing it."

"They can't climb that high. Too much meat on them."

"These clouds are low, though," insisted Liza. "You could graze them with a shot, and you can bet the dragons know to hide in clouds like these. Regular volleys, that's the only way of keeping the rails safe when the clouds are low."

"If it'll please you, make a pass with the gun. But you won't bring anything down, and then what? The whole town in a stir, just because you wanted to shoot something." And then Nastya would refuse them credit at the tavern and Kostya would charge them more for ammunition, and no one reputable would gamble or drink with them. Liza knew this just as well as her father did.

Vladimir Petrovich offered her a gap-toothed smile. It resembled nothing so much as an old battlement devastated by centuries of cannonades. It was the kind of smile that made children run for cover and dogs bark at him in the street. "Keep an eye on the rails, not the sky. The Moscow train will have our guests…and their rent."

"You could've asked more for billeting them and they wouldn't have said a thing against it. They have no idea what's reasonable rent in Russia, and I'd bet you my best pocketwatch they don't speak enough Russian to ask. You might've got double—"

"Their lieutenant writes good Russian, whether he can speak it or not," said Vladimir coolly, "and if he can't, Nastya knows enough French to take their money. Then what? She'd have their rent, and we'd have nothing but their strutting and prying. This vodka is swill." He didn't offer the bottle back, instead finishing it himself and then taking out his pipe. As he was filling it with tobacco, he remarked, "When you're my age, Liza, you'll be a better gambler. Today, though, you'll give me your best pocketwatch."

Vladimir struck a match and lit his pipe, then cast the match over the wall and into the courtyard below. Sweet-scented smoke rose from the bowl, the smell almost sharp on the chill air. To the east, the last leaves on the cherry trees and the plums clattered in a sudden, brisk wind. Liza pulled her muffler over her nose and let her breath warm her wind-chapped skin.

To the west, a smudge of smoke on the horizon signaled the arrival of the Moscow train.

Under her woolen muffler, Liza grimaced. Their guests were coming, and she wouldn't bother to conceal that they weren't welcome east of the Volga.

CHAPTER ONE

Innokentiy Vladimirovich Tarasov was called Kesha by his intimates, of whom he had very few. He lived with his brother in the spare rooms of a respectable widow, who lodged scholars at discounted rates out of a sincere approbation for classical education. She imagined herself a patron of St. Petersburg's intellectuals, a hostess of *salons* in the style of Madame de Staël (notwithstanding that the *salon* had dropped from fashion more than half a century ago). Among her regular guests were clerks and journalists, lawyers and surgeons; divinity students could be heard discoursing loudly upon the question of how sanctity manifested in the flesh, while fresh-faced radicals demanded that the church's traditional territories be remanded to the Tsar and redistributed among former serfs.

Her guests never spoke of dragons, or of gunnery turrets, or of gambling debts. They spoke of the Turks as abstractions, safely squared away behind a boundary line on a map. Kesha found such gatherings unfailingly congenial.

It was at one such gathering, while Kesha was listening with half an ear to a disquisition upon Tasso, that a stranger in a soldier's uniform tapped him by the shoulder and gestured him step aside. He found the prospect of a soldier's conversation even less enticing than the young wit's encomiums on *La Gerusalemme liberata*. "I'm engaged," he said, but as he tried to turn back to the conversation, the soldier held him fast.

"You're Tarasov, aren't you?" he asked. His accent was faintly but distinctly Polish. "You have their look. I have a letter for a Tarasov." He withdrew a rumpled letter from the breast of his uniform.

Kesha put aside teacup and saucer to take the folded paper. *To Pyotr Vladimirovich Tarasov*, read the outside face, and although it had been nearly six years since he had seen that handwriting, there was no mistaking the queer, left-handed slant of each upright.

Interesting.

"Yes, I'm Tarasov," he answered. "Thank you, Monsieur…"

"Jaworski. Captain Jaworski. I'll come at eight tomorrow for your answer," replied Jaworski with a cramped bow. As the stranger threaded through the gathered scholars, Kesha excused himself from the discussion of Tasso, pleading a sudden headache. Once he had burst free of the close gathering and stolen up the narrow back stairs to his room, he turned up the gaslamp by his writing desk and sat to examine his purloined correspondence.

Kesha worked free the string that bound the letter closed, carefully preserving the knots. The letter itself was almost insultingly brief, although his sister had clearly attempted to pad it with civilities.

Dearest Petya, (the letter began)

I hope you are well in St. Petersburg and are civil to your landlady, who is—you say—a good sort and deserving of civil treatment from a boy of your family and education. Things continue well at home, with six dragons redeemed since your last visit. Father's gout has been pretty severe, but he says, May God damn him if gout cripples him before a battle does.

I am writing because it is urgent that you return home at once, and I have entrusted our messenger, who is a reliable man, with funds sufficient for your ticket. We expect to be beset soon with the English, who have designs on our holdings, and if we are to make a fair showing, we must present them with the full strength of the Tarasov family, which they will have no cause to criticize. If you will not come, then I swear by my faith, you will no longer be my brother or my father's son.

Earnestly,
Elizaveta Vladimirovna Tarasova.

For a long moment, while the sounds of the salon filtered up through the floorboards, Kesha sat unmoving. His brother's fate lay in his hands. Even if Kesha had been disowned, Petya still had some credit with the family, and he might hope to inherit not only the name but also their goods and perhaps even the Tarasov estate—such as it was. To deny him the letter, or to counterfeit a response, would sever for good the tenuous ties that still bound Petya to father and sister, and thus bind him all the more firmly to Kesha and St. Petersburg.

The green light of the gaslamp shone soft upon the paper. Beneath it lay one of Petya's sketches for a flying machine, all intricately detailed gears and wheels and bolts. Petya was doing well in his studies, and in a year, he might easily gain a recommendation to whatever industry he cared to enter. It would be a kindness, truly, to keep Petya here, with his books and his playing-cards and his sketches of wheels. To return him to the borderlands, on so slight a pretext as the arrival of the English, would do irreparable harm to his career.

The moment passed.

Kesha folded the paper again, carefully sliding the string over the corners and rearranging it until it lay perfectly about the parcel. He imagined Petya's blunt fingers (no doubt stained with ink or grease) upon the paper. His own fingers were long, thick-knuckled, each nail bitten to the quick. Hardly any resemblance. They mightn't even be related.

Messenger will return at eight for reply, he scrawled neatly beneath the salutation. He blew on the ink to dry it, then placed the letter on Petya's pillow before he could change his mind.

With his heart pounding, Kesha turned out the lamp and undressed for bed by moonlight.

CHAPTER TWO

"Kesha."

Kesha muttered something unintelligible and turned over.

"*Kesha.*" This time, Petya caught hold of his shoulder and shook him lightly. At once Kesha's hand closed over his wrist, vise-tight and hot from the bedclothes. His eyes were wide and unseeing, pale as a dead man's in the moonlight. "It's only me!" said Petya, trying to unclamp his brother's hand. "It's only me."

Slowly, Kesha blinked. When his eyes opened again, he seemed to recognize Petya's face, and at length he released the wrist. "Petya," he said, and Petya nodded. "Have you *any* idea what time it is?"

"Half past one," ventured Petya, because if Kesha was being rhetorical then it wouldn't make matters worse to answer him, and if he was sincerely asking, it might make matters a good deal better. "We finished very late. Misha asked me to give you his—"

"I don't give a damn about his regards," said Kesha, levering himself out of the bed and groping for his matches. There came a scent of sulfur and a flare of light, and then the glow of the candle cast Kesha into shadow. "I suppose you've found your letter and want to speak with me about it, or else you wouldn't have shaken me awake at half past one in the morning. Well?"

On his own side of the bed, Petya drew up his legs to sit tailor-fashion, his thumbs fiddling with the string from the letter. Now, with his brother awake and irate, his red hair catching the candlelight like a saint's halo, it seemed utterly foolish to ask his advice or his blessing. Nonetheless, now that he had begun, Petya felt compelled to press on.

He turned to light the candle on his own side of the bed; it felt eerie to speak with Kesha without being able to read his face. "It's a letter from Liza, but I'm sure you've guessed that already," he began while his back was still turned. The match wouldn't strike. "She—well. She wants me to come home."

"And why does she want that?" asked Kesha.

"She says they're—oh, devil take this match!" His face heating, Petya took a second match and struck it neatly, lighting his candle at last. He shook the match out and set it in the chipped saucer that caught his candlewax, and since he could delay no longer, he turned to meet Kesha's eyes. "She says that the English are coming to drive her and Father out, and she wants to…"

With Kesha's eyes on his, Petya could not help being conscious of the import of what Liza wanted. It seemed suddenly cruel to him to beg his blessing, when Kesha would receive no benedictions in return.

"To bring the family back together," supplied Kesha, and his eyes were surprisingly gentle. "Of course."

"I *want* to stay. I love you, and I love my studies. I'd stay if I could—"

"But you're a Tarasov, and you'll never stop owing your life to your father."

Petya reached across the bed to press Kesha's hand. "He's your father, too, however angry he is with you. I know you both regret what happened."

Kesha's eyes flashed. His lips pressed tightly together, and he drew his hand away with more than usual violence. "I regret *nothing*," he said, low and dangerous as a serpent-charmer. "What I did, I did from necessity—a necessity to which he forced me. If he wants to see peace between us, let him send a letter calling me home. Let Liza call me her dearest—"

A cold sensation stole over Petya's limbs. He felt light-headed, as though he'd drunk too much wine, although he'd only taken tea at the *salon*. "You read my letter," he whispered, and somehow that whisper silenced Kesha's tirade. "You read my letter, and then you asked me why she wanted me home, but you already *knew*. Name of God, Kesha, sometimes I *understand* why Father won't speak with you!"

He realized that he was shouting only because his throat felt raw, and his hands were bunched into fists in his lap. Kesha looked as stricken as if Petya had clouted him across the face.

"We...we shouldn't speak of things like this at half past one," said Petya, when the silence had grown unbearable. "You read my letter. What of it? A man may read his brother's letters. I owe you so much—"

"You owe me no more than you owe him, Petya," answered Kesha. "What I give you, I give you because I love you. I'd be a miser indeed if I only gave away what I expected to see returned. I don't expect my gifts to be returned with interest, as our father does." He looked poised to take Petya's hand, his fingers twitching upon his knee.

The anxious anticipation grew unbearable, and at length Petya reached for his hand to still it. Kesha favored him with an ironic smile at the gesture, telling him with an air of feigned solemnity, "My metaphors are terrible after midnight. You really shouldn't surprise me when I'm not at my best."

"I won't. I swear."

"On your faith?"

"On my faith," answered Petya warmly.

They sat in silence then, listening to the settling of the house and the whistle of wind through the chinks in their window. Petya had tried to seal the gaps more than once, first with wax and then with melted lead, but the disaster of the second attempt had made their landlady bar them from further experimentation with her fixtures. The room grew colder than was truly comfortable in winter, but they'd secured a promise of curtains before the onset of the White Nights.

"You should go," said Kesha, drawing Petya from his reverie. "You didn't wake me for my advice. You wanted my blessing, so I'm giving you my blessing."

"I was just thinking…" He hesitated, unsure of whether to unburden his heart—or indeed, of why it felt burdened at all. "I was thinking of how much at home I've felt here. Of how I set the windowsill on fire—"

Kesha burst out laughing, his laughter ringing rich and loud against the walls. Over their heads, one of the servants threw something heavy at the floor to shut them up, and the sound only made him laugh harder. "My God," he said, when he could catch his breath long enough to speak at all. "My *God*, when you set the windowsill on fire—"

"Ssh," Petya said, elbowing him hard in the ribs. "You'll wake Madame."

"If *you* haven't roused her with your shouting," retorted Kesha. At length, he composed himself. "Will you go?"

"I'll go," answered Petya.

"Very well. Then I'll go back to sleep so that I can help you pack and see you off in the morning." With that, Kesha shifted over to his own side of the bed, blew out his candle, and drew his bolster over his head. Even beneath it, though, his expression was so grim and determined that Petya could scarcely stifle a laugh.

Kesha would find his peaceful repose if he had to hunt it down with a harpoon. He was, far more than Petya, temperamentally suited to their family business. If he hadn't been so determined to study in the city, then perhaps—

—well. There was no sense in *perhaps* or *might have been*. Petya blew out his candle and drew the bedclothes over himself, suppressing a hiss at the shock of the cold fabric on his warm skin. Although Kesha deplored the habit and would complain in the morning that his blankets had been stolen, Petya wrestled enough of the blankets free to wrap himself up like a well-swaddled infant.

This place felt like home. He knew the sound of his brother's breathing at night and the creak of the boards and the way the wind sounded in the cracks around the windowpanes.

He would miss it.

CHAPTER THREE

If Liza had entertained even the faintest hope that the English would be a help rather than a hindrance, she would have been disappointed. Even if they could be trained—and she admitted that most of them likely could—she would first have to find a language to train them in. Most spoke no Russian at all, and responded only haltingly to her broken schoolgirl French. These English might be some help if the Turks did cross the border in spring (as everyone suspected they would), but until then, they were painfully unprepared for dragons. Some of the enlisted men had never seen combat, and even those who had served in India or China had never fought nor even *seen* a dragon. Only one, a twitchy sort with thin whiskers and passable Russian, had caught a glimpse of a distant flight of dragons while on the way to a posting in Afghanistan. The English brought no weapons more substantial than their rifles, and when they had given a demonstration in the courtyard of the fortress, the Tarasovs had laughed outright.

Even Lieutenant Wainwright, whose Russian was every bit as good as her father had predicted, had pretended not to comprehend her when she'd said that his rifle would only tickle a dragon's belly.

"They should've been sent to guard the Nizhny rail line instead of ours," she groused to Osip Moiseyevich, an old gunner with fewer teeth than fingers. "Dragons never make it as far as the northern line. They might've been some use there. But instead we'll have Englishmen underfoot until Pascha."

"It's an insult," he agreed. "A plain insult, to you and to me. It used to mean something to fight a dragon, to protect the rails in your lord's name. Like being a kind of bogatyr. But now every fortress down the line is full of Englishmen looking to play knights-errant."

Had these offenses not been sufficient to set Liza's heart against the intruders, the English had been immovable as a glacier on the matter of board. "The crown has provided funds sufficient for our quartering," said Wainwright. Every Russian consonant was crisp. "If you think we came here to be extorted—"

"You came here against our wishes, with a pack of untrained pups and a bundle of pop-guns," Vladimir had answered, implacable as a cliff-face, while Liza had drawn herself up behind him and folded her arms over her breasts. She knew that she was tall and broad-shouldered, and even in a cincher and her finest evening gown, she easily outstripped half the soldiers in the hall. To his credit, the lieutenant didn't stand down—but Liza would credit him with nothing, and certainly not with bravery.

"We came on the order of Tsar Alexander II and Her Majesty Queen Victoria," Wainwright had said sharply. "If you want us to pay a hundred kopecks a week for board, sue the Tsar for it yourself."

"If you want me to sue for your board," spat Liza, "go ahead and starve to death."

By sunrise, the antipathy between the Tarasovs and their guests was undiminished. When the errand boy returned from fetching the mail, he informed Liza that Lieutenant Wainwright had been to the telegraph office and sent a message to Moscow, from whence it would no doubt be sent to St. Petersburg. Whether the telegram contained a complaint at the soldiers' ill treatment or a plea for board-money from Britain's precious queen, neither the errand-boy nor the telegraph master would say.

"The English aren't any more welcome to me than to you, but at least I have the sense to be civil in their presence," he told Liza, when she stormed into the office to inquire and flung her handbag down upon the counter. The man had been a postmaster for a decade before the telegraph had followed the railway lines to the borderlands; he had a narrow, leathery face pursed with wrinkles, and his every glance made Liza feel like a child. He regarded her handbag with a tranquil disinterest that made her long to strike him. "You're playing with fire, Elizaveta Vladimirovna."

"I'll play with as much fire as I damn well please," she snapped, then gathered up her bag again and turned on her heel. The door made a satisfying crash as she slammed it behind her.

A drink might have eased the knot of ire in her gut, but Nastya wouldn't sell her a drink at this hour, no matter how Liza flattered and tried to bribe her, and so she was forced to stop at old Olya's to buy another bottle of swill. If Petya were home, he'd have brewed a winter's worth of kvass, so effervescent it would tickle her nose. Hardly any alcohol in kvass, but at least it would have been cold and wet. The cook couldn't brew anything but plum wine and brandy, and Liza detested brandy.

Perhaps she'd offer the brandy casks to the English as a gesture of peace. Or perhaps she had no interest in peaceful gestures. The Tarasovs hadn't *asked* the English to come, and Liza didn't believe for a moment that the Tsar had, either. No, the English had been invited because if they couldn't come as guests, they would have come a few months later as invaders.

"At least we're getting a new railway out of it," old Olya said as Liza counted kopecks into her hand. "And they say the Tsar himself will come through on a tour, when it's finished! What do you think of that, eh? I remember when the rails first came to Yureyevsk, in your grandfather's day. Just think, soon we'll be able to take the train all the way to Bratsk!"

"I'd be happier if the English took the train all the way to Bratsk," said Liza. She tucked her bottle into her handbag and strode out of Olya's cottage, crossing the autumn-brown grass between the town and the fortress. Her bootheels stuck in the wet earth. It was warmer than it had been yesterday, but that did little to improve her mood.

She returned home no less irate than she'd been when she left, entering the fortress through the servants' door and descending at once into the dim halls of the keep.

The first Tarasov estate had been a palace, she had been told, with classical pillars and intricate moldings, crystal chandeliers and even a ballroom—but when the dragons had left it in ruins, the Tarasovs had gone to ground like badgers. Only the fortress towers rose above the cold earth, each one tipped with a heavy Gatling gun. Liza had grown up in rooms without windows, dreaming of watchtowers and gunnery turrets.

Her errands complete, Liza locked herself in her rooms and began to remove her day dress. It had been easier when she'd had a maid. She undid each delicate bone button with impatient fingers, then unlaced the cincher with a sigh of relief. Even the forgivingly light boning of the cincher had left deep grooves in her skin. In place of the dress, she donned a pair of hard-wearing wool trousers and boots with broad heels, a fur cap with moth-eaten lining. *Little Vladimirovich*, her father called her when she wore trousers and her uncle's old uniform coat. *My oldest son.*

She was just buttoning her coat closed when the alarm bells began to toll.

Liza sprang to the doorway at once, coat half-undone, door swinging open behind her; there was a hatch at the end of her hallway, and she unscrewed it and surged up the ladder. She had no gloves—the metal of each rung was cold and biting beneath her bare hands—but she gritted her teeth against the shock and flung herself against the upper hatch until it gave way. In the chill air, the alarm bell was still tolling, and from the apertures of the tower, she could see the villagers scattering for shelter.

Only a narrow iron ladder separated her from the great Gatling gun at the top of the tower, and she relished the way her hobnailed boots rang on each foothold. In moments, she was swinging into the gunner's chair, feeling more than hearing the well-oiled gears of the gun shifting beneath her. Her left hand gripped the attitude rotor. Her right hand closed on the trigger.

The gun was primed and ready. The Tarasov guns were always ready.

Come on, she thought, scanning the cloudless blue sky for that familiar flash of sun on scales, of mane and tail streaming in the swift-moving air. From a distance, dragons seemed slow and stately as dirigibles, their sinuous curves shifting with the wind like rippling banners.

Up close, dragons moved like a hailstorm sweeping down in the autumn.

Come on, you bastard. I'm ready.

From the east, there came an explosion that made her wheel wildly as the far wall buckled—and that was all the warning she had before the dragon was upon them.

It surged up and over the canted wall of the keep, screaming like all the fiends of Hell—its roar drowned out the cries from the other towers and the tolling of the alarm bell. Swift as thought, Liza whirled right, feeling the gun emplacement turning beneath her as she raised the massive barrels of her gun to track the dragon across the sky. Her right hand clamped down on the trigger, firing off a burst that made the whole tower vibrate. The magazine would run out in moments at this rate, and there wasn't a servant to reload her—there wasn't a single bloody person in the tower besides Liza, they were so *damnably* understaffed, and the next explosive would fall to the rails—

She adjusted her grip on the cold metal of the rotor. *Very well*, she told herself. Her eyes narrowed against the glare of sun on scales, against the way the dragon's scream made the very air vibrate. *Then I can't let myself miss.*

The gears spun madly beneath her as the rotor turned, and her next burst tore the dragon's belly open. It fell to earth like a leaf drifting down, spilling viscera and blood over the courtyard.

Liza let out a slow breath. Her heart was hammering. Her skin was cold-pricked, goose-pimpled. She couldn't feel her fingertips.

Slowly, she rose from the gunner's chair and surveyed the sky around her, shielding her eyes against the sun. Not another dragon in sight. Not typical, for the Turks to send only one where they could send four or five. Probably intended to be a reconnaissance mission, then. No other reason to send a dragon to certain slaughter.

She lowered herself down the iron ladder, hand over hand, then slid through the upper hatchway and into the relatively warmer air below. The lower hatch was closed beneath her, which was some relief; the men knew better than to leave the keep unsecured. She worked the heavy screw free with numb hands, then dropped into the hallway and closed the hatch behind her.

Her room, Liza noted, had *not* been locked up. If the English had sneaked into it during the confusion, then she would tear out their throats with her teeth.

Her dressing table appeared untouched, and her papers undisturbed. The bedclothes were in some disarray, but it was only to be expected at this hour. Their two servants had better things to do than make the beds, and Liza knew very well that she thrashed in her sleep. Her comfortable leather gloves lay just where she'd left them, across the chest that held her mother's wedding gown and her grandmother's jewelry. She picked up the gloves and slipped them on, flexing her hands until the joints ached.

If the English had crept in secretly, she'd have no way of knowing it, and so she drew no comfort from having found no overt evidence of invasion. As she left her room to investigate the dragon's corpse, Liza was sure to lock the door behind her.

Even for a dragon, this specimen was massive. Ancient; Liza would stake her last ruble on it. Its scales were bright as mirrors in the light of the noonday sun, its fur soft and light as gossamer. Its guts lay like slick ropes over the twisted grasses and cobblestones. A few of the English had been liberally spattered with dragon's blood, and it still smoked faintly in the chill air.

"We're lucky the damned thing didn't explode," muttered Vladimir Tarasov, nudging the dragon's muzzle with his foot. "They're known to do that," he said over his shoulder, carelessly drawing Lieutenant Wainwright in.

"To explode?"

"The gas in their bellies catches fire and explodes," answered Vladimir, with a cool tranquility that even Liza found compelling. She knew as well as he did that they hadn't any idea why dragons sometimes exploded when they were shot. For all they knew, the damned beasts ate explosives and then got themselves shot to spite the Russians.

"I've got a man who'd like to study its anatomy," Wainwright said eventually. "May we dissect it?"

"Do what you like with the corpse," said Liza. "Eat it, if you're still scraping for board. So long as the head gets to Moscow, the rest isn't our concern."

Wainwright looked up at her then with such an expression of consternation that she couldn't help laughing at him—but later, she would wonder what had dumbfounded him so: her trousers, or her shooting, or her utter lack of curiosity.

CHAPTER FOUR

When he was a boy, Kesha had occasionally chased trains along the tracks, waving madly at the conductors on their way west to Moscow or east to distant mining towns. He'd felt a kind of childish gratification when the conductor let the train whistle screech over the plains and low hills, imagining that the whistle blew for him and not to notify one of the fortresses along the rail line that a cargo was coming through.

As Petya's train pulled away from the Nicholaevsky railway station, Kesha watched it go and tried not to imagine that its going meant anything for him. "So much for that," he said to no one in particular, then turned and shouldered his way through the vaulted hall to the streets. There, he tightened his scarf about his throat and pulled a fold of thick wool over his mouth and nose. A few stray fibers caught in his teeth, squeaking unpleasantly against the enamel, and he grimaced at it.

It was surely his grimace that made others regard him with such wariness as they passed him in the streets, and nothing more. When he'd walked with Petya to the station, he'd seen no suspicious frowns or hollow-eyed, prey-cautious glares. Petya had been telling some story or other about an adulteress and a venal young minister, and the whole of St. Petersburg had seemed to laugh when he'd laughed. If Kesha were laughing, the people would surely have joined him.

It was his own fault that he was unhappy, and no one else's. He'd do well to remember it, when he longed to curse Petya for leaving and Liza for asking him to leave. His own fault, and his responsibility.

Kesha found that his mouth was watering, for he'd missed breakfast in order to help Petya pack his trunk. He could give in to the petty, self-lacerating urge to eat alone, or even to starve himself to punish his foolishness, and he weighed these options practically and morally as he walked. He chided himself with Burke's reflections on the sublime, since he had no living interlocutor to recall him to his senses—*such prefigurations of death*, he told himself, *"are delightful when we have an idea of pain and danger, without being actually in such circumstances."* It might give him a perverse pleasure to play the martyr for a few hours, but he had survived a separation from Petya before, and he would survive it again. It served no purpose to starve himself of food or company.

For this reason, Kesha found himself sharing porridge and coffee with Mikhail Dmitrievich Orlov, who was quite content to tender his regards in person and at a reasonable hour. "You oughtn't to have left the *salon* so early," said Misha serenely as he poured himself another cup. "We had quite a good conversation about translation after you left. I know you've a particular mania for the German and English writers, and we might've picked over your brain for an answer to the most difficult question."

"Which is?"

"Whether the language carries with it not only the sense, but also the spirit of the meaning—or, in plain terms, whether one can't understand German in translation not because Russian doesn't suffice to convey the same ideas, but because the language comes from a fundamentally different species of thought."

"Humboldt's national character question," mused Kesha. "How did you get to *that* subject? Was it the nonsense on Tasso?"

At this, Misha laughed heartily and refilled Kesha's cup. "If you were listening to the nonsense on Tasso, no *wonder* you had a headache! Oh, Keshechka, you'll wear out your intellect listening to idiots! No, no one but you was paying attention to the nonsense on Tasso. This was a far thornier problem. But here, perhaps it will make more sense to show you."

For a moment, Misha rifled through the inner breast pocket of his jacket until he could withdraw a sheet of paper marked with Cyrillic letters. The ragged edge suggested that it had been torn from a book. "Barbarian," sniffed Kesha, but he took the page and examined it carefully.

The piece was poetry, certainly, and from the poor quality of the versification, he surmised that it was poetry in translation. The Russian syllables seemed to grind against one another like blocks of granite in an earthquake, like flint and steel striking sparks—the translator had welded together ill-fitting words into unwieldy compounds, at times borrowing from Greek where Russian did not suffice. On a purely aesthetic level, it was an *ugly* poem.

In that ugliness, though, was something that struck Kesha to the heart and kindled a queer, inexplicable passion in him. "What was the original language?" he asked. The paper was shaking, and he recognized (as though from a great distance, a great height) that it was because his hand was shaking.

"Turn it over," said Misha.

On the reverse of the page, six intricate symbols had been scribed one atop the other, each one as delicate as the filigree on a crown or a ceremonial cross. "Arabic?" he guessed, for he had seen Moorish latticework and Arabic calligraphy that bore some resemblance to the…what were they? Words? Characters? Sentences coiled around one another? But at that guess, Misha shook his head.

"It's the language of the dragons," he answered, lips twisting half-wryly. "What do you say to that, Tarasov? The dragons have a *language*—they even write poetry, whether or not it's any good."

"Are you sure it isn't a hoax? A kind of...scholarly prank, devised by bored young men who know too much Greek and too little of the world?"

"Quite sure. I've been digging, you see, since I found this book." Misha's voice was low, and Kesha leaned in to hear him. The fine hairs on the back of Kesha's neck stood on end. He could see his eyes reflected faintly in Misha's spectacles, and they were wide and pale and staring. The morning's macabre reflections seemed very far away.

Misha closed his hand over Kesha's to keep it from trembling, whispering as he did, "There was a box of books in the university's library—quite concealed behind a bit of paneling, but the paneling had come untacked—"

"As it would, if someone had untacked it—"

"Will you *hush*, Kesha!" His fingertips traced circles on the back of Kesha's hand. "These books were at least a hundred years old, and the box was marked 'to be burned'." He didn't have to say that, in Russia, *at least a hundred years* meant *since the Turks turned the dragons against us.*

Kesha looked up, searching Misha's face for any sign of deception. It wouldn't have been out of character for him to fabricate some sort of elaborate hoax for his own purposes, whether he meant to make a point about linguistics or to needle Kesha about his family's history—and if he were attempting to be deceptive, then certainly he would pretend to be as earnest as he now appeared. "If these books are so very secret and precious, then why were you flashing your bit of paper about at the *salon* last night?" he asked. "Why tear out this particular page to show us?"

"Ah," said Misha, "I tore out the page to show it to *you.*

What it took the idiots four hours to determine in the abstract, you've deduced in a moment from the material. And *now* perhaps I shall have a proper conversation about language!"

"I need to see your box of books," answered Kesha. Even beneath Misha's hand, his own was still shaking, and he stood and thrust his hands in his pockets so that he could conceal their tremors. "Take me to wherever you've buried them; I need to see them—"

"Anyone would think I'd hidden them in a coffin, and not on a bookshelf," said Misha, but he stood as well. "Let me pay the reckoning and we'll return to my lodgings. Then I really *must* tutor a pair of young sparks, or they'll be using crib sheets for the rest of their lives—"

Kesha scarcely heard him. Something strange and mad was throbbing in him, and he couldn't say whether it was terror or elation.

Misha's box of books—or, to be strictly accurate, his half a shelf of books and his well-dismantled remnants of a crate—were everything that he had claimed them to be. Each book was at least a hundred years old, the dates neatly printed upon the title pages. The style of the quires, the pagination, and even the thickness of the pages and the residual tackiness of the ink all spoke to the great age of each volume.

The books concerned an ill-assorted hodgepodge of topics, with French treatises on governance packed in alongside Russian works of natural history and slim volumes of translated poetry in Russian or Russo-Greek interspersed with what might have been Old Russian. The style of the verse was unmistakably neoclassical, more concerned with imitating the works of the masters of antiquity than with producing respectable poetry or even accurate literal translations.

They were not books collected to investigate a particular question, or to suit the tastes and inquiries of a particular person's intellect. Rather, they appeared to be books that had been thrown together for no better reason than *that they were books*, and this fact somehow justified not only their compilation but also their preservation.

Which meant, Kesha soon recognized, that they contained no answers whatsoever.

Some books had tables of contents, and a very few (the drier texts) had indices to guide a new reader through them, but these maps provided no clues that Kesha could use. He recognized that he was seeking a particular answer, but he couldn't yet formulate the question that would generate it. Perhaps it was *Why were these books destined to be burned?* or perhaps *Why were they preserved?*

"The universities burned texts to do with dragons, after the Defection," Misha had explained, but both of them knew that it wasn't a satisfactory explanation. One could go to any reputable bookseller's and purchase an anatomical treatise on the physical makeup of dragons. Zoological journals regularly published proceedings of public dissections in the borderlands, and naturalists wrote learned articles on the relationship between the dragon and the pangolin. No history of Russia was complete without at least an attempt to account for the Defection, and popular novels and plays were stuffed so full of dragons that Kesha had entirely given up on reading Russian fiction. However mad the Germans were, they at least had the grace to confine their fiction to the dealings of madmen.

He was disinterested in dragons. The cities romanticized them, and the borderlands destroyed them; the anatomists cut them open, and the taxidermists sewed them together again. Kesha preferred to leave them entirely alone.

And yet, in the tortured verse of the dragons, he felt the edge of something like lightning in the vastness of the heavens.

There came a rap at the door, and Kesha nearly leapt from his chair at it. "Who's there?" he called, and a woman laughed.

"It's only Irina Abramovna," she said, at which he relaxed at once. Misha's aunt had no interest in his academic work, and certainly none in his contraband books. "I thought you'd like a bit of tea," she continued. "You've been shut away for hours with those dusty books, without even Mishka for company. Come downstairs and we'll chat over a nice dinner. Would you like that?"

"I would," answered Kesha, although he lay down the book only reluctantly. He opened the door on the warm air of the hallway, offering Madame Galiyeva a tentative half-smile. She was short and plump, pleasantly fleshy in the same way that her nephew was, and she had lost several teeth without any real damage to the vivacity of her smile. Her day dress was of fine silk, and it made Kesha painfully aware of the threadbare elbows of his jacket and the slight tea-stains at the cuffs of his shirtsleeves. "If you don't mind that I'm not dressed for dinner?"

"I never stand on ceremony," said Madame Galiyeva, which was a plain lie. But she doted on her sister's son and loved to spoil his friends, so Kesha didn't protest when she brought him downstairs to enjoy her well-appointed table.

They spoke of trivialities, of students who refused to master Greek and of the recent cold spell that presaged winter. Kesha told her of Petya's return to the border, and she told him of her husband's success in a recent, delicate legal imbroglio. "Do you think our Misha will make a good lawyer, Innokentiy Vladimirovich?" she asked, with an expression of suppressed hope that reminded him of his mother. She, too, had once imagined that Kesha would enter the legal profession, before he had dashed her hopes entirely by defecting to divinity school. It was not, she had thought, entirely *respectful* for a young man to inquire into the divine the way he inquired into the doings of men.

"I think," said Kesha, once he had drained his cup, "your Misha could convince a fish to swim in air, if he wanted to. And his Latin is impeccable. Better than my own. If he can tear himself away from his books long enough to attend a court session, he might be a lawyer yet."

Relief colored Madame Galiyeva's smile. "And you? What will you do, when you've finished your schooling?"

"He shall live in my library and tell me about the doings of God," laughed Misha from the doorway, and Kesha turned to him with a smile. His fair hair was spotted over with water droplets, which he shook free like a dog shaking. "It was snowing!" he told his aunt when she frowned at his ill manners, and she suffered him to kiss her cheek and sit down to eat with them. Although his cheeks were red and flushed, he called for a cup of cold kvass rather than tea or coffee.

"Well," said Misha, when he had settled into his chair and cleaned his spectacles on his handkerchief. "How are you enjoying my library thus far, Kesha?"

"I'm finding it bafflingly diverse," Kesha confessed. "If you expected me to see the connections between your books, I've failed your test."

"Ah!" The confession appeared to delight Misha, and he leaned over the table (which also occasioned a small frown from his aunt). "I imagine you checked the indices for topical connections."

"That was the first thing I did."

"And then looked for details exterior to the content—the publishers, perhaps?"

"Naturally, and the authors. And I looked for marginalia, since I'm sure you'll ask about that next—"

"And did you *read* the books?"

"If I'd had time to read all eight books," Kesha said sharply, "then I certainly *would* have."

"Then you won't have had a chance to see that the connection is *methodological*," replied Misha with an air of triumph.

In the silence that followed, Madame Galiyeva ventured, "Methodological?"

"They all use the pertinent sources in the same manner," answered Misha, and he glanced at Kesha to be sure that they both understood which sources were *pertinent*. Kesha nodded faintly. "That is, the way they'd treat Montesquieu or Locke. Is that hint enough?"

A chill weight settled in Kesha's belly like a stone. He recognized it as comprehension. "As people," he said softly. "Foreigners, perhaps, but foreign *people*."

CHAPTER FIVE

Petya disembarked from the train with his valise clutched in one hand, his other hand holding his hat in place. The wind was screaming over the low hills, driving discarded train tickets and faded advertisements across the tracks. On the northern side, smoke sifted up from the vents and smokestacks of the machinists' shop beneath the earth. South of the tracks, the town rose before him in ranks of faded timbers. He scanned the crowd for Liza's tall shape, or his father's distinctive red hair, but he saw neither of them. In truth, he didn't expect to. He and Captain Jaworski had wired ahead, but telegraph communication between Moscow and the border country was unreliable at best.

"They'll be happy enough to see you at the keep," said Jaworski, who had been smoking more or less continuously throughout their journey and with whom Petya would therefore forever associate the scent of tobacco smoke. As they stepped off of the platform and searched for a porter to take Petya's trunk, Jaworski refilled his pipe.

"I don't think they will be," answered Petya. "Happy, that is. Liza seemed very upset in her letter. She was nearly carving the paper with her pen, she was so angry—"

"She's a territorial minx," Jaworski laughed. "And you're right to be wary of that. Your father didn't call me in because he *liked* me. He called me in because he could trust me, and I'll venture to say that your sister thought the same of you."

"She did." Petya tried to smile in return. "She does."

They had delicately avoided the question of why Kesha had accepted Liza's letter in Petya's place and why he had not been invited to join them. Jaworski had served with Petya's uncles in the wars, and if he had no particular love of Vladimir Petrovich Tarasov, he knew as well as anyone that the Tarasov family valued loyalty above all else.

At last, Jaworski managed to flag down a driver who would take them and the trunk to the keep, and once they'd paid, they huddled in the cart and out of the gale. Even in the town, the wind made Petya long for the closed carriages of the city. Yureyevsk was hardly more than a village, after St. Petersburg. Petya had once thought it a very grand place, full of curious shops and raucous gathering-places, but he knew better now.

The road to the keep was broad and clear, made of finely ground stones that crunched under the wheels of the cart. Petya had walked it many times, but this was the very first time he'd let someone else drive him. The walls seemed to loom when he wasn't traveling under his own power. They stole upon him gradually, rising slow and grim from the hillside with the sunlight striking aslant the turrets. It was like watching a giant climbing to its feet.

"Hail, the towers!" cried Jaworski, hands cupped about his lips, and the wind stole his voice at once. He stood in the cart, then, and took off his hat to bare himself for scrutiny. "It's Ludwik Jaworski! For God's sake, open the damn gates, Vladimir Petrovich!"

Even from the ground, the watchman's smile was visible. Then came a great, shuddering sound of poorly oiled gears as the gates ground open, granting the little cart passage to the courtyard beyond. The Tarasovs had seldom had cause to open their gates in Petya's youth; they had few visitors important enough for coaches and few shipments large enough that they couldn't come through the servants' door. When Petya had been eight, a pack of Americans had wheeled the new guns into the courtyard and then built scaffolds to raise them to the turrets. Petya and Kesha had climbed over the scaffolds together and pretended that they were mountaineers traversing the Urals.

He couldn't help feeling very much a child, in the shadow of the walls that had closed him in for his entire boyhood. The place was thick with memories, clustering like gnats over stagnant water.

"*Petya!*"

The shout was the only warning he had before something heavy and warm slammed into his shoulder, knocking him flat in the cart. He made an undignified sort of squeaking sound and flailed at whatever was pinning him down, and in the process tore Liza's hair out of its updo and set it spilling over his face. Quite a lot of it got into his mouth, but that was probably all right, because in any case he wouldn't have been able to find words.

"L-Liza!" he said at last, and spat out a hank of her hair. "You're—" *wearing trousers*, he thought, but she'd been wearing trousers even before he left for St. Petersburg. *So damn strong*, but she'd been strong since they were children. "You're *here*," he said at last, with a half-surprised smile, and flushed at the inanity of it.

If Liza was offended, though, she only seized him by the shoulders and studied him with a ferocious grin, declaring at last, "You're damn right, I'm here. And so are you! My God, you've grown!"

"Not grown *very* much."

"A little around the waist," said Liza. Then, seeing Jaworski in the cart, she let her brother up and made a cursory bow. "Captain Jaworski! As quick as I'd hoped you'd be. How's your English?"

"You'll make an errand-boy of me, Elizaveta Vladimirovna," Jaworski said, laughing. "My English is as good as my Russian, since you ask. Do you need a translator?"

"I need a Russian who speaks English, and if I can't have a Russian, I'll take a Pole. They pretend they're harmless when I can't understand what they're saying, but I can *see* them sniggering behind their hands! If they think I'll be a good English hostess and ignore their disrespect, they'll learn how we host guests in Russia!" Liza began to twist her hair up again, thrusting each pin into place like a tiny dagger. When she finished, she readjusted her muffler and her coat and drew herself up to her full height. *Like a commander*, thought Petya. *She's become a commander since I left home*. He couldn't quite say why the notion disquieted him.

A servant came to take Petya's trunk into the keep. "Your old room, sir?" he asked, and Petya nodded absently. The man gathered up the trunk and departed, with the cool efficiency that Petya had learned to expect of servingfolk. He hadn't had servants in St. Petersburg—even his landlady's servants rendered her tenants little service beyond dropping irate shoes in the night when a conversation kept them up. Here, though, the domestic help had already ceased to be remarkable, or perhaps had become unremarkable again.

He would have to be careful not to fall into old habits of thought, while he lived in his father's house.

By evening, Petya had become intimately reacquainted with each of the gun turrets. He had peeled off the steel casing on the swivel mounts to oil and maintain the gears, cleaning away half a decade of grit and dust and, in one case, even an intricate swallow's nest. The mechanisms told him a secret story, one that Liza was too proud and their father too canny to tell: the fortress had lost staff since Petya went to the city, and there had been few enough dragons to fight that the castle had scarcely felt the loss. Six dragons since Petya's last visit, nearly three years ago. Lean years indeed for a family that depended on bounties.

Little wonder Liza had called him home. Little wonder their father was calling on his brothers' old comrades from the Polish rebellion. With the borders scant months from opening again, the Tsar had decided to shore up his southern margin. If Petya could believe the gunners' gossip, the Tsar might come to inspect the preparations himself. For the first time since the Defection, an outsider had come to supervise their border fortress—an outsider, moreover, with the ear of the English embassy and so of the Tsar. After the liberation of the serfs, the Tarasovs had earned no income from their lands, and so they relied on bounties and the Tsar's salary for their subsistence.

Vladimir Petrovich was a canny man. He would surely have guessed that if the Tarasovs ceased to be useful, they would cease to be supported. The Tarasovs must appear busy if they were to appear useful.

Although Petya's English was middling at best, he could nonetheless make out some of the conversations around him as he worked. The English wondered how much his father paid the "sappers," whatever that meant. They were impressed with the design of the fortress and the caliber of the weaponry. They were asking one another how much it cost to acquire and maintain such guns, and what the Russians had done before Dr. Gatling had sold them his cunning creations. *Tore the dragons' throats out with our fingernails*, thought Petya irritably, but he slipped his goggles back into place and set to welding a new tooth onto a broken gear.

Whether it signified well or ill that they were loitering about and watching him work, he couldn't have said. He suspected that if he waited for the English to leave the gun turrets in peace, he'd never manage any maintenance work.

"Did we ever have an engineer on retainer?" he asked

Liza when he'd finished clearing oil-clotted hair from the last of the mounts. He knew that he was smeared with grease and caked with dust, and there were probably bits of the swallow's nest still sticking in his scarf, but despite his shabby state, he felt a faint elation at all that he'd accomplished. "It's not that I mind doing this sort of work—far from it!—but I do wonder why you haven't brought in Lukin's people...."

"Because Lukin's people are union, and they won't be bullied into working cheaply," replied Liza, hammer-blunt. "We used to have a man come up when the guns locked up," she added, after thinking a moment. "He was a watchmaker, remember? A tiny little man, with a long, thin beard and spectacles that made him look like an owl. But when we couldn't pay him anymore, he packed up his shop and went away."

"When was that?"

"Two years ago," said Liza. If she wanted to add *While you were gone*, she bit her tongue, and Petya was grateful for it.

"You should bring in an engineer at least once a year. Someone has to clean the machinery out and tighten the bolts. It won't lock up as often or as badly if it's regularly maintained," he answered. "And a once-yearly visit isn't expensive."

"If *you* came back once a year, it would cost nothing at all," answered Liza, and Petya could neither refute her logic nor give her a wholehearted *yes*.

"Should I see what I can do with the gate?" he asked, when the silence had begun to stretch long between them. "Since I'm here, I could squeeze into the chain shafts and try to get the gears turning smoothly."

Liza threw her head back and laughed, and Petya hadn't the faintest idea why. "You can do that tomorrow. Tonight, dress for supper. The English are finally paying board, and I want them to see us looking our best."

Petya glanced back up at the turret where he'd been

working, flexing his fingers uneasily. "Are you sure it's a good idea? If we were attacked at supper, in our good clothes, without anyone at the guns—"

"Jaworski will be keeping watch, and we'll bring him a leg of lamb when we're finished. Stop *fussing*, Petya! Have a drink." She drew a flask from the pocket of her coat and passed it over. Petya took it and swallowed a mouthful before he realized that her flask was full of unadulterated vodka. Tears pricked at his eyes.

It was unkind of Liza to laugh at him as he doubled over and coughed. She had set his throat afire; she could at least have the courtesy not to laugh.

"You're not drinking enough, in the city," she informed him, when he no longer seemed in imminent danger of death. "What sort of student are you, not drinking in the city?"

"A *poor* student," he answered. His voice squeaked like a woodwind. "Kesha and I only drink when—"

Liza's hand closed hard on his shoulder. Her eyes were dark and cold. "Don't you dare mention that name."

The steel in her voice almost made Petya flinch, but he mastered himself and straightened. He was not so easily awed as he had been when last they'd met. "He's your brother, too."

"I have one brother, and he's here," said Liza. "Now wash your face and dress for dinner. Father expects us to make him proud." Since Petya had arrived, he hadn't once set eyes upon his father.

"Liza," he said softly, but she shook her head and held up a hand to forestall him.

"Not now," she answered. Her expression was taut, as though she had to restrain herself from striking him. "I can't talk to you now, Petya. Let me *be*."

She stalked away, her shoulders squared and her gait stiff as a soldier's. Petya watched her go until she'd vanished into the keep, then slipped his hands into his pockets and followed her down.

CHAPTER SIX

"He's gone soft."

"He's a hard worker," said Liza. Her father only snorted. Her hands went to her hips, and she could just barely feel the edge of her cincher beneath the heels of her hands. "So what if he doesn't drink or gamble? He'd barely settled his trunk before he was up in the turrets with a wrench and an oil-rag. He would've begged off supper to man the watchtowers, if I'd let him. Petya works *hard*, and I won't hear you calling him 'soft' because you don't think he's funny."

Vladimir's eyes flashed in the gaslight. He turned to her with his lip curling back over his teeth. The canines were missing, the molars lined with dark stains from half a century of tea and tobacco. "You sound like your brother," he told her. "We should never have let him go to the city. He's learned nothing but how to speak back to his elders."

"Has he raised his voice to you *once* since he returned? Has he said a single word to you that wasn't respectful? He is *not* like—" Liza made a disgusted sound and refused to go on. She was no more interested in discussing Kesha than her father was. "Petya is a good boy. He'll unwind in his own time, and until then we'll be *grateful* that he's home. If you want someone to drink with you, write to a few more of Uncle Sasha's friends. Jaworski was a good choice. He's as reliable as an old wolfhound."

Something changed in Vladimir's expression and Liza wasn't entirely sure she liked it. Her father was less sober than she was, or he'd never have complained about her brother. And she was less sober than she ought to be, if he wanted to pick a fight with her. "Ah, you like Jaworski?" he asked, too lightly. The lamplight made his skin look sallow.

"I like him as well as you do," she answered.

"I've been thinking that you ought to have a husband," said Vladimir. "We've passed down this fortress from father to son for over a century now. I'm getting old, Liza. If you want to inherit from me, I'd need to know that you'd pass the keep to your own son one day."

For a moment, Liza stood slack-jawed, as though he'd struck her. One hand went to her muffler and drew it closed over her neck, while the other hand went half-unconsciously to her knife. Whatever she had expected to hear—whatever mad games she might have supposed her father was playing—it wasn't that. "There's no way in Hell you'd marry me to *Jaworski*," she managed at last. If he hadn't been her father, if she hadn't been his child, she would have spat in his eye. "You're too proud of our name. I'm a Tarasov. If I inherit, I'll do it as a Tarasov."

"A Tarasova," Vladimir answered. "If I thought you could father a child on your own, I'd leave you to your choice—but we both know that you can't. And if I died? What then, Liza?"

"Then I'd make one of Petya's sons my heir," she said. "No one but a Tarasov will ever hold this keep. Not while I live."

"And if Petya doesn't have a son? *This* is why you aren't—"

"I'd bring in a *cousin*, damn it!" snarled Liza. The tremors racking her hands were anger, and nothing else. If they weren't anger, they would have to be terror, and she could not permit herself to be terrified. "Why are you asking me this? Is this some kind of test? Name of God, you've got easily another thirty years! Why dwell on death?"

Vladimir shook his head, though, and waved her away. They had reached his rooms, and he took the keyring from his waistcoat pocket and slipped the ancient iron key into the lock. "Go to bed, Liza," he told her. "I'm an old man who's had too much to drink, and it's made me gloomy. I look west, and I see the Kamensky boys getting old enough to have children, while you're just a few years from thirty… go to bed, my Liza. My good child, my good girl." With that, he swung the door open and vanished behind it. The door struck hard against the jamb, and then the bolt slid home with a heavy, final sound.

Good girl, thought Liza. She turned away from her father's rooms and toward Petya's, which were near her own. They'd had a wing of the keep to themselves, when the family had all lived together, mother and brothers and sister sharing a space with fine Oriental rugs and French furnishings from the last century.

Her mother had taken the rugs and the sofas to Moscow with her, when she'd gone, and what she'd left behind, Vladimir and Liza had sold piecemeal. They'd had debts to pay, between the payments of their seasonal salary, and Liza had no sentimental attachment to Kesha's favorite chair. His rooms stood all but empty, and even the spiders had long since given up on the bare bookshelves and the empty grate.

She rapped firmly at Petya's door. He answered almost at once, his stiff collar hanging by one button and his hair in slight disarray. He wrinkled his nose as though he thought she smelled of drink. "Oh, Liza," he said, smiling slightly too brightly after a pause slightly too long. "I was undressing—well, you can see I was undressing—"

"What did you think of the English?" Lieutenant Wainwright had tried to draw Petya into a conversation about the guns over dinner, but to his credit, Petya hadn't allowed himself to be drawn. He knew better than to share their secrets with strangers.

While Petya thought of how to answer, Liza stepped behind his dressing screen and struggled out of her cincher, then did up her dress again and flung herself into the nearest chair. She looked up at her brother, scanning his face for any hint of his sentiments. He was pacing, and it made him look anxious and excitable. His pale forehead was furrowed, dark brows drawn together until they nearly met in the middle. She noted that he had fewer freckles than she, which meant he hadn't seen the sun this summer. When they'd been children, they'd looked very much alike, and their aunts had exclaimed over Petya's dark, glossy curls and fine little hands—and they'd grown alike, too. Petya was a tall, well-muscled sort of man, but Liza was almost as broad-shouldered.

She'd learn nothing from dwelling on the past, and she dismissed those memories like overattentive servants. "Well?" she prompted. "The English?"

"I think they're out of their element," said Petya, finally. "Their lieutenant has been asking questions since they came, but they're the wrong kinds of questions. He's been asking about loyalty and how the gunners work as a team, but you and I know that the only real team on the towers is a gunner and his loader…and not even that, now, since we're too short-staffed for loaders. They say they aren't planning to invade Turkey in February, I suppose because they learned their lesson from Napoleon about Russian winters, but they won't be a dreadful amount of good to us until then. They do want to learn to fight dragons; they wouldn't be here if they didn't. But that doesn't make them better-equipped for it. And it's not that they're ignorant, although they are, or even *really* that they're inexperienced—but they haven't learned how to think if they want to fight a dragon, and they're not…not ready, yet, to start thinking that way."

"And how is that?" Liza drew up one foot to prop it on the edge of the chair, resting her chin on her knee and wrapping her arms about her leg. "Stop pacing, Petya. You'll make me dizzy."

Petya dropped himself into the remaining chair, although he clasped his hands together and leaned forward over his knees in a way that looked just as anxious. "The English have been a naval power for centuries, whatever they've been getting up to in Africa—no, let me finish. I promise it's relevant. They're used to thinking of enemy ships as…as floating regiments, I suppose. They can destroy or cripple a ship, but usually they'll be fighting a hundred or so soldiers just like them, who all answer to a single commander, just like they do. They don't *understand* how we fight, because the idea that they can't just chip away at a dragon with their rifles—and more than that, the idea that the dragon isn't constantly answering commands—that's *incomprehensible* to the English."

"And you got all of that from one conversation, did you?"

"I got it from a tutor," he answered, looking nearly ashamed. "The borders are opening again. The English aren't just here; they're also in St. Petersburg, asking what kills dragons. And my tutor had—well, when I heard the lieutenant's questions about the guns, they struck me as the sort of thing that my tutor had been complaining about. He said that the English would never learn to fight dragons properly, even if they could build the guns and the architecture, because dragons were too far out of their experience. He said it was a question of mentality, not of technology."

Liza realized then that Petya wasn't embarrassed because he had learned about the English from someone else; he was embarrassed because he'd learned it at *university*. He'd heard their father disparaging his education over dinner, and he'd assumed that she shared his prejudices.

It was a fair assumption. She shared most of his prejudices.

"I heard there were dragons in the Americas," said Liza, like a peace-offering. "Up in the north, keeping ships from finding a Northwest Passage."

"Maybe we should send the English over there to practice," said Petya. His hesitant, too-bright smile slowly crept up to his eyes and made them crinkle at the corners. Liza grinned to see it.

"Maybe we should send the English over there to *stay*," she answered. For the first time since he'd arrived, Petya laughed.

The chill wind screamed through the windows of the watchtowers, tearing Liza's hair free of its pins and whipping her curls across her cheeks. It felt like being struck by the string of a bow—when she'd been learning to shoot, her uncle had scolded her for holding her bowstring too close to her cheek, then passed the bow to Kesha. She'd never thought to question it. She had been just a girl, and it hadn't been her place to learn to shoot a bow. When she'd ceased to amuse her uncle, when he feared she'd start crying at a little unexpected pain, her lesson had ceased as well.

Her uncle had died in the Polish uprising, his ammunition spent and his horse shot out from under him. He'd taken a bayonet to the throat from some would-be Hussar, and that had been that.

Liza passed the flask of hot tea over to Jaworski. "Cold night," she offered.

"Bright stars," he answered, and took a long swig from the flask. "It was good of you to come spell me."

"I'm not here to spell you," said Liza. She knew that she was still too drunk to keep a proper watch, although the cool air was helping to clear her head. "Couldn't sleep. Thought you'd be cold."

"Well, I'm still cold. But it was good of you to think of me."

"Only practical. You're our best gunner, until I've slept." Liza leaned over the window ledge with her shoulders drawn up and her gloved hands clasped together, taking in the broad expanse of the stars overhead. They were, she had to admit, very bright. If she thought so because she was drunk, she wasn't particularly concerned. "My father's thinking of marrying us," she said, with a laugh that rang hollow on the thin air.

Jaworski didn't answer immediately, although she could hear his breathing hitch, then the sound of tea sloshing in the flask and a heavy swallow. "Thinking of marrying us." His voice was low, neutral. Liza didn't care to see his face.

"I'm not interested in marrying. If he asks you, you'd have better luck courting the Princess of Spain."

He said nothing for a long moment, and when she could bear the silence no longer, she turned to him. He was leaning out the next window, the spyglass pressed against his eye, his gaze fixed on the heavens. "Well?" she asked.

"I'm a widower, Elizaveta Vladimirovna." His accent thickened on her name. "I'd do my wife a disservice if I married again—and especially a wife half my age, who I didn't even love."

"I'm not ten years younger than you are," answered Liza, but relief stole over her limbs at Jaworski's reply. For the first time since she and her father had spoken, she realized how tense she had really been. "Uncle Sasha was the youngest of my uncles."

"He was a good man, Sasha," said Jaworski. It had the ring of a thing often-said. "A good soldier."

"A good dragonslayer. He could prepare a cannon faster than any man I've ever met, and he taught all of us how to man a ballista. You should have seen his face when we got the guns!" This time, when Liza laughed, Jaworski laughed with her. The shared laughter felt warm, like hot tea in her belly. "We used to say that Petya was going to grow up to be just like his uncle."

"What, a whoremonger?" All at once his expression grew shuttered, as though he thought he'd offended her. She laughed loud as a brass bell.

"You and your ceremony, Jaworski! Do you think I'm a little girl? I know what a whore is. I know my uncle fucked them. I probably heard him with a few of them, at that. He was as loyal to his wife as a soldier ought to be, and no more."

Jaworski's face was hard and still. It took Liza a moment to work out that she had offended *him*. "I'm drunk," she said, and they both knew that it didn't suffice for an apology. "I'll say anything if I think it's funny."

"You should get to bed," Jaworski answered. "If you fall off the tower, I'll have to tell your father why he's lost a gunner, and then he'll probably throw me off after you."

"And what then? He always says that—'and what then,' as though no one else in the world has ever thought about the future." Liza smiled. "I'm not *that* drunk. Not falling-drunk." The world was moving slowly, anyway. She'd catch herself if she started to fall. "Finish the tea and give me my flask back. It would be just like a Pole to rob a drunken woman."

Jaworski only raised his brows at that, then drained the flask and passed it over without comment or complaint. "Go with God, Elizaveta Vladimirovna."

"I don't need God to chaperone me," she answered. When she had tucked the flask into her pocket again and resettled her coat, she began to climb down the ladder, rung after rung. Her skirt caught at times beneath her feet. Perhaps she was more than a little drunk. She'd never have climbed up the watchtower in a dress, if she'd been sober.

Well, she thought, when she'd unlocked the door to her chambers and shut herself inside. *I've made a fool of myself.* It improved nothing to kick over her footstool and shatter a cheap porcelain vase, but it made her *feel* better, and that was what mattered.

CHAPTER SEVEN

After only a little pleading, and very slight self-abasement, Kesha managed to secure the book of poetry from which Misha's torn page had come. He took his leave in the evening, making solemn promises to return the book in as good a condition as he'd found it. He thought privately that this was not a particularly forceful promise, since Misha had no apparent scruples regarding the book's integrity, but it didn't do to borrow a friend's things without at least the *gesture* of swearing to keep them sound.

Misha never asked Kesha to swear on his faith. Like so many fashionable young intellectuals, Misha was an atheist, and he regarded the whole practice of religious oaths as an idle ceremony. "As fine to swear on a bit of carpet as to swear on one's faith," he had sneered once, and Kesha had been divinity scholar enough not to gainsay him.

Perhaps, one day, they would share a library and converse about the nature of God there, with a samovar and a tea service between them and overstuffed chairs that bore the impressions of their bodies. Indeed, they had enjoyed such conversations on many a winter evening in Galiyev's library, which was warm and dry even when the snow had begun to pile up on the outside window ledges. Misha stood to inherit his uncle's house and legal practice, since Galiyev had neither children of his own nor other nephews to give preference. He would surely lodge Kesha at very reasonable rates, if he were asked.

If Petya never returned from the borderlands, then Kesha would have no reason to delay asking. Although his landlady and her *salons* were intellectually stimulating, Kesha had no sentimental attachment to the room that he and Petya had shared for three years. Without his brother's clutter of engineering diagrams and wire models, his unwashed clothes lying in a little heap in the corner and his faint, wheezing snore at night...without all of that, the room was only a room, as good as any other and perhaps worse than many.

The housekeeper let him in and asked whether he wanted supper, but he waved her inquiries away and clambered up the narrow stairs to his room. The wire models lay scattered on shelves and tables or hung suspended from the ceiling, as though Petya would return any moment to take them down and tinker with them. His clothes were packed away in his trunk with his spare coat, his tools, and his favorite novel—*a partial evacuation only*, thought Kesha. *He'll return soon enough.*

With that faint reassurance, Kesha turned up the gaslight over his desk and slipped Misha's contraband book from his coat pocket. The cover was unmarked, and he suspected that the book had been rebound at least once since its publication. However, the title page named it *A Collection of the Poems of the Illustrious Dragon Race, Represented in Their Own Language, with a Translation into Russian*. It was a slim volume, barely larger than his hand, and the pages were so brittle that they creased at once when he bent them even a little. The editor had dedicated the collection to Tsarina Yelizaveta Petrovna, in gratitude for the establishment of a university in Moscow. The publication date only confirmed the age of the piece. This was a second edition, published in 1757.

More than a hundred years ago.

He carefully turned the pages, seeking the place where Misha had torn out his snatch of poetry. When at last he found it, he slotted the creased page in among its fellows and then returned to the beginning with a clearer conscience.

Misha's page had been representative of the quality of the whole. The Russian translations were truly *execrable* verse, stumbling over their own overeager tetrameter and too-neat rhyming quatrains. With each poem that he perused, though, Kesha became more and more convinced that the translator had done his best with an impossible task. The draconic symbols paired with each poem seemed strangely sparse, in comparison with the frantic, half-sublime rhetoric of the translations. Three to six roughly circular woodcuts, arranged single file in a column, like buttons on a winter coat or drops of blood on snow. If he had not known them for words (or sentences, or stanzas), he would have taken them for the printers' ornaments so common in such texts.

With a few leaves of his own paper, he drew each set of symbols at a larger size, attempting to copy every intricate curl and cross. By the second poem, his eyes were swimming, his fingers shaking with the exertion. Unlike Petya, he had never been a draftsman. His handwriting was cramped and precise, and he had never learned to turn his hands to beautiful works, or even *accurate* ones.

In an hour, Kesha had eight symbols drawn fully, each on a separate sheet of paper. While the ink dried, he massaged his aching hands and sat back in his chair.

For the past few years, St. Petersburg had taken part in a more general European mania for all things Oriental; Kesha had watched his peers pay more than they could readily afford for genuine porcelain from China and genuine prints (or at least, reproductions of genuine prints—or at least, reproductions of imitations of genuine prints) from Japan. Even Kesha himself had been lured into an opium den for a lark, although the experience had left him vomiting all evening and enduring anxious dreams for a week.

The trade in porcelain and prints and opium struck him as a rather mercenary affair, meant not to educate patrons but to extract their money in exchange for their wonder. The entire business had left an unpleasant taste in his mouth that was more than the lingering traces of bile.

But he'd studied the intricate stamps and careful inscriptions of the paintings hawked in the marketplaces, and he couldn't help feeling a kind of wonder at the minds that could see a single, delicate character and read an entire word's meaning into it. To learn to read each word as though it were the first word, complete in itself, containing its meanings like an egg contained a bird or a chrysalis contained a moth—he shivered a little at the memory. Long after his acquaintances had ceased to wonder at Oriental trinkets, Kesha still felt himself awed at the idea of pictographs and ideograms.

He could scarcely imagine the minds that could read meaning in the dragons' letters as easily as he read in Cyrillic.

When the drawings had dried, Kesha tacked them up on the wall, next to Petya's designs for fountains and flying machines.

The next day provided little opportunity for Kesha to study the copies that he had made, occupied as he was with the students he tutored and the development of his thesis. As old Starikovich liked to say, a thesis was like a stubborn colt. It would not begin to move without diligent coaxing—and once it had begun to move, if one did not rein it in, it would careen away too quickly to be arrested. "Which means, young Tarasov," he said, rapping Kesha's knuckles with his walking stick to punctuate his point, "you mustn't get so excited to have written anything at all that you let yourself write some stinking pile of horse shit."

Starikovich, too, had come from a border family—the youngest of eight sons, sent to divinity school because his family hadn't known what else to do with him. He was built broad and tall, and despite his great age, he was as spry as a man of half his years (and, the other students were inclined to remark, twice as sharp-tongued). It was said that he had left his position at the university to join the fighting in Poland, and although his military service was an article of faith among the older students, no one seemed to know *when* he had fought in Poland. All of this Kesha had learned by rumor and repute, for Starikovich never spoke of his past, and Kesha was disinclined to ask. He had no use for a mentor, beyond the necessities of preparing his thesis for defense, and he certainly had none for a father-confessor.

With his knuckles still stinging from the smack and his pride from the admonition, Kesha gathered up his early draft and left the meeting. The air tasted of coming snow, which was a surer prognostication than the low and heavy clouds, and there was no remedy for the chill like a heated conversation around a ceramic stove. With this aim before him, Kesha went to sift the coffee-houses in hopes of rousing Misha.

He found his friend holding court over a trio of young legal scholars at the second coffee-house in his search. Misha made an unlikely Socrates, for his round face lent him an appearance of earnest goodwill even in the midst of his most scathing critiques; however, he did have the old Athenian master's skill at posing incisive questions. At an unconsidered response, he would peer over his spectacles in a manner that made even Kesha feel like a fool, and for every thoughtful riposte he was prepared with a new question. These skills would serve him well when he came to practice law, but when Kesha watched realization break over the students' faces like sunlight over the eastern hills, he could not help feeling that Misha had been destined instead to teach. Catching Kesha's eye, Misha grinned broadly and gestured him over with his cup. "Ah, Kesha!" he cried. "Could you help me to explain to these fine young minds why it would *not* be politically advisable to sell our American territories to the United States?"

"I'm sure I haven't the faintest idea," answered Kesha as he slipped into the narrow space between his friend and the nearest student.

Misha passed him the cup, his eyebrows raised. "Not the *faintest* idea? Surely this isn't a difficult question! Let me jog your memory with reference to the Crimea—"

"I'm only saying, it would pay the war debts!" insisted a lantern-jawed student with pale eyes and a sort of faint whistle to his voice. "Russia can't ignore its deficits forever."

"Ah!" cried one of the others, a small, dark fellow whose features had a feminine cast to them. "Orlov's trying to prod us toward the old alliance between the English and the Turks!"

"And why would I be prodding you toward that?" asked Misha.

"Because. Well." The student licked his lips. "Because now the English are trying to make amends with us so that they can build their railway to China."

"Which is relevant, *why*?"

Silence reigned. Kesha finished his coffee.

"Because we might sell the American territories to *them*," offered the student who had been so eager to pay off Russia's debts. "They've got the bordering territories, and I'd think they'd want to solidify their hold on the continent."

Misha gave him a withering look over his spectacles. The boy's face crumpled in anticipation of the coming critique. "And I'm sure we want to explain to the United States why we refused their generous offer merely in order to sell the territories to someone else. You forget that this isn't only a political question. It's a question of *legality*, as any transference of property must be. I will see all of you tomorrow, and by then, I expect each of you to have discovered at least three *legal* difficulties with selling our territories to the United States. Alexander Ivanovich has taken the hint better than the rest of you, but even he is only guessing. How will you ever navigate treaty law, if you haven't learned the treaties that came out of the Crimea *by heart?*" He waved a negligent hand. "Disperse. We've finished."

Like doves startled from a rooftop by a thrown stone, the students rose and scattered. The small, dark fellow paused as though he had a question to pose, but he buckled under Misha's gaze and turned on his heel. The coffee-house door swung shut behind him.

"Alexander Ivanovich?" asked Kesha, when they were quite alone.

"A good boy," answered Misha affably enough. "The son of some minor functionary, and generally less of an idiot than the rest of them."

"A particular friend of yours?"

Perhaps something in his tone was sharper than he had intended, or perhaps the tense tapping of his thumb on the table had given him away, for Kesha found Misha regarding him as though he had proposed selling the territories in question to Sweden. Kesha was the first to look away, but Misha spoke slowly and deliberately so that he could not pretend to mishear or misunderstand. "A foolish boy," he pronounced, "with a decent mind, but no head for facts. And considerably better than some at drawing conclusions from the evidence available."

"Well. You *have* been known to suffer fools." Kesha passed the empty cup back. "Will you come to supper with me, Mishenka? I'd hoped we could discuss the poems you lent me."

The request made Misha laugh. Instead of taking the cup, he closed his hand warmly on Kesha's wrist. "So Machiavellian, Kesha!" he said, and the trace of a laugh still lingered in his voice. "To ask me after you've offended me, when refusing would only make me feel petty and childish. Even if you've forgotten your recent history, your argumentative logic is as sharp as ever."

"I haven't forgotten. Russia negotiated a moratorium on changing the national boundaries until February of 1881. That was the condition under which we agreed to remove our navy from the Black Sea to the Sea of Japan. The Tsar tried to extend the treaty last year, but the Sultan wouldn't come to the table. That's why the English are here now—because everyone expects that the warring will start again next year."

Misha blinked, and Kesha couldn't help smirking. "My father used to call the decade after the Eastern War 'the bounty years,'" he said. "Since they couldn't interfere with our borders without breaking the treaty, the Turks sent dragons across the border by the dozens. He used to have a taxidermist preserve the heads. We had nearly a hundred, before we ran out of places to hang them."

"You never speak about your father but to be smug at me," chided Misha, but with a particular gentleness that was softer for being little-practiced. "Perhaps one day you'll tell me why?"

"I might, one day," Kesha allowed. "You won't be able to help thinking less of me for it."

"I couldn't possibly think less of you than I already do," Misha said lightly. "Come, then. Let's have a look at that beastly poetry that's captured your heart so."

They rose together, and went together from the shop once Misha had settled the reckoning. All around them, a soft shower of snow fell from the lowering clouds.

CHAPTER EIGHT

"Excuse me, Pyotr Vladimirovich."

Petya would have flinched, but he was squeezed between a heavy length of chain and a rusted counterweight in the narrow shaft that held the gate's machinery. He made a soft, startled sound and freed a hand—still with a wrench in it—to wave to the English lieutenant. Wainwright, wasn't it? "Just a moment," he answered. "I need to tighten this bolt. It won't take more than a second."

"Of course. Take your time," replied the Englishman, and he leaned against the entry of the shaft to wait. He was not a particularly large man, but he had a way of positioning his body in the doorway so that it blocked all of the evening sunlight. Petya, who had been relying on that sunlight to inspect the more ticklish bits of the mechanism, resented the incursion immensely.

He tightened the bolt at a leisurely pace, then tested its soundness more thoroughly than was strictly required. The Englishman didn't move or comment on Petya's dawdling. At some point between yesterday and today, he had acquired a thick muffler and a fur cap that was slightly too big for him, which he wore with his faded pelisse as though he meant to look Russian in spite of his English uniform.

The English didn't know how to dress for a proper Russian winter. Wainwright would need a fur coat and heavier gloves, as well, in the weeks to come.

"Finished?" asked the lieutenant, when Petya had picked up his lantern and wriggled past the massive chain. Petya nodded. "Good. I'd hoped to have a chat with you, perhaps over tea. Would that be agreeable?"

"I won't be able to tell you anything my father or my sister wouldn't," Petya demurred, but the Englishman made an impatient sound at his hesitation.

"I don't plan to interrogate you about your keep," he said. His smile struck Petya as oddly mechanical, like the smile of a clockwork man in the Kunstkamera. "I was hoping for a bit of civilized company. I studied for a year in St. Petersburg, you see. At the Imperial St. Petersburg Academy of Sciences."

At these words, Petya could not help wondering (he was too suspicious; Kesha would have laughed at his suspicion) whether Wainwright said it only because he knew that Petya was a student there. He made as though to step past the lieutenant, and Wainwright made way for him. In the sunlight, his angular face lost some of the menacing sharpness lent by the deep shadows. "Very well," allowed Petya at last. "I won't be able to manage teatime, but if you'll let me finish my work, I could meet you later this evening. Perhaps at six?"

"Certainly, take your time," said Wainwright. "Is there a decent tea shop in the town?"

If some enterprising, cosmopolitan soul had opened a tea shop in Petya's absence, he didn't know it. He shook his head. "There's a tavern, but the tea there wasn't very good last time I had it. Very weak."

"It'll be a sorry day when an Englishman enjoys a weak pot of tea!" laughed Wainwright. "Then we'll brew our own from a proper Russian samovar. Christ, do you Tarasovs even have a samovar?"

They did, but Liza was pointedly denying the English soldiers any proper tea or coffee, and so of course Wainwright hadn't seen it. "Liza reserves it for guests she actually likes. If she won't let us use the samovar, though, we can boil water in a pan. Would that be" and he used Wainwright's word deliberately, "agreeable?"

"Very much so," Wainwright replied. "I don't mean to cast aspersions on your family, but it's a very mixed-up sort of house you have. Brandy with breakfast and vodka with supper, no tea for the asking—"

"If our drinking habits are more mixed up than the rest of our house, then we've done well," said Petya. "Now, if you'll excuse me, I have work to finish."

"Godspeed, Pyotr Vladimirovich," answered Wainwright. He gave a half-bow and turned to go, crossing the courtyard with a faintly uneven step that hinted at some old injury. Once Wainwright had departed, Petya went once more into the shaft that held the chain and counterweight.

Wainwright was no fool. Surely he could see that the Tarasovs were a fractured family, and that Liza held too tightly to her brother because she scarcely remembered how to hold him. The Englishman might plead a disinterested attachment to Petya's school and his city, but in these walls, no display of affection—not even Liza's—could be disinterested. He wanted to befriend Petya because he hoped to drive a wedge into that crack between him and the others, and thereby to weaken the whole. Liza had been entirely right to distrust him.

Petya hung his lantern from the hook high on the wall of the shaft, then began to winch up the great chain so that he could examine the portion that usually ran into the depths of the shaft. It was, as he had suspected, heavy with rust. He imagined that no one had cleaned out the chain-well in the last century, nor tried to keep out the damp.

The gates, like the rest of the fortress, were at the end of their useful life, sustained less by care than by disuse. Petya could replace the rusted links, or even replace the entire chain with one made of good steel, but then the place would only fall to some new ruin through its masters' neglect.

"No more hopeless thoughts," Petya scolded himself, smiling at how his inflection matched Liza's. Liza, at least, would never brook the ruination of the keep. She was a Tarasova not merely by birth, but by conviction, and if she had to hold the stones together with her will alone, she would do it gladly and then badger Petya into mixing mortar.

A steel chain, then. Modern and clean. Perhaps even a new counterweight. Certainly a new winch, since this one was so rust-choked and frost-weathered that he could scarcely make it turn. The machinists would charge him dearly for it, but it'd make Lukin smile to see that at least one Tarasov still cared about maintenance.

When he had finished his schooling, perhaps he'd return to the borderlands to service the guns and gates of the fortresses. Someone had to keep them running, and perhaps even improve them. There would always be dragons and wars with the Turks, and the forts couldn't be permitted to fall to ruin.

"Old habits of thought," he said wryly, and there was at least as much nostalgia as admonition in it.

The sun had slipped behind the heavy clouds while Petya completed his initial survey of the gate mechanisms; he could no longer delay his appointment with Lieutenant Wainwright. By this time, a light, hard snow had begun to hiss against the walls, and as he crossed the courtyard, the flakes beat against his face like grains of sand. He pulled his scarf up over his nose and his hat down over his ears, but that slight protection only heightened the sting as the snow lashed the soft skin around his eyes.

If he were in St. Petersburg, he could anticipate a hot cup of coffee or tea with marmalade to help him recover from the chill. But tonight he'd promised to have tea with the Englishman, which was enough to spoil the prospect completely. Steeling himself for disappointment, Petya descended from the wind-scoured courtyard to the deep recesses of the keep.

As he entered the main hall, though, a heavy hand fell upon his shoulder. "There you are, Petya," said his father warmly. "You're going drinking with me and Liza."

"But I promised to meet Wainwright for tea at six," said Petya, and his father's hand tightened in response.

"*Did* you promise it?" He chuckled as though Petya had told him a joke, but not a particularly funny one. "What do you think will come of that, eh? You'll have tea with him, and then you'll have yourself an English friend? Someone to laugh at the Russians with?"

If Petya had been a dog, he would have flattened his ears at his father's laughter. "I only wanted to be polite," he said. "He wouldn't let me say no. I told him there wasn't a tea shop in the town, and I told him you wouldn't want him using the samovar, but he—"

"Now you can tell him, when he asks, that you went to drink with your family. Even an Englishman can't begrudge you a few drinks with your family." *Ah*, thought Petya, as he apprehended his father's rhetorical mode. It had always been Vladimir Tarasov's way to speak his commands as though they were inevitable, no more to be opposed than the coming of winter—as though he did not even need to employ the imperative. Kesha had called him *a high-handed tyrant of a man*, and although Petya loved their father, he couldn't disagree.

He smiled faintly, then realized that his father couldn't see the expression beneath his scarf and tugged the fabric down about his neck. "I'd be happy to," said Petya, which made Vladimir grin. He noted absently that his father had lost another tooth.

"Good! I want to see my daughter drink my son under the table." He clapped Petya once on the back, squeezing on contact in a proprietary fashion, then turned to fetch his heavy coat. Petya's own clothes were flecked with rust and stained with grease, but he could see that his father was too much in a hurry to permit him to change into something cleaner.

The ringing beat of heeled boots on stone signaled Liza's arrival, and Petya had to smile at the figure she made in her gown. She had no interest in fashion; the cut of the dress was at least a decade out of date, too full-skirted for the esplanades and prospects along the Neva where the *beau monde* displayed their taste. She hadn't trained her waist to the slenderness that style demanded, nor had she a woman's winter cap to set off the ensemble—she wore a man's fur hat, which completed the rather ridiculous image. Petya thought privately that she looked far better in trousers and a masculine coat. In those clothes, at least, she seemed all of a piece.

"Is he coming?" she asked, then caught sight of Petya. "Are you coming?"

"I am, but I think Wainwright will be disappointed," he answered.

"Good!" Liza drew her brother into a rib-crushing hug, kissing both his cheeks. "I like disappointing Wainwright. It's better sport than shooting bottles. Why will he be disappointed?"

"Our Petya agreed to have tea with him," sneered Vladimir.

"Don't let that bastard near our samovar," she said immediately.

Petya burst out laughing. "I told him you'd say that," he answered, when he could catch his breath enough to answer at all. "He'll be so disappointed to miss a chance at real tea. You know the English pride themselves on it."

"They brew their tea into muck," Liza said, although they

both knew that she'd never tasted English tea in her life.

"They hardly brew it at all," said their father. Whether he had ever tasted English tea, neither of his children could say. "Let's go, Liza. I don't want to be talking about tea when I could be drinking spirits."

Petya offered Liza his arm, but she only snorted at his gallantry and fisted her hands in her muff, while their father threw his head back and laughed at the snubbing until his eyes watered. "What did you think would happen?" he asked, wiping his eyes. "Do you think she's an invalid who needs your arm? Do you think she's a *girl*? Name of God, Vladimirovich, look at the bad habits he's picked up in the city!"

As they passed through the door and stepped into the family's old carriage, Petya realized that his father had meant Liza when he said *Vladimirovich*, and more even than his sister's trousers and drinking and swearing, the patronymic made him shiver with a deep disquiet. If their father called her *Vladimirovich*, then surely it meant that she had replaced Kesha entirely in his heart. He had slotted Liza into the position of the first son and heir as easily as though Kesha had never been born.

The drive down to the town was cramped, claustrophobic, the smell of horse-sweat and musty velvet pervading their clothes from the closeness of the carriage. Liza traded outrageous barbs with their father, who gave a great, roaring laugh at the more profane retorts even as he parried them expertly. They spoke with the easy mirth of long familiarity, and even Liza's rough speech became half-musical with the wry wit of an experienced conversational duelist. It was then, her thigh pressed against Petya's and their father's knees nearly touching his own, that he realized that he, too, had been replaced.

"Come on, boy," said their father. "Don't look so glum! Anastasia Ivanovna will soon set you right. That smile will make you forget all about your tea and your foolish promises."

"I have no interest at all in Anastasia Ivanovna Vasilevskaya," demurred Petya. For all Nastya was the beauty of the town, and for all his father clearly wished to see them introduced more intimately, he couldn't help thinking it in poor taste. He'd broken with her sister Galya four years ago, not long before he'd gone to St. Petersburg, and he did not wish to appear as though he was working his way through their ranks. "I know you have my best interests—"

"His best interests! Do you hear that, Vladimirovich? He thinks he can resist Nastya's charms. Have you forgotten what a pretty girl's smile looks like, while you've been closeted away with your scholars? Have you forgotten, Petya?"

Liza shot her father a venomous look, and her lips parted as though she would speak. But then the driver opened the door, and instead she stepped out of the carriage without looking back.

Petya wondered what it was she had wished to say, and why she had bitten her tongue against saying it.

CHAPTER NINE

When the Tarasovs came to the tavern, they did so like lords from a bygone century. The patrons at their usual table cleared away at once when they saw Liza at the door with a scowl darkening her brow. Anastasia Ivanovna sent one of her younger sisters to take care of the other customers while she smoothed down her skirt and put on a smile. Catching Liza's eye, she went to attend to the Tarasovs herself.

Liza flung herself down upon the bench seat, her back against the corner where the walls met. "Bring me something strong, Nastya. I'm in a mood."

"Any fool can see you're in a mood," said Nastya, but then Liza's father pushed through the door with Petya close on his heels, and this seemed to satisfy Nastya's curiosity. She left the table with the grace of a battleship sliding smooth across the open sea, and Petya's eyes followed her as she went.

He would flirt with her, too, because he thought his father wanted him to flirt with her; Petya had always been the most obliging of sons. He had come home at no more prompting than Liza's letter, his trunk hastily packed and ink-stains still on his knuckles from university—and with no prompting at all, he had set to work on the gates and the towers, as though Liza had called him home for no other reason than to be their engineer. "Sit, before your eyes roll out of your head," Liza said, and (ever obliging!) Petya slid onto the bench beside her.

"Her sisters have grown up a bit since you went away," said Vladimir in a carrying undertone. He removed his gloves one at a time, tugging them off by the ends of the fingertips until they came free, and stacked them neatly on the table before him. "Was Vanya still alive, when he went to the city?"

Liza felt his eyes on her. She pushed her own gloves off from the wrists and dropped them into her lap. "I think so, but only barely," she answered. "Nastya had already taken over the business, and two of her sisters were tending the bar."

"No," Petya broke in, "They weren't. I'd have remembered if they were!"

"Ah," said Vladimir, his eyes dancing. "You would."

"*Enough*," said Nastya. "Name of God, I'll break a bottle over your head if you keep doing that. I'll eat with you, if you *must* balance your table, but you'll pay for my supper." With that she swept out again, seizing her second-oldest sister (Yulchik, Liza thought, all well-fleshed arms and broad chin) and drawing her back to the bar to whisper several sharp words in her ear.

Liza tossed back her drink quickly, longing for the wind-searing burn in her throat and the comfortable lassitude of drunkenness. Her father would drink until he was maudlin, and Petya would certainly be drunk within an hour and God only knew what he would do. As for Liza, she would drink until everything made her laugh. She couldn't bear these sober, jealous moods.

Petya drained his glass slowly, but even so, his eyes watered before he had finished. *Within half an hour*, thought Liza, and she poured another finger for him and then filled her glass again. The neck of the bottle clinked against the lip of the glass. The bottle was cold beneath her fingers and glistened like ice.

"Tell me something about St. Petersburg," said Vladimir, when they had settled in their seats. Liza tucked her shoulder against the place where the walls met and surveyed the room as though she were scanning for foes, only half-attentive to Petya's stories of scholarly bustle along the banks of the Neva. She cared nothing at all for libraries and faculties and museums full of clockwork birds and Hottentots, and at the moment she cared nothing at all for Petya, either. If she had known that her father would take it into his head to send Petya chasing after Nastya like a hound after a fallen bird—well, perhaps she wouldn't have come at all.

Two of the Englishmen were drinking in the far corner, laughing to one another in that quiet and half-ashamed way that she had begun to think was characteristic of the English. They would soon change their tune, though, when they had poured enough alcohol down their gullets. Liza had also begun to think that nothing was merrier than a drunken Englishman in a foreign land.

A party of young rail-workers had congregated near the center of the room, and they were toasting to something or other: a birth, a birthday, a marriage. A lanky, red-haired man accepted the accolades as his due, and only when she looked away did she realize that he reminded her of Kesha. There were always rail-workers in the tavern of late, whiling away the hours with dice and beer and then going out again in the mornings to join together the old rail lines. Soon they'd connect the tangle of railways to one great trunk, all headed east to China and to prosperity—*and what then?* Liza chuckled, low.

"What's funny?" her father asked.

"A woman can't clear her throat without something being funny?" replied Liza, and downed another glass of liquor. It burned a line of fire from her tongue to her gut.

"You drink it like *water*," said Nastya, with a snort of a laugh.

Liza craned her neck to meet Nastya's eyes, smiling. "For a Tarasov," she declared, "it might as well be water."

"It might for *you*," said Petya. "I'll be happy with kvass, or beer if you don't have any kvass."

While their father laughed and called his son weak, a woman, Nastya gathered her skirts and slid onto the bench beside Vladimir. She kept a careful space between them, neither too close nor too distant, but her entire body angled away from him as he leaned in to welcome her, and her smile was strained around the edges.

"My son has returned from the university in St. Petersburg," said Vladimir, as though St. Petersburg had only one university and Vladimir only one son. "He's learning to be an engineer. I might wish he'd chosen something else to study, but at least it's a *profession*. A man can earn a good living as an engineer."

Petya turned to his sister, confusion naked on his face. There was a crease between his brows that exactly resembled the one between her own. She could read his meaning in his eyes, clear as writing: *is he bragging about my studies? When did he become proud of my studies?*

Liza smiled across the table at Nastya. If Petya required any other answer, he was too much an idiot to be at university.

"Yes," answered Petya, when he had recovered himself. "Yes, I hope I'll be able to make myself useful. I enjoy working with my hands; it seems the most noble thing a man can learn to do—" On *noble*, she tipped her head back and laughed once, sharp and brazen. He shot her a wounded look. "Don't laugh at me, Liza!"

"Say what you like about the nobility of laboring like a gardener, with your hands," she answered, "but Russia was built on the labor of its *soldiers*, and not its workers. It demeans your heritage to say you want to be as noble as a *laborer*—"

"And what if he does?" The table quieted as Nastya spoke. Every one of them turned to her. "Oh, you all crowd around me like wolves! What are you waiting to hear? Are you waiting for me to say that my grandfather was bound to your grandfather's land?—but no, I won't speak for my family or my politics. I won't be drawn into this."

Seeing her withdraw, Vladimir stole Petya's unwanted glass and poured a finger of liquor, then passed the glass to Nastya with an expression of almost paternal tenderness. "We're friends here, Nastya. You and I are friends, you and Liza are friends. Why should we want to draw you into anything?"

Nastya sipped at her liquor. The drink lent her voice an unaccustomed roughness. "The English have been drinking here, and I've seen how Liza looks at them. I see you looking at them," she said, when Liza sat straighter and tightened her grip on her cup. "You don't like them here, and why should you? They don't belong in our town. They've put everyone's back up, worse than a raid. Dima thinks they're spies for the Tsar, and Seryozha says that they came here to turn us *against* the Tsar. Why shouldn't I be suspicious of everyone's politics, when the English are everywhere making a nuisance of themselves?"

"Ah, Nastyusha! You're above suspicion," said Liza, and cursed herself for the tenderness in her voice. "Your grandfather was bound to my grandfather's land; why should that matter? He was *loyal* to our grandfather, just like your father was to mine."

"Just like I'll be loyal to *you*, Elizaveta Vladimirovna?" Nastya laughed sharply. "You have unpaid bills standing in the way of my loyalty, and you come to my tavern in the morning to buy vodka from me—"

"I come to *see* you," Liza snapped. Blood rushed into her face, hot and shameful. How much had she had to drink in the past few hours? How many cups, while Petya wittered on about this German mathematician or that Polish chemist? "And you laugh at me for coming to buy vodka. Very well; laugh if it pleases you! I certainly never hear you laughing at anything else."

Nastya looked up from under hooded lids. Her eyes were flint-grey, cool, without mirth or mercy.

The bottle was half-empty. Liza's mouth felt very dry.

Nastya stood from the bench and nearly tripped as her skirt caught on the corner. "I apologize," she said to Vladimir, through a smile that pulled her mouth tight. Under her lip-paint, the edges of her lips were pale with the strain. "I can't balance your table. You can stay for dinner with your family, but I won't share it. Good day, Vladimir Petrovich."

With that, she swept away, drawing her shawl about her shoulders as though she'd been chilled.

Liza's heart throbbed painfully. She knew very well that she had humiliated herself, and if her father hadn't pressed Petya on their hostess—if her father hadn't leaned in so closely to greet Nastya, and if Nastya hadn't pulled ever so slightly away—

It was senseless to think of *perhaps* and *if only*. She had bared her heart like a little fool, and even Liza couldn't stand to see it so naked.

"She's a proud woman," said Vladimir at last. "She meant to wound you a little, and it irked her not to have drawn blood. It was no more than that, Liza. Bring her some pretty jewelry in the morning and soon she'll mend her manners."

"Bring her *jewelry*? Like a spurned lover! I won't barter for her friendship," Liza hissed, but she could feel the flush abating from her neck.

"Then pay our bill, if you won't give her a present. We'll be in poor shape if we can't get credit at the tavern for a girls' spat. We'd have to drink by ourselves, and what then?" Vladimir finished his drink. "Then we'd have no one but each other to dice with, and there's no money to be earned in dicing with my daughter."

"Do you hear something?" asked Petya suddenly. "Listen—"

Father and daughter sat straighter, listening intently. As though Petya's voice had let the sound cut through the laughter of the rail-workers and the singing of the Englishmen, both heard at once what Petya meant—and so did Nastya and her sisters, for in a moment Galya was ringing the brass bell behind the bar, and the patrons were rising from their chairs and pushing toward the steel hatch in the floor.

At the fortress, the alarm bells were tolling.

If Liza had been a sensible woman, or a sober woman, she would have joined the press of patrons into the shelter. She would have waited beneath the ground like a trembling mouse at the shadow of the hawk.

Liza was neither sober nor sensible, and she dashed outside, unsheathing her knife to cut the carriage horse from its traces. She yanked her skirt up around her legs and gripped the horse with her thighs, tangling her fingers in its mane and driving her heels hard into its flanks. With dragons somewhere in the darkness above her, she rode hard for the fortress.

CHAPTER TEN

As Kesha waited in the drawing room of Starikovich's house, he found himself continually on the verge of nodding off. He and Misha had sat up together until the early hours of the morning, studying the draconic symbols until the fire had died in the grate, and then they'd fallen asleep sprawled out on the sofa. He'd awakened early, too, when a charwoman came in to clean away the ashes and lay a new fire for the day. She had made a clucking sound with her tongue that had drawn Kesha out of strange dreams of wind and fire, and he'd pushed himself up from Misha's chest and run his hands through his hair.

And then, he reminded himself, resettling his portfolio in his lap, *I had to begin my revisions at once, or I'd have nothing to show Starikovich.* The morning had been one long, frantic sprint through his theological texts in search of a *modern* author whose views on immanence and the substantial soul weren't utter rubbish. Starikovich had castigated him yesterday for his reliance upon sources that had last been pertinent in the Renaissance, and reluctantly, Kesha had conceded the point. "How can you ground your argument in *Galen*, boy?" Starikovich had thundered, and rapped Kesha's knees with his cane. "Galen! And *he* was only pilfering from Plato, the scrounger. What were you thinking? Are we ancient Greeks? Are we living in Ivan the Great's era? Use your *head*, Kesha, and find an Orthodox source!" It was enough to make him want to abandon the question of immanence entirely.

Regrettably, Kesha's first, cursory search had only turned up grave meditations on Catholic heresies. These, he had dutifully compiled into a brief literary review in the (certainly doomed) hope of appeasing Starikovich. With unaccustomed anxiety, he reached into the portfolio to examine his notes one last time.

When he touched the edges of the pages, though, his blood went cold. He had written his revisions on the sort of thin paper that poor scholars favored, so light that Petya often used it to trace diagrams for his notes. However, the papers in his portfolio were thicker, heavier. He drew them out and saw that he had brought not his thesis revisions, but his notes on the dragons' poetry.

"What have you got there, boy?" Engrossed as he was in his own error, Kesha nearly leapt out of his skin at the sound of Starikovich's voice. He began to shuffle his papers back into the portfolio, but then the old man's hand came down like a vise and seized his wrist. "Hmm," he murmured, plucking the papers easily from Kesha's half-nerveless fingers. "Interesting. It's been *years* since I've seen a copy of the *Collection*. There was a better translation published around 1800, in Yekaterinburg. Had proper stanza breaks, but I see you've already figured out that these stanzas are organized on some madman's piece-of-shit odic scheme. Where did you find this?"

"A bookseller's stand," lied Kesha, although he didn't imagine that he could keep Starikovich in the dark for long. "In a box with other books. Quite honestly, it was some time ago. I've only just had time to read it."

"Well, it's a commendable line of inquiry for the thesis, if not something you'll ever squeak past the censors."

Starikovich let go of Kesha's wrist (the blood seeped slowly back into his fingers, with a tingling sensation) and settled himself in his favorite armchair, beside which he had piled a stack of heavy books that Kesha had never seen him open. "The dragons believed—probably *still* believe—that the soul's kept in a gland at the back of their necks, right against the spine—"

"How do you know that?" asked Kesha, when he could gather enough presence of mind to speak at all. "The universities *burned* their books on dragons; how do you know anything about them?"

"Just like a Tarasov, to think that the only books in the world are kept in *universities*," snorted Starikovich. "And the rest of us? Supposed to touch a match to our libraries, were we?" He took out his pipe and filled it, then lit it and puffed contentedly. The smell of tobacco smoke reminded Kesha keenly of home.

"I presume you were, but I can believe just as easily that you *didn't*," Kesha answered at last. "Do you read the dragons' language? Can you tell me what their symbols mean, or how I could *learn* what they mean?"

Blowing a smoke ring, Starikovich shook his head. "I could when I was a boy, but I haven't worked in the language for decades. I've forgotten all but a few words. 'Lamb' and 'mountain range.'" He drew his pipe away from his lips and made a sound like a horse's scream. It took a moment for Kesha to realize that he was actually *translating*, and by then Starikovich had tired of this line of questioning. "But this is all border nonsense, and you're here for your thesis. Let's see whether you've mucked out your last draft. Has Galen been deposed?"

"Eradicated," said Kesha, with perfect honesty. "I haven't found a good successor, though. Once our forebears stopped thinking of 'spirit' in terms of bodily fluids, all discussion of the material presence of the soul fell into a chasm of Cartesian logical puzzles and vague platitudes about heresy. As far as I can tell, it's never emerged again. Everyone wants to talk about theosis; no one wants to talk about immanence."

"Then perhaps you've got an untenable argument. What then, Kesha?"

The echo of his father's favorite words almost made Kesha flinch. He brought the portfolio up to his chest, clutching it tightly and striving to school his face to neutrality. "If my argument is untenable," he said, "I'll make it anyway. Someone needs to revive the question of immanence. There's little good in making only accepted, tenable arguments about the divine. The discourse is refreshed by a few mad prophets—"

Starikovich barked out a sharp laugh. "You'd call yourself a *prophet*, boy?"

"*—and heretics*," finished Kesha coolly. "As I feel no call to a religious life, the Orthodox Church may take what offense it pleases at my thesis. I might even cite dragons, simply to annoy the divinity school."

"If that's your plan," said Starikovich—Kesha braced himself for the inevitable rejection—"then I'll find you a *real* translation of the *Collection*, and see what other books my family will send west."

Kesha blinked. Smoke rose from the pipe. The house settled around them, and upstairs, Starikovich's wife walked across a carpet and onto tile.

Thwack! came Starikovich's cane. Kesha hissed and dropped his portfolio, sucking at his knuckles.

"Try not to look so glum, boy!" the old man laughed. "*Now* you've got a project!"

On his way back from Starikovich's house, Kesha called at the Galiyevs' for supper, then returned to his lodging feeling surprisingly refreshed by the interlude. Misha had been intrigued by the intelligence on Starikovich's family collection, and he had urged Kesha to share every scrap of new material that he could uncover. While Kesha pursued the problem from a more literary angle, Misha would do his best to investigate any changes in laws or policies dating from the years after the Defection. Very few things in Kesha's life gave him the same sense of peace and accomplishment that he felt at working through a puzzle with an intellect he admired, and Misha's intellect was one of the finest he knew. For that alone, he would have been grateful.

He unlocked the door to his rooms, hearing the familiar click of the lock turning over. On the windowsill, the remnants of Petya's ill-fated lead gleamed faintly in the twilight, then brightly in the gaslight. The scorch marks only set off the shine of the metal.

Kesha removed his jacket and his shoes, then settled into his desk chair and dipped his pen in the inkwell. The ink was sluggish—chilled, he supposed—but it began to flow more smoothly once he had stirred it a bit. He tugged a sheet of onionskin paper from his pile and spread it over the desktop.

Dearest Petya, he wrote. *It has been three days since you left for our family home, and I still expect to see you at every turn....*

CHAPTER ELEVEN

Amid the press of bodies, the confused shouting of Englishmen who'd never had to go to ground at a warning bell, Petya lost sight of his sister. "Liza!" he called, but if she could hear him, she didn't answer. "Father, we have to find Liza—"

From outside came a percussive blast that rattled the glasses on the table. A second, closer blast rang in Petya's ears and shook the bottles behind the bar.

"Get *down*, Tarasov," shouted Nastya from the hatch, as her four sisters descended the ladder to shelter. "Your sister knows what she's doing."

"But she's drunk; we have to find her!" Horror gripped Petya's heart, closing like a chill hand beneath his ribs. He felt certain—and why, he couldn't have said—that if they couldn't find Liza *now*, then she'd be lost to them forever. "Father, make her see—"

"Devil take the both of you," said Nastya, and she pulled the thick steel door shut over her head. Beneath the floorboards, in the stone that sheathed the shelter, the bolt slammed home.

The Tarasovs looked at one another in the sudden quiet of the tavern, with the warning bell still tolling from the keep. "I don't know what you expected me to make her see," said Vladimir, but he pulled on his gloves and started for the door. Liza's gloves lay where she'd left them. Petya scooped them up and put them in his pocket. If Liza survived the next hour, she'd want them again.

The carriage stood where they had left it, although the driver had run at the sound of the bells. The horse was gone. Vladimir put his hand to the traces, feeling the edges of the leather. "Hmm," he said to himself, and began to run for the fortress. He kept off the road, in the shadows of buildings, and Petya followed close behind. They knew better than to make dark shapes on the snow-dusted pavement. The going would be trickier when they got past the shelter of the town and to the hills beyond. The first snows lay white on the grass, and their dark coats would show at once to anyone looking down from the sky.

"Move your bones, boy!" Vladimir puffed as they emerged from the shadow of the last house. They were on open field now, cut across with the dark line of the railroad. Gunfire punctuated the continual clamor of the bell, round after round piercing the sky. Petya's breath came short; it had been years since he'd run more than the length of an alley, and he was half-winded already at the exertion. For all his age, for all his gout and his cough, Vladimir ran after Liza like an engine.

Overhead, the dragons began to scream.

The Tarasovs pelted up the hill, lungs burning and hearts pounding. The ache in Petya's thighs seared like hot iron. The world condensed to the razor-sharp keen of the dragons, the slippery earth and stone under his feet, the feeling of fire in his blood. *Liza, Liza, you madwoman!* he thought, and then they had reached the servants' entrance and found no horse or rider.

"She'll be inside," said Vladimir; "She's dead!" cried Petya at the same time. Neither could hear the other over the screaming.

A burst of gunfire cut the screams short.

A second burst, and a dragon came apart in plumes of gas and flame high above them. From the gunnery turrets, there came a joyous whoop like the crow of some foreign bird.

Petya closed his eyes against a spike of anguish. That voice hadn't been Liza's—in God's name, where was Liza? *Torn apart*, he thought, as he followed his father into the keep. *Eaten up—exploded—*

From a nearby corridor came the ring of bootheels on tile, and Petya whirled. Before him stood Liza, just rising from the crouch into which she'd fallen after jumping off the ladder to the gun tower. Her eyes were bright and her hair wind-tossed, her dress torn and her hands red and her cap missing—and she was *alive*, beautiful and real and *alive*. Petya laughed with shock as much as joy. "Liza!" he shouted, and then flung himself into her arms.

"No need to yell at me. I know my own name," she said against his hair, but she held him tightly in return. "I'm fine, Petya, stop *squeezing!*"

Behind them, Jaworski dropped from the ladder and then closed off the passage. "The English will be insufferable after this," he said without preamble. "One of them got the second. The one that exploded. They'll probably think this is a real *feather in their caps*," he concluded, drawling the English expression ironically.

"You should never have taught them to use the guns, if you didn't want them to fire them," said Liza as she prised her brother's arms off.

"I *didn't* teach them to use the guns," Jaworski cut in. He held himself erect, arms folded over his chest. He still wore his uniform, and it struck Petya then that the clothing was no affectation. Jaworski dressed as a soldier because, no matter what other work he might profess to pursue, he could never be anything but a soldier. "They are military men. I imagine they've used the occasional gun in their day."

"I'm surprised that they didn't fire their little popguns

at the dragons," said Vladimir, not bothering to conceal his disdain. "If they knew how to use our guns, then it was only by the grace of God. They certainly didn't come here equipped to fight dragons."

"God's ways are mysterious," said Jaworski. He smiled faintly, wryly. "It's not that they could *fire* the guns that surprises me. They're not so different from the guns the British use in their colonial wars. No, I'm surprised that they could *aim* them. You won't find these mountings anywhere else, and it takes weeks to learn to steer the things."

Petya, who had been listening in silence, broke in suddenly, "The Turks have them. The mountings, I mean. They used to use them for ballistae, before we had the guns. They're not identical, of course, but they work on the same...principle..." He trailed off, aware that the other three were regarding him with a new curiosity. Swallowing against the roughness in his throat and a coppery tang that he hoped wasn't blood, he continued, "They had a...well, a fascination for clockwork creatures, in the last century. The Kunstkamera has some of the earliest ones on display. But what I mean is, the Turks weren't only interested in the things as toys. They were fascinated with gears and mechanisms, and they had platforms just like ours, when *they* were fighting the dragons. For their ballistae. Not as modern, and probably not as sensitive or flexible, but ours weren't, either, back then. And even older models would have been enough to teach a soldier the rudiments. If he were clever."

Liza's lips drew back over her teeth. "I hate clever men," she said, low and dangerous. "And I especially hate clever Englishmen who take lessons from Turks."

After a dragon fell, there followed the arduous work of hauling its corpse clear of the fortress and restocking the gun towers, searching for undetonated explosives and making a preliminary assessment of the damage, and with one thing and another, Petya didn't manage to sit down for the tea he'd promised Wainwright until nearly midnight. As he poured tea into their cups, the clock was just starting to chime. By this time they were too tired for formalities, and both men were in their shirtsleeves—Petya with his sleeves rolled up over his elbows to hide the grease-stains at the cuffs, Wainwright with his top button undone as a concession to the warmth of the kitchen. Steam rose from the tea, hot and smoke-scented. "You've killed your first dragon," said Petya, by way of introduction.

"I did," Wainwright answered. He couldn't help breaking into a grin at the memory, like a child elated at the prospect of a festival. Despite Petya's reservations, the delight on Wainwright's face was infectious, and soon he was smiling across the table. "I didn't believe it when I heard it, but they *do* explode! Like a—" he searched his Russian vocabulary, seeking the most appropriate word "—like a bomb!"

"You're lucky it wasn't closer to the ground. I've seen those explosions knock over carts and scaffolds," answered Petya. He sipped his tea, trying to discern whether he was imagining the rusty flavor to the water. "I'm sorry I missed our appointment. My father asked me to go drinking with him and Liza, and I couldn't say no."

"Your father isn't the sort of man who likes hearing *no*, is he?" Wainwright's expression grew wry. He held his teacup in both hands as though to warm them on the porcelain. It was an oddly vulnerable gesture.

Against his better judgment, Petya found himself growing to like the man. No one who could cup his tea like that, with such a hangdog a look on his face, could be entirely without human feeling.

"Not really," said Petya at last. "You look as if you've known a few men like that, though, if you'll pardon me for prying."

"My own father had a bit of a reputation for intransigence," admitted Wainwright. "I can't blame Vladimir Petrovich for wanting us out of his house. My father would never have stood for quartering foreign troops on English soil, and he'd have made it exactly as difficult for you as you've made it for us. Although he probably wouldn't have plied you with such a quantity of excellent brandy."

Petya choked at that, spluttering into his teacup. He clutched at his throat and tried to cough, but at first he couldn't muster the air. Wainwright rose so quickly that he knocked his chair over backwards, then came around the table and clapped Petya manfully on the back. One powerful smack dislodged the small quantity of tea that had caught in Petya's throat, and with a hard, shuddering cough, he finally drew in a breath.

"Thank you," said Petya, weakly. "That's—" he tried to swallow "—that's the second time I've choked on a drink since I came home. By my faith, I was only trying to laugh!"

"Laugh at my father?" asked Wainwright.

"Laugh at my sister. She gave you the brandy because she hates it." Wiping his eyes, Petya settled back in his chair. Wainwright bent to seize his own chair by the leg and righted it. When he straightened, he was chuckling softly, as if he was too exhausted to know why he was laughing.

He was a different person entirely, with a cup of tea and a saucer and a table for two. When he wasn't looming in doorways and blocking the light, strutting about the courtyard in a jumble of Russian cast-offs, Lieutenant Wainwright seemed small and almost shabby.

Invite him to drink tea with you, Liza had hissed, *and get him talking about the Turkish platforms!*

How should I do that? Petya had asked. *It isn't a natural subject for a conversation. He'll know that he's given himself away.* He had imagined that Wainwright was a dangerous man, a canny strategist like his own father, and he had nerved himself up for the conversation like a man preparing for battle. To see Wainwright with his shoulders slumped and his eyes soft and tired, Petya felt almost ashamed of his suspicions.

He softened his tone, the way Kesha sometimes did when he wanted to make Petya stop fretting. It was a deliberate gesture, perhaps, but one kindly meant. "When you were in St. Petersburg," he said, "and studying at the Academy, what did you study?"

"I was a geographer," answered Wainwright. "I wanted very much to learn the secrets of the poles, and the empty spaces in Siberia and Lapland, where the dragons lived. It seemed as though there were expeditions departing daily, and the Royal Geographical Society had no use for a bumbling young scholar without any pocket-money. I thought I'd try my luck in Russia. The living was cheaper in St. Petersburg, at least."

"And did you ever go to the poles?"

"No." With the ease of a Russian native, Wainwright scooped marmalade from the little jar on the table and mixed the preserves into his tea. His eyes were fixed on something far away, something that Petya knew tacitly was beyond his understanding. "No, I never went to the poles—but one day, I crossed over into Finland and boarded a timber train to the north. When I reached the end of the line, I hired a sledge, and when the sledge would go no further, I walked. The sun never set on me, in those days; I slept under dancing lights, wrapped up in a thick blanket, my nose just barely poking out into the air...." He sipped his tea and grimaced, perhaps at the sweetness and perhaps at the bitterness. "It was the sort of foolish thing that you do, just once, in your youth. I lost three toes to frostbite, and I never saw anything that I couldn't have seen just as easily in St. Petersburg."

"But you're glad you went." Petya knew it the way he knew that Kesha was glad to have left home, despite all that he'd lost in doing it. "You learned something about yourself by going that you'd never have learned in the city."

Wainwright's lips quirked up at the corners. "I learned that I'm not the sort of person you want on an arctic expedition, if that's what you mean. No instinct at all for how to travel in the cold."

"That's not what I mean," pressed Petya. "I see it when you stand up to my father. You've learned that there's… there's something like iron in you. And you're proud of it, the way you're proud of your father even though you call him 'intransigent.'" He folded his hands in his lap, where the backs of his fingers brushed a loose thread that he couldn't remember having snagged. "Where did you learn to use our guns, Lieutenant Wainwright?" he asked, and then on the heels of that, "What's your Christian name?"

"It's Peter, just like yours," answered Wainwright readily enough, "and I learned from the Ottomans."

CHAPTER TWELVE

"What's he saying?" asked Liza under her breath.

"I can't *hear* what he's saying," answered Jaworski, casting an aggrieved look over his shoulder. The two of them were huddled over the vent in the earth where the smoke from the kitchen escaped, and the effusion of black smoke made it difficult for either of them to lean over the grate very long. Liza had turned away once already, doubling over in a heavy coughing fit, while Jaworski had wrapped his scarf thrice about his mouth in grim concession to the foul air. To compound their frustration, they'd discovered only *after* they laid their plan that the vent conducted sound very poorly from the kitchen.

"We could have asked them to have their tea in the dining room," said Liza as she flung herself onto a frozen tussock and wrapped her arms about her knees. "We could have listened from the hallway, and hidden when they got up from the table—"

"We could have, but we didn't. Now we can only hope that Petya's having better luck than we are. Are you ready to go in?"

"Let me sit outside for a bit." She smiled up at him, and perhaps she even meant the smile, a little. There was hardly any wind tonight. The moon hung low and full in a nest of thick clouds. The air in the courtyard still carried the scent of saltpeter and blood.

"Would you like me to sit with you?" asked Jaworski. Liza shook her head. "We could go up to the watchtower, if you like. If you need the air."

"I need to be *alone*, Jaworski. I've made a fool of myself in front of strangers—in front of my *father*—and I need to be alone, even for an hour."

He folded his arms, brows lifted and moon-touched eyes glittering as though he wanted to laugh at her. "Very well, but you don't need be alone in the snow, at night, feeling sorry for yourself. Just like a Russian, to make herself miserable because she's sad!"

"Just like a Pole, to think there's no use in being miserable," she retorted. "If your people had learned better discipline—"

"There are other kinds of discipline, Liza," said Jaworski. "When you want to train a pup to be a good hunting dog, you sometimes have to hit him and shout at him. But to reward his obedience, you can stroke him and call him pet names, and even feed him with your own hand. That's discipline, too, and I'll venture that beloved dogs will grow to be better hunters than dogs who know nothing but the flat of your hand. *That's* what the Poles learned under the Russians: how it breaks you to know nothing but being kicked."

Liza sat watching the smoke for a long moment, resettling her feet in her boots and feeling the chill, dry air on her eyes and the tip of her nose. She *had* been disciplined fondly, she thought, with pet names and good meals and her father's approval in all she did. She knew that many other girls wouldn't have had her chances. She had never considered, before, that she had been raised to be a faithful hound. *As reliable as an old wolfhound*, she'd called Jaworski, when her father had proposed that she marry him.

If she thought of such things any longer, her tongue would run away with her again, and so she locked the door on those gloomy musings. "When I came home," she said, "I dropped off of the horse, and the damn thing ran away the second I let go. Stupid thing. It probably got snapped up by the dragons we didn't shoot down."

Although Jaworski's eyes registered surprise at the change of subject, his voice betrayed none of it. "Would you like to track it? We're making no progress here, and the prints will be clear on the snow."

Liza rocked up to her feet, brushing the snow from her trousers and coat and settling her cap more closely about her ears. "We're more likely to twist our ankles than to find the horse," she said, but for all her misgivings, she strode toward the entryway. Perhaps it was foolish to track a horse at night, while the ground was slick with ice. For that, though, she had sensible old Jaworski.

"I'll fetch a bridle," he said. While she waited in the vestibule between courtyard and servants' entrance, he ducked around to the stables against the north wall. A few minutes later, he was joining her at the entryway.

Although Jaworski had clearly entertained hopes of following the horse's trail down the hillside as easily as he might have followed Liza's across the courtyard, they soon discarded the idea. Outside of the walls of the fortress, the wind was far less merciful. It had driven the fine, hard snow across the jumbled stones like grains of sand over a desert landscape. The stones themselves, which would have been very dark had they been wet, were pale and bone-dry in the moonlight, with the snow sheering over the sides and catching in the crevices between. Each stone cast a dark, jagged shadow over the rock and snow below.

The conditions weren't suitable for tracking *anything*, but Liza had got it into her head that they would find the horse tonight, and now that she had stepped out of the fortress, she wasn't inclined to turn away from the project. She stooped by a gravel-filled depression just past the track of the road, peering into the darkness until she could convince herself that she had found a hoofprint. "Here," she said.

"We should bring a lantern," said Jaworski.

"Never mind that. Come look at this," answered Liza. He was good enough to oblige her, and knelt at her side to examine the ground where she pointed. To her relief, he made a soft *mmm* noise of assent and followed the angle of the print with his eyes. Soon, he had uncovered what might have been a second print and might have been another gap between rocks.

"It was heading back to the town," he decided, but Liza took him by the shoulder and pointed to the long, black line across the hills. "Ah," he said. "You're right. Toward the rails." There was cover there, scrubby bushes along the north side of the tracks and plum and cherry orchards to the east. The leaves were mostly gone, but the branches might shelter a horse.

They picked their way carefully down the hillside, following the gentle curve of the road with the notion that they would pick up the horse's trail again once they had reached the relatively less hazardous ground at the foot of the hill. The tracks would be clearer there. The horseshoes would have gouged deeply into the grass, even if snow had caught on the tussocks.

Liza scarcely stumbled on the way down, although her limbs felt heavy and the stones shifted underfoot. The battle and its aftermath had cleared her head wonderfully, but it had also left her weary to her bones. She seemed to hear each crunch of stone beneath her boots a few heartbeats after it happened. The absurdity of the situation struck her then, and she laughed up at the moon. "What's funny?" Jaworski asked.

"Everything. This. Tracking a horse in the dark, because we can't eavesdrop on an Englishman."

"And you're still half-drunk."

"I'm not even a little drunk," she protested, but Jaworski was laughing with her, and his laughter made her feel warm and secure. Having reached the base of the hill, they began to follow its curve in the direction of the railway. In only a few minutes, they had picked up the trail again, clear as a scar across the plains. They pursued in companionable silence, then, Jaworski's hands in his pockets and Liza's breath clouding the air.

Although at first the horse's trail led in the direction of the railroad, it looped back toward the town just shy of the tracks. Perhaps a dragon had tried to snatch the horse up, or perhaps it had felt safe enough to seek not merely safety, but also shelter and perhaps a good meal. In its place, Liza would probably have done the same. Come to that, the warning bell had rung before her supper had arrived, and her stomach felt like a knot inside her. She suspected that she would wake with her head aching and her mouth dry and foul, but there was little help for it now. If Nastya couldn't be prevailed upon to sell spirits in the morning, she certainly couldn't be begged to sell hot meals in the middle of the night.

If I even felt like begging her for anything, thought Liza fiercely. She hadn't forgotten what she'd said in the tavern, and she doubted that Nastya had, either. After such a shameful display, Liza wouldn't be able to show her face there for at least a week.

"Jaworski," she said under her breath. "Have you ever made a fool of yourself over a woman?"

"I have," he answered. "I doubt there's a single man who hasn't, if we're honest. A courtship isn't about proving yourself wise, but about proving that you know how to manage your foolishness."

"Tell me more about it," said Liza. "A story, if you like."

"A story." They walked in silence for another long moment, the frosted grass squeaking against their boots and the wind whistling against their ears. Liza couldn't tell if the question had offended Jaworski, or if he was only searching for a suitable story to tell.

At length, Jaworski chuckled into his scarf. "I have a

story," he said. "A story from when I first fell for my wife. She was a spirited girl, with blonde hair that she wore in long braids down her back, and I was a foolish little boy who didn't have the first idea how to get a girl to notice me. I was just growing into my arms and legs, and she was already graceful as a doe, so I don't need to tell you I was too ashamed to ask her to dance with me. I'd watch her dancing in a circle with the other girls, with her braids flying out behind her every time she turned. Some devil must have got hold of me, because I thought—God only knows why—I thought she'd *notice* me if I only seized one of her braids and pulled it. But it's one thing to pull a girl's braid while she's standing still, and another thing to pull it while she's dancing…she turned faster than I'd expected, and suddenly she was lying flat on her back with her skirt flung up over her head. Oh, she cursed my name for years after that!" He laughed, and Liza laughed with him. There was only warmth in his voice when he spoke of his wife, and nothing at all of shame or regret. She wondered if that particular tenderness was common to all lovers, and if she could ever train herself to it.

Foolish woman, to think that one needs to train oneself to be a lover.

"I'd have done a sight more than curse your name, if you'd tweaked *my* braid," she laughed. "Would've cut off your hand at the wrist, to keep you from pulling girls' hair again."

"I never pulled another girl's hair," he confided. "I knew when I saw her fall, and my heart stopped in my chest, that she was the only girl I'd ever love."

"Sentimental," said Liza, and she clucked her tongue at him.

"Just as you say," Jaworski replied, but his smile never wavered.

The snow had begun to soften as they spoke. Heavy flakes gathered on the fur collar of Liza's coat and melted where her breath warmed them. The two of them knew without having to consult with one another that this snowfall would obscure any tracks, and they lengthened their stride in concession to the weather. From here, though, the trail seemed quite clear. "It headed for the railway station," Liza decided, "although I don't know why in God's name it would want to go to the railway station."

"There are porters near the station," answered Jaworski. "They keep horses stabled there to move goods and luggage when the trains come in. Your brother and I had to hire a driver when we arrived. Your horse might well have been foaled there, and in any case it will smell the other horses."

"I can't smell anything but smoke and gunpowder, but I'm no horse," said Liza.

A few seconds passed before what she'd said registered, but then she began to turn over the problem. There *was* some sort of problem, this she knew; something had sounded wrong…she realized then that the air had smelled only of ice and wet fur since they'd left the fortress, with its vent leaking woodsmoke and its stones red-washed with dragon blood. The smoke and gunpowder that she smelled, then, were *new* scents.

"Damn it, something's burning here," she said. "The dragons have hit something—"

"The attack was near three hours ago," said Jaworski, cursing softly in his mother-tongue. "It's probably finished burning by now."

Liza's chest felt tight. She willed herself to calmness, but with every instant she became more aware of the juddering beat of her heart. *You've failed*, said that heartbeat. "They've probably put it out. They know as well as we do how to manage fires. Better, probably. As soon as they came out of the shelters, they'd have put it out."

"We'd see fire, if they hadn't," said Jaworski, although even he didn't sound particularly comforted by this observation.

They reached the low palisades about the town and clambered over. Liza's skirt snagged on a pointed bit of timber and tore, but she only growled, "Name of God!" and continued on. She followed the taste of smoke on the air, searching the silent houses for sign of scorchmarks and the roads for crowding bootprints. The horse had been all but forgotten.

Slowly, they made their way through the streets, past the optometrist's shop with its sign flapping listlessly and the tavern with its lamps still burning. With a faint sigh of relief, Liza noted that the telegraph office was still whole. She wouldn't have relished waiting for the telegraph line to be reconnected. It was difficult enough to send for supplies even *with* the telegraph.

Jaworski took Liza by the arm then, pointing into the darkness—and then she became aware of it *as* darkness, for if any part of the town was lit at all hours, it was the railway station. "Dear God," she said softly, then took off for the station at a run.

The stone walls were blackened, the windows blasted out. The well-manicured square before the station was littered with ash and broken glass. A nearby warehouse's roof had caught fire and been put out almost at once. Snowflakes drifted through the gaps in the scorched shakes. Over the dismal scene, smoke still rose faintly to the moon, black against the whiter steam from the machinists' shop across the tracks.

Liza forced herself through the burnt-out entryway, to the hatch that—like in every other building in the town—lay concealed in the floor of the station. The roof-beams had been cleared away from the area of the hatch, and the door flung open. She pressed her toe to the striker on the shelter's gaslight, and in the yellow glow of the lamp, she saw that the hollow space below was empty. Whether this was because the station-hands had survived, or because their friends had taken their bodies away to be put to rest, she didn't care to contemplate too closely. The grating over the air vent hung off its hinges.

When she stepped out of the husk of the station again, Jaworski had left his post by the door, and she tracked him around the building to the rail lines. From a distance, the rails looked like a single track, but in truth, two tracks passed through their town: one eastbound, one westbound.

In the cold moonlight, she could see that both tracks had been ripped violently apart, as though by a giant hand—or a single explosive.

CHAPTER THIRTEEN

To cover his surprise at Wainwright's announcement, Petya poured himself another cup of tea. His hands were shaking, though, and the spout of the teapot clattered against his cup. "Peter Wainwright," he said. "Did they call you Petya, too, in St. Petersburg?"

"Why waste time on familiarities? You want to ask me about the Ottomans. I can see it in your eyes," said Wainwright. His own face bore an eager, almost hungry expression. Petya had seen Misha wear that look when he was baiting Kesha into some semantic trap. *Try me*, it said. *I'm prepared for you.*

The hairs on the backs of his arms stood on end, and he didn't relish the sensation one bit. "If you want to tell me about them, I'll listen," said Petya guardedly, "but it's your business. I do know a little history; the English and the Turks were friendly just a few years ago."

"Not so recently as that. I was only a child when we had our falling-out with the Turks—just a year after we'd taken their side against Russia, actually. They wanted India, so they thought they'd stir up our Muslim sepoys against us with damn stupid rumors about pig grease on the bullet casings, or some other nonsense, and soon enough we were up to our eyes in mutineers. I'm making light of it, but the truth is, that was a bad time for everyone. We did awful things while we were putting down the rebellion, to Turks and Indians alike."

"Not a friendship for the ages, the English and the Turks," answered Petya. *He wants me to be surprised that he spent time under the Ottomans; why would he want me to be surprised?* he thought as he stirred his tea. The click of the spoon on the porcelain came as regularly as the ticking of a clock. "But you were a child, you said, when the Turks made their bid for the Indian territories?"

"I was," Wainwright agreed. "Only four years old when the fighting broke out in the subcontinent. I lost family over there, but I'd never met them. I only knew that my mother would cry, sometimes, and I didn't know why."

Petya's father hadn't cried even once when he'd lost a brother to the Polish uprising. His mother often cited this as evidence of their father's inhumanity—*He never cried for Sasha*, she'd say, placid and detached. *Not one tear for his brother.* Petya had wondered, then, whether he himself would have cried if he'd heard of Kesha's death. He wasn't sure that he would be capable of it. "It was a bad time, for all of us," said Petya. "Bad years. My condolences for your losses."

"My mother had far more to grieve than I did—but thank you. You have a good heart, Pyotr Vladimirovich." The name sounded strange on Wainwright's tongue, and now Petya understood why. It was as though Wainwright was addressing himself, a few years younger and perhaps more foolish for it. "But to answer your question properly: while I was serving in Afghanistan, I happened to be captured by the Turks, and I learned to use their artillery mounts by watching them."

"An educational captivity," Petya replied. He might have said more, but then he felt a yawn welling up in his throat, and covered his mouth to stifle it. "I'm sorry," he said. "It is *very* late."

"You needn't apologize. We've all had our share of excitement, and now I've kept you up with tea and stories about Finland and Afghanistan. I wouldn't blame you if you were ready for bed."

"It's not that I'm ready for bed," said Petya. "I'd only lie awake, staring at the walls, waiting to hear the bells again… in St. Petersburg, we never worried about anything worse than a fire, or sometimes a murder nearby. I've lost the instinct for battle."

"May I ask why you haven't returned home since you began your studies?"

"Silly reasons," said Petya, and he tried to laugh. He longed to confide in Wainwright, and to unburden himself for this man who'd never offered him anything but kindness and openness—*or the appearance of kindness and openness*, he thought. "Just silly reasons," he said, more softly. "I didn't have money for a train ticket, or I had a project that kept me busy through the summer months. I always *meant* to return, but somehow I could never find the right occasion to."

Wainwright nodded, but his grip had tightened on his teacup. "If you'll pardon my temerity, that doesn't sound like the young man who came home and started fixing the machinery before he'd even had supper."

"And it doesn't sound like the Turks, to keep their captives in their artillery towers," answered Petya. He finished his tea and stood from his chair, making a respectful bow over the table.

"I'm not *lying*," said Wainwright, with some of the sharpness that he turned on Vladimir when he was being intractable.

"It's your business what you did with the Turks," Petya said, "but we have our business, too."

He turned at the doorway, and he would have departed—but there he crashed into Liza, who fixed her gloved hands on his wrists like bands of ice.

"*That man*," Liza snarled, "that *Englishman* has tried to ruin us!"

"I doubt he's tried to ruin you," came Jaworski's voice from the end of the hall. Over Liza's shoulder, Petya saw that he was very white. A point of chill-red stood out on each of his cheekbones and the tip of his nose, like the paint of a clown. "Calm down, Liza! I was in the towers, too. Blame me, if you're blaming anyone—"

During the shouting, Wainwright had stood from his seat, although he hung back by the fireplace with his arms akimbo. "What's this about ruination?" he asked, in the sort of voice that one might use to soothe a half-mad animal. His tone only enraged Liza, though, who bared her teeth at him and shoved past Petya, driving her index finger into Wainwright's chest.

"You," she said, soft and dangerous, swaying faintly like a serpent (or a drunkard). "*You* let them blast the rails. We gave you the *honor* of keeping watch, even though you'd done nothing to earn it. We trusted you to keep the skies clear and the rails safe, and *this* is what you do!"

Petya could see at once that Wainwright had no idea what she was talking about. "Please, calm down, Liza," he said, but she threw off his hand when he took her by the shoulder.

"Don't patronize me, Pyotr Vladimirovich," she snapped. "This man came to ruin our credit with the Tsar, and we were foolish enough to give him the opportunity—"

"Am I to understand," broke in Wainwright, "that the railway has been damaged?"

"That's *exactly* what you're to understand," answered Liza. "And you *allowed* it. You knew the principles of the watch! You knew better than to wait until they were so close to ring the bell, but you waited until they were right on top of us! Oh, you're lucky I don't strangle you where you stand—"

"Your Polish friend didn't catch them any earlier than I did," Wainwright said sharply. "It was dark; the dragons had been using cloud cover; there were three men on watch, and not a one of us caught them early enough to prevent them from hitting their targets. We shot down the lot of them *afterward*, and that's all we could have done. I didn't know until you *told* me just now that the railway station had been damaged, and I don't see how you can blame *me* when the proper masters of the watch were out getting *drunk*."

Liza dashed her fist across his face at that. There came a sickening sound of crunching bone, and when Wainwright looked up again, his nose was fountaining blood. "I won't stand for this," he hissed. "If you weren't a woman, I'd—"

She laughed, a delighted bray that made Petya feel queasy. "Don't let *that* stop you. I'm a Tarasov. Hit me if you can!"

"I'll do better than that," Wainwright promised. His lower face was a mask of blood, his lips slick and red and his teeth blood-washed. When he smiled, he seemed a kind of hungry ghost. "I'll report you."

"Go ahead," said Liza. "I'd love to see you called to account for the Tsar's railway."

With a significant glance at Jaworski, Wainwright replied, "I may well be called to account, but I'll take the rest of your watchmen with me."

For the first time since he had returned, Petya saw his sister at a loss for words. She followed Wainwright's gaze, her nostrils flaring as she drew in breath after breath. Without another word, she turned on her heel and stalked out of the kitchen, shoving past Jaworski on her way out.

The three men regarded one another in silence for the space of several breaths, and then Jaworski said, "Sit down. We ought to wash your face and set your nose."

Petya went to work boiling water again, while Jaworski gathered soft cloths and carefully cleaned away the blood from Wainwright's face. The Englishman's shirt appeared beyond salvage; nonetheless, his face looked better for the cleaning. The nose was visibly broken, and it would be a fearsome mass of bruises and burst vessels in the morning, but Jaworski set the bones with quick competence once the skin was clean. Wainwright only gasped once, low, at the pain of it.

"I'm sorry," he said thickly, once that business was finished. "I shouldn't have threatened you, Captain. She wouldn't see *reason*, and I—"

"No need for apologies," said Jaworski. "No one knows better than I or Petya here that the Tarasov family can be unbearable, jealous, suspicious—I mean it affectionately," he told Petya, who mustered a smile in reply. "Yes, I loved Petya's uncle, may he rest in God's bosom. No one could say that I didn't love Alexander Petrovich as though he were my own brother...but he did terrible things to his enemies without losing an hour of sleep. You'll have a difficult time convincing Liza that you're an ally, rather than an enemy."

"I'll be sure to remember that," answered Wainwright. "I'm afraid I've done nothing to dissuade her." He raised a hand as though to touch his swelling nose, then caught himself and dropped his hand to his lap. "You're a good man, Ludwik Jaworski. Thank you for your patience."

"It's no trouble. I think you're a good man, too, and good men should help one another. If you like, I can share your watches and be your gunner, so that no suspicion can fall on you." Jaworski's expression was genial, his voice kind, yet even Petya could hear the implications in his offer. *Choose to have my eyes on you at all times, or choose to have Tarasov eyes on you only when you fail.* If Wainwright missed that undercurrent of threat, then he was a less perceptive man than Petya had imagined.

The Englishman hesitated, the way he had hesitated to touch his face. He pressed his lips together, then nodded. "If Vladimir Petrovich agrees to the arrangement, then I'd be glad to have you keep watch with me. Thank you. If you'll excuse me, gentlemen, I think I'll go lick my wounds in my own quarters." He turned a strained smile on Petya, who returned it with the same discomfort. "It was a lovely tea. I hope we'll be able to drink together again."

"Of course," answered Petya, but he followed Wainwright with his eyes until he stepped out of sight.

At Wainwright's departure, Jaworski slid into the vacated seat. With the remaining hot water, Jaworski refreshed the teapot, then he swished the pot about to agitate the last of the flavor from the nearly-spent leaves. "Could have gone worse," he allowed, after a moment of sitting in silence. "I doubt he'll report us, now. What did he have to say about the guns?"

"He said he'd learned to use them while he was a captive of the Turks," Petya replied. "But as I told him, I didn't know the Turks were in the habit of letting their prisoners into their artillery towers." Jaworski offered to pour him tea, but Petya waved him away.

"It's not beyond all possibility. Some of their fortresses are situated on hilltops, like ours. A few of the higher ones don't even have towers. They don't need them. If he were captured in mountain country…but even if his story is true, I don't trust the man."

"Why not?" asked Petya.

Jaworski drank his tea without jam or sugar, milk or honey. He drained the cup in one go. "I don't trust him," he said, "because he said that the watchmen had 'shot down the lot of them,' when I could plainly see a few dragons returning south."

CHAPTER FOURTEEN

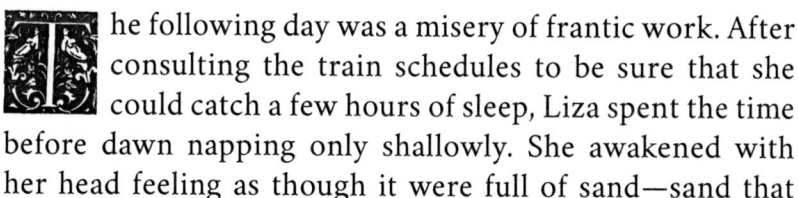

The following day was a misery of frantic work. After consulting the train schedules to be sure that she could catch a few hours of sleep, Liza spent the time before dawn napping only shallowly. She awakened with her head feeling as though it were full of sand—sand that someone was melting into glass, then pounding insistently with a heavy mallet.

Against her better judgment, she filled her teacup half full of brandy and doused the lot with lemon and honey. It did nothing to quell the aching in her head, but at least it warmed her throat. She also found that the foul taste in her mouth meant she couldn't taste the brandy. She filled a flask with the rest of her remedy and tucked it in her coat pocket against a future need.

With the sun still hanging below the horizon, Liza tramped down to the town to wake the telegraph master and had him wire a message to the next stations down the line: *Tarasov to Kamensky. Relay to Zaytsev. Rails out at Petrovsky Station. Station demolished. Detain all trains until further notice.* This accomplished, she corralled a pair of young English soldiers into painting signs on canvas. They couldn't read her Cyrillic, but they could copy it well enough, and they seemed appropriately contrite at their failure to prevent the destruction of the station. It didn't exactly mollify her—nothing short of a long sleep and a hot bath would have mollified her at this point—but it did incline her somewhat more favorably toward Wainwright's inferiors.

While the canvas was being painted, Liza gathered up a pack of rail-workers and sent them to the machinists to get them forging new rails. As she passed from the workers' flophouses to the station, she discovered her runaway horse, happily feasting on oats among the porters' animals at the stables. *At least one of us has had a fine evening*, she thought uncharitably.

By this time, Wainwright was awake, his nose swollen and red-purple under a bandage, and he volunteered to supervise the machinists' efforts. This freed Liza to manhandle a pair of handcars onto the tracks, one on the eastbound track and one on the westbound. As she was searching for a mallet to load onto each, the foreman approached her with her father in tow. "It will be three days at least before we get this repaired," the foreman told them. "The ties burned with the rest of the station, and the rails will be useless after that fire. We were expecting another shipment of supplies tomorrow, but now the trains won't be able to stop at the station. Until then, what can we do but clean up the debris?"

"Then clean it up," answered Vladimir, with a particular inflection that suggested he found the foreman incomparably stupid. It was at this point that Petya arrived with the soldiers who had been painting the canvas. In deference to Liza's instructions, they had firmly nailed the edges of each of the canvas sheets to a pair of sharpened poles. *Rails damaged, 3 verst ahead. Bring engine to a stop*, read each sign.

"Good," allowed Liza. Then, when they didn't cease looking terrified, she tried, *"Bon."* This seemed to relieve them somewhat more. "Petya, tell them that one of them is going with each of us. Three verst to the east and west."

In halting English, her brother conveyed her decree,

and the young soldiers nodded with expressions so politely worried and uncomprehending that Liza nearly laughed in spite of the direness of their predicament. However ill their fortune had been, however her head throbbed, however duplicitous Wainwright had proved, there was no better sport than baiting the English.

The soldier who accompanied her on the handcar was a fresh-faced, freckled fellow with pale hair and grey eyes. He looked almost painfully alert, which might have been because of the danger and might have been because he was sharing a handcar with the woman who had broken his lieutenant's nose. When she tried to question him, though, he shook his head and replied with a helpless little smile, "No…Russian."

They worked in silence, which suited Liza quite well. Down went her side of the pump; up went his; the car trundled slowly along the tracks, and as it went, Liza counted the cairns that marked each verst. Over the western hills, she could see smoke rising from the distant chimneys of the town of Kamensk, ten verst away from her own Yureyevsk. By the time they reached the third cairn, her arms were aching, but the day was warm and the snow had melted from the hillsides. The air was heavy with the smell of wet grass in the sunlight, and from the scrub thickets, birds called to one another anxiously. It was, she grudgingly admitted, a rather nice day.

With the young English soldier to help her, Liza unrolled the canvas and took out her mallet. While he held the poles in place, Liza hammered them firmly. Each jolt sent a bolt of pain through her temples, and again and again she contemplated offering the English boy her hammer. She couldn't help imagining him turning it on her, though, with sudden fire in his soft grey eyes. Even if he didn't want to murder her, she would still have shown herself to be weak before the enemy, and she couldn't brook any display of weakness. Therefore, she continued beating grimly until she had driven each post nearly an arm's length into the ground. Of course, even Liza's best efforts wouldn't be much help if the wind caught the canvas like a sail and sent it flying over the hills, but there was little she could do to prevent *that* but slash a few gaps in the fabric.

When the work was finished, she wiped her brow. Her pocketwatch told her that it wasn't yet eight in the morning.

"Name of God," she muttered, and took out her flask to drink. The tea had cooled a bit, and she could better taste the brandy, but it was the only remedy that she had to hand.

The soldier gave her a hopeful look, but she capped the flask and put it back in her pocket. "None for you," she told him. "I don't share drinks with spies and traitors."

His polite expression of disappointment did more than his denials to convince her that he knew no Russian at all.

Once they had rested a few minutes, they began the journey back to the station, with the handcar creaking mournfully the whole way. As they passed the last cairn before the station, Liza heard a long, low whistle from the west—a train, almost an hour ahead of schedule. "That was *damnably* close," said Liza to herself, and she began to pump at the lever with greater gusto at the sound. Catching the implication of the train's whistle and Liza's haste, the Englishman redoubled his efforts, and soon they were creaking and wobbling onto the last good rails before the station. There, she and her accomplice parted company, and Liza tracked down her father at the telegraph office.

"The half-past-nine train is early," Liza told him immediately upon entering. He looked up from his correspondence, then patted the stool beside him to urge her to sit. She did, feeling the muscles in her shoulders and her back protesting. Her body had frozen into a stoop, and sitting straight made her conscious of how ill she'd used her muscles this morning. Despite the balmy weather, her hands felt chilled; she longed for a muff to warm them. "We put up the eastbound sign, and when we were about one verst from the station, we heard the whistle."

"The train from Moscow, is it?" asked Vladimir, to which she nodded. "That's only to be expected; that one's only cargo and mail. It comes early all the time. The next will have heard that the rails are damaged. They'll be held at the next station. Go on—" he made shooing motions "—see if your mother's sent a letter! Bad things come all at once, you know!"

"Yes, Father," Liza answered, standing as quickly as she'd taken her seat.

She dearly hoped that her mother *hadn't* sent a letter. She'd had her fill of disasters for one day.

When Liza returned once more to the tracks, she could just see the train some distance away, its heavy gun pointing up at the sky. She thrust her hands into her pockets, knuckles knocking on her flask, and began to walk over the rough, black stones that lined the tracks.

The conductor met her two-thirds of the way along, then consented to walk with her back to the train. "You'll pardon my shock, Mademoiselle Tarasova, but it's been years since we had an incident like this," he said. His tone was unfailingly polite, but she heard the accusation in it nonetheless. This sort of thing was bad for business, and if the rail companies despised anything more than danger, it was lost business.

She bit her tongue against her first sharp retort and answered only, "I expect you'll be having several more, while the English stay in our watchtowers. They're overeager, untrained. Like a load of children who think their toys have readied them for men's tools."

If the conductor had any opinion on a woman in trousers talking to him of *men's* tools, he wisely kept it to himself.

Although the cargo trains weren't meant to carry passengers, every train bound eastward had its share of migrants aboard: men eager to make their fortunes in the mines or women seeking husbands (wedded or prospective), tax assessors and prostitutes and the occasional entrepreneur. By and large, this particular set of passengers appeared predictably working-class, mostly men between twenty and some indefinable middle age; among them was a pretty young woman with her hair tied up in a scarf. A well-dressed gentleman was dozing with his collar turned up over his cheeks, a valise at his feet and book in his lap. Some well-loved volume from a novel, no doubt, or some compiled dramatic serial from the city magazines. Liza, who hadn't had a new novel for nearly a decade, found herself inexplicably envious. *For God's sake, I hardly even have time to read!* she chided herself. "You'll have to lodge here for a few days," she told the assembled strangers. "Anastasia Ivanovna has good rooms, and she sets a decent table." Most of the guests took the news in stride, although a few insisted that they'd paid their fare and wouldn't spend more money for a delay they couldn't have helped. This was the conductor's business and not Liza's, though, and she ignored the complaint.

What do the rooms cost? asked one; "I don't know," she replied. *Are there any safer lodgings for a woman?* asked the girl with the scarf; "Nastya has a blunderbuss under the counter; try to convince her to let you take it to bed," answered Liza. *How long will we have to wait?* asked a third passenger, and at this Liza turned and snarled, "You will *wait* until the rails are *fixed.*"

This seemed to cow the passengers into silence. None of them dared to ask another question, at least, which suited Liza perfectly well.

Having attended to the obligatory niceties, Liza abandoned the passengers to collect the mailbag. Fewer letters went east than went west, but nonetheless, she had to sort through a fair quantity of communiqués between miners and timber-cutters and their families before she came across any familiar recipients. As she was tucking a letter from the munitions dealer's sister beneath her arm, she felt a light tap on her shoulder that made her whirl.

The gentleman stepped back a short pace at the violence of the turn, raising the book in his hand as though to shield himself from a blow. "Elizaveta Vladimirovna," he said, with a smile caught halfway between delight and sympathy. "It's been ages. Oleg Romanovich Kamensky."

"Kamensky," she said, with a faint bow of acknowledgment. He was an unexceptionable young man—the younger of the Kamensky boys, five years her junior, with dark hair and dark eyes. He'd finally grown into his nose, or else grown out of being ashamed of it. When they'd been children, she remembered, no one had let him forget it. *Madame Kamensky is a Jewess*, her own mother had observed when her father had talked of fostering Kesha with the Kamenskys, and Liza had never known whether she'd meant it as a criticism. In the end, Kesha had never been fostered at all. "I take it you got the telegram," she said, and rubbed her aching eyes.

"Just before I boarded, they said you'd taken a hit," he answered, matter-of-fact as only a border lord could be. "Bad business. That's not why I came, though. Your father asked me here to be witty at you—but I can see you've been on your feet since the small hours. Would you like to get a drink instead?"

Her lips tightened. "So you're a suitor. He's trying to marry me off again."

"I'm a son doing as he was told," said Oleg Romanovich, with a light shrug. "I know better than to argue, when the old bear of Kamensk tells me to hop to."

"Your father's young, for an old bear," she replied, the corner of her mouth twitching. "And you're only a cub."

"This cub will out-drink you, and he'll even buy," he said, offering his hand to shake. "We'll toast to swift repairs and to failed proposals, and I can catch the evening train back to Kamensk?"

"If you're willing to wait a week for an evening train," answered Liza, but she put down the mailbag and shook his hand anyway. "Let me wash and bring in the mail. If you out-drink me, I'll push you back to Kamensk on a handcart."

"If you push me back to Kamensk on a handcart, I'll owe you another drink!" laughed Oleg Romanovich, pocketing his novel and picking up his valise from the black stones along the rails. He sauntered off, whistling a cheerful march, and Liza found herself smiling despite her pounding head.

Her father could've chosen worse. Oleg Romanovich, at least, understood how things worked in the border country. He'd give her an evening's distraction from the ire of the rail companies and swap stories about dragons and guns, and he might even be persuaded to go shooting with her if he was too blind drunk to make it back to Kamensk. But go back to Kamensk he would, and for that most of all, she was grateful.

She returned to the mail, narrowing her eyes at the addresses on the letters. In the small bundle that she'd just withdrawn from the mailbag, there was a letter to Petya. The writer had tried to disguise his hand by writing with his left, but although he had formed the uprights quite neatly, he had wavered on the curves of the *O* and the *E*s. She knew of only one man who would write to Petya *here*, and with an apprehension that his handwriting would be recognized.

Tucking the letter into her empty pocket, Liza began the trek back to the station. Once she had dropped the rest of the letters at the telegraph office, she proceeded back up the hill to the fortress. By then, the wind had picked up, and it blew her coat hard against her legs. She had promised herself a hot bath after she'd dealt with this phenomenal cock-up, and she could look forward to good company after that, and damn it all, she *deserved* some peace of mind. Kesha's letter, though—

She took the letter from her pocket, placing it on her dressing table. Her first instinct was to burn the thing and deny she'd ever received it. She didn't *care* what Kesha had to say to their brother, because she already knew that it was all aspersions on the family and whining entreaties to return to St. Petersburg. Better to commit that to the fire at once, unread.

Her second impulse was to open the letter and read it. *Only to confirm my suspicions*, she told herself. Not because she had any hope that Kesha regretted his foolishness and wanted to be embraced again as her brother. Not because, since her childhood, Liza had wished to believe that one could always rely first on one's family—or because she still held out a childish hope that she'd placed her faith in something true, despite the slow fragmentation of the household.

In the end, Liza slid the letter under Petya's door, unopened and unread. What he did with it was his own business, and no concern of hers.

That unpleasantness behind her, she could at last reward herself with a bath. The lower recesses of the keep contained a spring of clear, cold water. It pooled in a little room to which Vladimir and Liza had the only keys, with a small pumphouse beside it that piped water to two reservoirs—one hot, and one cold. In Liza's childhood, before the walls had been shot through with copper piping, a servant would have had to heat water endlessly over a fire to ensure that she had a hot bath. The days of gas heat and lighting had come at last to the border country, though, and the Tarasovs had moved with the times. Now, when Liza wanted a proper soak, she had only to turn a tap and let her bathtub fill with steaming water.

Their mother had used to read novels in the bath. Suddenly, Liza had a very clear picture in her mind of Yelena Sergeyevna Tarasova reclining in her bath with one of Balzac's novels in her hands. She had been reading aloud to her daughter in French, a steady torrent of unfamiliar syllables without so much as a change in pitch to guide Liza through it.

Well. It had been a lovely domesticity, until her husband's little sins and cruelties had accumulated past bearing. She still called herself "Tarasova" in her letters, although Liza suspected this was a pose to make them more inclined to advance her money; Yelena Sergeyevna was as mercenary as her husband, and her blood ran colder.

It was, thought Liza, a very poor sign, when her mother could ruin such a fine thing as a bath without even being present.

She slid one bare foot into the water, then another. The water was nearly hot enough to scald, but she relished the ache as her cool skin heated slowly. *Peace of mind*, she thought, but even the words had grown bitter.

CHAPTER FIFTEEN

Two days after he'd sent his letter to Petya, Kesha began to feel that his life was resettling in a new and comfortable pattern. He had attended a lecture that morning on sacramental rhetoric in Orthodoxy, Catholicism, and Lutheranism, which was rather dull until one of the attendees prodded the speaker on the substance of the Eucharist. The lecture hall promptly exploded into a cacophony of outraged shouting, and Kesha didn't even bother to conceal his smirk as he jotted down notes on the implications of varying beliefs on transubstantiation. It was, he had to admit, more relevant for his thesis than he had originally supposed.

He left the still-raucous hall with a spring in his step and met Misha for coffee in a fine little coffee-house with colorful Tajik decor, where they had an agreeable conversation on the ethics of retributive and rehabilitative justice. He called Misha an atheist, and Misha called him a fossil of an outmoded feudal judicial system; they finished on the literary merits of *Titus Andronicus*, and neither could remember how they had got there. By now, he was beginning to reconcile himself to the possibility that Petya might never return from the borderlands, and considering the prospect no longer gave him a sharp pain in his chest. It would hardly be so bad, lodging with the Galiyevs and making Misha his daily companion. If they didn't understand one another as brothers did, then they might slowly build a fraternal trust—sharing midnight confidences, whispering secrets across the darkness for one another's ears alone.

They parted with tender expressions of goodwill and promises of later conversation; Kesha realized as he let go of his friend's hand and stepped out of the warmth of the shop that, against his expectations, he was *happy*. The shock of discovering himself to be happy was nearly as delightful as the sentiment itself.

On his way to a tutorial with a particularly bright young philosophy student, Kesha was seized with an impulsive desire to buy one of the midday newspapers from a boy who was hawking them on a street-corner. He couldn't have said, later, why he had done it; he might have blamed a sort of sympathy for the child, who wore a threadbare coat and whose voice was very hoarse with shouting, or he might have cited a renewed interest in the business of the world. Before Petya had come to live with him, Kesha had tried his hand at journalism, as many young scholars did to keep money in their pockets, but since then he had grown disinterested in the scandal-mongering and hunger for news that the profession entailed. Neither explanation would prove entirely satisfactory, and when he thought on the matter that night, he would remember Uncle Pasha's stories about their grandfather's uncanny foresight.

Whatever the reason, when Kesha had shuffled open the paper and skimmed the headlines, the very uppermost seized his attention at once. *Devastating blast at Petrovsky Station*, read the largest headline, and underneath in smaller print, *Rail trade with the east crippled*.

His knees felt suddenly weak, and he leaned against a nearby building to read further.

More careful perusal revealed that the explosion had

not been as bad as the headlines suggested. The station had been gutted and two station workers had died in the ensuing blaze, but Vladimir Petrovich Tarasov assured reporters that once supplies had come in from the foundries and forests of the northeast, "All will be just as it was before the accident."

He said *accident*, and the reporters said nothing of what had caused the explosion (although the editorials on the next page speculated that it had been the fault of dragons, Englishmen, or Englishmen employing dragons). Kesha, though, couldn't help smiling faintly at the boilerplate and bluster. *Dear old father*, he thought. *You haven't decided what story you want them to tell yet, and until you do, they'll tell every story that comes to mind.*

As Kesha had learned long ago, he could trust little that came from his father—and less, when the old man saw a profit to be turned.

He wondered if his letter was even now stalled en route to Petya. He had posted it just as the train was about to depart from St. Petersburg to Moscow, and that was a journey of twelve hours. It was another fourteen hours from Moscow to Petrovsky Station. If the timing were right, and the mailbag for the eastbound line were simply handed off from train to train, then it might arrive in a little over a day. If not…another four days wasn't so long to wait, and in any case Petya had never been good at answering letters quickly.

There was that nostalgia again. Kesha had been foolish to suppose that he could keep it at bay with coffee and Shakespeare and Eucharistic debates. *Very well—I'll grieve, if I must grieve*, he told himself. *There's something instructive in pain.*

The thought of pain and instruction made him push away from the wall, remembering his appointment with his student at the same time that he recalled Starikovich's promises of books on dragons. He couldn't remember whether Starikovich's family holdings were along the

Moscow–Kazan rail line, or the one that ran through Yaroslavl and Nizhny; if it were the Moscow–Kazan line, then the damage to the railways would hold up any shipments of books as surely as it had stalled the mail and the train cars loaded with iron and timber.

He met with his student at the university library, and even his high hopes for their meeting were depressed almost at once. The young man had caught a cold since their last encounter, and he spent the greater portion of the meeting sniffling pathetically into a handkerchief. At length, when Kesha had tired of deciphering the boy's mucus-laden musings on Aristotle's *Metaphysics*, he called their colloquy to a halt. "And, Vadik," said Kesha, just as the light of hope began to gleam in the student's eyes, "if you've recovered by next week, we'll be discussing the *Poetics* as well as what we didn't manage to cover today. You had best be *exceptionally* prepared."

The boy scurried away, still sniffling. His apparent terror at the additional workload gave Kesha a quiet thrill of satisfaction. If he couldn't rival Misha's reputation as a singularly ferocious wit, then he could at least derive some pleasure from being thought an utter tyrant.

Although Kesha knew very well that the library in which he now stood was not the only library attached to the university—and for that matter, that this university was not the only one with libraries that might have attracted a curious young legal scholar—he nonetheless found himself struck with an unquenchable curiosity. *Quite concealed behind a bit of paneling*, Misha had said, *but the paneling had come untacked.*

Kesha recalled that there had been a time, during the reign of Pyotr the Great, when the Twelve Collegia had been not an academic institution, but a governmental one. The place hadn't been absorbed by the Imperial University until the nineteenth century; when the dragons had defected, this building had housed politicians and their lackeys, Senate and Synod and colleges of war and commerce. If some long-dead bibliophile had hidden the books that now stood on Misha's shelf—if he had hidden them *here*—then he would have been a civil servant rather than a scholar. Perhaps a civil servant with a scholarly bent, but...

Turning over these ideas, Kesha pushed away from the table at which he and Vadik had been working. At first, he only circled the edges of the room, studying the paneling thoughtfully. He couldn't recall in what year the Collegia had been joined into one long structure. Had it been before or after the Defection? It must have been before. If it had been after, then certainly the books would have been found long ago. *I'm still assuming that this is Misha's library*, he cautioned himself, but his blood sang at the possibility of discovery. The paneling that lined the library was old, old enough to have been part of the original structure; it had a particularly Petrine character to it that Kesha had seen nowhere but in the university.

He ascended the stairs, repeating his slow circuit of the walls on the upper story. A few patrons glanced up from their reading with expressions of irritation, but he paid them no mind. Let them think him mad, tired, or absent-minded. None were his students, and none his instructors. Their opinions had no bearing on him.

On his second round, he caught sight of the faintest of cracks between panels. When Misha had said that the paneling had come *untacked*, he'd imagined some sort of easily visible gap in the paneling, swinging jauntily on a single nail raised from the surrounding wood. He had, in fact, been imagining the sort of ostentatiously "secret" hiding-place that all but cried out for the eye of the intrepid literary adventurer.

There was a gouge-mark in the paint near the base of the panel—just a faint one, as though someone had slid a pocketknife into the crack and prised the untacked panel up to see what lay beneath it. After casting a surreptitious glance about for nosy onlookers, Kesha took out his own pocketknife, inserting it over the mark of the knife that had preceded his.

Grudgingly, with a tremendous creaking of wood, the panel slid open. The empty space behind it was just large enough for a crate of books, but Kesha had only a moment to notice it before the sound of footsteps told him that he'd been discovered in his defacement of the Petrine architecture. Kesha hastily replaced the paneling and stood, pocketing his knife and affecting to lean against the wall just as an irate young scholar rounded a bookshelf.

"What's all *this* about?" he demanded, to which Kesha shrugged with what he hoped was an innocent expression.

"The walls creak," he said vaguely. "It's an old building."

"If you *must* go about acting tragical," answered the scholar in a sharp tone, "find somewhere more *poetic* to do it. Some of us are trying to read in here!"

"Of course," said Kesha. "I'm sorry for troubling you."

He descended to the ground level of the library again with his eyes still on the walls. Behind every panel, there might be caches of books just like the ones that Misha had salvaged; behind the bookshelves that had come with the university and the library, more panels might have slowly worked themselves "untacked" over the course of a century. The prospect was exhilarating in a way that he was powerless to describe. He longed to take a prybar to every old wall in the Twelve Collegia, strip the panels and bare whatever secrets they had concealed over the long years.

There would be a record, somewhere, of what had happened to the books and to the people who'd burned them. No doubt those records had also been burned, concealed, locked away from all who might come after with ethical inquiries; he could expect no better from a government that had responded to its allies' defection by pretending that they'd never had scholars or poets. Kesha didn't doubt that the great majority of the records were lost to him forever, and this grieved him not a little as he left the broad facade of the Collegia behind him.

He knew precisely where to search for records pertinent to *these* books, however. Misha was a sharp-witted, curious man with a keen eye for detail, but even Misha wouldn't have thought to lift that barely-untacked panel with a knife unless he had known what he'd find on the other side of it.

Whatever he had discovered that had led him to this library in the Imperial University, he hadn't deemed it necessary to share this discovery with his dear friend Kesha—the only man with whom he could have an intelligent conversation on linguistics. *He played on my pride,* Kesha realized, *and I let him use me.*

Kesha watched the birds that circled the shores of the Neva, and the well-to-do boys who threw them crusts of bread. It was a particular mark of privilege, to have crusts to share with the birds rather than with one's fellow-men, but Kesha didn't begrudge the boys their entertainment. Birds, too, had to eat. Better a boy's crust than a beggar's eyes.

Should I ask him how he knew? Kesha asked himself. *Would he tell me, if I asked him?*

He could come to no conclusion that would satisfy him. Surely it meant something that Misha had chosen to introduce the documents in his possession not as an ethical problem, nor as a mystery of origins, but as a *linguistic* quandary. He would have known that Kesha's keen interest in languages and meanings would make the prospect of a new language entirely too tempting, and he knew that Kesha had grown up in the borderlands. Other scholars might have been better equipped to puzzle out the meaning of the draconic symbols, but only Kesha had grown up learning to kill dragons. His guilt would ensure his silence.

And, of course, they were good friends—but Kesha had never trusted friendship as a guarantor of good intentions.

I'll ask him, Kesha decided, *but if his answer doesn't satisfy me, I'll conceal as much as he has.*

From the waterside came the laughter of boys and the screams of hungry birds. Along the banks of the Neva, there was never bread enough for all.

CHAPTER SIXTEEN

From the early morning until the evening, Vladimir Petrovich Tarasov camped out in the telegraph office, sending Petya to fetch him drinks and meals as he fielded increasingly insistent questions from Moscow, St. Petersburg, and Yekaterinburg. He seemed almost to revel in putting off his interlocutors, responding with vague and elliptical reassurances to even the most pointed inquiries.

Petya passed Wainwright more than once as he went about the town on his errands, but he could never *quite* catch the Englishman in the commission of a suspicious act. He always appeared to be strolling aimlessly, his broken nose swollen and bruised, his Russian cap slightly askew. The junior machinists said that he'd been supervising them, asking about the union and how they liked the work, which ought to have endeared him to Petya more than it did. Nonetheless, Petya could not help suspecting that his father had been right to take over the telegraph office, ensuring by his presence that no word of the disaster left the town without first passing through him.

Over the whole of the town, the thaw had worked a kind of magic. Children played in the streets, skidding giddily over the mud and tripping one another into puddles. The men had set off in the morning for their work in the mine or on the railway, but as the sun touched the horizon, they came home whistling and shouting to one another.

On the hillside beyond the church, kinsmen were digging graves for the two who had died in the blast at the station. Precious little remained to bury. A torso with an arm and part of a leg still attached. A shattered head and a blackened hand. The dead would be interred with all of the ceremony that the church could afford them, and the town would drink to their memories, and life would go on.

"A kopeck for your thoughts," said Wainwright from behind him. "Is that an expression, in Russia? In English, it's a penny—"

"—for my thoughts. I understand what you mean," answered Petya. "I was watching the gravediggers. Only a little Russian melancholy."

"And I was just thinking of how merry the town is, for a place that's seen destruction so recently," countered Wainwright. "The machinists work, the children play, the men sing, the women overcharge for good liquor…it's as though you'd never suffered at all."

"Life goes on," said Petya with a shrug, and he wished he had better wisdom than that to impart.

The door to the telegraph office swung open, and Vladimir stepped out with the telegraph master close behind him. The telegraph master locked the door, made a polite bow, and set off for his home; Vladimir turned and began to limp toward the fortress. The sight of his sloped back, his slow and dignified gait, made Petya's heart swell with an unaccustomed fondness. He seldom saw his father so vulnerable, and the sight awakened a tender, filial sentiment that he had thought long dead.

"The man can find a drink even in a telegraph office," Wainwright muttered with what sounded like grudging admiration. Petya turned at the remark. His confusion must have been readily evident upon his face, because

Wainwright frowned as though preparing an apology and asked, "Hasn't he been drinking?"

"His gout is bad," answered Petya. "He drinks to dull the pain, and sometimes it does help, but his feet still hurt even on good days. Mother used to say he should use a chair, but that was when he only had pains in one foot…and he ran after Liza last night. He must be aching awfully today. I'm not surprised he's staggering a bit."

"Well." The Englishman made a small noise of discontentment. Whether he was disappointed to have found some vestige of nobility in his host, or to have discovered the pettiness in his own spirit, Petya couldn't have said. "My apologies. It seems I've misjudged him."

Just as he finished speaking, the wind shifted. It had been blowing from the northwest, but now it came with sudden strength from the northeast. It carried with it a putrid scent like the reek of a charnel-house, and Petya covered his nose and coughed hard. The servants would have scrubbed the fortress clean of blood, but this scent was more than blood. It was a vast, horrid, and above all *familiar* scent that Petya remembered from the miserable summers of his childhood.

"The dragons are starting to rot," he said, nose pinched shut against the smell. He could still taste it on the air, though, and he swallowed against the gorge rising in his throat. "I hope your naturalist has learned everything he wanted."

"We've learned more than we knew before," Wainwright allowed. "This fellow served in the Canadian territories for a few years, and he's sat in on a dissection or two; he said the livers on these looked strange. Shriveled. And their eyes looked a bit jaundiced, he thought."

"Diseased?"

"That, I couldn't say. It could just be that Russian dragons have different livers."

The two men walked in silence back to the fortress, scarves wrapped around their lower faces against the smell of rotting meat. The dragons' heads would be in storage in the ice closet, where they'd be safe from the heat until the inspectors could come from Moscow to affirm the kills and award bounties. In the old days, when the family had been richer, Vladimir had brought in taxidermists to preserve the heads so that they could be hung about the dining hall, but he'd since sold his collection to pay off his mounting debts. The inspectors would take these heads with them, crated up with ice and straw to preserve them for the fourteen-hour train ride, and what they'd do with them in Moscow, God only knew.

In the secret parts of his heart, the parts which he had learned long ago to upbraid for cowardice, Petya preferred the dining hall without dozens of grinning dragons' heads peering down at him.

When he and Wainwright reached the keep, Wainwright went to the soldiers' quarters, leaving Petya to his own devices. On a whim, he followed a ladder-shaft upward into one of the watchtowers. He supposed that Jaworski was asleep, preparing for the evening watch, but he had some hopes of encountering a familiar watchman or one of his uncles' friends in the tower. Most of them were stoic men, not given to gestures of affection, but Petya would be glad of a little quiet company.

The watchtower was deserted. A few discarded bottles lay against the curve of the wall.

Within only a minute of peering out the windows, Petya apprehended why this particular tower was empty. The walls of the fortress acted less like barriers and more like buttresses for the towers, and one of the walls abutting this tower was badly scorched and fractured on the outward side. From the inside, peering up at the wall, he hadn't recognized the severity of the fracture, but this vantage point afforded him a better view of the damage. He considered the problem for several minutes more, attempting to devise a strategy for repair as though he were discussing a hypothetical problem in a tutorial.

Very suddenly, Petya realized that he was contemplating the problem from the tower *most* likely to topple and shatter should the wall give way. With startling immediacy, he imagined the long plunge to the rocks below, the stones of the tower grinding his flesh to a meaty pulp.

It didn't bear thinking about. He hastened back down the ladder and into the keep. Even if the place was as windowless as a tomb, at least it didn't smell of death.

When Petya swung open the door to his rooms, he heard a strange sound of paper scudding across tile. With the door shut behind him, he could see a small, hand-folded envelope secured shut with a neat black wrapper, of the sort that Kesha bought in packets to seal his correspondence. Although the handwriting was unfamiliar, it clearly read *Pyotr Vladimirovich Tarasov*, with his address beneath it.

The letter inside was written in a hand well-known to Petya, each character as small and precise as though it had been printed—but with a tiny, characteristic flourish at the end of each stroke, which Petya knew came from writing too quickly. He sat in the chair that he was just beginning to think of as his chair again, unfolding the letter carefully and examining its contents.

Dearest Petya,

It has been three days since you left for our family home, and I still expect to see you at every turn. Our room is duller without your laughter or the constant ticking of your clockwork creations, and if the silence allows me to concentrate better on my studies, I find I am less able to bear looking away from them. In your absence, I've begun imposing on the Galiyev family— Misha's aunt and uncle, whom you may have met at one of our landlady's salons. They are very kind and welcoming, with an infinite patience for their nephew's poor manners and worse taste in house-guests, and I am grateful beyond measure for their hospitality.

I had begun this letter intent upon using it to convince you to return to me, but I don't have the subtle talent for sophistry that Misha has—I cannot compel you so gently that you would imagine that returning had been your own idea. Nor am I so selfish as to ask or persuade you to return if it goes against your inclination. You've grown to be an intelligent man, possessed of sufficient discrimination to make wise choices. Indeed, perhaps you have made wiser choices than the rest of us.

Therefore, I will say in closing that I am well, here in St. Petersburg. I have your drawings tacked to the walls to remind me of you, and if I ever feel a kind of lonely longing for the sound of another being sharing space with me, I have only to wind the key of your music box or your model train and let them tick slowly on.

With all of my love, and my best wishes, I am,

Yours most truly,
Innokentiy Vladimirovich Tarasov

Petya folded the letter again and pressed it back into the envelope. He didn't know what to make of it; he was, he thought, too exhausted from the day's work to feel much of anything at all. Kesha might have adopted rhetorical helplessness as a pose to help him plead his case, but he might also be entirely sincere. Petya knew better than anyone how to read his brother's expressions and posture to recognize dishonesty, but with only these printer-neat words to guide him, he was at a loss.

It occurred to him, as he sat with his ankle crossed over his knee and his thumb on the flap on the envelope, that someone must have put the letter under his door. It couldn't have been his father, who wouldn't have let such a suspicious envelope pass by him unopened; it certainly couldn't have been the errand boy, who would have placed the envelope in his father's care. Perhaps Jaworski might have done it, but he'd come down from his watchtower only long enough to eat a breakfast of porridge with jam, and then he'd gone to bed at once. Their Kamensky guest wouldn't have known where to bring it, and he'd probably have shown it to Liza first, just in case it would win her heart to inform on her brother.

This left Liza, and she must have suspected the identity of the sender. She had known that Kesha was writing to him, and she hadn't interfered. She hadn't even opened the envelope; neither the paste nor the wrapper had been disturbed.

He wondered if it was usual for brothers to be grateful that their siblings *hadn't* opened their mail before passing it on.

Petya stood from his chair, then, and went to the door. He had every intention of going to Liza's rooms and begging her advice, and indeed, he had already locked his door behind him and taken a few purposeful steps in that direction before the foolishness of this plan struck him. When last he had mentioned Kesha, she had turned from him in a rage and demanded to be left alone. Surely it would only enrage her further to ask for her advice? Surely, after the disaster of the railway, she'd endured enough for one day?

He faltered, his hand raised to knock on her door. In the end, he lowered his hand again, knuckles tingling faintly in anticipation of a knock that would never come.

Instead, Petya slowly turned the screw-wheel that held the hatch closed, then flicked on the lamp at the base of the ladder-shaft. Even had the upper hatch been open, it would be too dark by now to navigate the ladder properly. Although Petya had learned to climb up into the turrets in the dark, he still didn't relish the prospect. He drew on gloves lined with rabbits' fur and pulled himself up and into the shaft, then drew up the hatch behind him. Caught between two steel doors, the light spilling up from beneath his feet, Petya felt a profound aloneness that soothed him in a way that he couldn't define. He found himself imagining a life in gear-closets and shafts, surrounded by cold metal that he could clean and rearrange and coax to obedience. Such a world seemed enticingly simple.

When he reached the upper hatch, he turned out the lamp again before unscrewing the hatch—a precaution against attack, his father had always said. The dragons would fix on any visible point of light as a target, and so the fortress had to remain dark at night. That kind of good sense would have saved the railway station, which must have looked like a beacon in the darkness. Whether or not Wainwright had "allowed" the dragons to strike the station, Petya privately conceded that such a strike had been nearly inevitable as long as the station master refused to black out their lights at night.

Nonetheless, when he crouched on the ladder with the lamp going dim beneath him, he could understand their hesitation. There was a kind of primal, irrational fear attached to the dark; Petya couldn't quite bear that sickening moment of utter blackness between damping the light and emerging into the cool evening air. The iron and steel of the shaft changed from a comfort to a cage in the darkness. He imagined the stones around him closing in.

The hatch swung open, and he climbed out and into the lower level of the watchtower.

It wasn't yet dark, although the sun was beginning to set on the western horizon. To the east, stars pricked the skies. One of their hired watchmen was keeping his eyes on the west, shaded goggles cutting down on the glare of the sun, with an English fellow manning the eastern windows.

A good division, thought Petya. *Dragons have been known to use the sun for cover, but never to come out of the east at sunset.*

Like Liza—and Kesha, although he seldom admitted it—

Petya had maintained his old habit of carrying a spyglass about with him wherever he went. He drew the glass from the breast pocket of his coat, extended it to its full length, and looked over the eastern hills.

In the dimness beyond the orchards, he could just make out two vast corpses, both dwarfing the men who scurried about them. Although the wind was coming from the northwest again, Petya couldn't imagine the breeze was much help to the Englishmen finishing their studies—but by morning, the beasts would have fallen prey to rot and stray dogs, and there was little recourse but to bear the stench and study the bodies thoroughly while the opportunity remained.

The English had slit the beasts down their bellies and pinned the skin to either side, like dissected snakes in anatomy texts. Petya wondered what they saw there.

Beneath him, he heard the servants' entrance creak open and then shut again; a broad-shouldered figure in a thick fur coat and hat made its way down the hill, keeping to the meltwater-darkened rocks rather than the lighter stone of the road. Whoever it was clearly didn't want to be seen.

Bidding the watchman a good night, Petya slid back down into the hatch, moving carefully so as not to draw attention to himself. He lacked the emotional wherewithal to think about his brother's letter at the moment, but he could certainly follow a stranger.

CHAPTER SEVENTEEN

When Liza stopped in at the tavern on her way into the town, she could see the lamps glowing softly through the filmy curtains. When she'd seen those lights last night, they'd filled her with a faint relief that she didn't care to dwell on—her pride had been too wounded, and Nastya's sharp looks too fresh in her mind. Tonight, though, Liza was sober, and she felt the same swell of relief beneath her ribs as she peered through the windows.

If the room grew quieter when she stepped inside, she thought that at least part of that was discomfort at her clothes. She seldom came to town in trousers, and when she did, it was on business. A Tarasov's business was good news to no one. Nastya glanced up from her patrons, smiling sharply. "Liza," she called, and came over to kiss the air beside Liza's cheek. "You left your father at home, I hope?"

"I just came to warn you," Liza began, but she faltered when Nastya looked up through her lashes and met Liza's eyes. Anastasia Ivanovna was the beauty of her family, a little tall and a little long of nose, but grey-eyed and pale-haired and always immaculately dressed. Since she'd inherited her father's business, many men had sought her hand, and she'd learned to put off their advances gently. Those who were her suitors were also her patrons, and she could afford to lose none of them.

Liza knew full well that she hadn't a chance of winning Nastya's heart, and that Nastya only bore her fumbling advances to keep her business. The knowing didn't make it easier to meet Nastya's eyes when she looked up through her lashes like that.

"I came to warn you," said Liza, more gruffly. "You need to put down your black curtains. I know it makes the place stuffy, but—"

"It's a necessary precaution, yes," agreed Nastya. "Thank you, Liza. Will that be all?" It was a pointed question, but Liza heard no malice in it.

"That will be all." As she turned to go, she added, faintly pleading, "I'm sorry for what I said last night."

If Nastya knew how rare it was for Liza to apologize to anyone, she showed no surprise at it. She offered her hand, and Liza took it and pressed it. Even through her glove, Nastya's fingers were very warm. "I'm sorry, too," said Nastya, after a pause just a hair longer than was comfortable. "I hope we can still be friends."

"I think we *can* be friends," answered Liza, and with some regret, she let go of Nastya's hand again. "Remember the curtains."

"I'll remember." She returned then to her work, pouring drinks and laughing with her patrons; she knew that her work was to ease their passages, and while men celebrated the lives of the dead or toasted to the newly-born, Nastya filled their cups to the brim. They drank in her presence like sharp, coarse liquor, until they knew nothing but the wanting of it.

Liza couldn't have brought Oleg Romanovich Kamensky here, where she'd have done nothing but stare longingly after Nastya and drink herself stupid. Better to drink herself stupid in the mess hall of the fortress, even if their vodka was swill.

Liza stepped out into the growing chill, pulling the door against the jamb until she heard it latch shut behind her. She drew the collar of her coat up about her neck as she stepped back onto the street—and if she hadn't chanced to glance up as she rounded the corner, she would have collided painfully with her youngest brother. "Petya!" she cried, seizing him by the shoulder. "What are you doing, creeping around in the dark?"

He had the grace to appear sheepish. "I was following a man from the keep. I thought it was Lieutenant Wainwright, but now I see..." His eyes fixed on her cap, her coat, her trousers; when she caught his meaning, Liza threw her head back and laughed.

"Name of *God*, boy, you thought I was *Wainwright*? I should be insulted. He's a whole hand shorter than I am!" She cuffed him fondly, and he made an endearing little squeak at the gesture. "Come on, then," said Liza, taking her brother by the arm and marching him down the street. "You got a letter today. What did it say?"

Petya regarded her with a dazed expression that she associated more with bewildered livestock than with university engineering students. "Are you still drunk?" he managed eventually.

"I'm sober as you are, and I've seen how little you can drink."

"But you've *never* wanted to talk about Kesha—"

"And tonight I do." She elbowed him in the ribs. "What did his letter say?"

His demeanor grew more thoughtful. Behind them, the tavern windows slowly grew dark as Nastya and her sisters let down the blackout curtains. "It didn't actually say very much," answered Petya, as though this fact surprised him. "Only that he missed me, and that he didn't want to persuade me to return to St. Petersburg if I wanted to stay here. And he wrote a bit about my drawings, and my models."

A breeze from the east brought the scent of putrefying

dragonflesh over the hills, but Liza didn't believe for a moment that *this* was what made her stomach twist.

"Will you?" she asked. "Will you stay here?"

Petya's hand closed on her arm. He pressed against her side briefly, like a cat begging for a stroke. "I might, when I've finished my schooling," he said. "I think that I can do good work here, and all along the southern rail system. I want to build such amazing things, Liza—such *amazing* things, things will that take us out of our fortresses and into the sky! But first, I have to learn everything I can about the principles of engineering, and I really do think that I can do that better in the city. Once the English are out, I'll go back to St. Petersburg."

Drawing in a breath through her teeth, Liza nodded. If it was a grudging nod, that couldn't be helped. "I can't fault your reasoning," she said. "And you came down after me because you thought that bastard was sneaking out in secret. If it's an insult, it's an insult to your eyesight, not to your loyalty."

"I do love you, Liza," said Petya, with an earnestness sharp enough to pierce.

She turned to him, snatching off his cap and ruffling his dark hair. "Petya, you damn sentimentalist!" she laughed. He tried to squirm away, but she held him fast by the arm, and in a moment they found themselves laughing and wrestling in the street. Liza had *nearly* got Petya facedown in the dirt with his arms pinned behind his back when a passing carter spat a long spurt of chewing tobacco over the both of them, and the indignity made Liza let her brother up in order to round on the carter with all of the profanity in her vocabulary. She only paused in her invective when she realized that Petya was laughing *at* her—and then she had to laugh, too.

It had been years since she had let herself look ridiculous, but Petya's laughter made her feel as free as a child again.

When the carter had passed them by, and when Petya

had wiped their clothes clear of tobacco and spittle, Liza drew him into a rib-crushing hug. "I've missed you, boy," she told him, and felt gratified beyond words when he smiled and answered, "I've missed you, too."

"Go on, then," she said at last, giving him a little push toward the fortress. "I have a few more errands in town before everything shuts down for the night, and then we'll have tea together before I take a watch. How does that sound?"

"That sounds good," said Petya. "Are you sharing a watch with Kamensky, then?"

Something in his inflection made her cock her head at him, brows lowering. "If you're implying—"

"I'm not implying anything! But you seemed awfully happy with him, and he seems pleased with you, and..." Helplessly, Petya threw his arms up. "I'm not implying anything. But if *you* are, then...then I'm happy for you."

"I'm not implying a damned thing," she answered, giving him a swat. "Get back to the keep."

That business complete, she checked her pockets to be sure that her hairpin hadn't been lost in the scuffle, then wound her way back through the town to the telegraph office.

With a bit of forcing, the hairpin slid into the lock of the office door. It was a touch too thick, but the pin was weak, and soon Liza had scratched it slender. Then it was only a matter of turning and pressing and listening for the click of the tumblers.

As she listened, she glanced up and down the street for watchful eyes. Half of the houses that faced the office had pulled down their blackout curtains or closed their shutters, though, and those that hadn't nonetheless had put up thick curtains of cotton against the cold. So long as no one stepped into the street, she would remain unobserved.

When she'd been a little girl, she and Kesha had picked the lock of their mother's wine cabinet and shared a bottle of her good French wine. They'd been sick for days after that, but they'd been so proud of their conquest…she imagined he'd be at least a little proud of her for this, although he'd scold her as though she were a criminal. It had always been his way to hide one kind of pride beneath another, uglier kind. Perhaps he thought that was virtue.

The last tumbler slid into place, and the telegraph office's door came open at a touch.

She would have to be quick. Petya was expecting her, and if he'd seen her making her way to the town, then God only knew who else had seen her. There would be metal shavings on the doorstep, and gouges in her hairpin, and she wouldn't be able to dissemble if she were questioned directly. *Quick, then*, she told herself, drawing down the blackout curtains and turning on the lamp before she made her way to the telegraph.

Liza had only used a telegraph once on her own. She had sent a message to her mother in Moscow, begging her to come home, tapping out a series of long and short beats with a crib sheet beside her so that she wouldn't forget any of the letters. Even so, she had misspelled the words, childish fingers stuttering and stammering on the lever; it had taken two weeks for her mother to write her back, and another two days for the letter to arrive. It had been a polite but unsympathetic refusal.

Perhaps it said something about her, that Liza was ashamed to be seen begging her family to come home.

This time, she had written down her message neatly beforehand, and her hands were sober and steady. She entered the codes that would see the telegram transmitted to the offices in St. Petersburg, then entered Petya's address. Kesha's address; she must think of it as his address, as well.

Three lines. *INNOKENTIY VLADIMIROVICH TARASOV. STOP. COME HOME. STOP. YOUR SISTER ELIZAVETA VLADIMIROVNA TARASOVA.*

FULL STOP.

There. Not such a difficult task after all, even if her heart was beating fast in her breast. She dimmed the lamp and put the curtains up again, then stepped out and convinced the door to lock—or at least, to latch soundly enough to pass a cursory inspection. If Liza had learned well how to pick locks open, she had far less experience in picking them locked again.

She had discharged her duty, come what would of it; even if Kesha refused to return now, at least he couldn't say that she had shunned him.

Slipping the hairpin back into her pocket, Liza straightened and began the walk back to the fortress. She took a crooked path, following the shadows of buildings in the evening half-light, noting the houses still lit and reminding herself to bully them into blacking out their windows on the following morning. Tonight, it would be their own damn fault if a dragon dropped an explosive on them.

From the tavern came the sound of singing. Something mournful-sounding, composed of many voices, with words that Liza couldn't make out. She smiled at that, wondering what Jaworski would say to hear Russians making merry with sad songs.

The stones of the roadway ground beneath her feet as she ascended the hill, and the light breeze ruffled the fur at her collar. With her hair tucked beneath her cap, she had passed for Wainwright, from a distance. Her own brother hadn't recognized her for a woman. *Or for a Russian, or a tall person, or for his sister by blood*, she reminded herself; she needn't be too proud of having fooled eyes such as his. No doubt he was so used to peering down at gears and mechanisms that he'd lost his ability to see anything farther than an armspan from his face.

Liza knew the way to the servants' entrance in the darkness. She could grope her way around the walls with her eyes closed, with her wits drink-addled, with her father's weight heavy on her shoulder. She knew every projection in the stone, every corner where the walls joined to brace a tower, every place where lichen had bloomed and mortar had crumbled. The brass latch was familiar beneath her hand—newly familiar, for they'd had it replaced last year, but familiar nonetheless. If she wanted, she could hold out her hands and trace the door's dimensions blindfolded. Without having to open her eyes, she knew what her home looked like. The fortress had written itself on her fingertips and the soles of her feet, on her shoulders and her cheeks and her palms. She'd written herself on the stones, too, with the blood from her scraped knees and split lips and once-broken leg.

She could recognize home. That Petya *couldn't* anymore alarmed her more than she cared to admit.

CHAPTER EIGHTEEN

Kesha straightened his ascot in his landlady's hallway mirror, then ran his fingers through his unruly red hair. It clashed abominably with the wallpaper behind him, which had an intricate pattern of pale and bright blues that Kesha found himself trying nigh-unconsciously to read. *Too long staring at draconic poetry*, he chided himself, and pulled at his hair with both hands; the chastisement did not in the least improve his reflection's appearance. Try as he might, he couldn't seem to help looking like a madman. He wanted only a long beard to appear a perfect hermit. There was nothing for it but to button the wide lapels of his coat closed, covering himself nearly to the chin and then wrapping a heavy scarf about his neck to fix the coat in place. If he looked a madman, at least he would be a *warm* madman.

The difficulty with accusing one's only good friend of dishonesty was, of course, that without him, one would have no good friends at all. Although Kesha might profess a kind of disaffected disinterest in the society of this world, preferring the company of long-dead philosophers and angels in which he only half-believed, he could not deny that he was anxious at the prospect of losing Misha's good regard.

Anxious enough to stare into a mirror like a fop, adjusting his scarf and brushing at his hair to put off the confrontation. At last, he wrenched himself away from his reflection and passed through the front hall, stepping onto the street with what must have been a very dire expression on his face.

He had offered his calling card at the Galiyev residence last evening, with an invitation for Misha to join him the next morning for coffee. It had been Kesha's first formal call since he'd come to St. Petersburg, searching for his mother's brother to beg for accommodations (and learning, to his sorrow, that the man had moved to Heidelberg some time ago without notifying his sister of his remove). He was out of the habit of offering pleasantries and invitations. He was, he supposed, rather out of the social habit in general.

The streets were busy with pedestrians and the occasional cab, horses shouldering past thickset women with their hair bound up in scarves and men dressed after the western fashion. The citizens of St. Petersburg seemed to move like leaves in a slow current, drifting inexorably together down the broad streets and narrow alleys; every now and then, a fine person's carriage would break through the flux with a glitter of gold and a flash of bright colors, or a priest's embroidered robes would make the crowd part like water around a stone.

Kesha stepped into the coffee-house, removing hat and scarf and coat at the door. Misha was early—but of course he was early; Kesha had never left him a card before, and he would have known at once that something was wrong. Indeed, rather than greeting Kesha with a laugh or an opening argument, he instead looked up from his cup with an expression of bemused curiosity. "A bit high-handed of you to summon me to coffee, when you knew you'd have seen me just the same if you *hadn't*," he remarked, when Kesha had taken the seat across from him. "Something's on your mind; let's have it out."

"Let me drink first," Kesha answered.

"Of course; you're surly before your coffee." Misha had taken the liberty of ordering a pot of thick, richly scented Greek coffee for them, and he poured a liberal dose into Kesha's cup. They tossed back their first cups together; Kesha closed his eyes at the bitter taste, in part to savor it and in part to shut out Misha's penetrating stare.

He couldn't draw out the moment much longer, though, and at length he put the cup back down on the saucer. When he reached across the table, Misha took his hand. "Why didn't you tell me how you *really* found those books?" asked Kesha, with the same forced softness that he had learned to use with his brother.

"Why won't you speak of your father?" asked Misha. There was nothing at all soft in his voice. "You've been a good friend to me, Keshechka, and I *am* grateful for that. But you can't say that you've trusted me any more than I've trusted you."

Kesha took a deep breath. "Something personal, then," he ventured.

"Yes," agreed Misha. "Something personal."

"Familial?"

"Yes." His inflection was half-wry, and he regarded Kesha over his glasses. "You've never asked me about my mother and father. Why is that, Kesha? Why have you never asked why I live with my aunt and uncle?"

"I'd thought it was your own business," answered Kesha. "I'd thought you were an orphan, actually."

"As good as an orphan," Misha replied. "My father was a political exile; they sent him to Siberia when I was a child, and my mother never told me what his crime had been or whether he could ever return. She gave me to her sister to raise and took the train east to be with her husband… there had been a radical strain in his family's history for generations, of course, but it was the polite sort of radicalism, if you take my meaning. The sort that wouldn't be out of place at *salons* today; an academic radicalism that never threatened the political order. My father's grandfather had even served on the Synod, but he did something or other to disgrace himself badly, and he was executed for it." With a faint smile, Misha broke off. "You're waiting for me to come to the point, aren't you, Keshechka?"

"No," said Kesha. "No, I've begun to apprehend your point."

"Then, to continue—a month ago, my aunt told me that my father had died, and my mother would return to St. Petersburg when she'd settled their possessions and saved money for the passage. The message didn't particularly affect me; I hadn't seen or heard from my parents since I was very small, and I'd begun to think of the Galiyevs as my proper parents. A week after that, I received word from the executor of my father's will. I'd come into an inheritance that had been waiting for over a century for me, which my father had concealed in a vault…and what do you think it was, Kesha?"

"Books," said Kesha at once. He could feel a thrill of discovery as he said it—a shivering cognizance of its *rightness* that struck him like an electric shock. "The books in the library."

"Wrong," said Misha cheerfully. "Those, I found later. What my father had left me was far stranger, and far more valuable."

With his fingers threaded through Misha's, feeling the pulse beating slow and steady against his own, Kesha released a pent-up breath. He had been trying to determine, as he listened to Misha's tale, whether he was being told the truth. If the steadiness of Misha's pulse did not convince him, or the admissions of an inability to grieve, that cheerful correction put him beyond doubt. "Very well, then," he said. "Let's hear about this strange, valuable thing your father left you."

"I can show you, if you like, once we've finished our coffee. I'd hoped to introduce you to it by degrees…no, that's not entirely true. I'd hoped to draw you out, once I'd hooked you with a puzzle, and to persuade you to tell me all of those secrets that I've been *mad* to know for years. And then, only then, would I begin to introduce you to my own little secrets—"

"Large enough secrets; your father was transported to Siberia, your father's grandfather executed for something unspeakable—"

"Very *well*, Kesha! Large secrets, then. But as I was saying, I'd hoped that you would invest some sort of trust in me before expecting me to extend it to you. We're too alike in temperament, though; if you had never asked, then perhaps we would have gone on guardedly circling each other until the end of our days. And I hope that we can learn to share confidences with one another." His smile was so earnest, his pale green eyes so bright with feeling, that Kesha could nearly imagine that he wasn't half a lawyer. *If he can't make a lever of my trust, he'll make a lever of my suspicions*, he thought, half-fondly.

Too alike in temperament. Kesha returned the smile, accepting the terms. "Share your confidences. Unburden yourself. You've strung me along like one of your students because you wanted me to come to your story in a particular frame of mind; I believe I'm in that frame now. What is it that your father left you?"

"He left me a copy of the dragons' letter to the College of War," answered Misha. "The letter in which they announced the Defection."

The same sharp shock of discovery went through Kesha at the revelation. Suddenly, clearly, he understood why Misha had chosen him of all of his acquaintance to look over the dragons' poetry. "And naturally, you could no more read it than you could read the language of the Arawak. You required a linguist to help you translate, but it wouldn't do to introduce the whole project at once; you had to lay a little trail of puzzles from my door to yours, and make me follow it until I'd uncovered enough material to prove my worth. And thus we come to the books, and how you found them."

Misha poured himself another cup of coffee with his free hand. He drank it black, the foam gathering on his upper lip and the grounds catching on his lower. Kesha had to restrain the impulse to brush his mouth clean. Dabbing at his lips with his napkin, Misha continued, "In his will, my father made an odd, elliptical reference to my father's grandfather and his legacy. Since I knew very little about the man, I went to visit my great-aunt on my father's side, who had taken up the curation of the family books and records. Oh, you'd laugh to see her house, Kesha! Books from floor to ceiling in every room, and a labyrinth of chests full of files with family trees to label to whom they belonged—and throughout the whole place, her great hounds stalking with their claws clicking on the floor. She'd sold her carpets, you see, to hire a man to build her more bookshelves. I would take you to view it, as though it were a public spectacle, but you'd only fall in love with the place and never return.

"But I see you're growing impatient," he observed, when Kesha shifted his hand to flex out a growing ache in his wrist. "To the point. I combed my grandfather's records with great diligence, but the man wrote nothing of note, and *nothing* to do with his father. It's all one long, dull record of nutriment consumed and properties sold or rented; I can scarcely believe I'm related to such a dull man—"

"I begin to see the resemblance," Kesha put in sharply.

"—but his *sister*," continued Misha, as though he hadn't heard, "His *sister* was a prolific diarist, and she recorded all of the sordid details of the affair. Their father—my great-grandfather, Alexander Alexeyevich—had led the negotiations to convince the dragons to maintain their alliance with Russia. I needn't tell you that he failed, and all of his books and papers were destroyed. His daughter, though, was a prodigiously brave woman, and in the dead of the night, she slipped into the very offices of the Collegia and prised free a panel—"

"—which she then tacked down again, once she'd hidden her father's books."

"Because if she'd taken them home, she'd only have been found out in it. And later, there was a purge," said Misha, half-dreaming, as though he were looking through time upon distant pyres. "The universities gave up their books on dragons, as did the fashionable families. No one forced them—or no one forced *most* of them; there were laws describing which books were seditious, but from what Klara Alexandrovna writes, the people of St. Petersburg *wanted* to burn their books. It was the patriotic thing to do. Even the universities were full of students dragging books to the square and throwing them on the fires. Any books, once they'd begun; they brought them out by the armload. She wrote that she saw poor people flinging holy texts into the flames, all because they wanted to burn something."

"Christ and all the saints," breathed Kesha. "It sounds like a massacre. All of those books—all of those *ideas*, gone—"

"Gone," Misha agreed. "I can't tell you how my heart sang, when I heard that Starikovich's family still had their books. The whole city went *mad* for burning, but if the east still has a few books—if Yekaterinburg really *did* keep printing and translators kept working even into this century—" He broke off there, voice suffused with unaccustomed emotion. The sound of it alarmed Kesha, who had never yet heard him in a state of true agitation. He folded his other hand over Misha's, clasping it as Misha had clasped his hand when the dragons' poetry had made him tremble.

Misha glanced down at their hands, smiling faintly at the sight of Kesha's long, thick-knuckled fingers stroking down the soft hairs over the back of Misha's hand. Kesha knew that look well. It was the one that Misha wore when he was curled up in the wing-backed chair in the library, his glasses gleaming in the firelight and his eyes fixed on some tome of foreign poems. When he spoke again, he had regained his usual tone of unaffected half-mockery. "If it's possible for us to decipher the letter, even after the purge, then perhaps it's possible for us to open negotiations with the dragons again."

He didn't have to say, *Perhaps it's possible to clear my father's name, and my great-grandfather's. Perhaps it's possible to make Klara Alexandrovna's bravery mean something.*

"I'll help you," answered Kesha. "You knew from the moment I saw the poetry that I would help you."

"No," said Misha, inordinately pleased at being able to correct Kesha twice in a single conversation. "No, I knew from the moment when you asked me how I'd really found the books. From that moment, I could see that you valued our partnership far more than anything in their pages."

Kesha withdrew his hands and folded them in his lap. Around them, the other patrons read newspapers and set cups down on saucers with a clatter; in the quiet, Kesha listened to the rattle of coffeepots over flames and the steady tread of serving girls' shoes on the floorboards. His own tale welled in his throat, tasting of ashes and acid. "I'm a thief," he said, when he could bear it no more.

Misha blinked. "Pardon?"

"A thief," answered Kesha. Once that had been said, the rest came easily. "When my father refused to let me go away to study, I was in a rage. I wanted nothing more than to spite him for denying me. So I stole all that he had—all that my family had—and fled on the next train. I didn't even have time to count it until I'd nearly reached Moscow, but it amounted to something very near four thousand rubles. He never brought the law against me for that. He only sent one letter, some months later, telling me that I was no longer his son." He sat back in his chair, steepling his fingers before him. "And that's *my* little secret."

CHAPTER NINETEEN

Upon closer inspection, the east wall appeared beyond salvaging. Petya was no structural engineer, and he had little experience with stone, but the fracture showed stark and pale against the soot-blackened wall, which suggested that the wall had begun to shift since the explosion. Structural engineer or not, Petya could tell that the fissure didn't bode well.

He rubbed his hands together and blew on them to work the feeling back into his fingers. The warm, buttery light of dawn did little to mitigate the sharp winds that swept over the southern hillsides—and Petya was foolish enough to come outside at sunrise to stand underneath fractured walls. Without gloves! Kesha would have scolded him for going out without gloves, even when the morning sunlight glanced warmly over the back of Petya's neck.

He turned away from the wall and began walking about the perimeter of the fortress, still rubbing his hands together in agitation.

In the keep itself, Petya heard the walls echoing with unaccustomed conversation. The English were at their breakfast in the mess hall, enjoying a hearty meal of porridge and some bacon that they had no doubt liberated from the ice closet. At first Petya thought they were saying "rations," but after a moment, he realized that they were calling the bacon "rashers."

Bemused at their terminology as much as at their temerity, Petya made his way through the mass of long tables and English soldiers in search of Wainwright. He could see his sister gesturing him over, her eyes a little hollow after a long night watch and an early morning seeing off Oleg Kamensky, but he waved her off and tapped the English lieutenant on the shoulder.

Wainwright turned, and to his credit, his genial expression faded only a little when he saw who wanted him. By now, his nose was considerably less swollen. "Well, Pyotr Vladimirovich," he said. "What can I do for you?"

"I was hoping that one of your men might be an engineer," said Petya. "I don't need a *good* engineer. A plain mason will do, if you don't have any better. But a wall's been damaged fairly recently, and it needs to be shored up. Our machinists don't really do this kind of work. I'd be very grateful for an expert's advice."

"An English expert?" asked Wainwright, half-wry, half-taunting. His Russian was very little accented, but a touch of the Anglophone crept into his *English*.

"An English expert, or Scottish, or Irish. Whatever you have to hand."

"I won't send you the Welsh, then," Wainwright answered with a smile. "I've got a few good sappers; they understand how to demolish walls better than how to build them, but they've bridged a few rivers in their day, and they might be of some use to you. The east wall, yes? That *does* look bad."

"And you planned to let it look bad, never saying a word, until—"

"Until your family did its duty? Yes, that was just what I planned. Your sister has made it quite clear that she has no interest in my help or my interference, and your father has scarcely said four words to me since he let us take the dragons' bodies. It wasn't *my* place to call attention to the state of your wall."

Wainwright's logic silenced him. He could imagine all too well how Liza would have responded to any critique of her family's fortress. Wainwright would have been nursing a black eye in addition to a broken nose, if she'd chosen to be gentle. "I do see what you mean," admitted Petya. "And the bacon? Where did you—"

"One of my men won it in a wager," answered Wainwright, and although he strove mightily to restrain the twitch of mirth at the corner of his lips, he couldn't keep the delight from spreading over his features. "Your Elizaveta Vladimirovna has some tricks yet to learn at the dice table."

"Only because our father hasn't taught them to her yet," laughed Petya. As though he had been given permission to laugh along, Wainwright was soon chuckling heartily. If they couldn't trust one another, Petya thought, then they could at least have a moment of shared laughter over bacon and porridge. It warmed his heart to feel even such a tenuous camaraderie with this man—this stranger, whom he had imagined for half an hour might be his friend.

Soon, though, Wainwright schooled his features to an expression of gravity. "If you can get your father's permission for my sappers to have a look at your wall, then I'll be glad to turn them over into your care. I'll even translate for you. But unless he allows us to help you, in so many words, I will *not* hazard whatever goodwill we have left here."

He wants to make me his advocate, his emissary, thought Petya, but even so, he grasped the rationality of Wainwright's ultimatum. He'd lost Liza's trust all but irretrievably when he'd manned a gun turret and shot a dragon from the sky; if displays of initiative were met with such strong disfavor, why should Wainwright trust his men and his reputation to Petya alone? What else could he do but solicit a blessing from the highest authority in the fortress?

The thought made Petya smile, a lopsided twist of the lips that he could feel in his cheek. Vladimir Petrovich Tarasov made an unlikely figure for a saint, if only because no one would have wished to paint his ikon. The red hair touched with grey at the edges, the loose-hanging skin of his jowls, the pipe in one hand and the bottle of drink in the other...no, Petya would never see his father's face when he knelt at the ikonostasis.

"You're laughing," observed Wainwright, which startled Petya from his thoughts. "Is it my face? Have I got something on it?" He offered a crooked smile, the mirror of Petya's own, and touched his nose gingerly. "Yes, right here in the middle. I think your sister tried to wipe it off for me."

"I doubt it," answered Petya. "If she had, there would be nothing left."

Petya found his father situated once again at the telegraph office, chatting with the master about laying down wires between the keep and the next fortress over. "I'm only saying that this is a very *flammable* building," Vladimir said, "and what if a mortar should hit? If we had to get word to the next tower quickly—"

"If you're threatening me with arson, Tarasov, then I'll ask you to think again," replied the telegraph master. He wore a placid expression as he said it, as though he habitually conversed with men who offered to burn his office down. "You know as well as I do that you're only interested in controlling who has access to the telegraph, and that's entirely against regulations."

"Hang regulations!" With an airy wave of his hand, Vladimir dismissed the entire imperial telegraph system and its bylaws. "Do you really think I'd forbid anyone the use of the telegraph? I'm thinking only of the *strategic* usefulness of having a line at the hub of battle; I don't have any other machinations in mind—ah, Petya! Here to bring your father some tea?" He sat back in his chair, folding his arms across his chest and smiling with false congeniality. "We were just discussing the prospect of putting in another line—*another* line," he said to the telegraph master, like a theatrical aside, "which would connect the keep to the telegraphic system, in case of emergencies. You're learning to be an engineer, boy; what's your opinion on the matter?"

Petya realized that he must be staring at the disputants like an idiot. His father's all-knowing smirk didn't dissipate in the least, and the telegraph master gave him a pitying look. He felt himself flushing, and he couldn't have said whether it was indignation or shame that galvanized him. "I think we'd do better to set up our own line, if you want my honest opinion," he said at last. "There's too much communication shuttling back and forth along the lines for the telegraphs to be useful as a warning system. But a private line, dedicated to emergency reports between the towers, would be heeded straightaway. And it would free us from suspicion of interference," he concluded. "Of course, it would be *very* expensive, and I'm not sure we could convince the Tsar to sponsor it—"

"You see? My boy's learning to dream rich men's dreams!" laughed Vladimir, rising from his chair to clap his son on the shoulder. "The engineer doesn't have to think of money; he only has to imagine what he *would* build if he *could*, and then spin his fantasies for his investors. A good living, if he can spin fantasies well enough."

He didn't say it, but Petya could see the question glittering in his bright, pale eyes: *and what then?*

"I think," said the telegraph master significantly, "that your son has something to say to you."

"Well, boy? You haven't brought me my tea, so you must want something." When he straightened to his full height, Vladimir was taller than his son. When Petya stood only a hand's breadth from him, breathing in his rancid-meat exhalations, he couldn't forget that he was still a child as far as his father was concerned.

He couldn't step back, though, without advertising his discomfort, and his father knew it well. "It's the east wall," he said at last. "I'd like to try to shore it up, or even rebuild it. The soldiers—"

"The *English* soldiers," interrupted Vladimir, as though it required clarifying.

"The English soldiers," conceded Petya, "offered to lend me some of their sappers, but only if you'll give me permission to have them work on our wall. They won't work without it."

"And why should I give them permission to work on our wall?" demanded Vladimir with a rough laugh (at Petya's naïveté, he thought). "Have you lost your faith in Russian workers, because they don't have your fine education? Haven't we got machinists who can work steel as well as any Englishman? Haven't we got miners enough in this town? Don't they know better than any scholars or sappers how to brace a wall? No, you'd have me let the English send their demolition men to dig up our foundations and plant mines—and what then, Petya? What will we do when the wall falls in?"

The heat that had grown in his face at his father's mockery now coursed through Petya's body. He had thought himself ready for his father's dismissal, but he was unable to bear his disdain. He took a sharp step back and didn't care what his father read in the gesture. "I didn't realize the English had brought *mines* to plant under our walls," said Petya, with an edge to his voice that he didn't bother to dull. "I'm surprised they haven't blown us all to smithereens already!"

Vladimir rose up like a thunderhead, broad shoulders rounded and countenance dark. "You'll speak to me with *respect*, Pyotr Vladimirovich Tarasov," he answered. "I won't hear your brother's insolence in your mouth—"

"You won't hear *sense*, either," Petya snapped. "I'm not disrespectful enough to countermand you. I'll tell them you refused, and that you think they're likely to blow up the fortress whenever they get the chance. And I hope they'll be grateful for the intelligence."

"They already know that I think *that*," Vladimir laughed. "But I have intelligence enough on them to curdle their milk. I know what questions they ask and what telegrams they send. Go on, then. Have your petty moment of betrayal. Give me up to your friend the lieutenant. If it will ease your little heart, then you've my *blessing*, boy." Behind him, the telegraph master was leaning over his desk with an interested look in his eyes, and Petya's anger expanded to encompass him, too. He longed to stamp his feet and shout, rave and rail and wave his arms like a madman.

He breathed in once, then twice, then a third time. With each breath, he exhaled slow and silent. On the third exhalation, Petya had regained himself enough to speak. "You're right. I was speaking in anger. Please forgive me, Father."

"None of that groveling," his father answered, lowering himself slowly (painfully) into his seat again. "Go find yourself some Russian miners, and *then* we'll talk about what to do with my wall."

Our wall, thought Petya, but he only nodded and bowed. "Thank you, Father."

He left the telegraph office with a coal of rage still burning in his heart. He nursed that coal, cherished it in his breast, as though he meant to start a fire with it one day.

CHAPTER TWENTY

Lieutenant Wainwright didn't whirl about when Liza's hand fell on his shoulder in the courtyard. He didn't startle, or jump, or suppress a small sound of apprehension. His hand was simply, suddenly gripping her wrist, and before she had a moment to respond, through some trick he had pulled her around until she was facing *him*. "Ah, Elizaveta Vladimirovna," he said, pursing his lips against whatever else he wanted to say. He released her wrist and made a brief bow. "Can I help you with something?"

Shaking out her hand, Liza frowned. She had meant to ask what he'd been speaking of so intently with Petya, but the excessive politeness of his response needled her like a burr at her hem, and the irritation drove that line of questioning entirely out of her mind. "Why did you let go? Because you saw that I was a woman?"

"Because I saw that you were my host," answered Wainwright.

"When I broke your nose, you'd said you wouldn't hit me because I was a woman. If I'd been a man, would you have hit me?" Even now, her fists curled at her sides and her wrist aching from the strength of his grip, she wondered what manner of fighter he'd be if he stopped holding back.

She licked her dry lips, tasting blood where they had cracked from the arid air. "Well?" she asked. "If I'd been a man—"

"You were *daring* me to hit you," answered Wainwright. His eyes narrowed. "If I've given you cause to dislike or resent me—"

"You made me so damnably angry!" she said. "If you'd swung at me, I'd have given you *such* a thrashing. And you might've thrashed me, too, but I could have respected a man who thrashed me in a fair fight. A man who lies and politicks and tells me he *would* have hit me *if I weren't a woman*...I thought you were better than *that*, Wainwright!"

"Are you asking me to hit you, Elizaveta Vladimirovna?" asked Wainwright, with a faint and flashing smile. If she had looked away for even a moment—if she had blinked—she would never have seen it at all.

They stood now at the edge of the courtyard, very near to the great gates. The gear closet door stood open, which probably meant that Petya was inside and working on his massive iron chains again; the ground below them was slick with melted snow and dead grass, mud and gravel mixed with decades of dragons' blood. Liza's lips drew back in a smile. "Just a friendly match," she said, dangerous, whisper-soft.

"We'll need rules," he answered, catching the seriousness in her voice. "I'd prefer if you didn't break any more of my bones."

"No more bones, then," she agreed. "I see you have a knife."

"So do you. What do you want to do with it, Tarasov?"

Not Tarasova. Liza folded her arms over her chest. "Swear to me on your faith you'll take *care* with it, if you draw it. And I'll do the same."

"I swear," answered Wainwright. "I'm ready. Until 'mercy,' then?"

"Until 'mercy.'"

She hadn't time to breathe before Wainwright's fist took her just below the ribs. She doubled over at the sudden pain, tasting bile, but caught his arm before he clipped her under the jaw—and with a heave that was all strength, no technique, she flung him hard against the gates. He tried to get his feet under him, but they found no purchase on the mud; he struck like the head of a battering ram, back colliding against the wood of the doors with a hollow thud. There was a strange, half-mad light in his eyes, and she knew the same light was in hers.

His knuckles struck her in the gut. She gasped, but she was laughing as she did.

Liza drew her knife, twisting the handle to make the blade catch the sunlight. She met his eyes, but he shook his head, and she sheathed the blade again. *On your faith, Vladimirovich.*

He launched himself from the wall, fists before him to guard against her attack. She drove a shoulder against him, though, and they smashed together like stones. *This* was what she'd wanted; this was why she'd hit him; she took a blow to the chest that nearly knocked the wind from her, and the breathless exhilaration was *glorious*.

Petya poked his head out from his little gear-closet with a horrified expression. If he shouted something (and she thought he shouted *something*), then she didn't hear him because Wainwright had given her a smart clout about the ear that made her head ring like a bell. She tasted blood and thought she'd bitten her tongue, split her lip; it didn't matter because she was pressing Wainwright hard against the doors with her hand at his throat, breathing, "Ask for mercy—"

—and then strong hands were fixing on her shoulders and yanking her back. "Get *off* him, Liza!" shouted Petya, his arms tight about hers; someone else had come to help pin her arms, and from the Polish cursing she thought it was Jaworski.

"It's all *right!*" said Wainwright, holding up his hands. He was breathing hard. "It was only a friendly sparring match.

Nothing to shout about. For the love of Christ, let your sister go, Pyotr Vladimirovich!"

Reluctantly, Petya released her, and after a moment Jaworski did the same. "You're sure she didn't attack you," he said, with a softness in his voice that was very like compassion.

"There were rules," she said. Saying it made her feel small. It felt like something a child would say. *We were only playing a game; there were rules.* "It was honorable. We wouldn't have hurt each other."

"Perfectly civil," Wainwright agreed, glancing over to her. "I couldn't have asked for a more honorable opponent."

"And two nights ago, she broke your nose, and you said that you wouldn't be made to hit a woman," Jaworski observed. It struck Liza then that what she had first thought was compassion was in fact a carefully studied neutrality. A politic voice.

"We agreed to it, like sportsmen. Like fencers," said Liza. "It was *gentlemanly*."

"Then you think your friend is a gentleman?" asked Jaworski. He shared a significant look with Petya, but Liza couldn't read their expressions.

"Hardly a friend," she answered. "But perhaps he's a gentleman; I'll give him that." With a bow to Wainwright and a civil "Lieutenant," Liza turned on her heel and crossed the courtyard. She didn't wait for her brother or Jaworski to pronounce their judgment. She and Wainwright both knew that they'd conducted themselves with dignity, and theirs was the only judgment that mattered.

Her gaze fell on the long shadow of a tower, which lay across the courtyard like the hand of a clock. *Speaking of judgment.*

It was simple enough, really, to solve the question of whether Lieutenant Wainwright could have seen the fleeing dragons from his perch in the watchtower. She had only to climb up herself to where he had been and look.

Each hallway of the keep contained a hatch that communicated with the towers of the fortress. Liza's mother had used to say that the corridors radiated out from the dining hall like the petals of a flower; *like veins from a heart,* her father had always countered. *Sending our young blood to arms.*

Liza knew every watchtower as well as she knew the backs of her hands. Which was to say that she knew her right from her left and how to use each one, but not the exact placement of every vein and freckle (or of every hatch and lamp). She knew, for example, that to reach the tower from which Wainwright had been firing on the night the railway station had been hit, she would have to take the north corridor from the dining hall, toward the rooms where her grandfather had bunked his forces in better days. Now, the English kept themselves in the north wing, with her grandfather's portrait hanging at the end of the hall and watching over the interlopers with a stern expression. She knew, as well, that the screw-door of the north tower's hatch always came unscrewed over the course of the day, no matter how often she tightened it. Perhaps Petya could repair it, while he was repairing the whole damned fortress.

This tower was seldom in use when Liza and her father were running the fortress on their own. It provided a worse vantage than the others; the Turks never came from the north, after all. The watchmen usually kept to the southwest towers, by the great doors and the road down to the town. To the north, there was only the dark line of the railroad and the hills sloping off into the distance.

It was possible that Wainwright really hadn't seen the dragons fleeing. Osip Moiseyevich hadn't seen them either, and she didn't think he was a spy for the Turks. Liza's leather gloves caught on the cold iron ladder. *I should've seen them—but I was barely off the first ladder before the battle was over. Stupid to have the whole family drinking in town like that.*

The bells had begun to ring no more than a minute

before the bombs had fallen. If Wainwright had been in the keep when the alarm had sounded, he would have had to unscrew the hatch, find the lights, and climb up the ladder (just as she had done, but without nearly a decade of practice). That would have taken him perhaps thirty seconds. Liza felt her toes flexing on the rung, though, and recalculated. Petya had said that Wainwright had lost three toes to frostbite, and even in good boots, that would have made him unsteady on the ladder.

He would have gone straight for the second ladder and the gun emplacement rather than lingering at the watch post; he wasn't the sort of man to dawdle and gape at the sight of a dragon, and anyway she'd heard him firing before she'd reached the fortress. He would have sat in the gunner's chair and gripped the attitude rotor—Liza lowered herself into the metal seat, pressing her spine against the backrest—and if every word he'd told Petya was true, Wainwright would *still* have been fresh as a virgin.

He'd learned by watching the Turks. Liza hadn't the first idea what the Turks' gun mounts looked like, but she was willing to wager a good silver snuffbox that they didn't look like *hers*. Wainwright would have sat in the gunner's chair, found the trigger first, possibly fired once to be sure he *could* fire it. Then he'd have put his feet down on the pedals, resettled his hand on the attitude rotor, and felt the gears moving smooth and easy to turn him and the gun. Petya had only just oiled them and cleared out the rats' nests; the gun would have turned swift as an autumn breeze.

Liza tried to remember what it had been like, when the gun mounts were new to her. She'd been twenty-two, grim-jawed and burning with rage at her brother; she'd wanted nothing more than to set him running across the hills while she showed him the range of the Tarasov guns. Her father had stood with his hands on the back of her chair, steadying her in the seat to keep her from whirling madly. His face had been a kind of blank in those days, as though he hadn't yet decided which expression to wear. *We can't waste ammunition for lessons,* he had told her, *or when a dragon comes, we'll have none at all, and what then?*

She tried to remember that anxious desire to please, and that feeling of spinning out of control.

She would scarcely have been able to look at the village; her eyes would have been fixed on the lever, the trigger, the long barrel of the gun. Her hands would have been shaking, and probably cold, too. She would have scrambled up to the turret without gloves, perhaps even without a coat. So eager to prove herself that she didn't care if she damn well froze to death.

He had cried out with joy when he'd shot the beast down, a great whoop of exultation that Liza would never have *bothered* with. Because she had been shooting down dragons for the past six years, and for her entire life, she had been a Tarasov. Dragons weren't creatures of legend, full of song and fire; they were damned nuisances, and killing them was her work and her legacy. She didn't imagine herself as St. George, his spear through a great lizard's throat.

Wainwright had been *surprised* to have shot the dragon down. Gears rotating under him, gun gyrating wildly, barrel nosing toward the night sky—and somehow, he'd managed to make the damn thing explode.

And he'd realized for the first time that this could be *his* work, too.

Liza rotated the chair to face southwest and pressed her spyglass to her eye, peering over the smooth curve of the gun and the neat, peaked rooftops. The train station stood on the northernmost edge of the town, its skeletal walls still a story high. Under her grandfather, the building had been the town's pride; its walls had been quarried from good stone, its roof built of strong beams. Even the windows had been finely made, the glass tinted faintly green and filmed over with coal smoke.

He wouldn't have been looking at the station, though.

He wouldn't even have been looking at the sky. He would have been looking at the beast he'd shot down, his eyes wide with wonder.

He hadn't seen the dragons fleeing. It would've meant tearing his gaze away from his triumph.

CHAPTER TWENTY-ONE

"Ah, Kesha! You can't imagine how glad I am to catch you today!"

Kesha had been Starikovich's student for some years, and he imagined that he knew the man's humors as well as anyone could. He had seen his professor in transports of delight and in towering rages; he could discern from the angle of Starikovich's eyebrows whether he planned to eviscerate a paper because he thought it had promise, or because he thought it was hopeless. This hard-won familiarity had taught him that, when the old man's eyes gleamed like twilight stars and his fingers tapped out a silent sonata on the head of his cane, any sensible person would quickly recall pressing business elsewhere. In another city, if at all possible.

Kesha, who could claim no business more pressing than a visit to his banker, trained his features to an expression of politeness and moved to one side of the walkway to let other pedestrians pass. "To what do I owe the honor, sir?" he asked, with all the good cheer that he could muster. He could feel snowflakes catching on his eyelashes.

"To whom, you might ask—to my nephew, bless his heart. He got my telegram and then had his books on the first train to St. Petersburg; I'd like to see a Tarasov step into line that quickly! I can't think he's read half of them, so it's all a jumble, but never mind that! There's a crate sitting in my parlor, waiting for you to cart it away." He tapped the backs of Kesha's knees with his cane, tilting his head to one side like a magpie sighting something glittering. "Well? Step lively, boy; Katya's been itching to get those books on the shelves, and if you don't take them, soon she'll have put them God knows where!"

Urged onward in equal parts by admonition and by judicious prods with the cane, Kesha found himself foregoing his trip to his banker and setting out for Starikovich's house. They scarcely even slowed when they passed Starikovich's acquaintances in the street; for a professor of philosophy, he had only a curt, half-growled *hello,* and he brushed past a pair of students who were clearly nerving themselves up to approach him.

For Misha's student, though, the hated Alexander Ivanovich with his face like a Romantic rendering of Cupid—his manner so earnest and devout, so blithely unaware of having interrupted—for this boy, Starikovich paused a full minute to chat on ecclesiastical law. He appeared almost to regard the young man with a kind of paternal affection, which made Kesha's blood boil in the most unaccountable way. *Jealous of Starikovich's affections, Tarasov? You have no need of fathers*, he berated himself, and soon he thought he had mastered his irrational irritation.

Nonetheless, Kesha barely restrained the urge to steal the man's cane and goad him on with it.

"There's a fine young scholar," said Starikovich, when they parted ways at last. "Knows how to treat his elders! You could learn from his example, I'll wager."

"I'm sure I could," answered Kesha, drawing his coat closer about his shoulders. "If I've been less than respectful—"

"He's not so damn *deferential* as you are," laughed Starikovich. "You'll seethe at me and still call me sir, and ask to what you owe the honor. He'll at least mention it, when I'm prodding him about like a straying sheep."

"And that's how I should treat my elders? Tell them to stop prodding me?"

Starikovich raised the cane, but at a warning look from Kesha, he only brought it down with a sharp *crack* on an iron railing. He was grinning, the sort of grin that made children draw back and women look quickly away, and for a moment he was the very image of Vladimir Tarasov. "Tell me to stop, if you think it'll do any good."

Kesha made a disgruntled noise in his throat, but this time he had the sense to stay out of reach of the cane.

Starikovich lived near the river, in a respectable district where every house had a small garden of salad vegetables and flowers, and only a very few people penned chickens in their yards. From the uppermost window of his house, one might have been able to peer out over the Neva waters and catch sight of the spire of St. Andrew's Cathedral and the tower of the Kunstkamera. The house wasn't far west of the Galiyev residence, and two or three minutes' brisk walking would bring Kesha to their doorstep; if Starikovich's crate was a large one, he thought, then he would leave the better part of it in Misha's care.

Thank you for sharing your secret, Misha had said, with more than usual coolness, and he had pressed Kesha's hand briefly. *I'll take a day to think on it, and then—then, I hope I'll be in a better frame of mind to answer you.*

"There's enough gloom in the air without your sulking about," said Starikovich, unlocking his door and shaking out his coat in the doorway. "Close that behind you. The heat will leak out."

Kesha closed the door and let it latch, then let Starikovich lead him into the parlor. A very small box of books sat in the middle of the floor, on a once-fine rug that might have come from Persia but had since assimilated to its surroundings. The box itself was really too small to be called a crate, no longer than Kesha's forearm and only a handspan wide; it could have held no more than five books, perhaps six if two were very slender. When he bent to pick up the box, he found it even lighter than he had anticipated. With his pocketknife, he prised the lid off, and found four slim books inside. "Ah," he said, and tried not to look terribly disappointed.

"These," said Starikovich, "are the books on the language. He's got more of the dragons' philosophy, but they're mixed in with all the rest, and—if you'll look at the covers—these are old enough that my sister's brood had the lot rebound. No titles on the spines; it'll take a few weeks to sort out the draconic stuff from the rest. Still, better than nothing, eh?"

With the box in one hand, his index finger tracing the title page of the first book, Kesha nodded slightly. *"The Language of Dragons, Rendered According to the Cyrillic System of Letters, with Notes for the Teaching of the Very Young*...name of God, did they actually teach children to speak this?"

"Better entertainment than Latin," answered Starikovich, chuckling like the clanking of old gears. "My brothers and I used to run through the courtyard screaming at each other and saying we were practicing our lessons. Didn't mean a damned thing, but our father was too proud to say he didn't understand it. He even tried to correct our pronunciation once; of course, we were very grave about the whole thing—"

"Do you think my grandfather learned to speak it?" asked Kesha, not caring whether he was interrupting the narrative. Beneath *The Language of Dragons* was the promised Yekaterinburg translation of the *Collection*, beneath that a volume of military training pamphlets from the 1750s, beneath that a book of quotations and aphorisms; he flicked through the pages, searching for the intricate circles that he had come to think of as draconic stanzas. "Was it...was it simply part of a young gentleman's education, or—"

"A young gentleman, perhaps," agreed Starikovich. "Particularly a young gentleman with a family tradition of military service. But you Tarasovs, you come from Cossack stock. I don't mean to say that you aren't one of the finest families in Russia; who could deny that? But your great-great-grandfather bought his lands and changed his name, and if you're a fine family today…"

"I'm a Tarasov, and Tarasovs think that all the world's books are kept in universities," said Kesha, with a touch of bitterness in his voice. "Yes, I see."

"You *see* that you're ashamed of your line, and it makes you think that you see me insulting your family," Starikovich told him, and with the head of his cane, he tilted Kesha's chin up. His eyes were bright as winter stars, and the metal atop his cane warm from the heat of his hand. "So see what I'm saying. I'm saying that no, it's not likely your grandfather learned to speak the language, because like every other man who hasn't got centuries of family wealth beneath him, he had other damn things to do. And I'm saying that you, who haven't got anything better to do, are going to learn this language from *spite*. To spite me, and to spite your grandfather, and to spite yourself—but you *are* going to learn it, and you're going to defend a thesis that will make every last one of your examiners shit his trousers."

They stood regarding one another, Kesha clutching the box of books to his chest, Starikovich leaning heavily on his good leg. The cane pressed uncomfortably against Kesha's trachea, but he didn't dare look away first.

At length, Starikovich turned from his pupil. "Go on, then. I want to eat dinner with my wife, and I'll never leave the parlor with you staring after me like an addled puppy dog. Go. Educate yourself."

"I will. Thank you." He bowed, not a perfunctory gesture of politeness but a deep, old-fashioned bow. To his credit, Starikovich didn't laugh, although he did raise his brows in amusement. Then, retrieving his hat from the hatstand by the door, he left.

As he walked, Kesha considered a detour to the Galiyev

residence, where he would no doubt be greeted warmly and plied with tea and conversation. Perhaps Misha wouldn't even be in; perhaps he could simply enjoy Madame Galiyeva's hospitality in peace, and forget his guilt for long enough to be a pleasant guest.

It was a comfortable enough sort of speculation, but Kesha knew better than to indulge it. He turned his steps homeward and didn't look back.

When Kesha arrived at his lodgings, he found a telegram waiting for him, which he accepted half-carelessly and slipped into his box. No doubt it was Petya, writing something earnest and urgent and heartfelt; he'd have run up a truly hideous bill in trying to make a telegram into a letter, and half of it would be sentimental nonsense with which Kesha was entirely unequipped to cope at the moment. He wanted nothing but to get warm and to read, and preferably both at once.

In his landlady's sitting room, a pair of Polish cartographers were having a quiet, earnest argument on the ornate French sofa. They'd kept most of the lamps burning, so he left them to their latitudes and he curled up on the ceramic stove to delve into the Yekaterinburg translation.

Gone were the awkward eighteenth-century iambs, the forced rhymes and ungainly stanza breaks. *This is no human poetry,* read the translator's preface, *and so I have not presumed to introduce human notions of what is poetical. If these words seem unbeautiful to the human ear, the fault lies partly in the errors of my translation, and partly in the human ear itself, which contents itself with the beautiful where the dragons seek the sublime.*

When Kesha made his way to the staircase, less than an hour and a lifetime later, his ears were ringing with the echoes of remembered thunder.

The first bend of the narrow stair was dark, which was hardly unusual. He might have brought a candle up with him, but he had grown accustomed to navigating the age-bowed treads in the darkness. Kesha rounded the hairpin turn halfway up, shifting his box of books to one arm so as to free a hand to fumble for his key, and then looked up from the landing into the half-darkness. The door stood slightly ajar.

Only Kesha, Petya, and their landlady had keys to the room. Kesha never left the door unlocked, Petya was in the borderlands, and their landlady wasn't at home. His grip tightened on the box, the rough edges digging into his palms.

Someone had picked his lock, secure in the supposition that he wouldn't return in time to interfere.

He put down the box in the shadow of the landing, then crept up the remaining stairs, one hand on the banister to steady himself. At the head of the stairs, a narrow corridor stretched to the right, its green-gold wallpaper washed grey by the afternoon light.

With the very tips of his fingers, Kesha nudged the door open. The hinges creaked, and a chill gust escaped through the entryway. Steeling himself for a confrontation, Kesha flung himself into the room—

—and Misha looked up from the desk, a sheaf of papers in his hands. He blinked, sliding his spectacles up his nose with an expression of irritation. "Ah," he said, as though he were faintly annoyed at having been interrupted while working upon a particularly tricky puzzle. "I'd been waiting in the parlor, but your notes were up *here*, you see."

"And so you did me the courtesy of testing my lock?"

"Condoning the occasional bout of petty criminality," answered Misha comfortably. "I see you've been taking your inspiration from your landlady's wallpaper?" He held up one of Kesha's most recent renderings of a stanza, a huge copy drawn on drafting paper; the strokes had all been outlined painstakingly in black ink. He had carefully filled the outlines with Petya's colored ink, diluting the red and blue pigment with water with each successive figure he identified, until six intertwined shapes showed clearly.

The circle that marked off the stanza; a row of stylized crosses snaking aslant the circle; a long arc like the brow of a hill that split the circle horizontally; two large, sinuous figures in the foreground, curved to parallel one another; a lattice of lines like a loom.

Marked out in watered-down ink, though, even Kesha had to admit that the dragons' writing looked rather like wallpaper.

"A pictogram, of sorts," pronounced Kesha. "And since you've had some time to study it on your own, I imagine you've already worked that out. How long have you been here, anyway? These," he indicated the crosses, "are the mountains; your translator identifies them as a very specific branch of the Urals, and the Yekaterinburg translator agrees, which makes me imagine that they're a sort of aerial map—"

"You *have* the Yekaterinburg translation?" interrupted Misha, putting down the diagram and standing from Kesha's chair. "Why didn't you bring it to me immediately? Where is it?"

"It's on the landing. If I'd tried to bring it to you immediately, I'd have missed you, because you were breaking into my room," answered Kesha, and he had the immense satisfaction of watching Misha dart past him and scurry down the stairs to retrieve the box. Misha, like many intellectuals of good family, made a point not to run where he could walk—and like many intellectuals of good family, he promptly forgot whatever genteel manners had been inculcated during his youth at the prospect of rare books.

While Misha leafed through the Yekaterinburg translation of the *Collection* to verify the geography, Kesha sat on the edge of the bed and drew his telegram from the box. A cursory glance showed it to be a brief—surprisingly brief—missive.

COME HOME.

"Misha," he said. "Mishenka, put that down. Come here."

With a long-suffering sigh, Misha marked his place

and put the book down on the desk, seating himself tailor-fashion on the bed. "Yes? What in God's name is so *urgent?*"

Kesha placed the paper into Misha's hands, watching as his friend's eyes lowered to those impossible words. He searched Misha's face for comprehension, or pity, or even annoyance, and he saw only a detached curiosity; Misha might have been reading a treatise on agriculture. He might have been reading a student's face, seeking an answer that he knew better than to expect.

Folding Kesha's hand in his own, Misha observed, "If they're calling you back to stand trial, I believe they've waited too long. They haven't a prayer of convicting you."

"I doubt that's what she wants," answered Kesha. "Look at the language she uses: our full names; 'your sister.' She isn't asking me to return to be accused, and she isn't threatening me with disowning, the way she did Petya. No, she wants to inspire me with… shame, I think. Familial obligation."

They sat together while the wind whistled through the cracks around the windowpanes and their hands grew slowly warm. Perhaps, Kesha supposed, Misha was thinking of his great-aunt's house, filled floor to ceiling with dead men's books and dead women's papers. Of no value, except for that the dead were family.

"Well," said Misha, at length. "Are you going?"

"I suppose I have to," Kesha answered. "As soon as the rails are open again."

"Very well." Pressing Kesha's hand in his own, Misha tried to smile; his cheeks strained at the effort, though, and Kesha was reminded for the first time in years that Misha was little older than Petya. "Very well. But until then—"

"Until then," Kesha agreed, "my time is yours."

CHAPTER TWENTY-TWO

The first trains began to pass through Petrovsky Station only a week after the lines had been blown apart—the station was still no more than a shell, a frame of fragile stone walls with the roof crashed in and the windows blown out, but the station master had rigged a makeshift shelter at which cargoes could be checked and tickets could be issued. The first trains to pass through, though, were troop trains. They blew eastward with no more than a mournful whistle to announce their passage.

Liza regarded the proceedings with a guarded sense of satisfaction. While Vladimir Tarasov had decisively blocked the English sappers from working on the fortress's wall, he had been much more sanguine about allowing them to help repair the station. Even Wainwright was more bearable with a purpose to guide him and his men.

Liza suspected that Petya was bringing the sappers to work on the wall in secret, while their father slept, but she had never caught them at it. Every time she looked, though, a greater portion of the masonry had been demolished, and even the swift work of the miners couldn't account for the speed at which the wall came apart.

On a particular snow-touched afternoon, a day after rail

traffic had begun to flow again, the errand-boy brought a brief missive from the town. It was written in that false left-handed script that she recognized from the letter to Petya, and it read, *I've arrived. Meet me at eight in the tavern.*

"So," said Liza, crumpling the paper in her palm. "You decided to come, after all."

She wanted to seize and shake someone—to call Wainwright down to the courtyard and make him duel her or shoot at bottles with her—but then Petya would accuse her of going mad and Jaworski would patronize her again, and she didn't have the patience to bear their condescension. She could do nothing with her restlessness but take to the towers and glare through her spyglass at the falling snow, watching for an invasion that never came. When the clouds obscured even the dim moonlight and she could scarcely see the hour hand on her pocketwatch, let alone read the time, she peered one last time over the town. With no little satisfaction, she noted that her warnings and dire threats had had their intended effect: every house and every shop, from the flophouses to the tavern, had obscured its windows with thick blackout curtains.

That much, at least, she knew was her doing. That much, at least, she'd done right.

She lowered herself hand over hand down the ladder shaft and into the hallway below, then slipped into her room to prepare herself. For the first time in six years, she'd share a meal with Kesha, and she intended to present herself as all that she was—the heir that he could have been, if he'd been less a duplicitous bastard. She took her hair out of the braid in which she had worn it for the day's work, then pinned it into a semblance of an updo; she unfolded her neatest shirt and trousers, and the embroidered waistcoat that she'd ordered long ago from France. Her bust had grown since she'd had any kind of spending money, but she could bind her chest easily enough, and the jacket and coat would close neatly over the whole. For Petya (or for Nastya), she might have worn a gown and a cincher and delicate boots with buttons up the sides, but Kesha deserved no such courtesy from her.

She studied her reflection critically, eyes narrowed. The person in the mirror was not at all the person she had hoped to see—it was a heavy-shouldered, inelegant person, dressed in rich but slightly ill-fitting clothes.

Liza left her rooms, her back straight and her hands thrust into her pockets. The air felt chill against her skin, as though she had just stood from a seat by the fire and turned her face to the cold. *This had better be worth it, she thought. You had better be worth it, Kesha.*

"Going somewhere, Liza?"

Liza wheeled. Her father stood behind her, hands shoved in his armpits to warm his fingers. She couldn't forget that, gout or no gout, he could still move like a cat when he wanted. "Just to the tavern," she answered, with what she hoped was credible nonchalance.

His eyes raked her from boots to collar, taking in the trousers and the waistcoat and the coat. "Dressed like that?" he asked. "Not your usual costume."

"I'm sick of making myself beautiful for the drunken asses," said Liza. "I'm a Tarasov; they ought to look at me with *respect* in their eyes—"

"You know, Liza?" Something in his expression brought her up short. She broke off her tirade. Her father looked uncharacteristically small, his shoulders sloped and his arms almost embracing him about the chest. "You know? I almost believe you. But that's not why you're going to the tavern dressed like that."

"Why am I, then?" she asked, half-hoping, half-fearing that he knew her purpose and meant to stop her. It would be easy to defer to Vladimir and shun her brother; it would be easy to shame him and abandon him the way he had abandoned the family six years ago.

Her father's hand closed on her shoulder. He smiled his

graveyard-smile. "You think you can send a telegram from here that I don't know about? You think I keep such a loose watch on my town? Tell your brother," said Vladimir, "tell him that, if he wants to, he can come home."

At first glance, Liza didn't recognize her brother among the faces in the tavern. There were more strangers than usual, a consequence of the renewed traffic on the rails, and a good third of them were tall, raw-boned men with hollow cheeks and reddish hair. She checked her pocketwatch, which informed her that she had arrived somewhat early, then cast about her once more for a narrow nose like her father's or hazel eyes like her mother's. When that proved fruitless, she took a table near the center of the room and ordered herself a pair of drinks. "Are you expecting a guest?" Nastya asked, raising one brow as she set the drinks in the center of the table.

"I am, but he can buy his own damned drinks," answered Liza. She downed one glass, took a breath, and then downed the second. Nastya regarded her with something very like sympathy—as though she knew well what sort of man required two drinks' worth of fortitude.

The other patrons cast aggrieved looks at Liza as she sat in her fine clothes; it was one thing to accept that the mistress of the fortress wore trousers when she was killing dragons or helping to rebuild the rails, but another matter entirely to see her dressed for dinner like a gentleman. She returned their looks levelly, resisted the impulse to prop her feet upon the table, and asked Nastya's third-youngest sister to keep her well-supplied with drinks. By the time Kesha descended the stairs, Liza had been waiting for only ten minutes, but it had felt closer to an hour.

Had her brother been seated among the rail-workers and transients in the tavern, Liza thought, she wouldn't have recognized him. His hair was shorter than he'd worn it when last he'd lived at home, and unruly, as though he'd been running his hands through it as he read (had that been a habit of his? Try as she might, Liza couldn't remember). He wore clothes that were very neatly kept, although even her untrained eyes could tell that they had been mended more than once when the seams and hems had come unstitched. This much, she might have recognized even after six years' absence, but his expression bore the marks of a new, alien avidity. He carried himself as though continually poised to startle into action, and she couldn't tell whether he seemed about to lunge or to flee.

"Well, then," she said, by way of greeting. "Sit."

He sat, and Nastya's sister brought them both drinks. Liza swallowed hers quickly, relishing the burn of it at the back of her throat, but Kesha left his untouched. "Well?" he asked. "You asked me to come home, and so I've come. What do you want from me?" His voice was touched with a St. Petersburg accent, and she couldn't tell whether it was a pretense.

"An apology might be a good start," she answered.

His lips pressed together at that, but then he nodded. "Of course. I'm—I'm aware of the grief and hardship I caused you, by leaving you the way I did—"

"By *stealing* from us—"

"By stealing from you," agreed Kesha. "It does little good to apologize for that, and I know it—but for what little good it does, I *am* sorry."

She studied his face, searching for a hint of the boy who'd helped her break into their parents' liquor cabinet and who'd learned to shoot a bow and a gun at her side. If she saw no trace of him there, perhaps he couldn't find his old accomplice in her hawk's eyes, either. "I accept," said Liza, although it pained her to say it. "I still expect you to pay us back every kopeck you stole—but I accept your apology."

"With interest?" asked Kesha, for which she had to flick alcohol at his eyes.

"What do you take us for?" Liza demanded, while her brother shielded his face from a second assault. "What do you think your family's become? A bunch of common usurers, demanding *interest*—how dare you insult your own blood?"

"Enough, I desist! Name of God, Liza, why can't you wear gloves like a proper woman—" said Kesha, but he was very close to laughing, and Liza found that she was, too. "No interest, then, if you're so set against it. I don't have anything like the money to pay you interest, anyway."

Liza licked her fingers clean, then admitted, "It was good of you to see that Petya got some schooling. Most of it is no good to anyone, but he's learned to take care of the gears, and that's something."

"You ought to see his designs," replied Kesha, and for the first time in ages, she could hear a real eagerness coloring his voice. "He's fascinated with the idea of flight; he's designing a set of improved hot-air balloons, as well as a sort of whirligig creation with spinning blades that doesn't look very promising—but it keeps him occupied. I'd brought a few of the better ones, in case...well."

In case he wanted them, thought Liza, but that wouldn't have made Kesha pause with his shoulders lowering and his eyes going flat and shuttered. He could only have meant, *In case he plans to stay.*

She was surely edging into drunkenness, if she was devoting any thought at all to what Kesha had meant.

"If you could deliver them to him, I'd be very much obliged," said Kesha, recovering himself.

"Why don't you deliver them yourself? I'm not your errand-boy, to carry Petya's papers back and forth for you."

"I would, if I thought I were welcome at the keep," he answered. "But I doubt our father will accept an apology and a promise of reimbursement. I stole a great deal more from him than his money when I left."

Liza felt her lips twisting into an ugly expression—she knew it was ugly, because Kesha's expression grew ugly in turn. "Before I came here," she said, "he told me that he'd welcome you home. After all that you did to us—all the indignity we've endured, all the *shame* you've brought us—he said that you could *come home*."

It was almost enough, to watch Kesha's disdain transmuting into shock. His jaw worked, as though he were chewing his words. "He said I was no longer his son," said Kesha, once the words had been rendered small enough to digest. "He *disowned* me—I never thought that he could—"

"Don't think it's a matter of love or forgiveness," snapped Liza. "It's only because even if I was his first child, *you're* his first boy, his first heir. He's comfortable enough with letting me inherit so long as you don't want to, but what then? The Tarasov name would die with me, or worse, be lost to some damn foreigner if I married—and *what then*, Kesha? He's cannier than that, our father is. He's *smarter* than we are. No, he might have told you in the heat of the moment that you weren't his son, but I've *seen* the will that he keeps locked away. I watched the lawyer draw the damn thing up! I might be his heir in name, I might hold the border against the Turks near single-handed, but who's the legal heir to the name? *You* are, you bastard, for all the good it does us!"

Her breath was coming sharp, her head growing light; she felt something like a scream welling up under her breastbone, and she squelched it with all her might. Drunk she might be, jealous she might be, but a Tarasov didn't succumb to a hysterical fit for no better reason than drunken jealousy. She forced her breath to regularity and sat back in her chair, swallowing the last of her drink. When she returned to the keep, she vowed, she'd gather up all the empty bottles she could find and then go out to shoot them to smithereens.

Slowly, she became aware that Kesha was regarding

her with an expression of mingled horror and wonder. "I never knew any of that," he said, when it was clear that she'd finished her tirade. He reached across the table for her hands, but she refused to offer them. "I swear to you—I honestly believed he'd thrown me out, and in my heart I congratulated you for it; you were always better suited to this business, anyway—oh, Liza, I'm sorry. You won't believe me, but I'm sorry nonetheless."

"I believe you," she said. "But I don't want to see any more of you tonight. Come to the keep in the morning and let our father scream at you for an hour—*then* I'll want to see you again."

"If that's what I have to do, I'll do it," vowed Kesha, and with that, he offered her his hands once more. Against her better judgment, she took his hands and clasped them, and she found them cold to the touch.

"You're the one who ought to wear gloves, Keshka," she said, soft and chiding. "I'll see you in the morning."

Before she could say another stupid thing, Liza stood from her chair and paid her share of the bill. Then, without once glancing over her shoulder, she swept out of the tavern and into the chill air.

CHAPTER TWENTY-THREE

This much, Petya would later be able to avow regarding the events of that night:

Liza had returned from town in a fine temper, the cause of which she refused to name, and she had seized up a biddable young Englishman from his supper and harassed him into carrying a sack of bottles out of the keep for her. She carried a second sack of her own, as well as two rifles over her shoulder, and Petya supposed that she was going (as she often did, when she was in a rage) to shoot bottles from the rocks on the eastern hills. It was too dark to see anything well enough to shoot it, but she didn't seem to like being reminded of that. When he finished his supper and went to join Jaworski in the western watchtower, the regular crack of gunfire and chime of falling glass only confirmed his suspicions.

"She must like the English boy, if she's taken him to shoot with her," Petya remarked; Jaworski snorted and shook his head in reply.

"It's less a liking for him than a disliking for being alone," said Jaworski. "She only wants to be alone when she's miserable." If Petya felt inclined to contest Jaworski's claim, he kept his sentiments to himself. Whatever her reasons, Liza was choosing to spend time with the English rather than wasting her waking hours trying to vex them, and he could only regard this as a welcome sign.

The sound of the guns echoed from the low hills around them, each report sounding and resounding on the clear, cold air. From the intervals, Petya supposed that they had made a game of setting two bottles up at a time, after which each would choose one to break. Every now and then, a third or fourth shot announced that one of the two had missed the mark, and at times Petya almost fancied that he could hear Liza's laughter.

By then, the light snow of the afternoon had become a fall of heavy, wet flakes. Even with the ground well-coated in snowdrifts, though, there was precious little light; once, when the wind turned suddenly, Petya caught the edge of the moon through the thick clouds. The watchtowers were dark, and the town was as well. He couldn't imagine how Liza and her new friend found their targets—but surely that, too, was part of the game.

A single report made Jaworski cock his head and turn away from the east-facing window, putting his spyglass to his eye and peering through the thick snow in the direction of the town. He must have seen nothing to alarm him, though, because he soon returned to his habitual spot.

"Did you hear something?" asked Petya.

"Probably just the way the hills echo," answered Jaworski, "but that didn't sound the same as the other shots. And I could have sworn it came from the west, and not the east."

The implication raised a strange, fearful heat in Petya's breast. "Perhaps the Englishman had another gun," he offered. "They were very proud of their guns, when they arrived; Liza kept saying that they were proud of their guns...."

Jaworski didn't answer at once, which did little to ease the misgivings that Petya felt. The interior of the watchtower was even darker than the world outside, and

Petya could scarcely recognize the man's face, let alone read his expression.

"I suppose he might," said Jaworski at last. "And I suppose that Liza would have wanted to see it, if he did."

"There," Petya replied. "It mightn't be anything." *He mightn't have murdered her in cold blood, in the sheltering darkness.*

Jaworski said nothing. The wind sighed through the windows, touching Petya's ears and nose with ice and chapping his lips raw. He took a long swallow of tea from his flask, then offered it to Jaworski; the both of them drew their scarves up over their noses again once they'd warmed their throats. For what must have been half an hour, they stood at the windows, ears pricked for the sound of the gun. They only heard the same pattern of shots—two of them, one after the other, and then a long pause. Two shots, then a third, and then silence.

And then silence.

It must have been very close to ten o'clock at night when Petya made out a pair of figures staggering toward the servants' entrance. They made their way slowly through the thick snow, and as they drew nearer, Petya could see why. One of them bore the other like a dead weight; whether it was Liza who'd succumbed to drunkenness or the English soldier, Petya couldn't guess. No laughter rang from the walls of the fortress, but who could laugh, with a drunken man (or woman) dragging behind? "I'll go to help them in," said Petya, to which Jaworski made an affirmative sound.

"Don't let her choke on her own vomit," Jaworski advised, but it was said with something like good humor.

Petya left the tea flask with him and then clambered down the ladder to the hallway, and from there made his way through the corridors to the servants' entrance. Grasping the knob in one gloved hand, he drew the door open to greet his sister.

Instead, he found Peter Wainwright with his arm braced on the doorframe, his face red with chill and exertion.

"In God's name, Petya," he breathed, but his teeth were chattering so that Petya could scarcely make out what he said. "In God's name, he was just lying in the street like this—I—"

"What's this?" asked Petya. "Where's Liza? Where's my sister, Wainwright?"

"Liza?" said Wainwright, plain incomprehension in his voice. "No, God, listen to me for once in your damn life—Petya, it's your father."

Wainwright took a fortifying breath, and with one last, colossal heave, he pulled Vladimir Tarasov's body into the entryway. Petya heard the crack of his father's skull striking the stones.

He saw at once the futility of protesting his father's rough treatment. The man's fine, thick coat was soaked with blood, his body stiff with more than cold.

Petya understood perfectly well what had transpired, even before Wainwright said, "He's dead."

END OF BOOK I

DRAKON

BOOK TWO

CHAPTER ONE

When the door of Kesha's rented room swung open, he had just put down *The Language of Dragons* and opened the book of rebound military pamphlets. He was sitting on the edge of his bed in his shirtsleeves, his suspenders hanging loosely about his waist and his shoes resting neatly beside the bedpost. The clatter of the door against the wall sent an icy chill through him, although he knew rationally that such invasions were only to be expected in a public lodging. "Who's there?" he demanded, willing himself to look up slowly despite the ice in his veins. If his guest *did* mean him harm, he'd gain nothing by advertising his fear; nonetheless, he freed a hand from the edge of the book to grip his pocketknife. The edge of the metal sheathing bit into his palm.

"Captain Jaworski," said the man in the doorway, and at once Kesha recognized the voice of the Polish soldier who'd delivered Petya's letter. "Innokentiy Vladimirovich Tarasov?"

"Yes," replied Kesha cautiously. He didn't release his pocketknife, although he loosened his hold on it. "What do you want?"

"You're wanted at the keep," said Jaworski, and he folded

his arms over the breast of his military coat as though he fully expected Kesha to accompany him in his stocking feet.

"Has my father sent for me?" Kesha asked, but Jaworski's face went dark at the question, and he raised his chin rather than answering. His point was plain, albeit tacit: further questions would be unwelcome.

Standing, then, Kesha shrugged his suspenders over his shoulders and buttoned his shirtsleeves, donning waistcoat and jacket, gloves and fur-lined winter boots. As he dressed, he couldn't help stealing glances at Jaworski's impassive eyes—but each time he looked, Jaworski's expression only grew more impenetrable. By the time Kesha had fastened the clasps of his coat and fixed his hat in place, he had ceased to look at Jaworski at all. He wondered whether the man had forgiven him yet for reading his brother's correspondence.

He wondered whether Jaworski even remembered.

At last, fixing his scarf about his throat and slipping his book into his pocket, Kesha nodded. "I'm ready," he said. *I'm ready*, as if Jaworski weren't staring at him like a gawker at a carnival.

If Jaworski found the remark as inane as Kesha did, he said nothing; he only made an affirmative sound deep in his throat and lit his pipe. The pipestem held between forefinger and thumb, he gestured with the bowl to the door. "You walk ahead of me," said Jaworski, and Kesha stepped through the frame without complaint.

He heard the click of a gun cocking behind him. For the first time since the door had crashed open, Kesha began to apprehend that his life was really in danger—he wondered in a half-abstract fashion whether he would conduct himself with dignity in the face of certain death, or whether he would fall to his knees to beg and snivel and clutch the hem of Jaworski's coat. For a horrifying moment, he could imagine that gesture of cowardice with perfect clarity. He could nearly feel his knees striking the floorboards, nearly taste mucus and bile in his throat.

The image disgusted him. He squared his shoulders and strode down the hall of the tavern's upper story, not permitting himself to falter or to glance even once over his shoulder.

Now the stairs, he told himself, counting them as he placed his feet on the faded carpet lining the center of each tread. *One, two, three—surely he wouldn't shoot me on the stairs?* Jaworski matched him stride for stride, and Kesha knew that if he hesitated, he would feel the muzzle of that gun pressing between his shoulder blades.

The main room of the tavern was nearly empty. The younger Vasilevskaya sisters would be sleeping upstairs, and only Nastya remained awake to scrub the counters and tally the stock. She glanced up as Jaworski marched Kesha to the door, but once she saw who it was, she trained her eyes on her accounting ledger again.

Kesha told himself that he had seen a brief flicker of guilt in her eyes, in that instant when they had met his own. It was easier to bear his own helplessness, if he could believe that she had *wanted* to help him.

Jaworski closed the tavern door behind them, shutting away the light from within. Blackout curtains hung in every window, just as they had during the years after the Polish uprising—Kesha remembered those days quite clearly, although he had been only ten years old. He remembered the way the boys from town had told each other stories about witches that came out of the winter darkness to swallow up sinful children. With the snow falling thick around him, suffused with an uncanny glow even in the near-moonless blackness, he could almost believe that Baba Yaga herself was waiting in the shadows with bloodstained lips and a skull lamp held high.

"Walk," said Jaworski, and Kesha could hear that he was speaking around his pipe. "You still know the way to the keep, don't you?"

"I still know it," said Kesha, although the houses were

not the same as they had been six years ago. He couldn't see more than a few paces in front of him.

He knew the carriage-road that led up the hill to the keep, and he knew the way the snow-wet gravel squeaked and crunched beneath his feet. When the keep loomed over him out of the dimness, he found that he knew that old presentiment of dread, as well. "The main gate, or—"

"The servants' entrance," replied Jaworski. "This isn't the time for formalities."

"Then I take it I'm not being welcomed back with open arms."

"You take it correctly," was all Jaworski said in answer. Kesha felt that aching anticipation of a bullet in his back once more, and he shivered to dispel it. Reaching for the handle (new), he drew the door open and stepped once more into his ancestral home.

Whatever feeling that entrance woke in him, though, it gave way to the sudden, horrifying consciousness that he was a second away from tripping over his father's corpse.

He believes that I killed my father, Kesha told himself, as he lowered himself to his knees under Jaworski's hawkish gaze. *Believes it, or at the very least suspects it—and he wants to see how I'll respond to the sight of his body, or he'd have brought it inside and laid it out on a table, the way civilized people do.* He caught the finger of his glove between his teeth and tugged it free of his hand, then brought his palm to rest along his father's jaw.

His thumb caught in the fold of a jowl as his fingertips splayed over his father's cool, whiskery cheek. This was, he knew, the face that he would wear in his own twilight years; there was his own narrow nose and his own widow's peak, the latter made severe by the receding hair at his father's temples. There were the crow's-foot lines at the corner of each eye—laugh-lines, Misha called them. Kesha remembered, distantly, that his father had been a man given to mirth.

Perhaps it made him a poor son, that he touched his father's face only because he knew that it was the sort of filial gesture that might ease Jaworski's fears. Kesha was inclined to believe, to the contrary, that it made him precisely the son that his father had always wished him to be.

"I heard a shot," said Kesha. He forced himself to look away from Vladimir Tarasov's face and down at his bloodstained coat, which Jaworski had not yet removed—it must have been Jaworski who'd decided to leave the coat in place, he thought. Petya would have fetched the delicate tweezers from his toolkit and fished out the bullet so that it might be identified, all the while wearing that peculiar, absent expression that always marked his face when he was engaged with a mechanical problem. Liza would have torn the coat away to bare the wound to all the world, coating her hands in the blood like a stage-Electra mourning for Agamemnon. "I heard a shot, but Anastasia Ivanovna told her lodgers not to push the curtains aside at night—I was reading in my room; she can vouch for me, if you like—"

It sounded like an excuse; worse, it sounded like an alibi.

"As it happens," said Jaworski deliberately, "I did ask Anastasia Ivanovna whether she could vouch for your whereabouts at the time when she heard the shot. She told me that she couldn't say where you were, and that she hadn't seen you since your sister explained the terms of your father's will."

Kesha only narrowly prevented himself from wincing. "Is *she* not a suspect? She had as much opportunity as I did."

"But unlike you, she doesn't stand to gain from your father's death."

It was true, and Kesha hated that it was true. If Nastya wouldn't or couldn't vouch for him, what hope did he have? He had no allies here to testify to the strength of his character—nor any real character to which to bear testimony—and he certainly had no witnesses to avow that he'd been shut up in his rooms. He could claim that he carried no weapon but his pocketknife, but he couldn't prove that he had *never* carried one; he could claim that he had watched Liza leave the table with no sentiment in his breast but a throbbing hope for reconciliation, but even he wouldn't have believed it.

His fingertips brushed the still-damp fabric of his father's coat, wet with snowmelt and blood. "You saw my boots when I put them on in the tavern," said Kesha slowly, and Jaworski nodded without lowering his gun. "You must have seen that they were dry, too—far too dry for me to have been out in the snow less than an hour ago. Even if I'd had a stove in my room, I couldn't have dried my boots in the time between the shot and your arrival."

"Try that argument with Liza," drawled Jaworski. "She might let you live long enough to finish it."

As though the mention of her name had called her into being, Kesha heard the distinctive ring of Liza's bootheels on the stone. He had only time to rise to his feet, his father's blood drying upon his fingers, before he felt her bare fist collide with his cheek.

He had expected the blow, but even so it sent him reeling; he knew from long experience that his right eye would be swollen shut by morning. "Liza," he said, pressing his gloved hand to the incipient bruise. "I suppose you think this is *my* doing?"

"I *know* it's your doing," she said, and seized his shoulder to spit in his good eye. Her breath smelled strongly of vodka and smoke and meat, as their father's had—and in a horrible, percussive moment, Kesha realized that his father would never breathe again. More even than the blood smearing his hand, more even than the impossibility of being forgiven, that simple cessation of breath made Kesha's throat tighten. He wanted nothing more than to throw up.

Instead he wiped his sister's saliva from his cheek with his coat sleeve and said nothing.

Behind Liza stood a fair-haired stranger, compact and

short of stature; the Tarasovs dwarfed him. He wore a British uniform and an expression of faint horror, as though he were hearing of a tragedy that had happened many years ago. "The English invader, I presume," said Kesha. "What's the nature of our relationship supposed to be? Am I working in collusion with him? In opposition? Did he help me to *murder our father*, or did he—"

"How *dare* you make light of this, you long stream of piss," Liza snarled, and spat again. "How dare you! The lieutenant carried our father's body through the *snow*, while you sat with your friends and toasted to the Tarasov estate! Oh, you must've thought you were such a clever bastard, to lure me into summoning you home with your cunning little letters and your harmless conversation—oh, you must have *laughed* at your big, stupid sister when she—"

"Lieutenant Wainwright is *also* under suspicion for your father's murder," cut in Jaworski, and there was a steely edge to his voice like the sharp end of a bayonet. "And the lieutenant has graciously agreed to defer the matter to a police investigation and a Russian court of law. I hope you'll do the same."

"And until we can summon the police or the law to our little patch of Hell?" Kesha sneered. He couldn't forget that they were speaking over the corpse of his father, and perhaps it would have seemed poetically appropriate if he hadn't felt so thoroughly inclined to empty his stomach. "Until then, what do you plan to do with your pair of murderers?"

"I plan to imagine how far you can run before I gun you down," said Liza. Her jaw was set as she said it, her voice perfectly steady; Kesha did not imagine for a moment that she was exaggerating.

"They plan to hold us," said the British lieutenant. "In the only room that locks from the outside rather than the inside."

"In the *pump room*?" demanded Kesha.

"No, you fool," said Liza. "In the ice closet."

CHAPTER TWO

The key turned in the lock, and the bolt clicked into place. Petya nearly flinched at the sound of it, although he knew full well that Kesha and Wainwright had consented to their confinement. They had been supplied with blankets against the piercing chill of the ice closet, and the servants had brought thick bundles of hay on which the two could sleep; when Kesha had requested a lamp, Jaworski had granted it over Liza's protests. "We aren't barbarians," he had said, and she had given him a look so sharp that it might have slit his throat open.

"Very well," she had answered, like a curse, before she had called for a lantern and a book of matches. She didn't say it aloud, but Petya thought that she was wishing Kesha might set himself afire with it.

At last, when Jaworski had gone to renew the watch, the two of them carried their father's corpse to the mess hall and laid it out on a long table. "We shouldn't disturb it," said Petya, when Liza reached for the top button on his coat. "When the inspectors come to study the body, they won't like it at all if we've damaged their evidence."

"We have to have him embalmed," said Liza tightly. "If we don't, he'll start to rot. We can't leave him outside."

"Yes, but we can't have him embalmed *tonight*. I'm sorry, Liza." She looked up at him, then, her eyes shadowed and hollow, and he wanted to draw her into his arms and stroke her hair until she could cry. But an embrace wouldn't help her cry any more than it would help him feel useful. Instead, he watched as she began to pace the empty room. With each step, her bootheels sent a low, flat peal echoing to the rafters.

"Why are you sorry?" she asked, when she had reached the wall and turned to begin another circuit. Drink and grief had roughened her voice, but still she managed to keep it from cracking. "I was the fool who summoned him from St. Petersburg. I didn't even have the courage to tell you, or the wit to set a watch on him—this is my fault, Petya, and I can never make it right."

"Then you really think that Kesha killed him." Even saying it made Petya's heart hammer, as though speaking made it real. "Why would Kesha kill him? He never wanted anything to do with the family name—"

"He *hated* our father!" On *hate*, Liza's voice broke at last, and a single sob wracked her before she regained herself. "He never wanted anything from the Tarasovs but our money, and in my foolishness I told him that it was his for the taking—I can't stop myself from babbling when I'm drunk; you know I can't."

For a moment, Petya waited to see if she would speak again, but she was preoccupied with her pacing. She fixed her eyes upon the beams and arches that supported the ceiling, or on the bits of silverware and potato still lying untouched on the tables. She looked anywhere but at their father's body.

"He never wanted our money, either," said Petya, more softly. "I've seen his accounts. Since he set himself up in St. Petersburg, he hasn't spent any of it—he takes work as a tutor when he needs a new suit or rent money, and he lets his friend Mikhail Dmitrievich buy him coffee and meals.

There are over three thousand rubles sitting in a bank there—" and when Liza looked as though she might answer smartly back, Petya hurried to finish, "—and he puts money in it whenever he has any to spare. He meant to pay it back when he could give you every single kopeck he took."

"So he told you," answered Liza, far too levelly. "And you always believe what you're told." Like a clockwork toy winding down, Liza's footsteps slowed on the stones. She braced herself on the edge of a table with her hands folded behind her back. "If Kesha didn't kill our father, who did?"

"Wainwright did." It was no easier to propose this than it had been to countenance Kesha's treachery, and yet in his heart he knew what he said to be true. "I can't believe you think anything else. He came here, and not a week later the rails blew—then when you brought us the evidence, he pretended he knew nothing about it—" He closed his lips over an anxious laugh. "You know that. You know that he lied about shooting the last of the dragons, that night."

"I know that he was *wrong* about shooting all of the dragons. Jaworski shouldn't have made it sound as though he was lying about it."

"Why are you defending him? In the name of God, Liza, you broke his nose, and then you threw him all over the courtyard—"

"He *agreed* to it!" said Liza, and although she didn't whirl on him, Petya flinched away nonetheless. "Lieutenant Wainwright is the first man I've ever met who had the decency to treat me like another gentleman—I can't expect a boy like you to know what it *means* to be treated like a gentleman for the first goddamn time in my life!"

Petya was dimly aware that his fingers ought to be trembling, but when he reached for his sister's shoulder, he felt them to be strong and sure. "You're not a gentleman, Liza," he said. "You're my sister, and I'm afraid of any man who doesn't treat you like my sister."

"I'm the heir," said Liza simply. "And the heir can't *be*

your sister, even...even if she wanted to be."

"Liza—"

If she heard the aching in his voice, she ignored it. "You think Wainwright is in league with the Turks, then. You might as well say it."

"I think he *might* be in league with the Turks. And he might be bribing the telegraph master to slip him secret messages from the British, or he might be taking money from the Tsar's railway company, or...there's no way of knowing why he'd lie! But he *did* lie, Liza, and that's flat!"

"That's not flat at all, from where I'm standing!" Liza's bootheel came down like a gavel. "And even if he did know— even if he did hide it—that means nothing at all about our father. He carried our father's body up from the town, in the snow—"

"Because he knew that it would tug at your heart and make you less likely to suspect him! Christ, will you forget your infatuation with the man and *try* to look at him logically!"

With that, she straightened and shrugged off Petya's hand. "To work, then," she said, removing two pins from her hair, and there was no mistaking the briskness of her manner. Whatever had made her sob and snap and stutter, whatever griefs or secrets or longings she bore, she had locked them away in a steel box beneath her ribs, and Petya would not see them again.

She pushed past him and began to undo their father's coat and jacket, his shredded waistcoat and shirt. "Help me with this," she said over her shoulder. "I haven't done this in years."

Since Uncle Pasha got himself shot on a hunting trip, Petya remembered, and then he understood what she meant to do. This would be easier, in some ways; Uncle Pasha had been gushing blood, and their father's blood had cooled. It didn't matter now whether Liza could pick the fibers from the wound. It didn't matter what she did with the flesh at all.

Where Petya had expected a single, neat wound, a hole

like a pipeline through the chest, he saw instead a grisly expanse of ruined flesh—even when Liza spat on her handkerchief and dabbed away the crust of blood, the flesh looked not so much penetrated as *shattered* with several large and ragged holes, through which Petya could see the broken edges of bloody bones.

When his father's chest lay bare, Petya held the cold skin apart so that Liza could work her hairpins into the wounds. "Not so deep," she said, softly. Reporting, without analysis. "The ribs and spine stopped most of the shot."

"Look at the angle," said Petya, and they turned their father on his side to examine the path the bullets (were they bullets?) had taken. "Steep—so the murderer must have been close to him, with the gun held low?"

"Or lying on his belly," said Liza in return, although she didn't take her eyes from the wound. "Or our father was lying down and got shot from near his feet. What do you know about gun wounds, that you think you can tell me how the murderer was standing? You're an engineer—when have you seen a man murdered?"

Petya could have answered, *I know something about geometry, even if I don't know anything about murder*, but he knew that Liza wasn't in a humor to hear it. Instead, he only watched as she teased free the first fragment of lead. "Not from a rifle, but even you've probably guessed that," she said. "Old gun—loads from the muzzle, probably. At least forty years old, probably closer to sixty. Short barrel, I'd guess, based on how deep the shot went. Loaded with more shot than was probably smart, too. It's a wonder the gun didn't explode in his face."

"You can tell all that from the…" What ought he to call that flattened bit of metal she'd prised out of their father's chest? "The bullet?"

"This," pronounced Liza, "is a pellet, or a ball. And not a Minié ball, either—those are for rifles, and they don't spray pellets like this. So the gun's probably older than I am, probably a soldier's trophy or an heirloom. Remember, Uncle Pasha had those old carbines up on his walls, from when he'd served in the Crimea?" Petya only nodded. He remembered those blunt guns, crossed over every door and every hearth. "They're easy to come by—every old veteran has one; I'd bet my best muffler there are over a dozen in this village. And that's not even taking the migrants into account. They aren't much longer than a cavalry sabre. A man could sneak a gun like that onto a train under a long coat, easily." She didn't have to add, *A long coat like Kesha's.*

Working carefully, Liza prised free another fragment of a pellet and placed it beside their father's shoulder. Petya felt a surge of helplessness as he watched her heavy, blunt fingers working the lead from the muscle and organs; although he had feared that she would do violence to the body in her haste for answers, she exercised the utmost care—delicacy, he might have said, if she'd been embroidering rather than extracting lead balls. He could do nothing but bear witness to her work, lending no expertise and offering only his trembling hands to hold the gaping wounds open.

He wondered if this was what she was like when she sat in the gunner's chair, all steely-eyed focus and precision, her jaw set and her teeth clenched.

"I would never have known that," he said, and his breath stirred the hairs that had fallen against Liza's cheek. "About the pellets, or the carbines."

"You never loved guns the way I did," she answered shortly. "And neither did Kesha—but he was a better shot."

"You were always the best of all of us at that." It was nothing like enough, after Petya had accused her of acting on a hysterical infatuation, but still he had to say it. "You said—if Kesha were found guilty, you'd..."

"I'd see him executed for his crimes." She said it in the same way she said that the wound was deep, or that their uncle had kept carbines on his walls. "It would be no more than he deserved."

Another pellet dropped to the table with the softest of sounds. "Ease up," said Liza. "No need to pull until your hands shake."

CHAPTER THREE

In his youth, Kesha had paid little attention to the ice closet. It was only a place for storing milk, eggs, autumn fruits, unsalted meat that inevitably became wormy when the ice began to melt in the summertime. Between visits from the Moscow inspectors, the ice closet was also the place in which the Tarasov family preserved its dragon heads—but in Kesha's youth, dragon heads hadn't been objects of any particular significance. There had been nearly a hundred of them ringing the dining hall, and the two or three that occasionally lay packed in straw in the ice closet were no more remarkable than the apples or the eggs.

Now, with the book of military pamphlets open over his knees, he couldn't help glancing over at the dragon's head only a few feet from his boots. Its eyes had filmed over, and its gossamer-fine mane was matted with blood. Kesha looked at that lolling tongue and those sharp, blood-crusted teeth, and he wondered whether the dragon had been a poet, in another life.

He couldn't look at the dragon any more than he could look away, and so he fixed his eyes on the British lieutenant instead. "What's your story?" he asked, trying out his rusty English and gratified to find that it still came readily to his tongue. "Why do they suspect you?"

"I had the bad luck to find your father's body," the man said, with no audible rancor in his voice. "Naturally I came under suspicion; your family's despised me since the moment my unit arrived. Nothing I did could help me to deserve their trust—if I was well-trained in Russian, it only meant that the crown had sent me to undermine them by winning their favor. If I knew how the Turks worked, or how the guns worked, then clearly I was an agent of the *Turks* instead. It's been..." he searched for the correct word, and when he found it, it was in Russian. "Vexing." Thereafter, he continued in Russian, and Kesha found his accent quite passable—suspiciously passable, he might have thought, had he been Vladimir Petrovich Tarasov. "I can't say how sorry I am for your father's death."

"Particularly because it makes your work much more difficult," observed Kesha, to which the lieutenant offered only a concessive shrug. "Your name is Wainwright, isn't it?"

"Peter Wainwright. Lieutenant." He offered his hand to shake. "And you'd be Innokentiy Vladimirovich Tarasov?"

"I would," agreed Kesha. Something in Wainwright's expression appealed to him immediately—something in the anxious wrinkle between his brows, perhaps, or in the way he chewed at his lower lip. It was the face of a man naïve enough, or brave enough, to hope that all might be right if only he worked hard enough to make it so.

Kesha couldn't help liking that face, and when he shook Wainwright's hand, his grip was firm. "If it will put you at ease," he said, "I don't think you murdered my father, and neither do I think you've come to undermine my family's efforts here. A plotting murderer would have no incentive to be friendly with me, since my sister so obviously despises me; it would do you no good to have my favor, and might even hurt your standing with her. She'd think we were co-conspirators, if we were too friendly when we came out of the ice closet."

"You're right, of course," said Wainwright, with a long, frosty sigh. "You and your siblings have been politicking since you were children, haven't you? Set against one another and everyone else—"

"Not against each other," Kesha answered, and he moved closer to Wainwright to avoid the dragons' sightless eyes. The skin around his own eye was swelling. "We didn't learn to turn against each other until I betrayed the family. Before then, our kinsmen were always above suspicion."

"It sounds an ungodly way to grow up." Wainwright sat upon a bale of insulating straw. "I hope you'll forgive me for saying this, but…well. You haven't given me any reason to suspect that you didn't murder your father."

In a gesture like assent, Kesha took a seat at his side. "And because you're an outsider, you have no reason to trust me if I simply *tell* you that I didn't—but I didn't, whether or not you can believe me."

"Until your family can bring in an inspector, I'll take it on faith that you're telling the truth. It will make lodging with you a little cheerier, at least." At that, Kesha couldn't help laughing under his breath, and Wainwright chuckled in turn. The thick stone walls sent even that low laughter resounding back like a merry, morbid chorus.

Wainwright shivered, and Kesha didn't think it was from the cold. "Let's think, then. Who else might have wanted your father dead, if the two of us are innocent?"

"I'm afraid I can't say," answered Kesha. "I've been away from home for six years; my gossip is out of date. I could tell you that Osya—that's Osip Moiseyevich, one of our watchmen—he lost his eldest sons when the dragons blew up the magazine, and my father didn't even help pay for their funeral. Or I could tell you about how the station master has always hated him for telling the rail company to use blackout curtains. The town has never liked my father, and from what I saw, they don't have any real love for my sister, either."

"She's an unconventional woman, to be sure," Wainwright admitted. "How is it that the Tarasovs are still in power here?—if you'll forgive the question."

"It hardly needs forgiveness," said Kesha. "It's the sort of question I asked myself, six years ago. The best answer I have is that the village is still fiercely loyal to the *family*, even if they don't much like this particular branch of it. My grandfather, Pyotr Alexandrovich, was a kind of saint to the people. They were his serfs, of course, but they also loved him dearly. They were ready to love his sons, too, but my father and my uncles weren't what you'd call saintly. They didn't have the good grace to keep their excesses behind closed doors."

"I see," said Wainwright. "Pyotr Alexandrovich—your brother's namesake, and Petrovsky Station's?"

"Yes," answered Kesha. "The rails came while he was the lord of the keep, and they brought most of the town with them. All the industry, certainly."

"And so when the station house blew—"

"—it was as though the dragons had killed him all over again. If he was our patron saint, the station was his shrine."

Wainwright sat a long while in thought, his gloved fingers tapping a tattoo on his knee. His breathing grew even and regular as his fingers stilled, and Kesha was on the point of taking out his book again when Wainwright spoke at last. "If the station house was a symbol of the 'good old days'—" the English expression slotted neatly into the Russian sentence "—then its destruction must have marked their passing. To a man who resented your father for not living up to the family name, the disappointment would have been crushing."

Kesha turned his gaze down to Wainwright and found the look returned. "You've taken my meaning," he said.

"You've offered me something to take," Wainwright answered. "You're the first person to do that—or the first since I came to Russia, at least."

They sat in silence for a long moment, and then Kesha said, "I'm going to fall asleep on your shoulder."

"If you snore," said Wainwright, "I'll be very cross with you."

Matters appeared no less grim in the light of morning—in part because the morning was not materially different from the night, in the ice closet; in part because the combined body heat of Kesha and his fellow prisoner had begun to thaw the ice and the dragon heads that rested on it. Kesha stuffed straw into his scarf and rolled it up over his nose and mouth, which itched abominably but which at least cut the scent of rotting dragon.

If it was dehumanizing to burn a people's books and to call them beasts, it was no less dehumanizing to dismantle their corpses. Even having read the dragons' poetry, even having been moved by it, he could scarcely imagine the dragons as anything but animate meat when their flesh slowly decomposed all around him.

"If I get out," he told Wainwright, "I'll never eat meat again. Not even fish. It would smell too much like this."

"At least you'll be capable of *eating*," Wainwright replied, with his arms clasped tightly about his knees. "I think even fruit would be too much for me. I'd subsist on air, like a chameleon."

At that, Kesha said nothing, but only wondered what the dragons ate. Sheep, he supposed, or goats—the pamphlets in his pocket were stuffed with instructions for the acquisition and distribution of livestock. The dragons had three words for *sheep*, none of which he could pronounce; he could trace the shapes of the words in the condensation on the metal shelving, though, and he did so to while away the minutes.

This symbol meant *a sheep lying down*; that one, *an old sheep*; the third, *a sheep on the run*.

He could render a stanza of the dragons' poetry on the slick, damp surface of the shelving, although it would be poor poetry to human ears. *I feel*, he began, and he drew the circle of the stanza with a diacritical "I" standing within the circle; *I feel akin to the sheep on the run*. The tail of that diacritical gestured to the third sheep-character, at the very bottom of the circle. Across that sheep he drew a line of crosses, and above it, a shape like the spine of a sea-creature.

I feel akin to the sheep on the run, who is harried over the low hills until death overtakes it.

"What's that you're scribbling?" asked Wainwright as he tilted his head to peer over Kesha's shoulder. Startling, Kesha wiped the circle away.

"Nothing," he answered, although he knew it to be untrue. "Only shapes," he said, relenting. "The sort of shapes a schoolboy draws during Greek lessons."

"I don't know what sort of schoolboy you were," Wainwright huffed. "*You* might've drawn shapes; I drew nothing but Greek letters in my lessons."

"Letters are shapes," Kesha allowed—but if he meant to say more, the heavy clunk of the bolt sliding back distracted him. In a moment, both Kesha and Wainwright were on their feet, brushing straw from their trousers with gloved hands. A slice of light spilled in from the corridor, and then there stood Petya in the gap between the door and the frame, wrinkling his nose against the foul scent of spoiling meat.

"Good morning," he said, as though that imported anything at all. "I've come because we're about to wire Nizhny to send in police inspectors, and I thought that you should both have a chance to send for lawyers, if you want them—and I suppose you'll want one, Kesha."

He meant Misha, of course, and he meant it kindly; in his earnest face, there was only a plain desire to see his brother comforted. Misha, though—God bless him—studied jurisprudence rather than criminal law; he would be precious little good as a lawyer, however comforting his presence might be. "I don't have a lawyer," answered Kesha, "And I doubt my friend Wainwright has one, either. Wire Mikhail Dmitrievich yourself, if you want him to come down here."

"I'm sure that your Nizhny inspectors will acquit us," replied Wainwright, although he looked considerably less sanguine than he sounded at the prospect. "I mean no disrespect at your preparations, of course—I've seen as well as you have how dangerous it is to leave lamps burning where the dragons can see—but had you simply imposed a curfew instead of putting up those curtains of yours, we might have had witnesses to acquit us *immediately*."

"You've *seen* it," said Petya flatly, and Kesha wondered at that peculiar twist to his lips on *seen*. "You see a great deal, Lieutenant Wainwright, and perhaps we'd like you better if you saw less."

Kesha watched the two men stare one another down, marking the subtle shifts in posture that he knew well from boyhood brawls and altercations with the St. Petersburg watch. Wainwright was a compact, bow-legged fellow, and with his chin thrust out he couldn't help looking like a wrestler poised to strike a blow. He was a hand's breadth shorter than Petya, and a touch ridiculous in his mismatched winter clothes, but Kesha didn't doubt for a moment that Wainwright would emerge the victor if it came to blows.

"None of that, Petya," he said softly, and Petya broke his eyelock with the Englishman. "We shouldn't make veiled accusations here. We can't afford it."

"Then let me make an open accusation," said Petya. His voice was just as soft, but it carried with it an undercurrent of power that Kesha could scarcely recognize. Was this the boy who swaddled himself in blankets like a babe, and who complained of cold feet and pointed elbows in the night? Was this his Pyotr Vladimirovich, who had set the windowsill on fire?

Wainwright offered a mirthless smile. "Make it, Tarasov. It would do me good to be *accused* of something."

"I think you let a few dragons escape on the night when the station burned," said Petya, "And you tried to hide it—and I don't *care* why you did it, or whose pay you're in, or whether you're working with the Turks or the English or the Tsar himself! I only care that you lied to me *just* when you wanted me to trust you, and now…now I can't trust you, even though I want to."

"I didn't—"

Before Wainwright could speak again, Petya turned and left the ice closet, shutting the door behind him. The key turned, and the bolt slid home again with a hard, final sound. "I'll wire Misha," he said, voice muffled by the thick door. "And I'll have someone bring breakfast for you. Good day."

Wainwright brought one leather-gloved fist down on the insulated metal of the ice closet door. "God damn it all."

Kesha seated himself again on a dry patch of straw, watching as Wainwright's brow came to rest on the door.

"What happened?" asked Kesha. His breath rustled over the straw in his scarf.

"I wish I could tell you," Wainwright answered. He shook his head from one side to the other, rolling his brow over the metal plating. "There was a raid. Your brother and sister were in town, so I had one of the guns. Thought I'd prove myself in the action, I suppose, and I'll venture to say I acquitted myself well." A huff of bitter laughter. "They told me afterward that I'd let a few of the dragons escape. Let them escape! If they'd seen me then…my blood was up, you see. I shot one down, and it bled fire. Great rolling gouts of flame. I felt like a mad little god—I wanted to empty the skies. I'd have shot my own grandmother if she'd had scales on."

"But some of the dragons escaped, Petya said."

"Did they? I can't remember. I really can't remember. I keep going over that night as though I expect to remember something different the hundredth time, or the thousandth time. I see the dragon sweeping in over the tower, and in my mind I can smell it. Like musk and lightning. Then I squeeze the trigger, and the dragon bursts into flame." His hand slid down the door and fell to his side. "I think I looked up. I must have. But I only remember thinking how cold it was, even with the low clouds. I didn't see any dragons. If I had, I'd have torn them out of the sky."

"It's a shame," said Kesha. "I think I'd have liked you better if you'd let them go."

CHAPTER FOUR

At the telegraph office, Nastya perched on the edge of the telegraph master's writing desk while Liza prepared a flurry of telegrams. Every so often, she kicked one leg in an anxious fashion, sending her petticoats fluttering and revealing the tip of a pointed boot. *She wants to be away from me*, Liza thought, but Nastya remained sitting upon the edge of the desk and held her gaze.

She had said nothing when Liza went to roust her that morning, but only rubbed her eyes and nodded as Liza told her to notify the village of the events of last night. She must have spread the news, because Liza could see through the office windows that men were surrendering their weapons to Jaworski in the square.

Nastya had brought Liza a pot of tea—the whole pot, and a cup with a saucer, and a little jar of marmalade that she'd stirred into the cup when Liza was too preoccupied to attend to it. She responded to that preoccupation with a volley of practical chatter, reminding Liza to notify her father's creditors of his decease and to arrange for a lawyer of her own to contest her father's will.

Liza let her talk. With her pen in her left hand, her right hand weighing down the paper, Liza focused on condensing her findings to a few terse and oft-repeated words. *Tarasov murdered*, she scrawled; *Please advise on discharge of debts.*

"And you'll want to send your mother a telegram, as well," Nastya was saying, at which Liza looked up. Nastya sat with her hip toward Liza, her pale hair spilling over her shoulder as she leaned in to glance at the paper. She met Liza's eyes with something like sympathy. "I don't care how good or bad a mother she was to you. She deserves to know. If nothing else, because she lives on your father's annuity."

"I suppose," Liza allowed. "She'll have to find someone else's charity to support her." To the Kamenskys: *Regret to reject proposed marriage. Best wishes to Oleg Romanovich Kamensky.* Rude, perhaps, to turn down a suitor by telegram, but Liza scarcely had the patience to draft a letter, and Oleg Romanovich hadn't entertained a hope of persuading her to marry him.

"Then you plan to cut her off?"

"I *plan* to pay the family debts," said Liza. "I don't doubt the creditors will come hounding us when they discover that my father's dead—and what chance will we have of hiding his death? He's the lord of a fortress, murdered on the streets; I'd be surprised if word hasn't made it to Yekaterinburg already."

"You *sent* word to Yekaterinburg," Nastya reminded her gently. "The munitions debts."

"Then I would be *surprised* if word hadn't made it," growled Liza. "What are you doing here, Nastya? You despise me; I know you despise me, but here you are with tea and goddamn marmalade, telling me to write to my *mother—*"

"I know what it means to lose a father," said Nastya, "even if I don't know what it means to have him murdered on the streets. However cruel I might have been to you in the past...I'm not heartless."

The letters on the page seemed to bleed and swim. "What are they saying in town?"

"They've been saying that you must have murdered him because he wouldn't make you his heir. Or that your brother must have murdered him for the fortress. Or that I must have murdered him because he wouldn't pay his bills. Only the stupid things that people always say when they don't know anything of worth."

Liza stood from the desk, thumb resting on the soft leather of her belt. She hadn't yet changed from the clothes she'd worn to shoot bottles last night, and now her shirt was wrinkled. The expression on Nastya's face suggested that some of the half-mad clarity of purpose she felt showed in her eyes. "*Did* you murder him? He was your lord," Liza said, tipping up Nastya's chin with a fingertip. "Your family always knew better than to cause trouble for your lords."

Nastya caught Liza by the finger; she gripped it tightly at the second joint—nearly too tightly. The pressure said that she was considering breaking it, and considering the consequences if she did. "I didn't lay a finger on him, and if you touch me again, you'll see how much trouble I'm ready to cause. I won't be used, Tarasova. Not this time. Not by you."

Liza found that she was curling her fingers through Nastya's, gripping them as tightly as Nastya was her own. Their hands were only a whisper away from Nastya's lips— close enough that Nastya could have kissed them.

Liza let her go. "I believe you. And I don't plan to use you. But I'll need your support all the same."

"My father was loyal to your father," said Nastya, her voice laced with scorn, "and his father to your grandfather."

"And now you're loyal to me?"

"I'm *not* Ivan Ivanovich Vasilevsky. We're not our fathers. If you expect my loyalty, you'll have to prove to me that you deserve it."

"I deserve your loyalty *by right of birth*," Liza said, but her hands were trembling. Nastya's grey eyes were very dark.

"You might have said that in 1861," Nastya replied,

holding her gaze. "But in *this* time, in *this* town, you owe us your money and your livelihood, and we owe you only our rent. Consider that, Elizaveta Vladimirovna—consider what you owe us."

With that, she stood from her perch. The hem of her narrow gown swept down about her ankles, covering the neat lines of buttons down the sides of her boots. "I didn't come to say that," said Nastya, "but you need to *hear* it. Do you think anyone will treat you as the lord of this town, now that your father is dead? You'll have to fight your people for every bit of ground, and if you refuse them anything, they'll call you a bitch and a whore—"

"They call me that already," Liza snapped.

"—and *you'll still owe them.*" Nastya's eyes flashed. "I know what it means to lose a father—just *think* for a single damn moment about what it means, for a woman to lose her father. If you think I'm heartless, then think of this: if you fail, they'll say you failed because you're a woman."

"Leave me be, Anastasia Ivanovna," said Liza, drawing in short, sharp breaths through her nose. Her chest ached with every inhalation, her lungs constricted as though with bands of iron. "Leave me to grieve in my own way—just leave me *be!*"

"Stop drinking, and stop gambling," Nastya said, straightening her hat and turning to go. "They'll forgive you for being mannish, but they'll never forgive you for being your father."

Petya came down to the telegraph office just as Liza finished drafting her missive to their mother, and he bore with him an address and a brief message. "Orlov?" said Liza, and she raised her brows.

"Mikhail Dmitrievich Orlov," agreed Petya. "Lodging with the Galiyevs. His aunt and uncle."

"And this is Kesha's lawyer? A man who lives with his aunt and uncle?"

"It's the only man he would trust to defend him before the law," said Petya, and even Liza recognized that this wasn't at all the same thing. "Wainwright didn't ask for a lawyer; he says that he trusts the inspectors to clear his name."

"So Kesha asked for a lawyer—"

"He asked that I *not* send for a lawyer," Petya broke in, pressing the message into the telegraph master's hand and watching as he began to tap out the codes. "It's only his pride that keeps him from asking—and I won't let him be condemned for his pride."

Liza tasted blood and bile in the back of her mouth at how Petya leapt to their brother's defense. She might have swallowed it down, but her ire had already been piqued by Nastya's presumption, and at this added insult she rose to her feet and caught her brother by the thick muscle between his neck and shoulder. "You won't let him be condemned," she said, low and feral. "And if the inspectors find him guilty? What will you do then, Petya?"

"'And what then?'" he asked. His teeth were tightly clenched; it looked nothing at all like a smile. "I haven't just come to make you send my telegrams. I want to use the English sappers to take the rest of the east wall down."

"You've been having them take the wall down in secret," Liza observed, to which Petya nodded wary assent. "Yes, then. Use all the sappers they can spare. I want that wall rebuilt, twice as strong as it was. I want to be able to use our east gun again, now that we have the men for it."

"And I want to write to Uncle Sasha's children and invite them to join us here. His son, at least—he's a soldier."

"He *was* a soldier," said Liza. "He's missing a leg." This was not strictly true; Uncle Sasha's son still had most of his left thigh, which was near enough to missing a leg—and if he came, Liza knew, he'd challenge her right to inherit.

He'd remember that Petya had sent for him, and that he and Petya had gone on hunting trips together when they'd been young and they'd both had ready money, and Liza would be left to seethe and sew while her brother took her seat in the gunner's chair, at the head of the table— "No. I've written to our mother. She'll spread the word soon enough. If you want to invite Uncle Sasha's children, invite his oldest daughter. She's sound; she can fire a gun."

"She's *pregnant!*"

"Only a *little*," said Liza, but this much she had to concede: even a woman who was only a little pregnant might miscarry at the sudden bark of a gun. "Very *well*, then. Uncle Pasha's oldest son? He's sixteen, isn't he?"

"A novice priest," Petya reminded her, "and our next oldest cousin is eleven. There's Uncle Vitaliy and Aunt Nika; they could learn—"

"Can you imagine anyone from Mother's side in a gun tower? I'd trust the both of them with my money, but I wouldn't trust either one with my life. It has to be our father's side."

And Aunt Katya had neither children nor skill with guns; she had been the youngest of their father's siblings, the only girl, the pet of the family. A woman who fancied herself a scholar, given to studying the stars and charting the paths of new comets—useless on a battlefield. "Useless," Liza said to herself, and she groaned. "Have we written to all of Uncle Sasha's friends from the war?"

"Since you and our father wrote them, I couldn't say," said Petya, "but I'd assume you went through his books thoroughly the first time."

"Thoroughly," Liza agreed. "Is there really *no one* left? Are *these*," and she gestured out the window, to where Jaworski collected and tagged weapons, "the only allies we have left? A handful of Englishmen and Poles?"

"Only a moment ago, you were saying we had men enough to man all of our guns," said Petya, with only the faintest trace of irony. "You mean to train the English, then?"

"I mean to train the troops they give me. If those troops are foreigners..." She crossed her arms, cupping her hands over her elbows. Nastya's rebukes still echoed in her ears, biting as a northeast wind. "They're sending soldiers to hold Kazan and Bratsk, but no one's going to send Yureyevsk so much as a drummer boy. You said yourself the English were useful. You'd trust them with our towers, and what are the guns without the towers? It's not *sensible* to let them build for us and not to let them shoot afterwards—"

"They could copy the designs," said Petya. "They could...I have no idea; they could mount them on their ships and attack our navy—"

"You think Dr. Gatling didn't sell *them* the design, too? Then you have a worse head for business than I thought, and a worse one than an engineer *ought* to have." She thrust one hand into her muff, then pushed open the office door and strode toward Jaworski with Petya trailing in her wake like a pup after its master. *Good,* she thought. *Let them all see how he follows me.*

"Jaworski!" she called across the town square. Jaworski turned to her with his hand propped on the handle of a cart. The cart lay loaded with weapons, rifles and pistols and carbines and a few elderly blunderbusses with barrels like trumpets. "Make your report."

"You Russians are a well-armed people," he replied, smiling faintly. "These are heirloom pieces, mostly—veterans' weapons, just as you said. Kept well, though. A good half have been fired recently enough to blow the dust out."

"Poaching," said Liza with a shrug. "We let them poach."

"Target shooting; ammunition is cheap, here, and cheaper for the older pieces," Petya added, to which Liza made a sound of assent. *He's already asked Kostya about the sales records,* she thought. *To see if he can find anyone else but Kesha to accuse.* Petya prodded the weapons in the cart with one hand, pushing aside a heavily ornamented pistol to peruse the guns beneath. "Are the Englishmen's rifles in with the rest?"

"Their rifles, pistols, and even their bayonets, all labeled as you asked," said Jaworski, and he patted the handle of the cart in confirmation. "Let's walk back to the keep, shall we? I'm frozen through; I've been knocking on doors for hours."

As the three of them began to wheel the cart up to the keep, Liza watched the town around them—she kept catching the people staring when they thought her eyes were elsewhere. An old woman peered out from behind a blackout curtain, her red shawl showing muted through the waxed paper of her window, her lips pressed together in a grim little line. A rail worker who'd been injured in the blast sat upon his front steps, thumb tracing a line over his knee where the stitches lay. *Bitch*, they were probably thinking; *whore, sending a Pole to take our guns away.* "They won't like it if we keep their guns for long," said Liza. "They'll want sheep for their pots, and they'll be restive without their Sunday mutton."

Neither Petya nor Jaworski answered her. The latter couldn't be expected to have an opinion on Sunday mutton, and the former was probably perfecting his damn pet theory on Wainwright's guilt.

Well enough, she thought, and asked, "Did you find anything in Kesha's room?"

"I didn't," said Jaworski, "but I *did* find a fine little gun in the lane behind the tavern."

"A carbine?" Liza asked. Her throat felt suddenly tight.

"A carbine," said Jaworski, his thin lips drawing up at one corner. "I'm not trained with these guns—but from the burnt paper and the traces of powder, I think I can say that it was recently fired."

CHAPTER FIVE

The inspectors arrived that afternoon from Nizhny Novgorod—to hear one of them tell it, the two of them had taken a trundling little car down a disused connector line between the northern rail system and the southern, watching the boiler bubble mutinously the whole way down. "The both of us were ready to jump clear of it the second it blew," said Polzin, the younger and stouter of the two inspectors. "The very second," affirmed Utkin, the elder and thinner. Both men introduced themselves as Ivan something-or-other, and before he'd entirely managed to learn their names, Petya had dubbed them Fat Ivan and Thin Ivan.

Polzin and Utkin, he reminded himself—they were both even-tempered gentlemen, polite and professional, and they deserved his respect.

Utkin insisted upon inspecting what he called "the scene of the crime" himself, and so while he went down to the town, Petya brought Wainwright out from the ice closet to give his statement. "It's highly irregular to keep a pair of prisoners locked up together, before they've spoken to an officer," said Polzin, dabbing his handkerchief over his green-tinted spectacles with a gentle sort of reproach. "They have a chance to compare stories and strategize, you see. Highly irregular. Now, toddle along, boy; you'll have to give a statement yourself soon, and I can't have you listening to this one's story."

Duly chastened, Petya went to kick about the courtyard, hands in his pockets and lips pursed tightly together. *I should have thought about what they'd say to each other*, he thought to himself, but at the time there had been no help for it—if Wainwright had been given the run of the town, he could easily have smuggled himself into the undercarriage of a train and been halfway to Siberia by morning. There had been no other choice but to lock the two of them up, and no room to do anything but lock them up together.

Liza caught his eye as she crossed the courtyard. The snow was falling thickly, and it had touched the shoulders of her coat—their uncle's old uniform coat— with unsullied white. "Utkin says we shouldn't have gathered up all the weapons. He says we should have waited for him to do that, so he could see where people had put them. 'Highly irregular,' he called it," she said, and tried to toss her hair. It was snow-wet, though, and it stayed plastered to the back of her neck.

"They don't like irregularities," Petya answered.

Liza freed a hand from her muff to clap it on his shoulder, and with a sudden pang he realized that she was trying to be sympathetic. "When Polzin asks you what you saw, you tell him *everything*. Don't leave out a thing. He can't see what you saw—"

"I didn't *see* anything—"

"Hear what you heard, then." Her lips twitched; she might have been stifling a smile or a sob. "We're lucky they came so quickly. The family name still makes them jump, in Nizhny—that's something."

"It's something," Petya agreed, although he doubted privately that it was the family name that had called the inspectors south.

Liza took his arm and drew him into a slow circuit of the courtyard, her elbow hooked through his and her muff hanging like a great bear's paw from one hand. "I've looked at the gun Jaworski found," she said, "and it hasn't been fired. Someone wants me to *think* it's been fired—whoever put the gun in the alleyway has scorched the right parts of the gun, and he's burnt a little paper in it and dusted it with powder—but on the poachers' carbines, the pattern of the scorching is different. It looks like something damn well exploded in the chamber. This one looks *wrong*. It looks like it's been held over a candle. And the soot has the same texture. Waxy." She rubbed her fingers together as though to scrub the soot away. "This is the wrong gun, Petya, and someone thinks he can play a trick on me."

"But who would—" began Petya, but then from the entrance there came a shout that halted him completely.

"Pyotr Vladimirovich Tarasov! It's your turn to give a statement. Please step this way."

Liza released his arm and gave him a push. "You heard him. Go on—give your testimony."

Fat Ivan—Inspector Polzin—had made the old study his base of operations. It was an ill-used and cramped little room in which there was very little to disturb. The few blank books that Polzin had salvaged were spotted with rot, and the ink had hardened in the bottles; Polzin was even now reviving it with a few drops of water and a burner that must have come from a lantern. The bookshelves were mostly bare and liberally coated with dust, and cobwebs stretched between the few remaining books. Petya thought he could make out Schiller's name on the cover of one, but the first few letters were so faded as to be illegible.

Polzin had dusted off the weather-beaten desk and placed a notebook in the center, and judging by the tidy spill of strange characters across the page—some form of shorthand?—it was here that he was recording his observations. "Ah, Pyotr Vladimirovich!" he said, taking the ink off of the burner and turning down the flame. "Very prompt, very good. I understand that you were on watch last night?"

"I was," Petya agreed, and he looked about the room for a chair in which to seat himself. Hadn't his father kept another chair here? He seemed to remember sitting in a narrow chair with a cracked-leather seat, listening to lectures on economy…in any case, the second chair was gone, and he was left to stand awkwardly before Polzin's commandeered desk. "Jaworski told you that? He was on watch with me. Or—he was on watch, and I wasn't scheduled to be, but I went up to watch with him anyway."

Polzin was jotting down what Petya said with every appearance of rapt attention, nodding as though encouraging him to go on. "Very good, very good," he muttered.

"And Liza—that's my sister, Elizaveta Vladimirovna—"

"I guessed you meant your sister."

Petya cleared his throat. "Liza. Ah. She had gone out with an Englishman to shoot. In the hills to the east, I think."

"You think?"

"Definitely the east," amended Petya. His palms were sweating beneath his gloves. "They had a lot of glass bottles, for, ah, for shooting. I couldn't think how they could see the bottles, since it was after eight, but I could hear the glass breaking. So they must've been close to the keep, on this side of the orchard, because the wind was coming from the other direction. From the west, I mean. I couldn't smell rotting dragon on it. It wasn't a strong wind, not where I was standing, but it would've carried away the sound if they were much further out."

"You were listening to the glass breaking, and there was very little wind, coming from the west," said Polzin. He made a sharp mark like punctuation, then looked up over his tinted spectacles. "Very good, very good. What then?"

"Then Jaworski and I heard another shot, and I thought—no, Jaworski *said* it sounded like it was another kind of gun."

"A different kind from the one your sister and the Englishman were using."

"Yes," Petya answered.

"And Jaworski was the one who noticed it."

"No—I mean, I heard it, too, but Jaworski mentioned that it was different. Different from the rest." Petya felt uncomfortably as though he was being examined by one of his professors. A wrong answer could be fatal, and it couldn't be called back again. "Then we listened to Liza and the Englishman shooting a little longer, and by then the snow was coming down fairly hard…we saw them coming toward the fortress, and I thought I'd go help them in."

He licked his lips. "I mean—we saw Lieutenant Wainwright bringing my father to the fortress. And we thought it was Liza, but it wasn't, and…ah. And then I went to fetch her, and when she came back, she said Kesha was in town, and she thought he'd done it. So Jaworski went to town to fetch him."

Polzin made another sharp, punctuating mark. Although Petya had finished speaking, Polzin continued to fill the page with his queer little scribbles; when at last he reached a stopping place, he dipped his pen again in the half-congealed ink and asked, "What next?"

"Well—Liza and I asked Wainwright where he'd found the body, and he said it had been in the alley behind the tavern, right by the back stairs. He said he went in to ask Nastya if anyone came in, but no one had, so he thought whoever it was had gone up the back stairs. He said he didn't expect us to believe he'd just *found* it, and he'd do whatever we thought best to find our father's murderer. Then Jaworski brought Kesha back, and he seemed…I don't know how to describe it. Surprised? Or maybe incredulous is better. He…it was as though he thought we'd staged it to make a fool of him, and he couldn't take it seriously. Liza was very angry with him, and hit him, and then we took him and Wainwright and locked them in the ice closet."

"Very irregular," murmured Polzin, but he was nodding as he wrote. "And then, hmm, then what?"

"Then my sister and I prised the bullets out of his chest. Our father's chest—the pellets, I mean. Liza said they were called pellets. We made a diagram of where they were, and how deep, and at what angle they'd gone in, but it wasn't… it wasn't very pretty. His chest was all torn to pieces. I'm sorry."

"You should have left them in the body," said Polzin, "but I think you know that. And then today?"

"Just what you've seen. We've slept a bit—catnaps, really. We've been sending for you and dealing with the creditors, and wiring our mother to tell her…and picking up the guns, of course."

"Which is—"

"Irregular." Petya smiled, and it strained at the corners of his mouth. If he didn't smile, he thought that he might scream and scream and never stop. "I'm sorry. This has never happened before."

"I don't imagine it has." Polzin continued to write while Petya stood, shifting awkwardly from foot to foot. "Now that you've given me your account, I'll ask you a few further questions, and once you've answered, we'll consider the preliminary interview complete. Can you do that, Monsieur Tarasov?"

"I can," Petya said. "If I know the answers."

"Very good. First, then, you say that Lieutenant Wainwright carried your father's body back from the town. Did either you or Jaworski see the lieutenant leaving the fortress?"

"No," Petya replied. "Or at least, I didn't see it. But he might have gone out before I went into the watchtower—and we didn't see my father leave, either. Or rather, I didn't see it; I don't know if Jaworski saw it."

"The lieutenant is given free run of the keep and the town? He and his men have no curfew, no posted hours?"

"None that I know of," said Petya. "You'd have to ask Liza about that. I've spent most of my time here fixing the guns and the rails. But no, apart from their scheduled watches, they don't have a curfew that I know of."

"Ah, thank you." The inspector paged back in his notebook, scratching some quick notes on an earlier page—was it a page from Petya's interview, or Wainwright's? There was no way of knowing. "And now, your brother's arrival. Did your sister tell you anything about it? Was it expected?"

"She told me, after Wainwright brought our father in, that she'd invited him...before that, no. She didn't tell me a thing."

"Did she tell your father?"

Petya thought, and even as he thought, Polzin jotted something down. *I've probably considered the question too long, and now he'll think I'm lying.* "I don't know that she did," he said, "but she must've, or else why would he have gone to see Kesha?"

"Why, indeed." The inspector's words had the inflection of an observation, and he briefly buffed his glasses with his pocket handkerchief before continuing. "What sort of sound does the entrance make when it opens?"

"The servants' entrance? The door squeaks a bit."

"Loudly enough that a watchman on duty would have heard it from the tower? In low wind?"

"Perhaps," said Petya, "But perhaps not, with the shots to the east. They were fairly close, as I said."

"And did your sister invite the Englishman to go shooting, or did he invite her?"

"Oh, she invited him," said Petya, although now that he thought back, he couldn't remember which direction the invitation had gone. Surely Liza would have invited the boy, and not the other way around? She'd made him carry a sack of bottles, after all, but then, she'd carried one, too—

"Actually, I don't remember."

"And your father frequented the tavern? He was known to visit it often?"

"Yes. Yes, everyone knew he liked to drink and gamble there. But when he took me drinking with him, we went in the carriage, and it was very grand and showy. If he'd walked down himself, I don't know that anyone would have expected him to be there. I'm sorry. I wish I could be more useful."

"You've done well. Commendable," Polzin answered. "And here's a final question, before I let you back out again: have you seen your father's last will and testament?"

"I haven't, but Liza told us what it said last night," said Petya. "She said it named Kesha his legal heir, and that she'd told him that when they spoke, yesterday. Told Kesha, I mean."

"And you didn't know before she told you."

"I didn't, sir. Inspector."

"'Inspector' will do," said Polzin, and he shut his book with a papery thump. "Very good, very good. You've been an excellent resource, and I'll contact you if I require further information. Tell the man outside to get Volkov out of the tower and bring him in to give a statement. Does that sound acceptable?"

"More than acceptable. Good day, s—Inspector." He reached across the table to shake Polzin's hand, but Polzin only regarded him with a mildly aggrieved expression that made Petya replace his hand in his pocket. The sweat was making the fur lining of his glove stick to his palm.

He left the study, passing Volkov's name to the guard as he went. Had it been any other day, he might have gone up into a watchtower to think, but the memory of that single report was too close to the surface for the watchtower to bring him any solace. Instead, he followed the dim lighting to the mess hall and settled down at a table far from the one where his father's body rested.

There would surely be a light supper soon; he could smell lamb and cabbage and plums cooking, and the mingled scents made his mouth water. Liza would probably go straight up into the towers after she'd given her statement, and someone would have to bring her a boxed supper and a flask of tea to make sure she ate.

Someone would have to bring a boxed supper down to Kesha and Wainwright, too, although they were sharing space with the meats and the cheeses and the late autumn fruits. Their lot was cheerless enough without a hot meal.

And will anyone make sure I eat? wondered Petya. But there was no sense in letting himself grow maudlin. He rose from his chair and followed the scent of supper to the kitchen.

CHAPTER SIX

Liza was very nearly drunk enough. She wasn't generally given to the finicky distinctions that her brothers liked to make—but tonight, as she rolled her head slowly from one shoulder to the other, she studied its weight and decided that yes, she was nearly drunk *enough*. "Fill your glass," she told the grey-eyed English soldier, whom she had begun to think of as particularly hers. "I've had my fill."

The grey-eyed soldier gave her a look of polite befuddlement, and she chuckled as she pushed the bottle toward him. He looked so very like a hound she'd once had, when she was a little girl and the family kept hounds; the poor animal had pricked his ears and tilted his head just like that. When the soldier leaned in to hear her better (as though he could learn Russian by coming closer—the idea!), she was struck with a powerful urge to reach out and scratch him behind the ears. She had been drinking to forget something, she knew, and what it was, she couldn't remember, so perhaps she'd done well. She wanted to do well, for her father's...

"Oh," she said. The mirth bled out of her like warmth on a winter day. "Oh, Christ." She swallowed against a wretched sound. If she started sobbing now, she wouldn't stop, and she couldn't bear to sob like a child at the head of the table. Jaworski would see, and Utkin, and Kesha would *hear* even if he couldn't see—and she couldn't bear the thought of him hearing of it. He'd laugh at her, sobbing into her beef with her elbows on the table and her hair in disarray. *When did I become a melancholy drunk?*

At her right, Jaworski frowned and laid a hand on her arm. "You should go to bed, Liza," he suggested in an undertone. "You haven't slept today; none of us have. You haven't even taken a moment to grieve."

"Why should I grieve?" she said, and swallowed again to banish the welling grief that pressed heavy at the back of her throat. There was no room for sentiment in the mess hall. Her father had taught her that. "We caught the bastard who murdered our father."

Petya said something too low for her to hear. "What?" she asked, quiet and detached. "Speak up, Petya. We'll have no secrets here."

She watched Petya straighten in his chair, squaring his shoulders as though *she* was the enemy. "Don't speak of Kesha that way," he said, and this time his voice carried throughout the mess hall.

"I'll speak of him how I like," said Liza. "He's a murderer and a traitor, and he's persuaded someone to cover his crimes. Transportation's too good for him. He deserves to go before a military court—they'll have the stomach to execute him."

"Even if it were true—"

"And who knew I was looking for a carbine?" she continued, cold and merciless. "My dear brother Petya, whom I've seen going to the ice closet to speak with the murderer—"

"*Stop*, Liza!" Petya pushed back his chair. "You can't really believe that. This isn't about our father—this isn't even about punishing his killer. This is about your damn vendetta against Kesha, and it always has been. Even if he were innocent, you'd still put a bullet in his back!"

"So what if I would?" said Liza—softly, she thought; it must have been softly, for she could scarcely hear herself over the rush of blood in her ears. "If I invited him back for no better reason than to shoot him myself, *what would you do*, Pyotr Vladimirovich Tarasov?"

He winced as though she'd slapped him, then dragged his arm across his eyes. Dry eyes—he wasn't wiping off tears. He was trying to hide the naked fear on his face, and he was failing badly. Had it really been less than a month ago that he had joked with her about dragons in the British territories? Had it really been less than a month ago that they'd wrestled like brothers in the streets?

"Please excuse me, *Lord Tarasov*," he said, stepping back from the table. His voice shook. "I don't think I'm hungry anymore."

"Go, then," said Liza. "Cool your blood outside. Come back when you're ready to apologize for your disrespect."

In the light of the lamps overhead, Petya's face was washed pale, his eyes darkly shadowed. She could see his muscles tensing, even beneath the thick wool of his jacket. Drawing himself upright, like a man facing the bayonet or the gallows, Petya said, "I won't apologize for trying to make you see sense." With that, he turned to go.

"Follow him," she said to Jaworski. "See that he doesn't set anything on fire."

"He doesn't seem likely to set anything on fire," Jaworski replied. His hand was fixed tightly on her arm, and she could see that he was more worried *she* would do something foolish. With her free hand, she prised him off one finger at a time.

"See that he doesn't *build* anything, then," said Liza. "He's never spoken back to my father, and he's never spoken back to *me*. He's in a dire mood, and there's no telling what damn stupid thing he'll do."

"He probably thought the same about you," said Jaworski. "You shouldn't have egged him on like that. He loves his brother, even if he's a villain. You knew what you were doing."

"I'm drunk," said Liza, but the calm detachment had faded, and grief was waiting beneath. She reached for the little vodka glass at the edge of her plate and found it half-empty. The clear liquid washed against the sides of the glass when she swirled it about. "I'm drunk, and he knew it. Follow him, Jaworski. See that he doesn't sneak onto the ten o'clock train and run to Moscow."

"He'll stay to defend his brother," said Jaworski, but he stood from his chair and shoved it flush against the table.

Slowly, deliberately, Liza pushed the glass away.

CHAPTER SEVEN

The bolt of the ice closet door slid back with a faint but audible clank that woke Kesha at once. The door swung open. On their bundle of straw, Kesha and Wainwright sat up straight. "Who's there?" Wainwright called, but Petya made a *hsst* sound to shush them.

"Kesha," he said. "Come quickly. Don't argue with me, just this *once*—she's going to kill you. She always meant to kill you; it's why she *asked* you here—"

"That's ridiculous," said Kesha.

Petya stepped over the head of a dragon, its eyes putrefying in the unaccustomed heat, and then seized Kesha by the wrist. "She's going to kill you," he said, "and she doesn't care whether or not you're innocent. Now, go—here, take these—" He thrust his free hand into the apple barrel, drawing out a pair of wizened apples and pressing them into Kesha's pockets. "Take this," he said, and took a matchbook from his own breast pocket and slipped it into Kesha's. "I don't know how long you have. She'll hunt you down when you run—"

"Why in *God's name* am I running?" Kesha hissed, but Petya was dragging him to his feet, and Wainwright must have absorbed a measure of that incomprehensible urgency, because he was pressing at Kesha's shoulders to make him stand. "What's going on, Petya?"

"She's at supper," said Petya. "They all are, except the watchmen, but you have time to run, if you edge around the wall and go to the east. Remember that—go *east*, where the wall is broken. No one will be foolish enough to climb into the east tower, even to hunt you down; no one will have a good angle on you. You can lay low in the hills until—"

"Will you tell me *why* you think she wants to kill me?" demanded Kesha, but then Petya was pulling the door shut with Wainwright on the other side. "Name of God, Petya, *explain* yourself!"

"She wants you dead," said Petya, with a peculiarly flat intonation that chilled Kesha far more than any of his former panic. "She asked me what I'd do if she'd brought you here for no better reason than to shoot you herself. I've never heard her sound so serious in my life. So *believe* me when I say that I think she's going to shoot you, and for God's sake, *run!*"

With kisses to Kesha's cheeks, a push to his shoulder, Petya shoved him in the direction of the stairs out of the keep—and Kesha couldn't have said why, later, but he loped off along the passage and took the stairs two at a time. His skin still felt tight with sleep, and his hands were half-numb from the chill of the ice closet, but he knew with a brittle clarity that Petya had no reason to lie to him. *Very well*, he thought, as he lifted the latch and slipped out of the keep. *Very well, Petya—I'll run.*

The air of the courtyard was shockingly cold, even after the ice closet; there, at least, he'd had Wainwright's shoulder to warm him, and the air had been still as a tomb. Here, the wind whistled through the gap in the wall and curled fiercely in the shell of the fortress walls, and even hugging the masonry, he could feel the wind tearing at his hair. Petya had given him two apples and a matchbook—he hadn't even thought to offer a decent hat against the cold.

At the gap, the moonlight glanced off the edges of broken stones. Kesha knew that in his black coat, on the pale snow and the moon-touched stone, he would be utterly exposed; he would have to—

"There!" shouted someone, and Kesha's blood froze.

He hurled himself through the gap just as he heard the crack of a rifle firing; behind him, a bullet chipped the stone and ricocheted into the darkness. His disused legs protested as he fled, pelting down the broken stone of the hill, and each time he put a foot wrong, his heart leapt into his throat—then his other foot caught and propelled him onward, downward, between scruffy winter bushes with needle-thin leaves and around stones half his height. He reached the first hill at full tilt and scurried up it and into the shadow of the cherry trees, scrabbling over the dirt like a dog where the ground grew steep. There was a thin copse of bushes beyond the cherries, too thin to shelter him in daylight, but the stone beneath them was dark with snowmelt. At the edge of the copse he staggered upright and began to run anew, doubling over as he crested the next hill to hide his shape from the riflemen.

He should never have run. Whatever Petya had said—whatever Petya *believed*, he should have stayed shut away in the ice closet, waiting like any innocent man for his name to be cleared. Only the guilty ran from the law. Only the guilty ran.

He sprinted onward, keeping to the valleys between the low hills. In his youth, he'd run these valleys with Liza, and she'd chased him and caught him a hundred, hundred times; he knew full well that she would catch him now. *Got you, Kesha!* she'd howl, laughing—but it wouldn't be her hand splayed at his back this time.

It had been almost a minute since he'd heard a gunshot. *She's preparing a shot*, he thought. *She knows where I'll go; we've run this valley a hundred times.*

He peeled off to the south, and by now his lungs were

burning. He tasted something foul in his mouth, bile or blood, but he spat to one side and kept running. How far from the keep was he? Two verst? Three?

Behind him, Kesha heard a sound like thunder. Later, he would wonder what it was—the blast of a dragon's grenade, or one train crashing into another—but on this night, as the clouds covered the moon, he could think nothing but the fugitive's mantra: *Run. Run as fast as you can, and don't you dare look back.*

CHAPTER EIGHT

Petya knew that he had to get away from the ice closet to avoid drawing suspicion to it, but for a long moment he dithered there at the heavy iron door. "I'm sorry," he whispered at last through the door. "But—"

"But you think I killed your father," said Wainwright from the other side, and he knocked once like confirmation. "I'm glad that Kesha's free."

Kesha knew the hills and rails around Yureyevsk. He could shelter long enough for the inspectors to clear his name, and then...then, however much Liza wanted her brother dead, she would have to see that murdering an innocent man would lose her the keep. She would have to.

Petya pulled away and thrust his hands in his pockets. His head and chest hurt awfully, as though he had a summer cold. He felt that any moment he might collapse in great shuddering sobs, tearing at the ground like a prophet in a frenzy—but he had an obligation to keep his sister from following Kesha into the hills, so he swallowed those burgeoning tears and strode down the corridor to the mess hall. He had just reached the entrance and pressed his hand to the doorframe when he heard the first shouts of alarm.

Liza's eyes met his across the hall, and she tipped her

chair to the floor in her haste to rise. *"What did you do?"* she demanded. "What the *hell* did you do?"

"There!" called Jaworski from the stair, and Petya heard the report of a rifle—for a moment his heart felt as though it was caught in a vise, but then Jaworski shouted, "God damn it all, he's headed east—"

"Who?" asked Liza, but her eyes burned into Petya's like twin points of flame. She knew, and if she made it to a gun turret...

He launched himself at her just as she made for the door, seizing her by the wrist and yanking—he swiped at her other hand to restrain it, but by then she'd twisted free and landed a fierce punch to his jaw. "Stop—" he said, but his mouth was full of blood and a piece of tooth, and her next blow caught him just under the ribs. Pain flared through him, burning the air from his lungs—he curled up, gasping, spitting blood on the floor. The next hit struck his temple, and he fell as though he'd crashed into a wall.

As though from far away, he heard Liza yelling, and he craned his neck to find her. "Name of God, Jaworski!" Liza shouted, and Petya watched (vision shattered, refracted) as she caught Jaworski by the throat and pressed him hard against the wall. "Why the hell did you do that? He was down—"

"He'd have stopped you," said Jaworski. "Now go. Get to a tower. You're running out of time."

She ran, but there were six of her running, and there was something *very important* that he had to tell her about the direction she was running, but he couldn't force himself to put words together. He could barely drag himself to his knees, then to his feet; he fought down the urge to retch when he stood straight.

Ducking his head against the dizziness, swallowing bile and half-digested brandy, he began to grope his way along the corridor to the stairs. When the stairs ran out, he threw himself into the icy courtyard, still stooping against the pain in his chest. Black spots swam across his field of vision, but he paid them no mind.

"Stop!" he shouted at the riflemen, who stood ranged at the gap in the wall— "Stop!" he cried, and whether they understood him or not, they stopped firing for that single blessed moment that he needed to hear...

...God. Name of God. *No.*

The telltale click of the gun mount's gears rang like a knell on the still, cold air. "LIZA!" shouted Petya, hands cupped at his mouth, although his throat was raw and his ears were ringing. "Liza, *no—*"

She didn't hear him, or she didn't care to hear him. Atop the eastern gun turret, she sat in the gunner's chair, one hand on the trigger and one hand adjusting the angle of the barrel. Her six shapes coalesced into one—one single, perfect woman atop a tower, wind tearing at her hair and pale face shining in the moonlight, with no damn idea what she was about to do.

She squeezed off one burst, and the gun mount absorbed the kick the way it was *engineered* to—sent that kick shivering down the tower, where the walls would absorb the force—but on this tower, this one tower out of all of the towers, there were no walls to buttress it against the blast. The turret shuddered like a lightning-struck tree. With a sound like snapping bone, the tower fractured.

The riflemen saw that long crack running the length of it, mortar torn apart and stones gaping. They dropped their guns and scattered, and still Petya stood with his hands cupped at his mouth and blood streaming down his chin. "*Liza!*" he shouted, but she never once turned to look.

The click of the gears sounded, and the gun swiveled to point low. Low, into the valley between the hills.

"Get down from there!" Petya screamed, tears stinging his eyes. "You'll kill yourself! Liza, get down—"

He thought he heard her shout *Go to Hell* before the second burst shook the tower apart.

CHAPTER NINE

Liza woke to the taste of blood and mortar.

She coughed, and that cough hurt like a *bastard*. With greater care, she began flexing her fingers—none broken, which was as close as she was ever going to come to a goddamn miracle. Next, she flexed her arms. Bruised, and from the pain in her shoulder she'd probably snapped a collarbone, but it was on her right side, and she could afford to favor that arm. She brought her left hand up to feel for broken ribs.

Three, by her count, all on the right side. Nothing punctured, as far as she could tell, but best not to press them too hard.

"I'm here," she said, but it came only feebly through the thick paste of blood and dust coating her tongue. Leaning heavily on her left hand, she tried to pull herself up. "I'm—"

She remembered the fall. She remembered Petya, shouting something that she couldn't or wouldn't hear—and she remembered the kick of the Gatling gun.

The barrel of the gun pointed up toward the moon, which was because the gun mount was embedded in the earth only an armspan from her face—and gradually, she realized that this was because the mount had crushed her leg.

Liza woke with blankets wrapped tightly around her, her head throbbing with a low, even beat that wasn't quite painful. "Ugh," she said, and she extracted her hand from the blankets to push her hair away from her face.

"I wouldn't," said a voice not quite familiar. "Try to lie still, Mademoiselle Tarasova. You'll only agitate your injuries."

"God damn my injuries," said Liza, and she noted as she did that her chest and shoulder were bandaged. Someone had tried to put her right arm in a sling, but she'd wriggled out of it in her sleep—and that someone was probably the town druggist, who was sitting at her bedside with his narrow chin propped on his hand. "Have they caught my brother yet?" she asked. "Has Petya started fixing the tower?"

"It's been two days since your fall," said the druggist. He had a thinning beard in the old Russian style and a heavy mustache; it gave him the look of a walrus eating a lady's veil. "Your brother has been recovering adequately—"

"So he was hurt, too—damn fool." She began unwrapping the blankets with her left hand, untucking them from beneath her waist and hips. She knew that sitting would be hell on her ribs, but if she could draw back the blankets enough to see her leg… "What happened to him?"

"Someone struck him in the head," the druggist replied. "He was concussed, at first, and we had to keep him awake all through the first night. I think the danger's past, though. I can bring him in, if you like; he was in and out yesterday. You spoke with him. Your mother's been in, too. I take it you don't remember."

"Keeping an eye on me," said Liza, and she laughed—the laughing hurt as though her ribs were breaking again, but breaking beneath a hundred layers of silk and gauze. "I don't remember."

The coverlet came away, as did the linens beneath. Thus freed, she raised the stump of her left leg to examine it. The whole thing was bandaged, of course, but even so, she could assess the features of her injury in that odd equanimity that the druggist's concoctions lent her.

Amputated below the knee rather than above, which was heartening. She'd never yet met a veteran with a good prosthetic knee joint, and she would have to climb the damn ladders into the gun towers when she recovered. The bandages appeared mostly clean of blood, which probably meant they'd been changed recently—another heartening thought. The druggist had probably been assigned to her care, and one of the soldiers had probably sawed her free of the gun mount if they couldn't shift it. She hoped for her own sake that it had been someone who'd done it before, who knew how to cut to keep the leg from suppurating. Losing a leg was bad enough; she wasn't sure she could watch it rot away.

"Have they caught my brother yet?" she asked again.

From the doorway, Jaworski answered, "We haven't been tracking him."

"Haven't been *tracking* him!" Liza cried, and damn her ribs, she was sitting upright. She pushed herself up on one elbow, teeth clenched against that peculiar, distant pain in her chest. "Why in God's name haven't you—"

"Inspector Utkin has evidence to suggest that your brother is innocent," Jaworski cut in. "Innocent of the murder, I should say; his other crimes, the inspector refuses to take into account."

"He *can't* be innocent," said Liza. Her throat almost closed up against the words. "He was at the tavern when my father was shot—my father died the same night *he* arrived—"

"But his boots were dry when I came to collect him, and Nastya confirmed it in her statement," said Jaworski, and although his expression was bland, his tone said that he was no more happy about the business than she. "Utkin and

Polzin are very interested in the status of his boots, in fact. They claim that your father was lying on his back when he was shot—"

"That would explain the low angle," muttered Liza to herself, at which Jaworski nodded and continued.

"And they found a pair of bootprints, frozen in the mud where they claim the shooter stood. Smaller feet than your brother's; they measured them when they interviewed him." He tugged off his gloves one after the other, fixing his teeth in the tip of the middle finger of each to pull the leather free. "I don't care for their evidence, but they seem to think it's compelling," he said, once he'd tucked his gloves into his pockets. "They even took a tailor's tape to my boots, even though Petya has told them that I was on watch that night. They'll probably come to measure you, when they hear you've recovered."

"Then I've lost my leg for nothing," said Liza softly. She traced her hand along a fold in the coverlet, feeling the way the calluses on her palm snagged in the fabric. "Let him rot in the hills. Let him freeze to death. I don't give a damn what he does."

"I'll be happy to," answered Jaworski. "We'll beat the hills in springtime and see if we can find his bones—"

"No," she said. "No—I won't be convinced of it. It would be easy for those to be someone else's bootprints. All kinds of people go through that alley. It would be *easy*, Jaworski— and if I can't convince the inspectors, I know that *you* believe me. You're the—" her breath hitched. "You're the only man who was loyal to me from the first moment, without question. I can count on you, can't I?"

"I'm your man," he said, and he knelt at her bedside to take her left hand. "Tell me what you need me to do, Elizaveta Vladimirovna."

"Damn the procedures, then," she said, and she pressed his bare hand in hers. Despite his gloves, despite the almost oppressive warmth of Liza's chambers, his skin was cool to the touch. *I must have a fever,* she thought. "Find my brother. Hunt him down and bring him back. Innocent or guilty, he needs to be brought in. You're the only man I can trust with this, Jaworski; you're the only man who would do exactly what I would, in my place."

"I hope I'll do it more soberly," he said, for which she had to release his hand to cuff his shoulder. She could feel the impact run up her arm and into the lax muscles of her body, where it faded into an aching warmth.

"More soberly, then," she conceded after a moment. "Choose three men who are above suspicion. Take them into the hills to hunt my brother down. Don't come back until you've found him."

"I won't," said Jaworski. "And if he won't come, when we find him?"

Liza drew in a rattling breath. "If he won't come—you have my permission to kill him."

Yelena Sergeyevna Tarasova stood at the threshold of her daughter's rooms, her greying hair demurely concealed beneath a black lace veil and her figure cloaked in layers of black bombazine. "You're awake," she observed from the doorway, unsmiling. "They told me you wouldn't keep the leg. I see they were right."

Liza looked up from Utkin's plaster mold of the compelling bootprints, just barely managing to suppress a snarl. "Mother," she said coolly. "My leg is fine. The amputation was clean, and they've given me morphine."

"This is just like when your cousin Borya lost his leg," continued Liza's mother, as though she hadn't heard. Her eyes were fixed on something distant, and Liza longed to shake her into the present. "His mother kept the bones in a jeweled box, like a relic."

"Most of his leg," said Liza. She spared a brief moment

of contrition for forbidding Petya to invite their cousin, and for such petty reasons. *Ah, Borya—if I'd only known!* "And this is completely different, Mother. I still have my knee. Only give the damn thing time to heal."

"Your father taught you such language, I'm sure." Liza's mother took the druggist's chair, drawing it close against Liza's bedside. The folds of her bombazine gown made soft whirring sounds against the rough wool of Liza's favorite blanket.

"I'll go on swearing if I want," said Liza. "And I'll go on working the towers as soon as I'm well. I'm going to get a leg I can use to climb the ladders and work the gun mounts, just as soon as I can get fitted." *Just as soon as I've healed enough that they'll let me*, she thought. The druggist had carefully redirected the conversation every time she'd tried to bring it around to prosthetics, and eventually she'd thrown an empty bottle of laudanum at him. She hadn't managed to shatter it, but she'd sent him running, which was near enough to a success.

Thank God she had strong arms. The collarbone and ribs would make matters more ticklish, but surely they'd let her go about on crutches as soon as the bones started to knit. They were already letting her sit, her back propped up against a nest of old pillows; surely they'd let her out of bed once the bones began to knit?

Her mother had been watching her as she took stock, her hands folded in her lap. When Liza met her eyes again, her mother smiled thinly. "You'll go to Nizhny while you convalesce, of course."

"I'm staying here, Mother," said Liza. She reached to the bedside table for the bottle of vodka that Jaworski had so thoughtfully left her. Her mother watched her without comment. *She looks like a vulture watching a dying lamb*, Liza thought. "It's medicinal," she said to fill the silence. "If I can't have a cold drink when I've lost a leg—"

"Indeed."

"'Indeed,' you say! God damn it all, do you even care whether I drink or not?"

Yelena rose smoothly to her feet, her face as placid as an ice-encased lake. "Soon this rage will burn itself out, Elizaveta Vladimirovna. When it does, perhaps you'll find you've tired of living like this."

Liza rolled onto her good hip, her free hand steadying her against the headboard of her bed. Slowly, deliberately, she rose to her one remaining foot and stood erect.

She was taller than her mother; she had her grandfather's hawk nose and broad shoulders, and even with her hair falling loose about her shoulders, she knew that she made a fearsome figure when she looked down her nose. "Living like this?" she said, sharp as a gunshot. "Living as my father's heir? Is that what you want me to stop doing, *Mother?*"

"You know that you were never your father's heir," said Yelena.

"I know that," said Liza, and with the morphine still faintly warming her blood, she could say it without rancor. "But in his will, I stand *second* in line to inherit, and not last. That *means* something, and you can't take that away from me."

Liza's mother neither blinked nor looked away. "You're bleeding," she observed, and looking down at the stump of her left leg, Liza could see that it was so. "I'll go to fetch the druggist."

"Do," said Liza. As her mother departed, skirt rustling like crows' wings, she sat heavily on the edge of the bed and watched the bandages staining red.

The druggist brought Petya with him, trailing behind like a heavy shadow. All at once, Liza remembered the accusations she'd flung at him on the night of the fall. They seemed ridiculous now, on the far side of that dire moment; if Petya loved his brother, he loved the truth more, and he would never sacrifice the one for the other. "I see you've recovered well," said Liza. "Hand me my bottle, Petya."

The druggist knelt by the bed and began undoing the

bandages, making a soft *tch, tch* sound at what he saw there. "Give her the bottle," he said, and Petya obeyed him at once. "We'll have to cauterize again; the wound has reopened. It will hurt, I'm afraid."

Liza pressed the still-cool glass against her brow before she put the mouth to her lips, and the liquid washed down her throat like ice and fire. Petya sat at the edge of her bed and watched his hands as she drank. "I'm sorry," he said eventually.

"What are *you* sorry for?" asked Liza. Putting the bottle down, she reached across her lap to take Petya's hand. "I accused you of planting evidence. You! The only honest man in the keep. *I'm* sorry."

"I set our brother free. I ruined your wall. I took your leg." He pressed her hand tightly, as though he, too, was bracing against a sudden pain. "All of those things. I've taken away something that I can never give back, all because I didn't *trust* you enough to believe that you'd…oh, Liza. I'm sorry."

"You were probably right not to trust me." Liza tugged her brother close enough to fix her thumb at the hinge of his jaw, then turned him to meet her eyes. "But you're an engineer. If anyone can give me a new leg, it's you."

CHAPTER TEN

With Liza riding upon a cart, a pile of pillows beneath her to shield her from the jolting, the Tarasov keep made its way to the cemetery behind the church. She had insisted that she come, although the druggist had just burnt her leg again to stop the bleeding and she was numb and sleepy from the morphine. She had begged them to let her help carry her father's coffin, too, but no one would indulge her.

Petya bore one corner, although his head still rang from the blow he'd taken to the temple. His feet fell heavy on the frozen earth, and he watched them break the crust of snow so that he wouldn't have to look across the coffin and see a near-stranger bearing the pall.

Kesha should have been there, and it was Petya's fault that he wasn't. He would have been able to find the words to eulogize their father, even if he hadn't meant them, and Petya was tired enough not to *care* what anyone meant so long as someone could speak his father to rest. *Someone needs to speak well of the dead*, he thought, as the pallbearers passed through the great gate in step. Below them lay the town, low and drab and close-huddled against the surrounding hills. The black stones along the rails cut the rough plain in two, and on every rooftop, smoke had stained the snow grey. That dim landscape filled Petya with a sense of futility that he couldn't quench. *Someone needs to tell us why we should remember him*, he thought, *or else we'll all forget.*

The church rose into view, with its roof of rough shakes and its hopeful little onion dome. Another relic of his grandfather's era, beloved by the people; they named their babes before the ikonostasis, married their children on its steps, and buried their dead beyond its walls. The Tarasovs had interred Petya's uncles here, and he had watched the townspeople digging graves for the rail workers after the blast, carving at the barely softened earth.

The coffin was heavy, but the grave lay near to hand. Someone had scored the ground in the family plot until there was a hole big enough to lay a body in. It seemed a small hole, for such a heavy body.

The pallbearers put the coffin down for the priest to bless. As he straightened, Petya surveyed the churchyard. When he had buried his grandfather, it had been full of mourners, but his grandfather had died in summer—*and beloved*, he thought, before he could silence himself. The telegraph master stood at a distance with his arms folded over his chest and one hand tangled in his wispy beard, the lines of his leathery face pursed into an unreadable expression. Anastasia Ivanovna and two of her sisters watched from their father's grave, as though to say, *This is our place—keep to yours.* They were dressed in severe gowns of black so faded as to be grey, with their hair hidden under plain, dark scarves and their faces muffled.

To one side, Petya saw Liza's cart roll close enough for her to survey the proceedings. To the other side, Petya's mother stood with her chin held high and her black gown stirring faintly with each breeze.

The cut of the dress was some years out of date, Petya realized. The torso was too long, the skirt cut too close. His mother must have had it tailored some time ago in anticipation of this day, and when she'd received the telegram, she had only to pack it.

She had given up on her husband years ago—and that was what brought Petya to tears.

"Will any speak for this man?" asked the priest, once the blessing was finished.

No one spoke, and after a long, cold silence, the pallbearers lowered Vladimir Petrovich Tarasov into his grave.

In his rooms, with a fire fading to embers in the grate, Petya sat sketching his sister's body. He drew her seated at the gun mount, the way she'd sat when he'd cranked the gun for her; he drew the way the ball of her foot pressed against the footrest, working the brake that brought the barrel of the gun to a sudden stop. He drew her climbing the ladder to the tower, the toes of one boot catching on a new rung, the heel of the other hooked at the rung below it.

He drew the muscles in her good right leg—his own calves were shapely, smooth-muscled, but hers went tight like thick knots when she flexed her foot and rocked on her ankle. Grotesque, he might have said, if she'd been a stranger; she would never turn heads at the flash of an ankle, and not only because she wore boots that went nearly up to her knees.

He drew her boots, too, and how they fit against her flesh. There were wrinkles in the leather at her ankles, the crests of each wrinkled line worn nearly white with long use, and there were rows of buttons to fix the boots in place over that muscled flesh.

Pulling off one stocking, he held his foot out before him, rotating it at the ankle, flexing it at the arch until it cramped down the middle. He rolled it along the bare floorboards, heel to toetip, and drew it in each attitude of flexion.

When the last embers faded, Petya let them die and drew a blanket over his lap. Only when the inkwell ran dry and his pages were full did he put the work aside.

His eyes were heavy, and his head ached dully. He thought the ache might be hunger, although he hadn't been inclined to eat. Liza hadn't eaten today; she had only had morphine and vodka, and vomited up the gruel that the druggist had pressed on her.

It was foolish, perhaps, to refuse to eat simply because she couldn't yet. Petya wouldn't dispute its foolishness.

He fell asleep only moments before the clock struck four-thirty, hand splayed across his lap desk, one stocking on and one stocking off.

***

The alarm bell yanked Petya from his sleep. He stumbled out of bed and into his trousers and coat almost before he'd woken properly—put his boots on with only one stocking, left his gloves bunched up at his wrists—then sprinted out the door and onto the ladder and into the tower, because Liza would be finished with her first magazine by now and someone would have to load her—

No, she wouldn't. He realized it and kept climbing without a pause, skidding across the floor of the watchtower and up the second ladder into the gun turret, where he flung himself into the gunner's chair—*it should have been Liza's chair*—and wrenched the barrel around to the sky.

Dawn was just breaking, and the dragons came screaming out of the sun. There were six of them, moving in a pack, all glittering scales and claws and teeth as they descended to drop a volley of bombs on the towers. The first one struck the north tower and glanced off, and the blast only chipped the stone—then Petya brought the gun around and clipped the dragon smartly behind the ear, and it fell in a shower of its own blood. He raked its corpse with a quick burst of gunfire to be sure it stayed down, then turned his barrel to the skies again.

His throat was half-numb with cold. His wrists were bright red where he hadn't pulled his gloves down properly. He was only beginning to wake; he was only beginning to *think*. He didn't have the instincts to do this half-asleep, and where was the watchman who was supposed to be in this damn tower—

Liza was supposed to be in this tower.

The second dragon fell to someone else's shot, hitching like a wind-caught scarf and falling to earth in a tangled heap. It screamed on the ground, thrashing, smashing a cart with a powerful blow of its tail, and Petya emptied his magazine into the dragon's head. It seized up as the shots smashed its skull, forelimbs contorting, teeth bared in agony.

A dragon cried out over the fortress, and the other three answered in unison; they went screaming eastward, the long hair of their tails trailing bannerlike behind them. Soon—sooner than Petya might have expected—they were only shining specks in the distance.

He didn't take his hand off the trigger, although he knew that it would be useless to hold on to it. He couldn't shoot them from this distance. He couldn't *see* them from this distance.

Slowly, feeling every single one of his fingers protest, he prised his hand free and climbed down again. His hands wouldn't close entirely on the rungs of the ladder, and whether that was because they were cold or because he hadn't put the gloves on properly, he didn't know. Swearing softly to himself, he climbed down the second ladder and into the relative warmth of the tower, shutting the hatch behind him. He braced his back against the inner wall of the ladder well, paused to realign his gloves, and then continued down into the hall below.

Liza would be sorry to have missed it. *Everyone* had missed it, Liza in her sickbed and Wainwright confined to the ice closet and Jaworski off chasing after Kesha, Kesha being chased. Petya realized for the first time how very alone he was. He went to knock on his sister's door and found the druggist waiting there with Thin Ivan—with Utkin—who waved him on with scarcely a second glance.

"If you'll let me in to see her, I could measure—" he tried, hopefully.

"She's sleeping," the druggist replied. "So you really mean to design her a prosthesis? Can you even…?"

Petya hated the polite dismissal in his voice. "I think I can, yes," he said, schooling himself to humility. "I've never designed a prosthetic leg before, but I've built dozens of other mechanisms with the same kinds of joints. It's only a matter of calibrating springs so that they'll respond to the right pressures—when she walks, or puts her foot against the footrest of the gun mount—"

Utkin made a sound that was more a cough than a laugh, but too quiet to be identified easily as either one. "She's still insisting on going back into the towers, is she? Very irregular. Very irregular. We'll see what she says when she's not taking morphine."

"I think she'll say the same thing," said Petya. Indignation swelled beneath his breastbone, like a breath held too long. He wondered if this was what Liza felt like all the time—if it was, he understood why she drank. "The fortress is her life. She was always our father's child. I couldn't imagine her any other way, and I don't think she could, either." *I want to put her right again,* he thought. *I want to make her the same woman she was when I found her.*

After a long, uncomfortable silence, the druggist tugged at a loose button on his jacket. "You could measure her for her leg?" he prompted at last.

"Yes," said Petya, relieved. "That's exactly what I could do."

"Then fetch your measuring tape," said the druggist, and Petya scurried back to his room to do just that.

On returning to Liza's door, he pushed it open carefully so that the hinges wouldn't squeak. Liza lay still on her mattress, but she opened her eyes to slits when Petya stepped in. "I heard the bombs," she said by way of greeting, smiling in an easy, lax manner that he didn't recognize at all on her face. "Couldn't hear the shots. Did you kill any of them?"

"Two," he said, then sat on the edge of her bed to bare her good leg.

"You want the other one," she informed him.

"No, I want this one," Petya replied. He brought out his measuring tape and measured her shin, following the bone from the kneecap to the ankle joint. "I've got designs for your leg—"

"Show me," she said.

"I don't have them *here*."

"Then *bring* them and show me." With a light push to his shoulder, she pressed him away from his measurements. "That can wait. You can measure me when I'm asleep. Now I'm awake, and I want to see your designs."

Her narrow brown eyes were deeply shadowed, but there was an openness in them that Petya had never seen before. He couldn't have said what it was that made them foreign to him—he could have measured the diameter of her pupils, or gauged the slackness of the muscles around her eyes, but those quantities would tell him nothing at all about the effect of that unguarded expression.

"I'll bring you my designs," he said. "I'll be back in only a moment."

When he returned, though, Liza had drifted to sleep again. He took his measurements on her sleeping form, noted them in scrupulously tidy handwriting, then went to his room and shut himself in to work.

CHAPTER ELEVEN

By dawn on the third day, Kesha had devoured his last apple. He gnawed each to the core, then ate the cores as well; the seeds, he ground down between his teeth and swallowed. They did little to quell the ache in his belly, but he wasn't inclined to waste even an apple seed from a misplaced sense of delicacy.

His pursuers would know that he was following the rails eastward, and if they had any sense at all, they'd have boarded a train and stationed themselves in the next town. He'd given the next fortress a wide berth, never allowing himself within sight of their guns. More than once, he considered pelting down the grassy slope of the hill to catch a passing train, seizing the ladders on the side of the car and hauling himself up and into an empty coal car. At least if he could sling himself aboard, he would be out of the wind.

The scrubby pines had faded to a sweep of long, dead grasses, dotted here and there with winter-withered bushes. Over the low hills, the wind moved like a living thing, breathing and scenting and hunting. At night, when he huddled in his coat beneath a stand of firs, Kesha had felt its teeth seizing at his extremities.

As his stomach had grown tight and hollow, he had

begun to accept that he wouldn't make it as far as the next fortress before he had to surrender himself or drop.

Settling down within sight of the rails, his body flat to the ground to hide his shape, Kesha weighed his options. He had left a clear enough trail from the Tarasov keep to wherever the hell he was now; he had to assume that if he was being pursued, he would be found. His sister would hunt him to the ends of the earth, if she had to—if she hadn't been convinced of his guilt before, she would believe it with a nigh-religious conviction now that he'd run. He couldn't hazard his welfare on her mercy.

He could run down and swing himself onto a train, he thought, and he discounted the possibility immediately for the same reason he'd discounted it every other time. Even if he could manage to run alongside a train and catch the ladder without crushing himself (unlikely, given how weary and underfed he was by now), slipping onto a train could never hide his tracks well enough to make him *harder* to find rather than easier.

He could give himself up, of course. Kesha had no idea what that would do.

He glanced off to the west, where the hills slowly mounted skyward and cloaked themselves with pines. He thought he could make out a thin pillar of smoke, which suggested that a train was approaching. When he turned his head to the east, he saw only the hills and the sun stretching all the way to Siberia.

Misha's father had been sent to the work camps for sedition, or treason, or some other crime that was only holding unfashionable opinions. "I wonder whether he did anything at all," Kesha said to himself, dragging his body upright again. His tongue stuck to the roof of his mouth.

As he stood, the book in his pocket knocked against his thigh.

He paused, then drew the book out of his pocket and studied it with new eyes.

It was only a collection of military pamphlets from the last century, hard-bound in a blue canvas cover that had been stamped with the Starikovich crest. The first pamphlets were full of practical considerations of quartering troops with dragons, stratagems for defusing tensions among the soldiers, and recommendations on requisitioning sheep and chickens and zinc, but in the lattermost half, he'd seen... what had they been? Words, certainly. A soldier's practical Draconic vocabulary. Phonetic spellings and diagrams for how to write the characters out.

But why would soldiers have to write the characters out? What possible good would it have done them to be able to write individual words in the language of dragons, without any of the grammar to join them? They could scarcely put together an official missive, let alone a personal letter or a poem—

—unless they weren't writing works with grammar. If they weren't writing letters, but *signs*...

He leafed back to the final pamphlet in the volume, studying the characters drawn there. *Sheep*, said one. *Water*, said another. *Warning*, the third said; *North*, said a fourth.

Help.

He pressed his lips together, then slowly, deliberately, he began to walk through the shallow snow. His boots broke the crust and bared the dead grasses beneath; he tracked a single shape like a *Ze* across the ground, consulting the pamphlet when he'd finished to be sure that the shape matched the one in the book.

Ink, now. He didn't have any ink, and the stones here were all pale—except the dark rock along the railroad. Thrusting the book back in his pocket, he dashed down the hill; his legs were aching with the unaccustomed strain, but he could scarcely feel the burn in them any longer. He knelt alongside the tracks and spread his coat out like a fishing net, scraping in a load of heavy black stones. His hands were blue-touched at the tips, and the black rocks coated his palms thoroughly with a dark, gritty dust, but he could scarcely contain his laughter.

And why should he contain it? There was no one to hear it.

He bore his bundle of stones to the top of the hill and filled in the letter he'd tracked, laying out the stones evenly over the bare grass—when his supply ran out, he stumbled down again for another load, and then another, until he had blacked in a shape just like the one in the pamphlet.

It was the one thing his sister could not expect. The one escape that had a prayer of being real and final. *My one chance to find the answers that Misha asked me to find, before my life went to Hell*, he thought, half-bitter.

Then, curling his hands between his arms and his ribs to warm them, Kesha sat down to wait.

At first, Kesha thought they were a flock of birds—late to fly south, darting out of the rising sun and swooping against the pale blue of the sky. He didn't realize until they slipped behind a low cloudbank how high the dragons flew…and thus, how massive they must be.

They were heading west along the rail lines. Toward the fortress of the Abramovs, and beyond that, the Tarasov fortress. As he watched them go, he felt a tight, cold sensation in his viscera that had nothing at all to do with the snow; he had been raised to kill creatures just like these, and he had done so with a young boy's determination to excel. He couldn't help feeling the same old bloodlust at the sight of a flight of dragons winging toward his home, and that longing for a gun burned hot behind his eyes.

With a dust-blackened hand, he traced the circle of a poem atop the crust of the snow. *Help*, read the character in the center—help, which looked like a dragon twisting in agony. He remembered the heads slowly putrefying in the ice closet, their eyes clouding over and their skin peeling back.

What would he tell the dragons, if they saw his sign and came for him? If any survived who'd spoken Russian, they would be a century out of practice. But they would remember the name *Alexander Alexeyevich Orlov*. Perhaps they would even remember the man himself. They might look kindly on someone who came to them bearing his name.

To the west, the whistle of a train echoed over the hills. Aboard the train, the men in the engine would be pouring on coal; the men in the second car would be readying their heavy Nordenfelt gun, that endless whistle making them frantic as they loaded and fired. Even the conductor would probably be getting out a rifle, for all the good it would do. From his boyhood, Kesha had recited his father's admonitions more dutifully than he had ever said his prayers: *a rifle is nothing against a dragon*. A bullet from a rifle might penetrate a dragon's hide, yes, but if the first shot missed, there wouldn't be time for a second. *And what then?*

A flurry of shots, and then a blast that resounded like thunder.

So much for the train. So much for the brave men with their gun.

Kesha found that he was rocking, hands balled up in his coat pockets. If he'd had anything in his stomach, he thought he would have vomited; as it was, his stomach heaved and clenched, and he tasted bile.

It wasn't his affair any longer. Perhaps it never had been. Those were no more his people than the dragons were; he had severed his ties with them when he'd run from the fortress. To be theirs meant to be subject to their laws, under which he must necessarily die or be transported for his crimes. *What had Misha's father done?* wondered Kesha. *Had he done it knowing that it meant abjuring his family and his people?*

In the west, a column of black smoke rose where dragons had blown the train apart. It was in the Abramovs' territory. It was their affair. It wasn't his.

After something like an hour, when the sun hung low and yellow over the eastern plains, the dragons returned—closer to earth now, pale bellies flashing as they skimmed beneath the clouds. He raised his eyes to them, afraid to move lest they should know him for a Russian, and for the first time in years he said an earnest prayer under his breath.

Kesha heard a distant clash of high, thin voices, like sopranos vying in an *imbroglio*. Then the smallest of the dragons peeled off from the rest and dove, osprey-swift, with a scream that made Kesha grope at his waist for the gun he no longer carried. His blood grew cold at that uncanny shriek. He stumbled to his feet. His knees had locked from cold and ill-use; his back had cramped from hunching until he couldn't straighten. Doubled over, knees bent, Kesha lifted his chin until he could meet a pair of brown eyes like a horse's.

The dragon alighted on a weathered grey stone, drawing its long body up into a neat coil as though to preserve its warmth. It turned its head from one side to the other, then brought a surprisingly muscular forelimb up to scratch at the ruff of fur about its neck. When it seemed certain that Kesha was watching, it screamed once, long and high.

In the back of his mind, he could hear Starikovich keening the word for *mountain range,* and with a quiet thrill, he realized that the dragon was speaking to him. He raised his hands, slowly, then caught the dragon's gaze and shook his head. "I don't speak your language," he said, enunciating each syllable.

The dragon scratched again at its mane as though considering the problem anew. When it spoke a second time, although its voice was shrill, Kesha could recognize human phonemes—not in any order that he could decipher, of course, but even that barest trace of recognition gave him hope. "I don't speak that language, either," he answered in German. "German? *Français? Lingua latina?*"

Something shifted in the dragon's eyes. "*Salve, vir,*" it said, hissing on the sibilant and drawing out each vowel.

Latin. Kesha fought down a laugh. *I'm speaking to a dragon in Latin.* "What is your name?" he asked carefully. "How—*what* are you called?"

"Men call me Aysel. You wrote in the language of the dragons; you asked for help. My comrades believe that your letter was a..." The dragon tightened its claws meditatively on the stone, as though searching for vocabulary. "...ruse. However, I do not believe that you would speak to me in the Latin tongue if it were a ruse."

"I am called Innokentiy Vladimirovich Orlov," he answered. "I am running from...men are pursuing me. I want to escape them."

"A criminal?" Aysel made a sound like a snort. "We see many criminals along the road of iron. They do not wish to die in the east; thus, they die in the hills."

His heart hammered beneath his breastbone. If he didn't think quickly and speak well—and the dragon's Latin was infinitely superior to his own—then he, too, would die in the hills. *What did Misha's father say that made them deport him to the east?* "A criminal," agreed Kesha, "And an orator as well. I desire to establish peace between Russia and the dragons, and for my crimes they pursue me with fire and sword."

"With fire and sword!" laughed Aysel; its laugh was an awful sound, like the scream of a dying beast. "You may withhold your gestures of rhetoric, my little Cicero. I shall take you to the Voice, and you will be questioned—with neither fire nor sword." With that, the dragon uncoiled from the stone and climbed down, resting with its belly flat against the snow. When the dragon lay stretched upon the earth, shoulders bunched in anticipation of contact, its sheer bulk became apparent. Kesha was a tall man, but Aysel was at least five times as long as he was tall, and he couldn't have encircled its ribs with his arms. He had seen dead dragons many times throughout his youth, and he had even helped to drag the corpses out of the courtyard on occasion, but he had never apprehended the pure physical power of a dragon before this moment.

Only an hour ago, this dragon had helped to blow up a Russian train. He couldn't permit himself to forget that.

Aysel tossed its head, indicating its back with a long, equine jaw. "Sit, man. Hold my hair, or I will drop you."

Hunched over as he was, Kesha could scarcely sling a leg over the dragon's back. He fisted his hands in that long mane, and as he did, he felt its heat—where long hair met skin, it was uncomfortably hot, and the scales were so warm beneath his bare, frozen hands that he hissed at the contact. "Some of our scientists thought you were cold-blooded," he said in half-dazed Russian.

"What's that?" asked Aysel, and he remembered himself and reverted to Latin.

"You are warmest," he said. "Very warm."

"And you are *rudest*," replied Aysel sharply. "Your grammar depletes my patience. Sit, man. My charity is finite."

Beneath him, the ridges of Aysel's spine dug into his flesh. He gripped the mane tightly, until even his numb fingers could feel the bite of the hair where it twisted around them.

Under his thighs, the dragon's ribs expanded as though at an inhalation—and slowly, carefully, they rose into the chill air. At any other time, Kesha might have watched the ground drop away with an undisguised fascination; today, though, he was tired and cold, and Aysel was as warm as his landlady's ceramic oven beneath him. They cut through the sky like a boat through swift water, Aysel at the helm and Kesha no more than a passenger.

CHAPTER TWELVE

Liza woke when her little mantel clock chimed noon, and on waking, she sat upright in her bed. "Now," she said, as though saying it could make it true. "Now, Tarasov, you've got to pull yourself together."

She called out for the druggist, but he didn't reply; neither did Petya come when she shouted for him. "Fine," she said, and she dragged the druggist's chair close enough that she could use it as a crutch. Leaning heavily on the back of the chair, lifting it with every step to advance it across the rug, she crossed the room to her wardrobe and withdrew a hard-wearing pair of trousers and a pair of stockings. The chair was a doubly useful walking aid, since she could sit when her limbs felt weak and pull on her stocking and her boot there.

That finished, she stood and removed her nightgown. It was a gauzy thing, more to her mother's taste than her own, and she wasted several minutes in searching out the laces and clasps to release it. With every movement, she discovered new sore places at her ribs and shoulders—the broken bones, and the tender flesh over them. She'd have to be careful of her right arm if she wanted the collarbone to heal. A crutch wouldn't be sufficient to her needs, but she knew where her father had stowed the old wheeled chair that he'd never used. Her aunt had bought it for him when the gout started getting bad, like an insult wrapped in a peace offering.

She let the nightgown fall to the floor and drew a shirt over her shoulders instead, buttoning it one-handed. A right-handed woman would have had difficulty in buttoning her own shirt without a maid, with her collarbone broken on the right; Liza was left-handed, though, and she hadn't had a maid in years. She closed the shirt one-handed and pulled a robe over it, then her long coat over that.

Her brother had left designs on the bedside table, beside the little bottle of morphine and the half-full bottle of vodka. *Stop drinking, and stop gambling*, came Nastya's voice, echoing in Liza's memory as though Nastya were speaking at the far end of a long corridor. *They'll forgive you for being mannish, but they'll never forgive you for being your father.*

How many days had it been? She'd been injured not yesterday, nor the day before, but the evening before that—and on that morning, as they'd shared tea and marmalade in the telegraph office, Nastya had counseled her against vice. Against foolishness.

Liza swept the bottles into one hand and deposited them in her coat pocket. She would leave them in the kitchen when she passed it; if the drink weren't ready to hand, perhaps she would crave it less. "Now, the chair," she said aloud, and if her limbs still swung lax at either side, she liked the renewed strength in her voice. Fixing her hand under the backrest on the druggist's chair, she slowly made her way to the door and then out into the hall.

When she and her brothers had been children, their mother had curated their "library" with great care. It lay across the hall from the study, so that when she had finished her accounts and her latest novel, she could simply slip from one room to the next to pick up a new volume of Balzac. Liza and her brothers had been tutored there, in the leatherbound presence of Galen and Machiavelli and Avicenna and Sophocles, as though Herr Schulze had believed that a child could learn through mere proximity to great works. Kesha had often shut himself away in the room, after their mother's departure, and propped a chair just like the druggist's beneath the door handle to keep Liza from bothering him.

And after Kesha had abandoned the family, the library had fallen into disrepair. Liza had filled it with empty crates that would one day ship dragons' heads to Moscow; broken furniture and worn saddles had found their way into the room, awaiting only the return of the Tarasov fortunes to be restored to their former glory. It was a room for things too damaged or too useless to sell, but too valuable to burn.

She braced her good shoulder against the heavy door and forced it open. The hinges groaned in protest, but she pushed at the door until it stood fully ajar and then turned up the dimmer on the gaslamp.

In a house above ground, like her mother's house in Moscow, the wallpaper might have faded with sunlight and neglect. In this little tomb of a room, though, under a thin patina of dust, it was the same vivid green it had been in the days of Liza's childhood.

The wheeled chair lurked in a corner, beneath a threadbare sheet and a box of rusted bolts. She'd concealed it so that her father wouldn't have to look at it, never wondering whether it was folly or courage to refuse the chair when the pain nearly crippled him. Now she knew full well that it had been pride, and the same pride made her lift the bolts aside and whisk away the sheet.

Beneath it, the woven cane chair was almost entirely free of dust. A few moth carcasses lay on the seat, but she swept them away and lowered herself onto the cushion. She closed her hands on the armrests, hearing the cane protest after years of disuse.

How would she move, without someone to push her?

Liza let her hands fall to the wheels, which were sharp-edged as new cart wheels under her palms. "Push yourself, Tarasov," she said, and with a powerful push at the spokes, she urged those old wheels to turn. They groaned like the hinges—one more piece of unused metal; one more ancient tool, more rust than iron—and then slowly, slowly, she began to roll across the floor.

"Good," she said, as she passed the druggist's chair and then wheeled over the slight lip at the doorjamb. "Good. Now, to find Jaworski."

You can't find Jaworski, she remembered. *You sent him to hunt your brother.*

"Petya, then," she told herself. "And I'll send for Nastya, and see if anyone has a pig ready to slaughter."

Fastidious as Utkin and Polzin might be, Liza had to admit that they managed their evidence with a commendable efficiency. She found the cartload of guns laid out upon a clean sheet in her mother's office, each piece photographed and the photographs annotated. Leaving the revolvers and the hunting rifles upon the floor, Liza rolled the sheet over the carbines and muskets and the blunderbuss and set the bundle on her lap. She folded a notebook and pencil into a flap of the sheet, then knotted it so that they wouldn't fall free.

She would have to see if Petya could build a pair of saddlebags for the wheeled chair, or at the very least find a satchel to throw over the back. It was damnably difficult to carry anything when she needed both hands to move herself.

Very well. Her hands were sweat-slick and raw by now, and her shoulders burned from the exertion. At her breastbone, a kindling ache reminded her that she was meant to be keeping her arm immobile. "Very well," she said, and rolled herself out of the office and down the hall.

She had never paused to reflect, before, on how far the office was from the stairs, nor on how uneven the flagstones were in the mess hall—as her chair lurched and caught at the lip of each stone, though, she cursed her ancestors' architects in the most colorful language she knew. More than once, she nearly spilled her bundle of guns over the floor, and more than once she gathered them laboriously to her chest and wrapped them tightly before proceeding. If Petya couldn't build her a new leg, she vowed to herself that she would plane down every goddamn gap between the flagstones on her own hands and knees.

When she had nearly passed the final long table, Liza heard bootheels on the stone. She froze, trying to catch her breath; the prospect of discovery was at this point more potentially humiliating than the prospect of being stopped. For the Englishmen, her Englishmen, she could never permit herself to be seen in a state of weakness—if they had sawed her free of the gun that had crushed her leg, it was only what soldiers did for one another on the field of battle. A woman in her long coat, panting in an invalid's chair, could never be a comrade to them.

Their shadows fell across her own. It was only willful ignorance to imagine that she hadn't been seen.

"Mademoiselle Tarasov," came a soft voice, and invalid though she was, she raised her chin at the address and turned to stare down the soldier.

It was her grey-eyed boy, the one whom she had taken to plant a sign along the rails so many weeks ago—the freckled young man whom she had taken shooting, on the night when her father died. She hadn't yet learned his name. "What is it that you want?" she asked in ungainly French.

"I want to aid you, if you will permit," he said. "Where do you wish to go?"

"To the top of the stairs," she said, hating her own helplessness and his helpfulness in equal measure. "To the heart—to the *court*, damn it—"

"Good, then I shall carry you, when we reach the staircase."

She felt him tilt the chair gently back before he wheeled her to the stairs. Once they had reached the foot of them, he gestured for her to rise and gathered her in his arms. To his companion, he said something in quiet English that she couldn't comprehend—but he must have asked that the other man follow them with the chair, because he came after, the chair clattering as it struck each step. Liza clung to the bundle of guns until her soldier set her down again, this time in the cold of the courtyard.

Petya or his agents had thrown open the gates to let in cartloads of new stone. It was impossible to miss the scaffolding around the shattered silhouette of the tower, nor could she miss the shapes of workmen swarming busily over it. From this vantage, she could see how far she had fallen, as well as the great furrow that the gun had gouged in the earth.

She had been in the gunner's chair the whole way down; the pole on which it was mounted had absorbed the force of her fall and snapped in two. It had tipped her onto the ground just as the crazily canting gun had wheeled over her.

There was no immediacy to the memory. It might have happened to some other woman.

"Take me to the other side," she said. "Petya's sent for a pig. They'll be bringing it—oh, *damn*." She brought a hand up to her throbbing temple and tried a second time in French. "I wish to go to the wall close to the door. The big door. My brother will bring me a...an animal, a sausage animal..."

"*Porc?*" offered the grey-eyed soldier, to which she nodded. The cold air pricked at her eyes. "Why a pig?"

"So that I can shoot it." The second soldier laughed as though she'd told a fine joke, and he only laughed harder when she turned a look of ire on him.

At this her grey-eyed boy frowned and gestured her to sit. She obliged him warily, half-certain that he would refuse to take her where she wished to go once he had her in his power, but he only began to wheel her across the unyielding grass. Her wheels caught on dry stems and softer earth alike; she preferred the frozen ground to the slurry of mud and ice where the workers had been. "Must it be a pig?" asked the soldier. "Why not a bottle? And why so many guns?"

"The gun—the pieces make holes in the skin," she said, pinching her own sleeve as though it were loose-hanging skin to demonstrate. "The pieces, the pebbles..."

"*Balles?*" offered the second soldier, and then in surprisingly clear Russian, "Bullets?"

"Pellets, more than bullets," she replied, delighted at having made herself understood and half-aghast at her own delight. "Pellets. If I can find an animal with skin like ours, I can shoot it until I find which gun killed—"

The second soldier threw up his hands, though, and shook his head. "Russian only for guns," he said, enunciating each word carefully. He spoke again to his companion, consulting in that impenetrable English, and then told her solemnly, "Keep watch now."

As the two of them tightened their scarves about their throats and crunched back across the courtyard, Liza reminded herself that they were attempting to honor her by speaking to her in Russian. It felt no less patronizing for that.

From her seat near the gate, she watched a woman in a fur cap lead the pig that she'd requested. They strolled up the gravel path, the spotted pig trotting along with its nose close to the earth. After ten long, cold minutes, the woman drew near enough for Liza to make out her sharp features.

Nastya. Of course.

Liza thrust her hand into her coat pocket, where her gloved fingers brushed the neck of the vodka bottle. "Anastasia Ivanovna," she called, when Nastya halted in the lee of the fortress walls. "I have a present for you."

"Your brother said that we could keep the pig when you'd finished with it," Nastya replied. "And he paid the man who owned it."

"*Another* present," said Liza, and she withdrew the vodka and the morphine from her pocket. Nastya frowned at the sight of the bottles until a line sliced between her brows, but she crossed the space between them and took the vodka in her free hand.

"Am I here to share a drink with you, Elizaveta Vladimirovna?" she asked. Her voice was hard and cold as glass.

"Until you pull the cork from this bottle," said Liza, "I won't drink again." She opened her hand slowly, letting the weight of the bottle shift into Nastya's palm, and then rested her hands in her lap.

Nastya's expression didn't soften, precisely, at the gesture; that blade-thin line between her brows stood out as starkly as ever. She nodded as she tucked the bottle away, though, and she answered, "I'll hold you to it." That was better than a smile.

"Take the pig to the place where the wall meets the next tower," said Liza, pointing. "Tie him or leave him; I don't care."

"Why can't you shoot a bottle, if you have to shoot something?" asked Nastya, but she did as she was bidden and tugged the pig by his string to the corner of the courtyard.

Liza carefully unrolled her bundle of guns, setting them to one side. She selected a blunt carbine with a tag dangling from the trigger guard: *Sergei Afansyevich Zhukov*, it read. Seryozha, who'd insisted that the English had come to stir up a rebellion. She raised the gun, careful not to brace the butt of it against her injured shoulder, and sighted along the barrel toward the curious little pig.

"Because," she said, "I need something that bleeds."

CHAPTER THIRTEEN

The tracks stood empty; the two o'clock train wasn't due for nearly an hour. On the platform, Petya hesitated as the wind caught at his portfolio and made the fastening string tick against the cover. *I can't expect charity*, he reminded himself. He glanced from the tenements on one side of the tracks to the smoking chimneys on the other.

Along the railway clustered low buildings of soot-streaked timbers that housed the workingmen and their labors. Some of them Petya knew to avoid; in their youth, he and Kesha hadn't been permitted to visit the flophouses that huddled close along the railway, although of course Kesha had never listened to his father. There, he had listened to the laments of battered unionists from the cities and shared his books with miners' sons, and he had returned home with unanswerable questions about why God left such children in poverty.

For Petya, the most urgent questions had always concerned engines and mechanisms. Before the dragons had destroyed it, he had played in the old switch house some distance from the station, learning from the engineers how to shift the course of a train. After the switch house burned, though, Petya's free hours were devoted to the machinists' shop very near to the tracks, where a team of dour men prepared replacement parts and took in battered engines to be refitted. The shop had once been a favorite target for the dragons on their raids, and like the Tarasovs of old, the machinists had taken their business beneath the earth and shielded themselves with thick cement. During the day, the low smokestacks of the shop vented noxious fumes and thick smoke, staining the wood of nearby buildings with a faint patina of grey.

With a fortifying breath of chill air, Petya stepped down from the platform and onto the black stone around the rails. He crossed the tracks from the skeletal station to the maze of vents on the far side, where the yellowed grass lay damp and clear in a broad rectangle. All around it, the snow still crusted the ground, but atop the machinists' shop the earth was still uncomfortably warm and smelled faintly chemical.

At the entryway, he heaved open the heavy metal door and descended a narrow stone stair, flexing his gloved hand on the portfolio. "Lukin," he called at the foot of the staircase; the sound of hammers and hydraulics drowned him out, though, and he raised his voice. "Lukin, are you here?"

A grindstone stilled, and an old man put his work aside and pushed his spectacles up his nose. "Why, is it Pyotr Vladimirovich?" laughed Lukin. "We thought your days in the shop were over—look, everyone! It's little Petya come back to us! That must mean he wants something."

Over the laughter of the machinists, no one could hear Petya reply, "I *do* want something." Lukin must have marked how his lips shaped the words, though, because he stood from his work table and crossed the floor. With every step, he crushed metal shavings beneath his boots and kicked aside fragments of scrap.

"Well, boy," said Lukin, arms folded over his potbelly. He smacked his lips as though enjoying a sweet. "Well, well.

We've seen a damn lot of Englishmen around, but not a glimpse of you. What brings you to the shop?"

"I need parts," said Petya, "And although some are standard—bearings and bolts—some aren't in standard sizes, and others are entirely new—" He withdrew the portfolio from under his arm and unwound the string that fastened it shut, laying out his designs upon the nearest work table. He had drawn each part separately and to scale, carefully noting its dimensions; Lukin could not miss, though, that these parts in conjunction could only form a human leg and foot. "I can pay you to make the new dies and molds, and of course I'll pay you for the labor, but..."

"We all saw your sister," Lukin replied, and his expression gave nothing away. "When she came on the cart. They put a blanket over her legs, but everyone could see what had happened to her. Little Galya couldn't stop talking about it."

"Galya knows it's not a secret," answered Petya with a weak laugh. "It's never been a secret. Would I have come to you, and trusted you to make these parts for me, if I didn't want you to know what I was making?"

"You might've," said Lukin, but he was already tracing the bearing that would articulate foot and ankle. His fingertips were touched with grease and iron filings, and they marked the page where his index finger brushed it. "That's what they do, you know. They have us each make a piece of a thing, and never the entire artifact. If I didn't cross the tracks every day, who's to say I'd even know what a train looked like? It doesn't look like anything in *my* shop."

Petya's heart seized. "We're friends, aren't we?" he asked, and it came out so softly that he could scarcely hear it. "You were so kind to me, when I was younger. You were like an uncle to me."

"And I hope you'll remember that, when it comes time to divide the fortress between you and your sister." A trail of grease tracked the coil of a spring. "We've got long ears, in this town. We hear, for instance, that she's not the legal heir—and we think about who we'd like to see running the keep." At this, Lukin raised his eyes from the design, looking up at Petya over his spectacles with naked interest in every line of his face.

"You want *me* to run the keep," said Petya slowly. "You... you want me to take my sister's place."

"The way we see it," Lukin answered, "she's had a chance to show us what kind of woman she'll be—and she looks no better than your father, God rest his soul. The older people in this town look at you, and we say, 'There's the spitting image of Pyotr Alexandrovich. There's the man who can bring us back to the good years.'"

For a moment, Petya's heart beat in time with the rhythm of the hammers and the whine of the grindstones. Even with the vents overhead, the machinists' shop was oppressively hot and smelled of rust and oil. *Refuse him*, he thought. *It was never your place. It was never what you wanted.* His tongue stuck to the roof of his mouth, though, and he only licked his dry lips.

Before Petya could muster a reply, Lukin shook out the design sheet in a businesslike fashion and then folded it in half. "Well—I'll make your parts," he said. "And I'll even assemble them, if you like. But keep in mind, someday you'll have to pay back a good deal more than the cost of labor."

"I'll keep that in mind," Petya answered, and shook Lukin's hand.

He couldn't say why he paused on the point of turning to ascend the stairs. "Actually," he said, "I have another design, if you have the time to look at it. I can't get a model to work, and if you have any advice..."

"Let's have it, then. I'll make some copies and tinker with the design after my shift."

Petya unfastened his portfolio again and pulled out the design for the flying machine. "Thank you," he said, passing the drafts into Lukin's hands. They felt ancient, fragile, made of onionskin paper and hope.

When Lukin tucked the design away and turned back to his grindstone, Petya knew that it was time for him to leave. He took the steps at a quick clip and emerged into the cool late-autumn air, breathing hard as though he'd arisen from a drowning.

Crack! came the report of the gun, resounding from the inner walls of the fortress and issuing forth through the gates. A long pause followed—so long that Petya couldn't doubt his sister had kept her promise to remain in the chair—and then, as he was crunching up the gravel path to the hill, a second *crack!* of a different timbre.

He passed Nastya on her way out the gate. "She wants a second pig," she said, when they were close enough to speak. "Tell her you won't pay for one, Pyotr Vladimirovich. She needs to go back indoors before her fingers lock on those damnable guns."

"A second pig? What does she want with a second pig?"

"What did she want with the first pig?" scoffed Nastya. "To shoot it, of course. What does she ever want with a thing? This is only a new sport for her, and she'll tire of it if you take the toy from her."

"Did your sisters tire of their sports, when you took their toys?" Petya replied, lips twisting wryly. "I doubt they did."

"My sisters," said Nastya levelly, "knew when the time for play had ended."

"I'll talk to her," promised Petya, and he pressed her wrist—a narrow, bony wrist, he couldn't help noticing; Galina Ivanovna's wrists had been the same, when the two of them had danced together. "How are your sisters?"

"Well," said Nastya. If she were inclined to conceal the calculation in her eyes, it was visible nonetheless; when she spoke again, there was an edge to her voice. "They're ready to see the end of investigators from the city and Poles beating down our doors to take our guns, and being summoned to the keep like criminals to explain in a thousand different ways why they couldn't have killed your father. I know *I'm* tired of being called a murderess behind my back. You've buried your father, Tarasov. Put him to rest."

"That's why you want her to stop shooting things," said Petya, releasing her wrist and tucking his hands into his coat pockets. "Not because she's been hurt—because she's still as obsessed with our father as ever—"

"And that festers," Nastya agreed readily. "If she doesn't like the answer that she gets from shooting the pig, what next? Will she shoot men to see what *that* tells her? Will she dig up your father and wrest the secrets from his bones? He's a wound in her, Pyotr Vladimirovich, and a worse wound than her missing leg. We'll be at war in less than a year, if the word from the city is true. She could turn this town into an engine of war, but so long as she chases at his heels like a little spaniel…"

Here, she touched a heavy pocket on her coat—an unconscious gesture, thought Petya; he couldn't say what it imported. "I see what you mean. Or I think I do," he said.

For an instant, with the marbled grey of the clouds at her back, Nastya looked like a statue of a sybil. With her black coat framing her pale neck, her lips cold-white, she looked as though she would speak a prophecy. "Then see this: the men in this town will follow her, if they think she's worthy of their allegiance. But they won't follow her into your father's grave."

"I'll remember that," said Petya. For all his efforts at gravity, his throat tightened so that he squeaked awfully on the last word.

That squeak broke the spell, and Nastya's cheeks flushed red as she laughed. "Name of God, Petya! It's only advice!" Still laughing to herself, she continued on her way to the village, black coat and black hat and silken hair blowing loose in the breeze.

At the gate stood Utkin with his broomstick arms folded over his narrow chest. His icy eyes followed Liza as she conferred with the errand boy, taking the ammunition that he proffered and then sending him scurrying for powder. "I'm sorry," Petya said, and he began to twist the string fastener of his portfolio around one fingertip. "I know this is—"

"Irregular," Utkin agreed, raising one hand as though to wave away the apology. "It's terribly irregular. It's also a damn good idea." In her chair, Liza poured a clattering half-handful of balls into the barrel of an ancient gun. "You'll see in a moment—she's a very good shot, even with the older weapons, and between the two of us, I wouldn't even be sure of hitting the pig from that distance. Your Elizaveta Vladimirovna, though, hits a separate part of the animal with each gun, and she *records the pattern of the wounds*. It's terribly meticulous. Terribly orderly. Not the wounds, of course; they're a wreck. But she studies them well."

"And you aren't angry that she's taken your evidence?"

"Furious," Utkin replied. Petya could hear no trace of rancor in his voice. "I shall most probably file a complaint. And speaking of filing complaints, you might want to hear what your Lieutenant Wainwright was doing on the night of your father's murder."

Together, they watched Liza align the barrel of the gun. Utkin might not recognize how Liza favored her injured side, but Petya marked it well. Without her shoulder to brace the butt, she had to manage the recoil with her arm muscles alone, and the kick of these old rifles sent a shock from fingertip to heel. In her place, Petya was sure he'd have developed a flinch.

With a world-shattering crack and a plume of smoke, Liza fired. She grimaced as the force of it rocked her in her chair, but she put the gun aside and let the errand boy push her across the grass. "What was Wainwright doing?" asked Petya.

"He was sending a telegram to a particular address in Moscow," said Utkin, "with the stipulation that it be forwarded to St. Petersburg, and from thence to London. We suspect that the message was in English, of course—of course it would be; he's an Englishman—but we can't be sure. It's unlikely to be in Russian."

"Don't you speak English?" asked Petya. "I can speak a little, and when Jaworski comes back, he and Kesha are fluent—"

"What makes the matter difficult," said Utkin, "is that we can't say positively what language it is, because the message is ciphered. A cipher with a key, my colleague suspects, but certainly ciphered. As it should be, since the Moscow address belongs to a prominent British diplomat."

"Could you give me the message?" asked Petya. "My English could be better, but I'm good with puzzles."

"Inspector Polzin will have the message in our office," Utkin replied. He hadn't yet taken his eyes from Liza, who sat with her head bowed over her notebook and her unbound hair falling into her eyes. Every now and then, she brushed it back irritably and returned to her sketches.

She gestured the errand boy over again, indicating the pig; he turned it over obediently, baring the undamaged flank to the cool air.

Petya couldn't help seeing his father's body on the frozen earth, heavy and inert and soaked with blood.

He wondered what his sister saw as she prepared the next gun to fire.

CHAPTER FOURTEEN

Three hundred feet in the air, Kesha drifted out of sleep once more. He had bound his hands in the dragon's mane, lest he should slip off while he slumbered; now, he undid the knots and combed the tangled hair with his fingers. He hadn't the first idea how dragons groomed themselves, but he could at least do Aysel the courtesy of a human grooming.

They had tracked south along the Turkish-held half of the Volga, where ice had begun to form like thin glass sheeting in the shallows. A hundred or a hundred and fifty verst, he thought dimly, but he couldn't say how long he'd dozed on Aysel's back. They had passed over tranquil towns without even gun turrets on their walls—towns that hadn't feared dragons for over a hundred years, where the churches with their onion domes stood shoulder to shoulder with the minarets of mosques.

When Aysel began to descend at last, he sat straighter on its back. "Where are we?" he asked over the rush of the wind.

"Täteş," the dragon replied without turning its head. *Täteş, on the Volga,* he thought, *which the Russian maps still call Tetyushi.*

The town lay nestled among rolling hills, with horse-drawn carts plodding over the roads and chimneys smoking gently as housewives prepared the evening meal. Between the houses stood ramshackle fences of wood, with early-winter gardens between and chickens pecking hopefully for grain. It might have been any quiet neighborhood on the outskirts of Moscow. There was even an Orthodox church with its bell tolling three in the afternoon.

"Täteş," he said to himself, tasting the sound of the word. He could bear to call it that.

Aysel set them down in a field outside of the town, which Kesha thought might be growing beets. He let himself down, feeling Aysel's ribs draw in beneath his legs as he slid unsteadily to the earth. "My comrades will have told the Voice to expect you," said Aysel, with a catlike yawn that bared the roof of its mouth. "Still yourself, human. You will have caretakers soon enough."

Even as Aysel spoke, Kesha saw a pair of men crossing the fields from the town, making their way over the rows of low beet hillocks. They wore uniforms that Kesha could not identify, although he supposed that they were Ottoman; the necklines of their jackets made neat vees from their shoulders, and beneath those they wore white collared shirts that came nearly to their chins. On their heads were fur-lined caps, so very like the caps of Russian men—and indeed, Kesha might have passed men like them on the streets of Moscow or Kazan without a second glance. One had cheekbones like Madam Galiyeva's under his dark Kazakh eyes, and the other had a singularly Russian nose. They paused six paces from Aysel, saluting in unison and waiting for the dragon's bow.

The Kazakh soldier said something in the language of dragons, at which Aysel tilted its head thoughtfully before answering in kind. It spoke at some length, at times gesturing with claws or chin or tailtip—and for the first time, Kesha began to hear the structure of a language in that long, modulated scream. The vowels shifted and flowed between half-swallowed consonants; the rise and fall of pitch seemed to communicate meaning as well as feeling. Whatever Aysel said made the Kazakh soldier grin, and he was still smiling when he turned back to Kesha.

"We understand you've had trouble," he said. "You'll understand if we can't take your word for it. Not many in Russia know how to write signs that the dragons can read." *In Russia*, he said, as though he wasn't speaking easy Russian with only a trace of an accent.

"Aysel told me that I would be brought to the Voice," Kesha replied. "And if I could beg a bowl of broth and a crust of bread—"

"You'll eat what Söz sees fit to feed you," said the soldier with the Slavic nose. His accent marked him Tatar, although his Russian was very nearly as good as his comrade's. "I'm very sorry, but we would do the same for any stranger. Täteş is at war, you see."

"I thought there were laws against attacking Russia's borders," said Kesha, but he let the men take his arms and escort him along the row. The withered beet leaves rasped against his boots as he crossed the chilled earth. "I thought that the borders were locked in place until the first of February—"

"It only breaks the treaty if we occupy the land. And the dragons aren't interested in occupying land, are they?"

Glancing over his shoulder at Aysel, who sat watching him with its head cocked to one side, Kesha allowed, "I suppose not."

He followed docilely as they brought him through the town. He could smell baking bread or roasting meat when a woman opened her door to shake out a rug, and over all hung the warm, comforting smell of woodsmoke. As they approached the center of the town, they moved from well-beaten dirt tracks to paved roads, more humble than those of St. Petersburg but more neatly kept than the roads that converged on Petrovsky station. Although smoke rose in plumes from distant smokestacks, the factories themselves were hidden from view. Here, he thought, was a town that had been little touched by the coming of the steam engine or the rise of industry; here was a town to which the Volga brought nothing but water.

His custodians led him to an inn, with a common room on the lowest story and a narrow stair leading up to the next. The look of the place reminded him of the eighteenth-century coffee-houses that he had frequented when he'd first met Misha—a touch of the rustic *izba* in the steep roof, the rectangular windows with heavily ornamented wooden shutters. This building had been Russian, once, as had the rest of the town. Perhaps, in a few months, it would be again.

"Ah," said a woman's voice, and Kesha turned at it. At a table beside the entryway sat a woman of middling age, with a pot of tea and a sheaf of papers before her. She was trimly built, with deep-set eyes of a very pale brown and thin, thin lips, and despite her Ottoman uniform, she wore a matronly blue scarf over her hair. When she spoke, her Russian was slow but unaccented. "So this is our young writer of signs, is it? This is the man who requested a dragon's help."

"So I am, madame," said Kesha softly. "Are you the Voice? Are you...Söz?"

"You may call me Söz, if you wish, or you may call me the Voice. In Turkish or in Russian; it does not matter to me." She gestured to the seat across from her own, which was crossed with afternoon sunlight. "You look tired, cold, and hurt. Sit, and share tea with me. Tell me your name and your troubles."

Kesha lowered himself into the chair and let her pour him a cup of tea, which he took in both hands without waiting for a saucer. "My name is Innokentiy Vladimirovich Orlov," he said, before he raised the cup to his lips. The first swallow swelled the parched tissue of his throat, and he downed the second greedily. "I'm a political dissident—or that's what they called me when they arrested me. I believe that Russia must make peace with the dragons and atone for a hundred years of war." He let a bitter note creep into his voice. "For those crimes, they sentenced me to be transported to Siberia."

"Orlov," said Söz thoughtfully, circling the rim of her cup with the tip of one finger. "That name still has currency, in draconic circles. They still speak of Alexander Alexeyevich Orlov, who—"

"Who spoke before the College of War. He begged them to negotiate with the dragons, and he lost his life for taking their side."

"So you do know the name." Söz sipped at her tea, her eyes never leaving Kesha's.

Yes, thought Kesha. *And I know his daughter's name, and his great-grandson's. Perhaps that will be enough.* "I do," he said instead, "and I want nothing more than to honor his legacy."

Söz quirked her lips at the declaration. "His *legacy*. Tell me, what do the Orlovs say of Alexander Alexeyevich's *legacy* today?" He couldn't tell whether she emphasized *legacy* to mock him, or to familiarize herself with the taste of the word.

"My great-aunt keeps records," Kesha said. "In a house packed to the gills with documents and diaries, with hunting hounds pacing the floors." In the privacy of his heart, he thanked Misha for his interminable anecdotes; they would lend verisimilitude to his story. "Alexander Alexeyevich's daughter, though, wrote of his execution, and of the book-burning that followed after—she saved a dozen books from the flames, boarding them up in the walls of the Collegia—"

"Now part of the St. Petersburg Imperial University," Söz cut in, smiling thinly. "But doubtless you know that."

"I was studying in St. Petersburg when I came across the records," said Kesha. "The College is a library now. I couldn't help untacking the siding to see whether Klara

Alexandrovna was telling the truth. To think that anything had survived the burning…I'm a scholar, madame. I couldn't bear the thought of leaving those books behind."

"And from thence, to political dissidence? Quite a leap," said Söz. "Ibragimov, will you bring our guest some bread? He must be famished."

The soldier with the Russian nose saluted, then went to have quiet words with the innkeeper. Kesha's eyes followed him for a moment, and then he turned once more to Söz. She raised her slim, dark brows, folding her hands upon the table. "Go on when you are ready," she said.

Kesha looked up at the Kazakh soldier, who stood sentinel at Söz's shoulder. "If I may ask, some of your soldiers seemed to understand the Draconic language."

"The local dialect," Söz agreed. "It differs from the Anatolian or the Balkan, and the three are for the most part not mutually intelligible."

"Where did they learn it?"

Söz smiled thinly. "Some, from the dragons themselves. Others, like Orazbek," and the soldier inclined his head at his name, "I taught. Do you understand the languages of dragons, Monsieur Orlov?"

"Less well than I would like. So many books were burned, and so much was irrecoverably lost…in St. Petersburg, I wrote articles and essays," he said. "I tried my hand at publishing translations of the dragons' poems—I thought that it would be impossible for my people to kill the dragons, if only they could read their poetry again."

"Your people kill Russians for writing poetry, and many a Turkish soldier has died with poems to his sweetheart folded in his breast pocket. I fail to see why dragons should be any different." Indicating her papers and inkwell, she asked, "May I write down your testimony, Monsieur Orlov?"

"Testimony?" asked Kesha. He looked to the papers, but their neat rows of Arabic script defeated him. "Am I to be tried, then?"

Söz laughed, dipping her pen. "Ah, testimony was the wrong word, was it not? From the Latin *testificari*, to bear witness with an oath on one's manhood—no, you are not to be tried. I am the Voice, Monsieur Orlov, and words are my business; you of all people should know that a thing that goes unrecorded goes unremembered. I wish only to remember what you say." Although her expression held nothing but sympathy, the lines around her mouth relaxing and the soft folds of her blue babushka shadowing her brow, Kesha knew better than to accept her kindness on faith.

"Write whatever you like," he said eventually, finishing his tea. "I only wish I could read it."

"Few can," Söz replied. "Turkish flows poorly in Arabic script, and only somewhat better in Cyrillic. If you ask our linguists, they will tell you that the Arabic alphabet is on its way out. In Istanbul, some of my correspondents have begun to employ the Latin alphabet or the Greek."

The innkeeper brought a plate of flat bread to their table, with steam rising gently from the cracked crusts. A jar of preserves stood to one side of the plate—fig preserves, thought Kesha, by the color and the shape of the seeds—and a few slices of cold mutton lay on the other. "Eat," he said; his Tatar accent was stronger than the soldiers' had been, and Kesha thought that he must be a native of Täteş. "Söz will pay."

With a negligent gesture, Söz indicated that he should obey the innkeeper's instruction. "We'll resume your story when you are no longer ravenous. Do try to eat slowly, or you will make yourself sick."

"Along the railroad, I ate bark and grass," said Kesha as he spread a piece of bread thickly with preserves. "I expect that my stomach has shrunk to match my diet."

He scarcely tasted the first bite; he tasted only the acid of anticipation. The first mouthful went down badly, and he thought that he would vomit. He swallowed, though, and washed it down with another cup of astringent tea, and in a moment he was able to take a smaller bite. This time, he could appreciate the tang of the preserves. He chewed carefully before swallowing. "Unleavened bread," he remarked, as though to himself. Söz did not reply; she only perused her notes and then jotted down a new line in Russian. *The Old Man approaches the stage*, it read, which meant nothing at all to Kesha. But she'd written it in a language he could understand, and large enough that he could read it even upside down and across the table. She wanted him to see.

When he had finished a piece of bread and an equal quantity of meat, Kesha pushed his plate aside and folded his hands on the table. "I'm ready," he said, to which Söz nodded.

"Very well," she said. "My dragons report that they destroyed a train bound eastward. Was that your train?"

"It wasn't, although I heard the blast," Kesha replied. "I was being held in the keep two towns to the west of where Aysel found me."

"So you spoke with Aysel." *Scratch, scratch*, went Söz's pen on a clean sheet. "In what language?"

"In Latin," said Kesha. "As I said, I can't speak the language of the dragons, although I'm learning to read it. Aysel's Latin is very good."

"She is a very young dragon," said Söz. "The older ones remember your language, but she was raised to speak only mine among humans. You are lucky that she knew another. Tell me, then—how did you come to escape the Tarasov keep?"

At hearing his own name spoken in such a plain and knowing fashion, Kesha could scarcely restrain a shiver. "You know which families hold the fortresses, then."

"A general knows which commanders he will face in the field," answered Söz, and here she steepled her fingers with the pen nib spearing skyward. "You do your race a credit, Innokentiy Vladimirovich. You lie fluently and without scruple, and you know your history and your politics well enough to concoct a plausible story. I do genuinely believe, I must add, that you are a champion of the dragons, and that you imagine that their poetry might save them. This genuine belief is what makes you such a fluent liar. But it is my business to trace the flow of information, and word has already come from Kazan that a suspect in the murder of Vladimir Tarasov has escaped, and that his name is Innokentiy Vladimirovich Tarasov."

CHAPTER FIFTEEN

Liza's mother found her in the courtyard with the snow catching on the loose strands of her hair. Liza's cheeks were probably chill-red and her lips felt chapped from the wind, but she straightened in her chair like a queen at Yelena's approach. "Mother," she called genially. "We've made good progress today—"

When she spoke, Yelena's voice was cold and low and flat. "I can see you've made progress."

"And look, I haven't done myself an injury. My collarbone is fine, my ribs are fine," Liza replied, although they ached all along her side. The morphine was wearing off. *Good*, she thought. *Let it wear off*. "Petya, tell Mother that my ribs are fine."

It was Utkin, though, who crossed the snow-touched earth to lay a hand upon Yelena's arm. "She's been very careful," he said, in that clear and belling tone that Uncle Sasha used to take with panicked serving women. His voice, she thought, had a tone that spoke of years of comfortable command. "She lets herself be carried and pushed, like a good girl."

"She never lets the gun rest against her shoulder. She's very careful of her collar," put in Petya, and although she couldn't turn comfortably to look at him, Liza knew that he would be wearing that eternally gormless expression that he so often wore with their mother. "I don't like it any better than you do, Mother, but if she *will* get out of bed, then I'm glad she's taking such care."

Behind her black veil, Yelena's face was cold. She still wore her widow's bombazine gown, all black lace trim and ungainly princess-form cut and dyed pearl buttons holding it closed, but beyond the graveyard, it had no power to impress.

Liza laid the latest gun across her lap and crossed her gloved hands over it, palm against knuckles. Snowflakes tickled at her cheeks, and their coolness reminded her that she was damnably weary. "Tell me what you want, Mother," she said, praising God when her voice didn't crack.

"I've spoken to your father's lawyer."

"To disinherit me," said Liza sharply. "Let's be clear on what you want."

"To discover whether he had ever authorized a second will and testament," Yelena countered, nonplussed. "You might well have guessed that no such document exists, and so at present your brother remains the legal heir to your father's estate."

"And of course you'll convince him to name you his executor, even if he *did* murder our father—"

"That's for the inspector to decide," said Yelena.

Liza's hands closed over the long gun to stop them from shaking. Under her gloves, she was sure, her knuckles would be standing out whitely. "Even if he didn't murder our father," she replied, "he will never be innocent. He stole from us and he betrayed us, and it's my legal damn *right* to demand redress for that."

"It was your father's right. By now that business has passed, Liza, and you'd do well to let it lie."

When the errand boy ran up from the keep with a box of pellets, Liza beckoned him close and handed him the gun.

"Put these away," she said. "Keep the ones I've used separate from the ones I haven't. I'll need to finish the rest on a new pig."

Yelena glanced along the wall to the bloody heap in the corner. The pig was, even Liza had to admit, completely shattered. She'd blasted every corner of its hide with sprays of pellets and shot, until it scarcely resembled a living creature at all—until it had become only a kind of canvas on which she inscribed in words of blood, *My father was murdered thus.*

Yelena Sergeyevna Tarasova turned to study the corpse, and for the first time since she had arrived at the keep, she smiled.

Liza's lips cracked. She tasted blood. "You've been waiting for years to see my father dead," she said, and licked her lips clean. "You want to see this whole place razed, and me with it—"

"Liza." Yelena raised her eyes from the pig's corpse, her hands tucked neatly into her muff.

"What do you want Kesha to *do* with the fortress, Mother?"

The errand boy began to tuck the guns away in the snow-frosted sheet, rolling the used ones first in the fabric and then rolling the unused ones after them. *Good*, thought Liza. *At least one person around here can follow simple orders.*

Yelena turned away in a rustle of half-silken skirts. "Take her inside," she called over her shoulder. "Put her to bed, and see that she stays there. Take her away until she's rational."

"I'm completely rational," said Liza. "I'm rational enough to go to bed if I *feel* like going to bed, because I choose it. Boy—take me to the stairs. Petya, carry me down when we reach them."

The errand boy looked from sheet to chair, torn between the two orders. Utkin, though, took the handles at the back of the chair and began to push it over the uneven earth. Every stone, every deep patch of mud, sent a jolt through

Liza that she felt in her knitting bones. "You've done well today," Utkin said as they crossed the courtyard.

"Thank you," answered Liza, and she couldn't help feeling her heart give a lurch at the words. Her father would never praise her like that again. He had praised her precious little in life.

"I've put in an order with the machinists for your leg," said Petya gently. "It shouldn't be very long at all before we have a model that you can use."

A keen yearning lanced through her like the burn of an open wound; she longed to stand, to run, to climb—and even as that longing woke in her, she thought of Nastya's fingers closing on the bottle of vodka. *Not yet.* "If I put my weight on this stump, I'll only ruin it," said Liza, with a huff of breath. "I'll wait for it to heal before I try your new leg in the field."

They had by then reached the stairs, where Petya threw open the door and released a cloud of warm air that melted the snow on her coat and her hair. He bent to her, putting one arm under her shoulders and the other under her knee. "You don't know what good it does to hear you say that," he told her, with such a peculiar seriousness that she felt inclined to laugh at him.

"Keep your good," she replied, leaning against his broad chest as he gathered her close enough to carry. "Let me sleep."

Just before the door closed behind them, Liza heard the whistle of the three-o'clock train.

Liza opened her eyes on a stranger's face. The man was plump, bespectacled, and handsome in a faintly cherubic way, with blond hair that he wore lightly pomaded back. He wore a suit that must have been expensive, for although Liza knew nothing of city fashion, she knew enough to recognize costly wool when she saw it. "Are you the doctor?" she asked, drawing down the bedclothes about her waist. "Petya said they were bringing a doctor—"

"I'm Innokentiy Vladimirovich's lawyer, Mikhail Dmitrievich Orlov," said the man, entering Liza's room with a polite bow and extending a hand over her coverlet. "May I shake your hand?"

Liza glanced down at his hand, then up again at his face. His eyes were a pale shade of green, and they wrinkled at the corners when he smiled. His palm was warm against hers; he shook firmly, and with the handshake she felt a measure of the lingering, bone-deep ache go out of her.

"Your men tell me that you have a party out searching for my client, Lord Tarasov," he said. "I've been given to understand that they aren't particularly concerned with his safety."

"Jaworski will bring back the important parts of him," said Liza. She rose enough to tuck a thick bolster behind her back, then padded it liberally with pillows. Thus fortified, she met Orlov's eyes. He was a short man, and hers was a tall bed; they were level with one another when she sat upright. "Can you speak to your *client's* character?"

"Unless your brother is standing for a trial," Orlov replied, "I'll refrain from giving testimony. I didn't come to see you to convince you of his innocence. I came because I hope that I can expedite your efforts to find him, and I'm willing to provide whatever resources you require in order to ensure his safe return."

"*Expedite,*" she sneered, but he only folded his hands over his broad stomach and kept his eyes on hers. "Have you spoken with my father's lawyer? I should say my mother's; she has him in her pocket—"

"I came to the fortress as soon as I'd left the train," said Orlov. "You can imagine that I've had little opportunity to catch up with the local legal community."

Liza felt at her side for the near-empty morphine bottle,

knuckles knocking against the cool glass. "Such careful words," she said under her breath. "No wonder Kesha chose a boy like you—you can't be older than Petya, but you've already learned how to speak without saying anything at all."

Someone had brought the druggist's chair back, and now Orlov seated himself on the yielding cane seat. "Do you earnestly believe that your brother is guilty?" asked Orlov. His voice was very quiet; it resonated in the hollow places of her cheeks and her forehead and made her feel as though she were buzzing. (*That was the morphine, she told herself. It could only be the morphine.*)

The bitter taste lingered. She swallowed against it. *Eat something*, she told herself. *Something that isn't alcohol and morphine.* "I don't know whether he's guilty," said Liza at last. "I believe it. In my soul, I believe it—but I don't *know* it."

"And why do you believe he ran?"

"Because my damn fool of a brother told him to run—what do you hope I'll say, Orlov? Do you think you'll build a case against me by painting me as a vengeful bitch?" The bottle spun over and over her deft fingers, its length easily manipulable.

"I hope you'll tell me the truth," answered Orlov, with the most disarming of smiles. "You Tarasovs have been taught that you have so much to lose if you speak the truth. It discourages you from that honesty which I consider fundamental to your character."

At the base of Liza's sternum, a dull heat kindled. "Call me a liar again," she said, dangerously low. She gripped the morphine bottle until the lip ground against her palm.

"Not a liar," said Orlov. He didn't raise his hands to placate her, as Petya might have, nor did he school his expression to gravity. That infuriating smile played about his cherub's lips, and she wished to smash them into his teeth. "I don't think you're a liar, but I do believe that truth is malleable on the borders of Russia—and no one is as well-suited to the borders as a Tarasov."

Her lips drew back over her teeth. Her hand arced up from her side, flinging the morphine bottle sidelong like a skipping stone.

Orlov ducked the bottle, which shattered on the stone behind him. A sharp scent of opiate rose from the broken glass, and he wrinkled his nose at it. "We want the same thing, Lord Tarasov," he said when he rose. His voice was soft, but there was a quality of the implacable to it—a teacher's voice; a lawyer's voice. "We want just the same thing, and it's in my interests to *help* you to get what you want."

Liza raised her chin. If she could have, she'd have made the sickbed into a throne—but since this was all the audience chamber she could expect, she sat up straighter against the pillows that propped her up. "You can say we want the same thing, Orlov," she replied, "and you might even be right. We both want to find him, eh? That makes us allies, eh?"

He smiled. She hated that guileless little smile of his.

Her eyes held his, and she knew he saw the pain there. *Let him see*, she thought; *it means he sees my strength, too.* "But when we get to the base of it, you want Kesha alive, and I don't care if he's dead."

The mask never slipped. Orlov kept smiling, unperturbed as a summer day. "We can debate the logistics once we've found him."

CHAPTER SIXTEEN

When the westbound five-o'clock train stopped at Petrovsky Station, Jaworski was on it. He returned to the keep and commandeered a table for himself and his party of searchers, all of whom were ill-washed and chilled after days in the field. "Give us tea and brandy," he told the cook as he peeled his gloves free. "I don't care how you brew it, so long as it's hot. And some meat; I don't care if it spoils our supper. And tobacco for my pipe."

Turning to Petya, Jaworski raised his eyes from his hands. "Fetch us bacon and some kind of fruit," he said. "Search the prisoner for writing supplies, while you do it."

"Writing supplies? What's happened to my brother?" asked Petya, but Jaworski gave him such an aggrieved look that he pressed his lips together against a third question. "Yes, sir. Right away."

If it rankled to be treated as a servant, Petya could forgive the slight; Jaworski was a commissioned officer, and doubtless he had become re-accustomed to giving orders in the field. Forcing himself to think charitable thoughts, Petya turned on his heel at once and departed the mess hall.

Petya was by now intimately familiar with the route to the ice closet. From the mess hall, he had only to follow the narrow servingman's corridor toward the kitchen and take a left turning rather than a right, just as he had done on the night when he'd released Kesha to whatever hellish fate Jaworski had uncovered. Beyond that turning stood the narrow door, all impenetrable thick iron and wood, each edge nearly flush with the frame. When he and Liza had fought over where to keep their prisoners, he had insisted that they would suffocate in the ice closet. "There are mouse holes enough to let the air in," she'd told him, and when he had inspected the closet more carefully, he'd seen that it was so.

He and Liza had the only keys. She hadn't demanded his yet, presumably because there was no one left in the ice closet whom he might want to free.

At the left-hand turning, Petya halted at the echo of unfamiliar voices. They spoke in low, swift English, one voice muffled by the door, the other resounding plainly down the hall. Petya had to strain to catch their words.

"...couldn't possibly expect the old man to be safe in a place like this," came the clear voice. "And what else could we do? We've no business—"

"Lower your voice," said the muffled voice, and although it spoke through a layer of iron and wood—and in English, at that—Petya knew it to be Wainwright's.

After a few unintelligible words, though, the other man remarked, "I can't hear a word you're saying. Could you repeat that, sir?"

Petya heard Wainwright sigh. "Word mustn't be permitted to get out about the old man. I know your Russian is less than perfect—"

"Abysmal, I believe you mean."

"Abysmal, then. Abysmal as it may be, you *must* sound out the sympathies of the townspeople. There will be factions, and none more pronounced than among the tradesmen. Pay careful attention to what people say near the station, in particular. It's no secret how long they've resented the old man."

"The human heart always resents a tyrant," mused Wainwright's interlocutor. "And naturally some would show their appreciation for an assassin, if he could paint himself as a hero—"

"Go practice your Russian with Andrews, and then speak to me of heroes and assassins," said Wainwright, laughing. In that laugh, Petya suddenly heard the man who'd put on a sardonic look and then leaned in the doorway of the gearshaft, blocking out the light. Deep in his belly, anger tightened like a fist.

Their conversation was by now concluding. He couldn't permit himself to act upon what he'd heard. If either man saw the rage upon his face or felt it rising from him like heat, he would lose his chance to learn anything more. He raised himself to the balls of his feet and padded quietly down the corridor. Only when he could no longer hear their voices did he stride down the hall again, letting his bootheels ring out on the stone floor.

He met Liza's favorite, the grey-eyed young soldier, at the turning. On meeting him, Petya dipped his head respectfully. "Hello," he said in Russian, to which the other man replied with only a hesitant smile. His pale, soft cheeks were freckled over, and the skin under his eyes was unlined. *He can't be more than nineteen*, thought Petya as they passed one another by. *And it doesn't matter how old he is. He helped to murder my father, and now he'll make whatever use he can of it.*

"I've come to fetch some bacon," he called at the door, and Wainwright (ever the gracious host) replied, "Excellent. Do come in."

The iron bolt on the door clanked as Petya slid it back, but by now he'd oiled the hinges well enough to keep them from groaning. "Was your friend here to feed you?" he asked as he found a hunk of meat for the cook. "I was meant to have your food in an hour…"

"Elliot was only updating me on the status of the mission," answered Wainwright. "Your sister favors him, and far be it from me to ignore her favor. He'll be my liaison until my name is cleared."

"Elliot," tried Petya. "Could you write the name in Cyrillic to help me sound it out?"

"I don't have anything to write with," said Wainwright. He gestured to the metal shelving, though, where he traced the letters Ельот beside a set of uneven smears. "Does that help?"

"Elliot," Petya repeated, although his eyes were fixed on the smeared shapes beside the letters. A circle, he thought, with pictures inside it. "Elliot—I'll remember."

In the thickening silence between them, the rage in Petya's stomach slowly came unclenched.

Wainwright hesitated before speaking again, twisting his hands in the fur-lined ends of his sleeves. Petya was struck then by how diminished he was. Wainwright looked rake-thin and sallow in the faint lamplight, like a mannequin made of straw and ill-fitting castoff clothes. He looked nothing like a murderer, with his pelisse hanging loosely from his shoulders. "If you could tutor him in Russian, I'm sure he'd thank you for the lesson," said Wainwright at last. "He's a capable boy, and very eager to please."

"I don't have any real skill in teaching," answered Petya. He took down a few jars of cherry preserves and tucked the cool glass under his arm. He couldn't bear to bring Jaworski apples, after sending Kesha away with only two apples to line his pockets. "I'll do all I can, though. If nothing else, I'm sure Liza would like to hear him speak it."

"How is she? Is she recovering?" The question was quiet, but an earnest little light shone in Wainwright's eyes as he asked it.

"She's Liza. She's recovering less well than she pretends, but far better than you or I would in her place. I can't ask more than that."

Wainwright raised one hand as though he meant to touch Petya's shoulder in sympathy. Petya drew away, though, and

Wainwright dropped his hand at once. "Go with God, Pyotr Vladimirovich," he said.

Petya bolted the ice closet's door behind him, then locked it.

He left the bacon with the cook and returned to the mess hall. There, he dropped the jars of preserves on the table, and they went rolling across the polished surface to Jaworski's hands. "What did you find out about writing?" Jaworski asked, taking up one jar and twisting open the lid to plunge his spoon into the red flesh.

"They seemed to have been writing in the condensation on the shelves," offered Petya. "Or at least, something had been written there before; I could see the grease where it had been swiped away. They had nothing else in the room. But that's not important—"

"Yes, yes, your brother," said Jaworski. Taking a folded leaf of paper from his breast pocket, he passed it across the table and gestured for Petya to unfold it. "His trail went cold east of the Abramov fortress. We could find nothing but this sign—at least as long as you are tall, and written in black stones from along the rails."

Petya unfolded the paper, noting the sinuous shape drawn in pencil. It looked like no letter in any alphabet he knew. Whether it was Arabic or Chinese or no language at all, he couldn't have said. But Utkin and Polzin had found a book on speaking to dragons among Kesha's belongings, and Petya wondered if he could find this shape in its pages. "You've copied this exactly?" he asked. "You couldn't have mistaken it?"

"He copied it exactly," broke in one of the watchmen, who had received the first plate of bacon. "Made us stand in the snow for ten minutes while he was getting it right."

"You'd have been standing in the snow regardless of what I'd been doing," said Jaworski. "And that's another thing—the dragons blew the rails east of here."

"We got a telegram from the Abramovs about it, earlier today," answered Petya. "But you don't seem to have been delayed in returning—"

"They hit the eastbound train; the westbound line was relatively intact. I can't think why they would've done that, if they meant to disrupt trade—everyone knows that nothing goes east but workers and mail—but I'm straying from our subject. To your brother." The cook offered a cup of tea, which Jaworski gladly took. He drank it without cream or jam, as though its tart heat alone sustained him. "It's my surmise that he was taken shortly after the dragons destroyed the train. Whether the dragons ate him or rescued him, I couldn't say, but the time of the explosion aligns too neatly with the last fresh signs on his trail. In short, I'm saying that he's as good as vanished into thin air."

For a moment, Petya sat and let Jaworski's story wash over him. He knew, dimly, that he ought to feel something at what he had heard, but no matter how he probed at his heart, he could find nothing resembling fraternal feeling. Where he had expected grief or fear for his brother's safety, he found only the queer ache of absence. *I've never been without him*, he thought. *All my life, he's been my brother; we've shared a bed since I was small. Even those three years apart—* "He'll be halfway across Turkey by now," said Petya, because he couldn't imagine that Kesha had vanished entirely from the earth.

"Then you think your brother is colluding with the Turks," said Jaworski softly. In his eyes there was a look of curiosity carefully shuttered. It was the look that an engineer wore as he worked on a puzzle, permitting himself no hope of easy answers. "Do you believe that the Englishman has anything to do with this?"

"I *don't* believe he's colluding with the Turks," Petya replied, "and I never shall. But I could believe that Wainwright taught him to write the symbol—to summon the dragons?—after all that he said about serving in Turkey...and after what I just heard in the ice closet..."

Having served Jaworski's men, the cook brought Petya a

cup of tea as well, and he spooned in marmalade and stirred the mixture. Jaworski sat with his teacup pressed against his bottom lip, waiting for Petya to go on.

"They were talking about the 'old man,' and saying that it wasn't a secret how the people resented him. And they mentioned that there would be factions...I really didn't hear very much," admitted Petya. "They were speaking in English, faster than I could follow. But Wainwright *laughed* when the other man mentioned assassins—Elliot. The other man's name is Elliot."

Jaworski's cup came to rest on the table with a cool porcelain clink. "You believe the old man is your father, then, and that they were sharing news about his murder. A common enough pastime, in a town where a prominent man has been killed."

"You had to hear it," said Petya, although he couldn't raise his eyes from the swirling scraps of orange peel in his teacup. "The way he laughed—it was as though he didn't care one bit about my father's death. I've never heard a man *laugh* like that at a murder, even if I've heard men gossip about deaths. This was different, Jaworski. I know that you don't believe Wainwright is the murderer—"

"It doesn't matter what I believe," Jaworski cut in. "Tell your inspectors what you heard, and let them decide how to use that information; that's their job. My job is to man your sister's watchtowers, and I can't do that properly until I've had a smoke and a few hours of sleep."

At the mention of Liza, Petya fell silent. "She's much better," he said, after a moment of watching Jaworski devour fat slabs of bacon and wash them down with more tea. "She's so much more lucid than she was when she sent you away. She found Father's old chair, and she let the boy take her around the courtyard. Inspector Utkin let her test the guns they'd collected, and he seemed really pleased at what they found...it would do your heart good to visit her. She's nearly herself again."

"She's a rare woman, Liza. A rare woman. I wonder what sort of creature she would have been, in a different life." With his empty teacup, Jaworski toasted their absent comrade, and Petya brought his cup up to clink against it.

"You two ought to marry," said Petya. "I know she's willful, and mannish, but—"

"No." Jaworski said the word simply, flatly; it was no rolling knell over the mess hall table, and yet there was a final quality to it nonetheless. "Your sister and I discussed this. We're not inclined to marry."

"I think you'd do her good," answered Petya. "She listens to you. She makes everyone else listen to her, even when she's in the wrong, but she *listened* to Father—and she listens to you."

Jaworski rubbed at his temples; the light of the gaslamps washed the grey strands there the same ruddy color as the rest of his hair. "I haven't slept enough to listen to you wooing me for your sister," he said. "I'll sleep now and keep watch when I wake. As to Liza, the matter is closed. Devote your energy to finding your father's murderer, if you want to give your sister peace. She'll thank you more for that than for arranging her marriage."

Petya's heart sank at the reproof, but he rose to his feet with Jaworski and shook his hand across the table. "Sleep well, Captain," he said. "When you wake, I'll tell you what the inspectors think about what I heard." Petya withdrew his hand and put it in his trouser pocket, where he felt the slim slip of paper with the Englishman's ciphered message on it.

As Jaworski turned to go, Petya felt a faint but perceptible thrill of inspiration. He withdrew the paper, studying once more the row of orderly, unintelligible characters.

WWR TZS GCS CP BJZF BFOWO JPFF CJ.

If it were in English, might the first words be *the old man*? And, knowing the first words, might he not be able to discover the key to the cipher?

Taking out his pencil, he began to scratch letters and sums over the paper. He didn't notice the watchmen as they dispersed, nor did he notice how his tea grew cold at his elbow.

CHAPTER SEVENTEEN

Kesha froze in his seat, fingertips still plucking at the edge of a piece of flatbread. "If you know who I am already," he said, "then you only asked for my story to learn how I would lie."

"It was an interesting lie," said Söz, shrugging. "You chose to approach me not as an operative of the imperial government, but as a person interested in dragons. Perhaps as a person who had some sympathy for them and some understanding of their cause. It was not the sort of choice that I would have made, but it was an effective choice nonetheless—and I kept listening, Innokentiy Vladimirovich, because I have some use for a liar who makes effective choices that I would not have made." She smiled a faint, obscure little smile and steepled her fingers again. "If he can counterfeit the accents of St. Petersburg, as you do, so much the better for me."

Kesha slowly, carefully permitted himself to relax, and he tore the burnt edge from the bread and brought it to his lips. *If she has use for me, then I'm not immediately destined for death; that's something.* "Why do you need a Russian liar?" he asked. "I've done nothing that might make me trustworthy in your eyes."

"You are a wanted man, which gives you no incentive to return to your native country," Söz replied. "Such men, I have found, are less likely to turn their coats again, once they have been turned a first time. Since you have run from your family, you cannot return easily to their bosom. You can read a little Draconic, which I understand is forbidden knowledge in the cities of the west. Since you choose a political radical as your pose, I must suspect that you have some sympathy for the position, which suspicion your studies only confirm. I cannot trust you, but neither can you trust anyone else, and this makes you useful."

It was politic to pause to consider the implicit offer, and Kesha knew enough to be politic. He finished his burnt crust and studied the tea-stained white cloth upon the table, attempting to summon the reluctance of a man who had been asked to betray his country. It was appropriate to show reluctance, for even bad men were often patriots; could a good man be anything less? "I would require a guarantee of safety," said Kesha at last.

"You would have it. If you required compensation, I would be authorized to compensate you, as well. At first, with room and board; after continued, successful service, with something more substantial."

Söz raised her dark brows, and Kesha noticed anew how deeply set her eyes were. The skin about the lids was thin and creased and dark as a bruise. "The only compensation that I require is the chance to work with the dragons and to learn their language," he said. "You of all people should know that information is a currency, and I'm nothing if I'm poor in mind." He drew in a breath to still his rattled nerves, watching Söz dip her pen in her inkwell and bring the tip to hover over the paper. "I was in earnest when I said that I wanted to restore Alexander Alexeyevich Orlov's name, although he isn't a relation. His great-grandson is my friend—my only friend in the world, perhaps. If I can do nothing else, and help no one else...I want very much to help him."

He wondered what Söz heard in his voice; he wondered whether she thought his desperation real or feigned. Whatever it was she observed, she scribed a careful note in a language that he couldn't read.

"Very well," she said, and she gestured for another pot of tea. "Then let us conduct our business. For information, it is customary to trade information. Tell me all you can of the people in the Tarasov keep. I am particularly interested in the English."

"I couldn't tell you very much about them," said Kesha. "I know that my sister resented them; she summoned me and my brother home because she didn't care to see our keep overrun with foreigners. Almost as soon as I arrived, my father was murdered—" let Söz decide for herself whether he had done it "—and she had me brought to the keep and shut in the ice closet. I only had a chance to meet one of the Englishmen, but he was a very decent fellow named Peter Wainwright."

Something shifted in her expression at that name, but what that fleeting emotion had been, he couldn't have said. In an instant she was composed again. "Go on," she said.

"What more can I say? We spoke about literature, mostly, and history. He told me of his fondness for Shakespeare and Pushkin, and nothing more than that. It passed the hours in the ice closet, but it's of little political import."

"Then he was imprisoned with you?" asked Söz carefully. "He is not at his liberty."

"He was, but I suspect he's innocent of my father's murder. It's only a matter of time before the evidence of the inspectors exonerates him." At this, Söz drew out a well-marked sheet of paper and scrawled a short note in impenetrable Arabic letters.

When their tea arrived, with a little ceramic pot of honey accompanying it, Söz pulled the innkeeper down to say something in his ear. He went in turn to the guards to huddle with them behind the counter, where they commenced a frantic whispering that Kesha could not fail to observe. *That's something she didn't know*, he thought. *That's something she can use.*

Then Söz was turning back to him with a faint, ironic smile and asking, "Tell me about your family. You say that your sister resented the coming of the English. Does her word carry weight in the fortress?"

"Her word is law—it has been since she was a child," said Kesha. "She was the oldest of us, my father's favorite, and he encouraged her in learning to command the keep. I can only imagine that she became more high-handed after I left; she was heir in all but legal title…my brother said that she and Father dismissed most of the servants and over half the garrison in the months after I left. They hadn't the money to keep them on, and the men got suspicious when their pay kept getting delayed. It had been delayed more than once in the past, but never this long or this badly." When Söz made to pour him tea, he accepted and mixed in a generous scoop of honey.

"Your brother, though, is not the heir," guessed Söz. "You take jam with your tea, no? Is that not the Russian custom?"

"On Turkish soil, I'll take honey," answered Kesha. "Pyotr Vladimirovich is not the legal heir, no. My sister told me that I still had the title to the family holdings."

"If she knew it," said Söz, "then he wished her to know it so that her resentment for you would burn all the hotter. It is a common tactic for manipulating one's inferiors: to prefer an undeserving vassal, all the while praising the deserving one, and thereby to direct the deserving vassal's ire toward her rival rather than her patron."

"That sounds like our father," said Kesha wryly. The honey was heavy-tasting and dark, incomparably sweet, with none of the tartness of marmalade or pineapple compote. It struck him viscerally, as it hadn't when flying over mosques and onion domes, that he was truly in another country.

"Your brother, then. Tell me more about him—he is the youngest, is he not?"

"And an engineer, or he soon will be," said Kesha. "He came to stay with me in St. Petersburg to study mechanics, and he designs all manner of things: steam engines, boilers, flying machines without gasbags—the whole gamut of engines, really."

This time, Kesha caught what had changed about Söz's expression. It was not so much a flicker of movement as a brief moment of stillness. Her lips neither pressed together nor parted, and her next blink came a fraction too late on the heels of the last. She held herself in abeyance, anticipating some further response and retreating from whatever it might make her feel. "A common subject for study, when your people are attempting to bridge the continent by rail. Has he any influence among your engine companies?"

Had he any? Kesha realized that he hadn't the first idea how Petya's studies translated to influence. "Only through our mother," he decided. "Our grandfather is one of the directors for the Imperial Rail Company's Moscow branch, and our mother is his favorite daughter. If she wanted him to fund the development of my brother's designs, I'm fairly certain that he would."

Söz put down her pen with a satisfied nod. "If you were to go to Moscow, would you be recognized as your grandfather's grandson?"

"I doubt it," said Kesha. "My father had charge of us, when my mother left. After our childhood, we seldom visited, and we spent most of our visits in the company of the family. We weren't faces about the town—and certainly no one would recognize me with a beard."

"Very good," said Söz, with a sharp little smile. "Then, since you have given me information, I shall give you a task."

"What sort of task is it?" asked Kesha. "In Moscow, or so your questions suggest. It will require me to pretend to be a man from St. Petersburg—"

"Not necessarily a man from St. Petersburg. Ryazan might do, as well, so long as you do not sound like a man from Moscow or the borders. You have learned to cultivate a good western accent, and it will serve you well in this work." Söz shuffled through her papers and withdrew one written in neat rows of Cyrillic characters. She passed it across the table, and Kesha took it and perused it. "Examine this document as though you are an actor who is learning his part. Your task will be to lie fluently and inventively, based upon the particulars that we have outlined."

Yazikovich, read the document. "Son of the Tongue," said Kesha, aloud.

"Son of Shame, in Turkish." The little light in Söz's eyes suggested that she had intended the name to carry both meanings.

Kesha had to smile at the pun. "A fitting agent for the Voice, then. Fluent in French and English; married; despises shellfish...is this pertinent?"

"It is a question of verisimilitude," said Söz, although she raised her brows in faint amusement. "The question is not whether it is pertinent for Yazikovich to despise shellfish, but whether he will seem more a person than a fabrication if he has foibles unrelated to the task. When Yazikovich visits his contact in Moscow to deliver the news that we have prepared, he will be expected to speak particular codes and to remember particular cues, but he will also be expected to be a person utterly different from Innokentiy Vladimirovich Tarasov."

Tell your contact, as though casually, "Peace, Kent!" The quotation was written in English, and Kesha marked it and committed it to memory. *He will answer, just as casually, "Come not between a dragon and his wrath." By these signals he will know to trust you, and you will know that he relies upon you to deliver true tidings of the political status of the border country.*

"These are spies' watchwords," he said. "Will you make me a spy for the Turks?"

"Only a spy's agent," said Söz. "You will learn no more than you know already of English politicking, and thus you will espy nothing. You will serve only to deliver information, and no more."

"And what will the consequences be for Russia, if I deliver this information? What good will it do you?"

Söz only raised her brows and smoothed the line of her scarf. "You are the Son of Shame, Keshka." She used the harsher diminutive easily, without even a pause to recall it to mind. "What right have you to know the consequences of your actions? What right have you to paint your name across the canvas of state? You are right to say that information is currency, but this currency, I will not give you."

"Then I'm to enter this conversation blindly. Without knowing whether I've accomplished your aims or foiled them."

"It is the choice that you must make," agreed Söz. "If you cannot bear the choice, then my Tatars can simply take you up the Volga under a flag of truce. I do not imagine that the Russians will look unkindly on us—Turk or Tatar though we may be—if we return to them a patricide."

With bread and tea in his belly, Kesha considered the decision before him. Perhaps it made him a bad man, that the prospect of being a traitor gnawed less at his conscience than the prospect of never knowing whether he had been a successful traitor. He felt in that moment an acute awareness of the pawn's dilemma as it crossed the board, incapable of retreat or redirection. *Liza will kill me if I return, whether or not I'm guilty*, he thought. *And if I don't return, if I lie as fluently as Söz might wish, how many others might die?*

The thin curl of steam rising from his teacup recalled the plume of smoke from the blasted train, cutting thick and black across the morning sky. He remembered the crack of gunfire as though it had come from a lifetime ago. *How many others will certainly die, if I can't make peace between Russia and the dragons?*

"I'll take your offer," said Kesha at last. "Blind or sighted, it makes no difference. Whatever you'll have me say, you'd have someone else say in my stead if I refused. I'll be your tongue, and I'll speak as you direct me. But you must promise to let me speak to the dragons."

"That, I will permit. I will use you, Keshka, but I will not use you up." She folded her hands upon the table. "I will not set you against anything that you profess to love—and you bear little love, I think, for Russia, but much for the dragons."

"And for my brother and sister." Söz raised her brows again at that, but she did nothing to stop him from continuing. "Can you promise me that what I do won't put them in danger? That I won't be the instrument of their destruction?"

"I cannot promise that no harm will come to them," said Söz, after a moment's consideration, "but I can promise that I do not have their harm immediately in mind. The Russian borders are fixed in place for the next three months, and much as I might wish to aggrieve the Russians, it does not do to bring all of Europe down on my head. Will that satisfy your fears?"

She hadn't answered him—and both of them *knew* that she hadn't answered him. There was something mutually revelatory in their pact to maintain the delusion. "It satisfies me," said Kesha. "What news will I give your contact in Moscow?"

Söz's English was nearly as flawless as her Russian; only the faintest sibilance on the S gave her away. "Only this: *The old man dies in the last act of the play.*"

Söz was as good as her word, and Kesha was given a cramped little room on the upper story of the inn. The ceiling of the room sloped so sharply that Kesha could only stand upright near the door and the washstand. The bed lay tucked into the angle between ceiling and floor. A narrow window let in the afternoon sunlight, but its glass panes marginally diminished the chill.

Kesha closed the door behind him and sat on the edge of the bed. The thin upper mattress gave like wool, and beneath it, he heard the rustle of straw. As he took off his shoes and lay down, Kesha drew in what felt like his first full breath in days. The linen sheets smelled of soap and herbs. He pulled the quilted coverlet over himself, and with his former enemies to guard his rest, he fell into a deep and dreamless sleep.

He woke to find that night had fallen. In his stomach, the now-familiar pangs of hunger warred with the need to relieve himself. Kesha went to the washstand feeling like nothing so much as a hollow tube for nutriment, and when he had attended to the more pressing of his body's demands, he ventured downstairs to seek out supper.

At the head of the stair stood a heavyset man who nodded as Kesha passed. *My watchman*, he thought. *It would have been foolish for Söz not to set a guard on me.*

Laughter rose through the floorboards and echoed up the narrow stairwell, which told him that the hour was not yet late. Indeed, in the common room, he found every low couch occupied and every table full. At some, working men smoked together in relative silence, and at others, soldiers joked and elbowed each other as they downed cups of steaming tea. He smelled tobacco on the air, mint, meat cooked almost to burning; he heard at least two languages and recognized neither of them. Amid the merrymakers sat Söz at her table, papers spread before her and inkwell close at hand—a small island of order in an ocean of sound.

Unwilling to resume the day's interview, Kesha scanned the room for the soldier who'd known the language of dragons. Orazbek, with his Kazakh eyes and easy laugh; at the memory of that laugh, Kesha found him.

Orazbek and his companion had shed their uniforms

and donned high-cut jackets in the local style, but even so, the set of their shoulders marked them as military men. The people of Täteş seemed to see it, too. Civilians left them as wide a berth as they did the men in uniform. When Orazbek's laughter broke above the low rumble of conversation, old men glanced over and then muttered darkly into their tea. *Täteş is at war*, the soldier called Ibragimov had told him, but the people here knew well who had brought the war to their town.

Kesha crossed to Orazbek's table, very conscious of how his own height and the low level of the table made him loom over the two soldiers. "May I join you?" he asked.

"If it isn't Söz's Russian liar," observed Orazbek in easy Russian, with a grin that softened any malice in his words. He shuffled over to make room on the couch, and his comrade shifted with him. "Shall we call you Tarasov, or Orlov? Which name have you chosen tonight?"

"Tarasov," Kesha replied. "And your friend?"

"This is Selim Kaya, but you must call him 'chorbadzhi' now. He just got word today."

"My rank," clarified Selim, who was an older man with threads of grey in his dark hair. He looked quietly mortified at the introduction. "In Russian, I believe you would say 'colonel.'"

"Congratulations on your promotion," said Kesha. "Is this your celebration, then? I apologize for intruding."

"No celebration. My previous commander suffered a terrible accident, and I was next in line for his command. There is nothing to celebrate in the death of a man one respected." Although Selim did not meet Kesha's eyes, there was a trace of grief in his voice that Kesha did not think was feigned.

Orazbek pushed the teapot across the table along with a tarnished silver teacup. "So, Tarasov the liar. You want to learn about dragons, do you? You want to learn their language, their poetry."

Kesha poured himself a cup of mint tea, letting the subject be changed. "And you speak the language. Why did you want to learn it?"

"At first, only because it was a language." Orazbek dipped a bit of bread in a bowl of buttered beans, then took a bite. "But the more I learned, the more I found myself stealing across the rye fields to hear what the dragons had to say. The old dragons have good stories, and most of them don't translate. They used to be nomads, herders, warriors—like my father's people, before the reforms. They have so many words for raids, sheep, travel. They have different words for traveling toward something and running away from something, another for wandering aimlessly and another for seeking without finding. You have to use a dozen words in Turkish to say the same thing. But when I hear their stories in their own words, they remind me of the kind my father used to tell me when I was small. The Kazakhs in the cities are starting to forget how their people used to live, but the older dragons remember, and sometimes it feels like meeting my ancestors."

"Is that how you want to live? A nomadic life?" asked Kesha.

Orazbek laughed softly and leaned back, hands on his knees. "I like trains and running water too much for that. My mother told me when she sent me to university, 'Learn something that will keep you in the city. Become a doctor, an engineer.' But all the same, I don't think a people should forget where they came from."

Kesha toasted with his teacup, remembering his own Cossack ancestors and wondering what stories his family had forgotten. "Did you? Become a doctor, that is?"

"No, my mother and I had different dreams. Myself, I wanted to be a statesman one day," answered Orazbek, a touch wryly. "I learned French, Russian, and German. I wanted to be representative in Parliament, a diplomat, a voice for the people...no, if I'm honest, I wanted the Sultan to name me a paşa so that I could rub shoulders with the grandest men on three continents. But then I was conscripted, and that was that."

Selim, who had clearly heard this tale before, replied, "You have already earned your commission. One day, you will distinguish yourself in the field. Many paşas were once soldiers."

"Most came from rich Turkish families, though. They never had to distinguish themselves in the service; they only had to keep from disgracing themselves too badly. No, the only way to rise from nothing is to have the right friends—or to do something so impossible that it could only have been done by Allah's hand."

"I would not discount your friends just yet," said Selim, raising his eyebrows and glancing in Söz's direction.

"No, no," laughed Orazbek. "She might speak my name into the right ears, it's true. But some favors come at too high a cost."

CHAPTER EIGHTEEN

The knock came at nine o'clock at night, when Liza was finishing a bowl of strong pork broth. "It's Orlov," said a man's voice, not yet familiar. "I understand that you're probably not entertaining at this hour—"

"Come in," said Liza irritably. "What do you want?"

"Your brother had mentioned that you were awake, and so I thought I might attempt to catch you in a better frame of mind." Mikhail Dmitrievich Orlov hesitated before Liza's armchair, asking, "May I take a seat?"

"Sit," she said. She put her broth aside. "Speak."

If it ruffled him to be commanded like a dog, he concealed his ire. "I have a proposition for you, which I believe will be agreeable to us both. On the condition that you guarantee me Kesha's safety—"

"You call him Kesha now." Orlov folded his hands at the observation, but he didn't attempt to deny or downplay it. "Trying to make me think of him as a friend instead of a legal rival, are you?"

"That's actually my offer," he answered.

At this, Liza tilted her head. It didn't quite bring the man into focus, but it did remind her forcefully of how her collar ached from the day's exertions. *A drop of morphine*, she thought. *A little glass of vodka to dull the pain.* "Go on," she said.

"If you guarantee me your brother's safety, I will take you on as my client and represent your interests in acquiring legal title to your family's property," said Orlov. "Moreover, I will help you to open a civil suit against him for every last kopeck that he stole from you, all those years ago."

"Petya said that he didn't spend the money," said Liza, half to herself. "He said our brother had shown him ledgers to prove it. I didn't believe it. Any man can make a ledger. Father taught me that. Any money I can't carry isn't real." *Not that it stopped us from asking for credit.*

"I'm not inclined to believe it, either. Your brother didn't know Kesha when he first came to St. Petersburg. He spent money on coffee and opium and expensive Chinese pottery, put rubles into beggars' bowls and collection tins at church—as though he hadn't the first idea of how to spend such wealth, try as he might to waste it. He wasn't at all cut out to be a hedonist."

At Orlov's faint, wry smirk, Liza found herself smiling in turn. "Our Kesha was never a prodigal. Whatever his sins, he didn't know how to waste money. Not even a taste for gambling."

"Quite the poor specimen of martial nobility," remarked Orlov. "And not at all inclined to take over the holdings here. We've a standing agreement to share a townhouse with a library in St. Petersburg. It would be disagreeable in the extreme for him to be tied down to a dismal fortress halfway to Siberia."

"You," Liza said deliberately, "are trying to get me to like you."

"I am," Orlov said, with a laugh that made blushing apples of his round, plump cheeks. It was a less offensive laugh than she had expected.

"It's working. You'd take my case for no payment but my brother's life?"

"I would, and I think we'd have some luck in making

that case. Even if you aren't the legal heir, your cause isn't hopeless. Your father's will excludes your mother from all properties and movables not already in her permission, and now our only concern is to keep your brother from naming her the executor of his estate. You may be certain that he'll listen to my counsel in this matter."

Liza shifted at the itch in her side where the bandages bunched together, bringing one hand absently to scratch it. Orlov scarcely blinked at the display. "You're assuming that he's innocent."

"Of the murder? I suppose I am, but it makes no difference in either case. If he transfers the estate to you, it scarcely matters whether he does so from a jail cell or from the Tsar's palace." He met her gaze and held it. "If he is guilty, though, you'll have to excuse me for declining to bring the civil suit against him."

"That sounds fair." Liza offered her hand, and Orlov reached across the gap between bed and chair to take it. "Put it in writing. My mother will insist that I'm in no state to be making agreements, let alone agreements that would cheat her of my father's estate. It'll need witnesses."

"You'll have a document and witnesses to our contract," said Orlov, releasing her hand with a tenderness for which she could not account. "I want the best for you and for your family. You have my word on that."

"Keep saying such pretty things, and my brother will try to marry us. Petya," she clarified when he frowned. "Not Kesha. Petya keeps trying to marry me off. If you can put in a clause about stopping him from making matches, I'd be grateful."

With a conspiratorial smile, Orlov replied, "My aunt has the same fascination with making matches for me. She'd have me married to the most illustrious legal partnership, the most accomplished young woman, the most attractive carriage with the best-bred horses…I really have begun to suspect that she doesn't trust my judgment."

"You do keep company with my brother. I'm not inclined to trust your judgment, either."

"My aunt adores your brother. She likes him quite a bit better than she likes me."

Liza smirked and took up her bowl of broth again. "No accounting for taste."

"From the smell of it, there's no taste at all in that broth. Shall I slip you something more substantial? Meat, or some sort of pie?"

Liza considered the bowl, then considered Orlov's pale and smiling eyes. "I hope you aren't this transparent in the courtroom," she said at length. "Even I can see that's a bribe. Very well. Give me meat."

"I'll give you more than meat," said Orlov. "I'll help you reclaim your liberty and your dignity. No one else in the keep will promise you that—and whatever you might think, that promise is the farthest thing from a bribe."

Liza brought the bowl to her mouth and drained the last of the tepid liquid. "Perhaps that's so," she said. "But after I've reclaimed my dignity, you'll be in St. Petersburg, and I'll have to keep my dignity on my own."

Orlov smiled at her as though she weren't in a nightdress, as though she weren't drinking broth straight from the bowl, and said, "I can think of no one who'd do it better than you."

"I don't *care* what you think I ought to do, Mother. I'm eating my morning meal with my men, and then I'm going out and shooting another pig."

"Are they your men, then, Lizochka?" Yelena leaned down to tuck a lock of Liza's hair into her bun, and Liza barely kept herself from twisting back that too-familiar hand. "I doubt they'd agree."

"Is there a problem, Madame Tarasova?" came Orlov's

voice from down the hall. Both Yelena and Liza turned to face him, and Yelena lowered her hand at once. Orlov was dressed ostentatiously for an informal breakfast. He wore a well-cut black waistcoat and a fine silk cravat in white, which together made him appear less plump and diminutive than he really was. "I believe Elizaveta Vladimirovna had meant to attend breakfast with you to advertise her goodwill for your son," he cut in smoothly. "After the shock of her father's murder, she wasn't at all in her senses, and her excellent recovery has made it absolutely clear to her that she was too hasty in accusing her brother of wrongdoing. The family must stand together, in such a troubled time as this—and since you are the heart of the household, Madame Tarasova, she knows that she must first make her amends with you."

A muscle fluttered and twitched at the corner of Yelena's smile, but smile she did. "Of course you're right," she said. "There's no cause for bad blood."

Liza felt the chair rock slightly as Orlov gripped the back of it. "Your blood and my blood are the *same blood*, Mother," she said under her breath. "Don't forget that, when you go making accusations."

Orlov's fingertip brushed her shoulder as though to quell her. "Shall we go to break our fasts?" he suggested brightly as he began to wheel Liza down the hall. "This business will seem much more palatable after a bit of kasha with cream."

"I believe this business is concluded," said Yelena. It was like agreement.

"That was good work," murmured Liza, when Yelena had taken her seat at one end of the table. Orlov sat beside her, gesturing the errand boy over to bring them kasha and sausage, and then poured out tea for her.

"Yelena Sergeyevna is a woman of society—have you any coffee?" asked Orlov, searching the table. "No matter. She responds better to maneuvering and indirect speech than to plain speech, even though she knows it to be manipulative. To speak to her in that way is to indicate that you believe her to be *worth* manipulating, which is nearly the highest form of flattery that she can imagine."

Liza thought of her mother's grim, blank face, of the smile as alien as a scar upon it, and she couldn't bring herself to believe it. "And she responds to that—even knowing it's manipulation."

"She probably wouldn't respond to it if she *didn't* know." Orlov gave a faint sigh and took a teapot from its place beside the samovar, pouring himself a measure of black tea and taking a sugar cube to go with it. "I shall miss coffee while I'm here," he said wistfully, putting the cube between his teeth and drinking a careful sip of tea.

His plain, ridiculous disappointment tugged at Liza's heart, and she had to smirk at him with his pathetic little teacup and his dissolving sugar cube. "We can send for coffee," Liza answered, laying her hand beside his on the table. It was better than reaching for her own tea; she knew that her shaking hands would rattle the cup on the saucer. "Nastya probably has a few sacks tucked away in her cellar, anyway. She's as well-stocked as they come."

Orlov must have seen her trembling, though, because he brushed his knuckles against hers and asked in a low voice, "Was the morphine you threw at me your last?"

"I've decided to stop drinking," answered Liza, more loudly than she would have liked. Certainly more loudly than was polite. "Not a drop. Not even morphine."

"You've lost a leg, my lord," said Orlov. "No one would accuse you of weakness for taking morphine."

"It's not a matter of *weakness*—it's a matter of respect." She drew in a breath that sent an ache all along her ribs. "Before my accident, someone told me, 'They'll forgive you for being mannish, but they'll never forgive you for being your father.' If I'm to hold the Tarasov keep, I can't do it with my head clouded—I can't *think* with the morphine in me. It's worse than drink. I've killed dragons with a bottle of vodka in me, and never wasted a shot. The morphine…" She reached for her tea and raised the cup from the saucer. The surface of the tea shimmered faintly in her grip, but at least the porcelain didn't clink.

"I see," was all he said. Their kasha and sausages arrived. When Orlov gestured with his fork and knife as though he meant to cut them for her, she waved him away. It was hard going to saw the sausages into manageable pieces when her shoulder jostled her broken clavicle at every stroke, but true to his word, Orlov granted her the dignity of serving herself.

"You might do well to recommit yourself to God," said Orlov, after a moment of quiet eating.

Liza swallowed a mouthful of sausage and washed it down with unsweetened tea. "I'm not sure I believe in God," she replied.

"I'm quite certain that I *don't*," Orlov answered. "It's as useful to swear on a tea service as to swear on a god. But if you mean to reform—publicly—to gain your men's respect, you'd do well to tie that reformation to an instrument that they understand. You needn't alter your beliefs, but you might let yourself be seen at services once a week. It would also excuse your disinterest in marriage, in the eyes of your men."

"It doesn't need *excusing*."

"Not to you," he agreed, "but you've said yourself that your brother keeps trying to make matches for you. An unmarried woman without a father is a legal threat, as an unmarried woman *with* a father can never be. She answers to no one. Her virginity allows her to retain her sovereignty. Men will seek to marry you off because it makes you *safer*, and the worst part is, they won't even realize that they're doing it."

Liza looked down the long table to where Yelena and Petya sat sharing poached peaches and cream. The errand boy plucked Petya by the sleeve and leaned down to speak to him, and he glanced over the table to meet Liza's searching eyes. His expression was unreadable, complex, and laced with something halfway between guilt and longing. "I suppose," she said reluctantly. "This is how you'll earn me my liberty, is it? You'll teach me to be as political as my mother?"

"I'll teach you to be as political as your father," answered Orlov, as Petya rose from his seat and went to the door.

"You've never met my father."

The hardness in her voice barely ruffled Orlov. He cleaned his hands on his napkin, absurdly urban and unabashed about it. "I've met you, and I've met your brothers. I've had a day to walk through your town and speak with the people. I'll never know your father, but a man such as that leaves his mark on those around him—and as a political man, I must teach myself how to read such marks."

"And you'll make a political man of me, will you?"

Whatever Misha might have said in reply, however, he stifled as Petya swept across the room with a long box in his arms.

CHAPTER NINETEEN

Liza studied the leg for a moment, extending a hand to trace the joints. "I didn't think you'd have it finished this soon," she said, gripping the ankle and lifting the leg into her lap. "It's heavy."

"Its girders are steel. Steel is denser than bone," said Petya. As she tested the springs at the ankle and the ball of the foot, pressing the sole against her palm and rolling heel to toe over her hand, he felt suddenly and irrationally convinced that she would despise it. When he had brought her poetry and watercolor paintings as a child, she'd never had time for them. *Show them to someone who cares for art*, she used to scoff. Now, with the well-oiled springs compressed under the steady pressure of her hand, he wondered whether she had any eye at all for the smooth lines of the foot or the brushed-steel simplicity of the ankle. She slipped her other palm into the cup where the remains of her lower leg would go, frowning at what she saw.

"It's a good design," she said after some consideration, "but it'll put too much weight on the stump. If you could put a hoop around here—" and she hiked up her skirt to indicate the flesh below her knee "—and a joint at the knee, with another hoop just above it, my whole leg would be bearing the weight, and not just the injured part. I could wear it sooner."

"It would shift and chafe you," said Petya. "I could pad the hoops, but you might have to wear it over your clothes to keep them from snagging on the hinges—" At the mention of clothes, she whisked her petticoats over her legs again, and the rustle of fabric made him go still and quiet.

"I'd planned to wear it over my clothes," she said, with a peculiar, steely note to her voice that he remembered from a dozen foiled childish schemes. "I'm not interested in pretending that I have two legs. So long as I can run and climb again, I don't care how it looks."

"I designed it to let you run and climb," said Petya tightly.

"And that's what this does. The foot moves like a real foot. I don't know how you made it catch on tiptoe and then release—"

"There's a set of gears built into the ball of the foot." He turned the leg to show it to her, taking a watchmaker's screwdriver from his pocket and undoing the plates over the top of the foot to reveal the mechanisms underneath. "Look here—this is a sort of pawl for the ratcheting mechanism, but when you flex the—"

At the first hint of explanation, though, Liza only laughed and pushed the leg away. "Tell that to your friends at the machine shop," she said. "It works. That's all I know and all I care to know. I want to *use* this thing by the time my collar heals—another month at the least, they tell me. A month and a half, maybe."

"You'll wait a whole month?" He exchanged a glance with Misha, who only shrugged as though it was none of his affair. "I'm glad to hear it, but it's not at all like you to wait for a month...."

"When I was small, I fell from a scaffold and broke my leg." Liza brought her tea to her lips again, then held the cup out for Misha to refill. He obliged her readily, filling her cup to the brim. "You were only a baby then. You wouldn't remember. But I tried to run on that leg only a week after I broke it—and I ruined it. Uncle Sasha had to break it again and reset it so that it would heal straight, and do you know what he said? 'God almighty,' he said. 'A soldier would never struggle like this.' A good soldier would know better than to ruin himself for war."

"Was it the…"

"Same leg," said Liza. "God didn't want me to have a left leg, I suppose." She glanced at Misha as though the two of them shared some impenetrable secret, and then looked back to Petya.

"I'll have the modifications finished in a month, easily." He tucked the leg back into the box, more discomfited by her easy compliance than he had ever been by her disapproval. Heaving the box under his arm again, he cast about for some other topic of conversation. "I should tell you—I overheard—"

"Utkin told me," replied Liza. "I'll make Elliot wheel me around the courtyard. That should keep him close. Might even make him my adjutant."

"Make him trust you," said Petya, and at this, she nodded. "Was that your idea, or Utkin's?"

"It was *mine*," she snapped. "Name of God, Petya, what must you think of me, if you don't think I can have ideas of my own?"

"You have excellent ideas!" he said, raising his hand between them—as though he expected her to strike him, he realized an instant after he'd done it. "But your ideas are… well, they're military. I just didn't think you'd…I didn't think it would occur to you, to flirt with him to distract him."

"I'm not suggesting I *flirt* with him, I'm suggesting making him tend to an injured comrade," said Liza, teeth clenched. "If you want to stop putting your foot in it, think of me as a man, and that should clear up all of those damn stupid ideas about *flirtation*."

"Elliot won't think of you as a man," said Misha, low and light. "If a woman came to your brother and asked for his help, and asked him to stay near her in preference to every other man, wouldn't he suspect her of flirtation? And wouldn't he be right to suspect it, nine times of ten? At least one time of a hundred, he'd be right to suspect even if it *were* a man—"

"You oughtn't to speak of such things at the breakfast table," said Petya, with a glance down the table at where their mother was finishing her peaches. "It's not decent. She'll hear."

"Nothing I say will be decent in that woman's ears," said Liza, as though the comment had been hers rather than Misha's. "Go back to make excuses to her, if you like—and let me manage Elliot in my own way."

Misha inclined his head toward the box then, and Liza turned to him as though expecting a cue. Whatever his gaze suggested that she do, though, she was blind to such subtle prompting, and in the end she only put down her tea with a clack of cup on saucer. "Damn it all," she muttered.

"Thank him," prompted Misha.

At that, Liza fisted her hand in her skirt. "Thank him for what? For making a coquette of me at my own damn table—"

"For making you a leg, and for making it well, although he didn't have to."

"It's his damn fault I *need* a new leg," she said under her breath, but he could see the hectic flush fading from her cheeks. He wondered idly whether she thought he hadn't heard it. "Thank you, Petya. It's a good leg. When you've fixed the top of it, I'll be happy to use it."

She gives praise just like our father, thought Petya, and he turned to go. For the second that it took to pace to the entryway, he considered excusing himself to his mother— but by then he was halfway out, and whatever offense he might do her was already done. He could do nothing but go on, out of the mess hall and out of the fortress, into the crisp air of morning.

By this hour, the workingmen had already trooped off to the mines and the machine shop, and the children were at their studies or their labors. At the stroke of nine o'clock, the streets were mostly occupied with women running household errands with scarves over their hair and coats lined with heavy fur.

Petya knew that he ought to go at once to the machine shop—indeed, he was still carrying Liza's new leg—but his sister's tepid displays of gratitude made him loiter despite the cool air. From the baker on the main street he bought a palm-sized tart, which he ate to warm himself as he walked. He had left without donning his coat or his gloves, and his hands felt thick and numb as he paced between shops. Inside the shops, though, the pot-bellied stoves radiated warmth and inspired him to linger.

The old watchmaker's shop had been emptied of clocks and filled anew with eyeglasses, and there he bought a packet of tiny screws and chatted with the optometrist about grinding lenses. "I'm thinking of going into the glazier's trade, between the two of us," said the optometrist, a second-generation German by the name of Beutel. "There's more call here for good windows than for good spectacles. The poorest are still using waxed paper and shutters." It delighted Petya in the most private parts of his heart that Beutel thought him concerned with the living situation of the poorest. It recalled to mind Lukin's intimations that, should Petya wish to take his father's place, he would find men enough to back his claim.

"Have you come to pick up the latest shipment of ammunition?" asked Kostya the munitions dealer, who brought out his father's ceramic samovar to make Petya some tea. "I've heard such things about the goings-on at the fortress—such things, and still months before the Tsar comes to bless the rails!"

"You're fishing, Konstantin Bogdanovich," laughed Petya. "There's nothing to hear but that my sister's recovering."

"And your brother's lawyer has come all the way from St. Petersburg—"

"Nothing has come of it yet. My brother's lawyer and my sister have struck up a very congenial friendship, and no one is more surprised at it than I am."

"Not even your mother? She's been nosing about among the legal types, and I heard from Vova that she means to disinherit our Liza! He has it on very good authority that she won't stop pressing until she's sure that Liza won't see a single kopeck. Such a scandal!"

"You're terribly well-informed, for an arms trader," said Petya, finishing the weak tea and putting the cup on the counter beside an old musketoon on a stand. "How is it that Jaworski let you keep all of your weapons? He went about collecting every single gun in the town, or so he and Liza said—"

"Because at that hour, no fewer than three men were with me in this very room, all of us playing cards, and we all swore on the Holy Scriptures that the guns had stayed right where they were. Not many men can swear like that, but the Polish fellow went all up and down the town asking my friends to confirm my story, and when the fourth man had sworn to it on the Holy Scriptures, he had to admit that it wasn't his place to take away my livelihood on such a slim chance of guilt. I'll say this, Petya: I've done a brisk business since then! God rest your father, of course. So many of the hunters come to me for a gun these days. Only to rent, of course, at a negligible price, until they can have their old guns back. I'll tell you, old Kostya will be a wealthy man! To say nothing of your sister's purchases. She had the errand boy running back and forth all yesterday, to the keep and to the shop and back again. Some of those old pellets, I'd thought I'd never be able to shift, but she sent the boy down and bought them all up. No, if I were to guess, I'd say it was that Anastasia Vasilevskaya who murdered the old man, may he rest in Abraham's bosom—"

The bell over the door rang once. Both Petya and Kostya looked up. On catching their eyes, though, Galina Ivanovna Vasilevskaya ducked out again with a fierce blush. Guilt washed over Petya at being recognized, and more than that, at being so nearly caught gossiping about her sister.

"Go on," said Kostya, nudging Petya's arm. "She was your sweetheart, wasn't she?"

"Four years ago!" said Petya. He shied from the touch and took up his parcel again. "We were only children then. What does she want with your shop, anyway?" He remembered the glow of a blush on her cheeks, and then he looked upon Kostya with new eyes. "Is she *your* sweetheart...?"

"By all the saints, no!" laughed Kostya. "Her sister's sent her to rent a gun, you mark my words. You know that Nastya and her sisters keep a gun beneath the counter, and that crafty Pole no doubt has *that* one as well. Nastya doesn't like to be kept waiting, you know—and I shouldn't like to be the one who made her wait!"

"I'll catch her," said Petya, and at that, he darted to the door and followed Galya down the street. She was walking quickly, but the blue-grey of her checked woolen skirt let him keep track of her as she hurried away. "Galya!" he called. "Galya, it's Petya!"

She turned, and at the sight of his face, her hands went up to her mouth. She had fine, thin hands like her sister's, and nearly as fine a face. In that first, striking moment of recognition, he remembered how dear that face had once been. Her eyes went wide, and then she was gathering up her skirts and running to fling herself into his arms.

"Petya!" she cried, brushing each of his cheeks with quick, darting kisses. Her voice had that familiar, breathless quality that he remembered from their teenage years, and it charmed him now as it had after Pascha dancing four years ago. "I hadn't thought I'd see you today at all—what luck, to see you today! I have to hurry, though, or I'll be late for an errand—"

"I won't keep you," he said, and kissed her cheeks in turn. "I only thought I should tell you to go back to Konstantin Bogdanovich's shop, if you need a gun for the tavern. He's more than happy to rent one to you until you get your own back."

"Oh, I only meant to say hello," she demurred. "But does he offer guns for rent? I might go back. Nastya has been complaining about wanting her gun, when your sister has all of the guns in town. It's so rude of me to complain, after you gave us a whole pig that you bought yourself, but my sisters and I were all night picking bits of metal out of the poor beast's skin. And it's not safe for a woman to run a tavern without a gun."

"Here," said Petya when she paused for breath, reaching into his pocket for the last of his money. "Rent a gun, if you want. Buy it, if this will pay for one. I'd hate for you and your sisters to be in danger."

She heaved a breath not quite loud enough to be a sigh. "You're still the kindest man," said Galya, and here she stepped back as though remembering her place. She cupped her elbows with her palms. When she spoke again, her voice was low and deferential. "I know you mean well when you offer such things, but what honest woman would take charity from a man like you? I shouldn't speak ill of the dead, but after the way your father spent his money, and what people said about women who took money from him…"

Petya pressed his lips tightly together. "I see. Excuse me, Galina Ivanovna. I seem to have forgot my coat. I ought to go to—"

"Call me Galya," she whispered, half-plaintive. "It made me feel we were children again, when I heard you calling 'Galya!' down the street."

"Galya, then," said Petya. "If I ever suggested—"

"You never suggested it," she said at once. "Never."

"Then forgive me, for…" He could not finish; there was nothing to say. *Then forgive me, because if it would have made my father proud of me, I'd have prostituted myself for a smile from Nastya.* Or perhaps, *Then forgive me, because women shouldn't have to safeguard themselves at every turn from the cry of "Whore."* "Forgive me," he said weakly, "for delaying you."

"You're forgiven," she answered, and with that they parted: Petya, to the machinists' shop, and Galya, to parts unknown.

CHAPTER TWENTY

The call to morning prayer woke Kesha from a fitful slumber, and he lay listening to the plaintive notes of the summons until he felt ready to stand. Then, chafing his arms to warm them, he levered his legs over the side of the narrow bed.

Söz had provided him with an Ottoman uniform. "You'll have Russian clothes before you go to Moscow," she had promised, but today he put on the high-collared undershirt and the vee-necked jacket. It was a somber, deep blue that stood out all the better against the scattering of reddish hair over his chin. He studied his face in the rented room's little mirror, examining it for some trace of the familiar.

He would dye his hair before he went to Moscow, he supposed. Strangers remembered a red-haired man all too easily. The beard, he'd keep until he had delivered Söz's message, and then he'd carve it from his cheeks with a razor blade. He splashed water over his face and patted it dry with a towel, then descended the narrow stair to the front room of the inn.

When he stepped outside, he found the streets oddly empty, although he could smell breakfast and a faint tang of ironworks. Half of Täteş was at prayers, and the other half—the Orthodox half, he supposed—had already begun the morning's business.

He began the trek westward with his eyes on the sky, lips aching where cold and wind had cracked them. Soon he had passed out of the village outskirts and found the beet field again, its hillocks lightly crusted with morning frost. His Ottoman boots made a faint creaking sound on the frozen earth, but he tucked his hands in his armpits and followed his shadow over the rows. Soon, just as Orazbek had said, the beets gave way to low hills covered with fields of winter rye, the stalks still pale green despite the late-November chill.

Kesha, though, had grown up in a border town, and knew that queer, inexplicable verdure. In the soil where machinists and farming families had gone to ground, where their cookfires and forges heated the earth above them, he had seen long grasses clinging to life just like this.

The dragons lived beneath the rye fields, then. If these lands had been cultivated for as long as Kesha thought they had, the dragons had probably been living beneath the rye fields for *years*—perhaps the fields had grown up over the dragons. "Vaster than empires, and more slow," he muttered to himself. In the absence of human voices, with the sky stretching endlessly above him, he felt he must speak or go mad.

He hooked his thumb in his belt. It was loose; there hadn't been eyelets enough to tighten it around his narrow waist. The oppressive quiet of the abandoned beet fields and the hollowness in the pit of his stomach reminded him of nothing so much as the last, miserable days of running.

Still dwelling on those long, solitary hours, Kesha hastened to the first of the rye fields. He walked a circuit of the hill until he found a sort of broad, round door of wood and iron, and this he tugged until he could crack it open.

Did the dragons build this? he wondered—for when he had passed the round door, it was at once utterly clear that someone had built the space beyond it, and that an inhuman aesthetic had gone into its making. The hall was circular and surprisingly cool, lit at long intervals with tinted gaslamps. The floor had been tiled with pieces of ceramic, each piece painted with fine, minute designs in shades of blue.

When he knelt to examine the tiles, Kesha found to his surprise that he recognized words and even whole sentences there. *Beauty*, said one glyph, and a second tile quoted a poem in Misha's book—spread out into a sentence rather than circled into a verse, but the meaning was the same. The words of that neoclassical translation came as though unbidden to his lips: "Here rest we exiles of the world / By thunder driven o'er the hills—"

"Terrible poetry, in your tongue," came a sibilant voice from above him. Kesha raised his gaze from the poem until he met the dragon's eyes. In the dim glow of the gaslamps, they reflected the light like the eyes of cats.

Kesha bowed, as he had heard his ancestors bowed a century ago. In reply, the dragon dipped its head. Aysel had been copper and brown as good earth, but this dragon was the black-flecked white of snow over wet stone. "My name is Innokentiy Vladimirovich Tarasov," Kesha said. He could scarcely force his voice above a croak. "Is it better poetry, in yours?"

At the question, the dragon drew itself up on its forelimbs with a cry like a death-wail. All along his arms and across the back of his neck, Kesha's hair stood on end. At the height of the cry, the dragon's eyes went wide and it pawed the tile, flexing its talons until the cry faded into the scream of wind through shattered crags. Something caught in Kesha's throat, smooth and cool and impenetrable as a stone. "That is the poem, in my language," the dragon answered, with a faint sound that might have been a laugh.

"Hardly neoclassical," said Kesha, swallowing. "It would never suit iambics."

"We haven't had a good translator since China," replied

the dragon. "And not a good poet for a hundred years. Not one of my comrades cares to read old poetry—and why do you?"

Kesha knew that he ought to lead the dragon on to politics. He ought to ask, *Why China?* or *Why Russia?* or even, before anything else, *Why Turkey?* He felt the echo of the dragon's cry in his skin, though, and he could say no other thing but, "Because nothing is more important to me than your poems. Nothing is more true."

The dragon snorted, then added, "You may call me Boris Baivich. I must admit, yours is a novel approach to winning my trust. I'm half inclined to grant it. You promise to be entertaining." As Boris Baivich led Kesha deeper into the cavern, he paused now and then to point out a particularly poignant line on the tiled floor. He paused at each translation, claws tapping the enamel over the porcelain, as though he was considering not only the correct words but also the correct voice for the translation. *Long lay we upon the breast of the steppe, listening to the new grass breathing,* said one, or so Boris Baivich rendered it; *The hills rise up in a crest like the crest of a beloved,* read another, the two crests doubling and redoubling until they became a ridge of mountains along the back of a dragon. *They scoured the citadel with flame and silver, until the air itself burned away.*

With ash and snow, the poets shaped eight new words for grief. As Boris Baivich spoke, the corridor echoed with the screams of far-off conversations.

"This is all a single story," ventured Kesha. He traced his hand over the crooked curl of the snow-glyph. "Of how you came to this place."

"Most histories are," said Boris Baivich. He scratched at the rough mane along his collar, nostrils flaring briefly. "Even among your people, I'd thought it was a basic principle that the past and the present are contiguous."

"I hadn't realized it was a history."

"Your people seldom do."

My people, thought Kesha, and in his mind's eye he saw

the dragons' histories burning.

At the center of the hill—or so Kesha supposed, judging by the distance he'd walked—the passageway opened up into a broad atrium, the round of it lined with what might have been Doric columns. There, dozens of dragons rested at their ease. Some rose on their haunches to scream snout-to-snout, and others curled in close knots that glittered in the gaslight like ropes of polished granite. Their shared heat made the room almost soporifically cozy. Kesha found his eyelids drooping although the morning was yet young. "Is this how all dragons live, here?" he asked softly, turning again to Boris Baivich when he realized that he had been staring at the assembly long enough to be rude. "All packed together in—"

"Caves?" Boris let out a light laugh that made the nearest knot of dragons raise their heads and yawn at him. "No more than you do."

"I did grow up in a cave, actually," said Kesha.

At this, Boris scratched beneath his chin and yawned. The roof of his mouth was mottled with black spots. "Well," he said, after a moment. "Then a little less than you do. If we had a *proper* society, we would follow herds across vast swathes of land, returning home only when we had a new idea to share or when we'd run out of sheep. It's barbaric to *live* in the place where one builds a culture."

Kesha remembered Orazbek's praise of running water, always paced by his fear of forgetting the past. "In human societies, we consider the construction of dwelling-places a sign of civilization."

"As I said. *Barbaric*. This—" With a toss of his head, Boris took in the entire atrium. "*This* is a garrison. It's not a place where people *choose* to live."

"And yet you wrote your story on the tiles?" asked Kesha. From a niche near the ceiling descended another dragon—narrower than Boris Baivich, and a warm copper. Aysel, Kesha thought. She drew herself into a loose coil very close to him. "We paint our stories in places sacred to us—murals on church walls, or in stained glass—"

"I *know* where you tell your stories, human," said Boris. "You also carve them into trees and fenceposts, when you're left to your own devices. Consider this," and he gestured to the entryway with an elegant flick of his wrist, "an exceedingly elaborate fencepost."

"It is very rude to speak in the language of the Russians," Aysel said in Latin, with a yawn of her own that seemed too pointed to be accidental. At the corner of her jaw, her mane was beginning to bristle. "Such private conversations, with a human whom *I* brought—"

"If you had bothered to study—" Boris Baivich raised his voice and his shoulders, lips drawing back from his teeth.

"Please," Kesha broke in. At the sound of his voice, both dragons turned slightly, each pointing one great dark eye at him. He gathered his rough Latin and continued, "I have come to ask questions of you, and I would be glad of answers."

"Ask," answered Aysel, turning to face him with a toss of her head.

"In Russia," said Kesha slowly, "I could not find a book about the history of your people. The people of my city burned them many years ago, with the books of philosophy, and of poetry as well. I believe that my countrymen did not choose to…did not choose to converse with yours. No laws forbid me from learning the language of the dragons, but choosing to learn your language was more difficult nonetheless. If I had learned it, then I would not have found books to read or countrymen who could speak it with me."

"Your people never spoke the language of the dragons with skill," sniffed Boris, but Aysel snapped at him to silence him. "Continue," she said, with a low and rumbling growl.

"I can find no histories of the dragons in St. Petersburg," Kesha went on, although he could feel himself quailing at the strength of her jaws and the bulk of her torso. "Thus, I cannot learn why your people chose to give their loyalties over to the Turks, and..." he cast about for a verb that was not *betray*; his Latin lessons had taught him nothing of how to soften political speeches. "I would have you tell me, if you can, why you fled your compact with the people of Russia."

"Is *that* why you came to the land of the Turks?" laughed Aysel. "To ask a very simple question—"

"A question to which he lacks the answers," replied Boris. "Do you know the reason, Aysel? Or are you too young to remember?"

"I am too young to *remember*," she said sharply, "but not too young to learn. We left the people of Russia because they did not honor our agreement. That much is easily said. They pledged land to us for our use, and then they put souls on that land and sold it to their veterans."

My great-great-grandfather was one of those men, thought Kesha. "Nonetheless, the dragons asked Russia to hear their case again. They wrote a letter to the senate."

Aysel tucked her tailtip beneath her folded hands—and they were hands, Kesha realized, long-fingered and slight of palm but otherwise jointed much like his own. "The senate chose not to hear them. Our allies were cast down from their seats, and the dragons saw that they would never be citizens of a human empire."

"Not entirely true," Boris interrupted. "Here we are, in a human empire, with some of the rights of citizens. Murdering us is a crime, at least, which is more than I can say for any of our previous hosts."

"A slave is not a citizen," said Aysel coolly.

"Slaves are property," countered Boris. "Whatever else you may say about our status, at least we own ourselves."

"Quiet yourself! Let me tell him our story. You will not make poetry of our flight from Russia, and so I must in your stead."

"It was a brutal, ugly little incident, not worthy of a poem," Boris grumbled, but he let Aysel go on.

She turned her head to regard Kesha with one eye, then the other. Although her face was as fine-boned as a doe's, there was nonetheless a certain firmness to her flesh for which youth alone could not account. Her scales were brighter than Boris's, and Kesha guessed that they would be more supple if he were to press his fingertips against them. She looked as though she ate better than Boris did. "I told you that our people saw that they would never be citizens of a human empire. Our own alliances broke when we realized this."

"Alliances? With whom?"

"With the other dragons," she answered. "Even within our clans, many could not agree on a course. Some desired to sue for peace anew. Others claimed that they would never again serve human masters, and fled singly and in clans. Still others were filled with rage at this betrayal, and they sought to repay it with blood."

"Only a few of them actually called for the empress's head," said Boris. "Four, in my clan. Five at the very most."

"Other clans were more…I do not know the word in Latin. What is the word for when you burn with anger, because you long for justice?" She gave a whistling trill that made several other dragons look up with clear concern.

"*Try* to speak softly. The word is 'radical,'" supplied Boris in Russian, and Aysel nodded.

"Radical. Our people were splintered then, and some who had long desired power and influence sought to deepen the wounds. Dragons hunted men and other dragons. The senators who had defended us were called traitors, and executed or sent away. Our books burned—and the men of Russia would not defend us."

Kesha looked to Boris for confirmation, but he only gave a very human nod. "Aysel can make poetry of it, because she did not see it," he said. "What use is it to tell you what I saw? I could speak for a thousand years, and you still couldn't imagine it. Neither of you were there."

"I'm sorry," said Kesha.

"I would prefer that we spoke of something else," Boris answered. Aysel leaned against his shoulder, and he pressed his cheek to her neck. What that gesture imported, Kesha couldn't have said. He knew only that when their Uncle Sasha had died, Liza had leaned on his shoulder in just the same way.

Taking Boris's cue, Kesha asked, "And thus, you joined forces with the people of Turkey?"

"No other people knew better how to fight dragons," said Aysel. "They promised us protection from our own when our people splintered. They let us use their land, although they did not make us citizens. In payment for this kindness, we have fought in their wars for a hundred years—and now we help them to make angels."

Boris rolled one eye, glancing over the assembled dragons. He lowered his voice. "But a garrison is not a citadel, no matter how one dresses it with tiles and pillars. The last brigands went east half a century ago. One might be tempted to wonder how long we will be expected to repay our hosts, and how much their protection will cost."

CHAPTER TWENTY-ONE

In his mother's study, Petya once more considered the code. Polzin sat across the desk from him, taking what appeared to be detailed measurements of Wainwright's boots and the plaster cast of footprints that had so excited him. "The sole is the key," he kept saying to himself. "The fit is nothing; the sole is the key."

With that mantra echoing in the little room like a prayer, Petya turned the slip of paper over and over between his fingers. He had tried direct substitutions, seeking common letters and making them E or S; he had tried reversing the order of dots and dashes, but still the cipher refused to crack for him. *WWR TZS GCS CP BJZF BFOWO JPFF CJ,* the text read, once the telegraph master had translated it back out of English Morse code. Most of the letters were at the end of the alphabet, which suggested that Wainwright had generated the code by treating the letters as numbers and then adding or subtracting a key rather than by direct substitution.

WWR TZS GCS. Once more, he returned to the hypothesis that had struck him yesterday before supper: were those first three words a coded form of "The old man"? If he knew the beginning of the message, he might be able to find the key that would decode the rest. The English alphabet had twenty-six letters, and he could use simple arithmetic to derive the key to the cipher from the coded message. He had only to substitute 23 for W and subtract 20 for T, substitute 23 for W and subtract 8 for H. For G and C, the code would cycle about again after 26; 7 (G) minus 13 (M) took him back to -6—or rather, 20 (T).

Dipping his pen once more in the inkwell, he took a fresh leaf of paper from Inspector Polzin's neat stack and began the work of subtraction. A moment's work yielded *COM ENO TBE*.

Petya blew on the ink to dry it, absently gnawing at a thumbnail as he considered the new series of letters. It was a start, but no more than a start. He had no choice but to wring the rest of the key from Wainwright some other way. "Come not be," he offered, but Polzin only looked up from his plaster and asked, in accented English, "Be what?"

"I don't know," answered Petya. "It's the first part of the key; there's more to it than those nine letters."

"Try something with feeling," advised Polzin. "'Come, not be sad,' or 'Come, not be so angry.'"

"'Be not' is English poetic syntax," said Petya with a little laugh. "My brother taught me that. 'Come not' is the same. It's like 'Do not come.'" Polzin had returned his gaze to the sole of Wainwright's boot, though, and Petya felt his inattention like a wall. He ducked his head again and studied the letters, their shapes rough and more than half-Cyrillic in his unpracticed hand. *Come not be.*

Once the ink had dried, he folded the paper and tucked it into his waistcoat pocket. "I'll see if I can get Wainwright to tell me," he said at last, to which Polzin nodded absently.

"If he is a spy," cautioned Polzin, "he won't give up his secrets at a question."

The memory of that conversation in the telegraph office struck Petya suddenly, and he said, "Maybe not at a question—but a month ago, my father told me that he had intelligence that would put Wainwright in his power. 'Curdle his milk,' he said."

Polzin tilted his head at that, sweeping back his dark curls from his forehead. He had a bald patch at either temple, exactly where thumb and forefinger tracked across the skin, as though repeated rubbing had worn the hair away. "I wish you'd told me that earlier. Opportunity, we've established; means, we haven't ruled out; if your father had intelligence on Wainwright, that gives us a motive. 'Curdle his milk,' indeed. A very good motive."

"I didn't remember it until now," said Petya. "If I find anything else—"

"*If* you find anything else, bring it back. But he may not let his secrets slip a second time." Polzin pinched a magnifying lens between brow and cheek, then waved him away. Petya scarcely needed the cue. He heaved himself off of the chair and toyed for a moment with his jacket, at last leaving it draped over the back cushion. The ice closet was scarcely cold any longer, after Wainwright had spent a week in residence there, and Wainwright might be put less on his guard if Petya approached him casually.

And with tea, he thought, diverting himself briefly to the kitchen to have the cook prepare him a tea tray. "Thank you," he told her, which only made her shake a teaspoon at him.

"I'll have you in here later to brew the next season's kvass, see if I don't," she said firmly. "We need to get her drinking something other than that swill she calls vodka."

"I'll come—I promise, I'll come," said Petya, and then he bore the tea tray down the hall to the ice closet. When he slid back the bolt, he found that the lantern was out in that cramped little room.

"Ah, Petya!" exclaimed Wainwright, sounding rather cheerful despite the darkness. "I'm not a bat; I just recognized your silhouette. My lamp has run out of oil."

"What bad luck!" answered Petya, putting down the tea tray. "Hand over the lamp and I'll fill it for you." With a cup from the tea service, he collected a measure of oil from one of the lamps in the hallway, which he poured into the lamp's oil reservoir. He drew out a match from his pocket and lit the lamp anew, hanging it once more in its accustomed place. "There—now you can enjoy your tea in the light."

"You've brought me *tea*! An Englishman isn't himself without tea."

"Nor is a Russian," answered Petya, with a forced little laugh. "I'll let you choose which you want to be today, since I've got lamp oil in my cup."

"We'll share a cup, then," said Wainwright, pouring himself a fragrant cup of tea. "Jasmine," he said, after a moment. "I hadn't thought the Tarasov keep was a household for jasmine tea."

"My mother brought it with her from Moscow," said Petya, kneeling amid the insulating hay and watching Wainwright busy himself with cream and marmalade. "She likes more delicate teas than my father or my sister."

"And more delicate than you like?" Wainwright took a sip, then passed the cup into Petya's hand. The porcelain was warm from tea and touch, and the drink was sweet and rich on his tongue.

After a moment, Petya realized that he hadn't answered. "I don't really prefer it either way," he said, shrugging and returning the cup to Wainwright's hand.

"When he was here," said Wainwright carefully, "your brother told me that the Tarasovs didn't turn against one another until he left you. That's not true, is it?" He laced his fingers together over the cup as though to shelter it.

"He was always our mother's boy, and Liza was always our father's girl," Petya replied. "Uncle Pasha used to say that Father never forgave Mother for naming him Innokentiy instead of Pyotr. 'You'll make a priest of him,' he used to say, and she'd always say, 'You'll make a soldier of my daughter.'" An old, familiar uneasiness rose in him at the admission. His throat constricted, and his heart pattered against his breastbone as though seeking escape. "No one forced us to turn against each other, but we did anyway. What else could we do?"

"What *you* did, I suppose. Take neither side, and end up with no side at all."

Petya glanced up at Wainwright. In the lamplight, his skin had a sallow, almost waxen cast, and his cheeks had grown rough with a week's worth of stubble. His hair was lank and oily, although he had clearly attempted to dress it without a comb or mirror. Drawn a part along the left side of his skull with his fingernails and then swept his hair to either side, by the look of it. "I suppose that's what I did," allowed Petya. He reached for the cup, draining it to the dregs. He poured out another measure of tea and drank it plain.

The scent of jasmine wasn't nearly enough to drown out the stink of the dragons' heads. "The inspector will be coming tomorrow for those," he said, gesturing toward the heads. By now, beetles or rats had worried at the flesh until it hung slack on the bones. The eyes had been eaten out, and the empty sockets gazed sightlessly across the narrow room.

Wainwright gestured for the teacup. "When will I be free to go?" he asked. "I've never complained. You've shut me in an ice closet with those stinking things, you've kept me from my men, you've even taken my boots, and I've never said a word against you. I've done everything in my power to help your investigation go smoothly—and do you have a single concrete reason to keep holding me here?"

"No," admitted Petya, although his hand went to his pocket nonetheless. "It's just caution."

"Just fear," corrected Wainwright. He reached for Petya's hand, pressing it against the seam of his pocket. "Do you have something there? Something that you think will convict me?"

"Matches," said Petya, drawing one out. The moment he had released the pocket, though, Wainwright darted two fingers in and pulled free the folded paper.

"Matches!" he scoffed, unfolding the paper to read the neat columns of letters and numbers. "You're a bad liar, Petya—at least your mathematics is better. You came here to find the key to my telegram, didn't you?"

"I did," Petya admitted, and a heat crept from his cheeks to the back of his neck. In the slight chill of the ice closet, it felt like being dashed with warm water. "They believe you're a spy. I believe it."

"Can an Englishman in Russia be anything *but* a spy?" With a laugh, Wainwright folded the paper again and passed it back into Petya's hands. "You never trusted me. I say that I spied on the Turks, and you thought I was their agent; I put myself in your hands, and you suspect I'm scheming to play you into *mine*. When will we trust each other, Petya?"

"You keep calling me that, as though you want me to think you're a friend. You haven't earned my friendship."

"It does neither of us any good to be playing games with names. You want to know that you can trust me? Then here is the key, *Pyotr Vladimirovich Tarasov*. Take it to your inspectors and prove that you're the good son. Earn your place on their side, and use what you know to acquit me once and for all." He closed his eyes, lips moving briefly as though seeking his place in an unseen text. "'Come not between the dragon and his wrath.' Use it to decode my telegram—or *ask* me what it says. I could tell you, if you only *asked* me."

"Tell me what it says."

Wainwright finished his tea and let the cup fall on its side on the tray. "It says, 'The old man is well taken care of.'"

Petya's hand tightened on the paper. "You killed my father."

"I watched your father die at my feet!" snapped Wainwright. Something kindled in his hollow eyes, and Petya rose to his haunches in case Wainwright meant to do him violence. "Maybe the shot should have made me come running, but it didn't. There were dozens of shots that night. One more didn't strike me as remarkable, so I wasn't watching out as carefully as I should have been. I found him in the street with the snow on his coat—at first I thought he was a drunkard, but he reached for me, and then I saw the blood. I stood watching him, thinking that if I touched him, I'd never be able to convince you that it wasn't my fault. 'I should have chosen her,' he said. Those were his last words, Pyotr Vladimirovich—and when I heard them, I thought of how your sister would feel if he were left lying in the street for hours. Out of respect for her, I carried his corpse *on my back* up from the town to the keep. He's easily twice my weight. Almost a foot taller. Can you imagine how it felt? Watching a man die at your feet—even a man you despise—and then carrying him on your back, in the snow, with nearly an hour to think about all the reasons you should've done *anything* else—"

"*King Lear*," said Petya softly. "Your key was from *King Lear*."

"It was."

"An old man with three children, each of them vying for his inheritance?"

"A king, with traitors in his court and Englishmen vying for his lands."

"You killed my father," Petya said again.

Wainwright answered, with an incredulous look, "You think your *father* is the old man. You think that, when I said he was taken care of—"

"Who else could it be? What *else* could you mean?"

A shadow appeared in the doorway. Petya stood at once, turning with every expectation of seeing Elliot framed against the lights of the hall. Instead, to his relief, he saw Polzin with his thick fingers curled around the edge of the door. "A word, Master Tarasov," he said. "Only a word."

"Quickly, then," said Petya, sighing and slipping the paper into his pocket. He shut the door behind him, leading

Polzin down the hall and gesturing for him to keep his voice lowered. "What is it?"

"I'm quite sure," he said. "The impressions are beyond all doubt—a sort of scoring along the sole, almost too faint to be made out, but it matches the print exactly, exactly. And if that's not enough, the boots are very distinctly stained—"

"Get to the point, Inspector Polzin." Impatience left a sour taste in Petya's mouth.

"The point," said Polzin, raising his voice, "is that the footprints are most certainly Wainwright's, and while he stood by the tavern, your father was still bleeding. It puts him at the scene of the crime at the time of death, which you can imagine is no coincidence. Your testimony provides us with a motive. At the risk of overstating my case, I believe that will close the book on his culpability. To have been so close, with the victim so direly wounded, and not to have been the culprit or to have witnessed the culprit…"

"It is hard to believe," admitted Petya.

"Have you made headway on the cipher?"

"Another minute," said Petya, to which Polzin only nodded and said, "Of course, of course." He patted Petya's arm and left him standing in the middle of the hallway.

The door to the ice closet was ajar, Wainwright's face peering around the iron edge of it. He looked up and met Petya's eyes, thin lips pressed together until they went white. "I don't believe I'll tell you who the old man is," he said, "until I have a lawyer."

CHAPTER TWENTY-TWO

The errand boy began wrapping the last of the guns in the cloth again, and Liza fought down the urge to scream imprecations at him. He had done nothing wrong. He'd been the most reliable of servants, fetching everything she requested at once and in gratifying silence. And even if he'd been a bad servant, Nastya was watching. "If I'm no longer a suspect, may I have my gun back?" she asked, and Utkin nodded and waved her to the bundle.

"Not *one* of these!" said Liza, with a high noise of frustration. "Not a single one—not a blunderbuss or a carbine or a musket—not *one* leaves the right wounds! No matter how much powder I give it...."

"Or how much you skimp on powder," agreed Utkin. He folded his arms again, tilting his head at Liza's notebook of sketches. "Tell me, based on what you've found so far, what are the features of the gun you're seeking?"

"Something like a carbine, just as I thought," said Liza, while Nastya knelt and sorted through the tags. "But a shorter barrel than any of these had. Flared, too, or so I'd guess. They're easier to overload. The blunderbuss was closer than the carbines, but the barrel was too long. Something like a musketoon?"

"A difficult conjecture to prove, without the right kind of gun to test," said Utkin, tapping his fingertips one-two-three-four on his inner elbow. "If you were to—"

"Vanya!" came the shout from the keep, and Utkin pivoted at the cry. Soon after, Polzin's heavy tread sounded on the stairs, and Utkin strode across the courtyard to huddle in the entryway.

"Out of the wind," said Liza, smirking faintly. "At least *someone's* found something."

"And now, perhaps, we can all get on with our lives." Nastya shouldered her gun, snapping free the tag that read *Anastasia Ivanovna Vasilevskaya* and tucking it into her pocket like a souvenir. "Have you had a drink since last we spoke, Liza?"

"Morphine," Liza admitted, spitting to one side at the bitter taste of the word. "Take the guns down to town, boy. Give them back to their owners."

"Yes, sir," he answered with a little salute. He was very small, and very thin; the bundle of guns was very nearly half his size. He staggered a bit as he bore them away.

When Liza looked up again, she found that Nastya was studying her with something inscrutable in her dark eyes. "You don't have to *confess* that you've had morphine," she said, oddly gentle. "You've lost a leg. Anyone would take medicine to treat it."

"How am I to know what *anyone* would take? A week ago, I wouldn't have given a damn what anyone thought. If I care at all, it's your doing. Yours and the lawyer's."

"The *lawyer's*!" There was scorn in Nastya's voice, yes, but Liza thought she heard something new there—something on the verge of breaking. "Do you have a lawyer now?"

Liza folded her hands in her lap, ignoring how they shook and ignoring likewise whether it was from the cold or a craving for morphine. "He's my brother's lawyer. The one from St. Petersburg. What do you care if I have a lawyer?"

"Any woman of substance has a lawyer," said Nastya, tilting her head up with a faint laugh. Her eyes were closed against the snow, and her laugh was clear as a little silver bell. Liza gradually came to realize that Nastya hadn't answered her at all.

"You want to be the only one who has my ear," said Liza. She peeled back her lips over her teeth; it felt something like a smile. "You think he's a threat."

"I think he doesn't have his ear to the ground here like I do. Here's something; the machinists want *Petya* to head the keep! They think because he's one of theirs, and a man—"

Her half-panicked tone suddenly struck a familiar note beneath Liza's shattered breastbone, and Liza cried, "Oh!" before bursting into laughter. "Oh! Now I see it—I *see* it, Nastenka! To think that I've spent so many years afraid that you hated me, and the whole time, I only had to *listen* to you—"

"You've gone mad," said Nastya simply, and she wrapped her fur-lined coat more tightly about her shoulders.

"The scales have fallen from my eyes," answered Liza, and in her heart she praised Orlov to the heavens. "All your politicking and prompting! All your implications! You prod me and mock me because you want me to *love* you!"

Nastya drew herself up at the accusation—for accusation it was; Liza couldn't call back the triumph she felt at making it. Her eyes flashed, and her gloved hand clutched at the barrel of her gun. "I don't care whether you love me," Nastya said, softly and deliberately. "I don't give a damn what you feel about me, so long as you take me *seriously*."

"Kiss me," said Liza, her voice just as soft. She freed a hand to beckon Nastya closer.

At that, Nastya spat. She spat badly, against the wind, and she wiped her mouth when she had finished, but she stared Liza down until she was quite sure they'd both understood the gesture. *I spit on very few offers*, her look seemed to say, *but for this one, I'll make an exception*. "What will you offer me for a kiss? Will you offer to protect me and my sisters?"

Liza put her hand on the arm of her chair. "Kiss me because you want to kiss me—don't kiss me if you don't. I won't haggle for your kisses. You aren't my whore."

At the word, Nastya turned her cheek as though recoiling from a slap. She lowered her gun and raised a single hand, but she paused with the gesture half-complete. "I am not and never will be your whore," she said, low as the thrum of a heartbeat, and then she braced herself on the free arm of Liza's chair and leaned down to kiss her.

Nastya's lips were cold, and her teeth chattered beneath them. Her cheek was cool, but above her muffler, the skin radiated a faint and livid warmth that made Liza gasp to feel it. As her lips parted, Nastya caught her teeth on Liza's lower lip, biting down sharply enough to crack the chapped flesh.

Liza's heart pounded at the back of her throat. She tasted blood. "Nastenka—"

"Come to find me when you're well," Nastya whispered. She straightened. At some point, Liza had caught her by the wrist, but Nastya shook herself free without a struggle. "I can't come to your fortress every hour of the day," she said, shouldering her gun again. "Have your brother send a cart down with the other pig. In a month or two, we'll see what kind of fortress lord you make."

"For your sake, I'll be a dozen times better than my father."

"For your own sake," said Nastya, "you'll be a thousand times better than your father."

Liza watched her walk away, the ache of that kiss still lingering where Nastya's teeth had scored her flesh. They had kissed as lovers did, in a courtyard with workmen to one side and inspectors to the other; they had kissed beneath the eyes of the watchmen and the eyes of God, and not a one had come to part them.

"Elliot!" called Liza, ebullience welling from her throat as though from a vast spring. "Elliot, take me back to the keep!"

From his post by the wall came her grey-eyed English soldier, and he grinned at her as though he, too, understood the triumph of that kiss. He took her chair by the back, and when she gestured him to the door, he pushed her across the courtyard with the most pleasing complaisance.

Utkin looked up to her from the foot of the stairs with a faint, thin smile. "Polzin's found the evidence that will put the last nail in Lieutenant Wainwright's coffin," he confided. "He's calling for a lawyer even now."

"It's a shame," said Liza, although she couldn't bring herself to remember why it was a shame with Nastya's taste on her lips. "I was starting to like him."

CHAPTER TWENTY-THREE

A part of Kesha burned to ask what Aysel had meant about angels, but then the implications of what Boris had said caught up with him. "You have no reason to remain with the Turks now?" he asked.

"We have *reasons*," Aysel answered. Her nostrils flared as though she had caught a foul scent. "They feed and house us. If humans harm us, we may seek restitution. My elders tell me that these are reasons enough to remain in the caves."

Boris laid a claw on the back of her hand, the point pressing hard in a depression between her bones. "Some of our elders still remember the remove that brought us to Russia. They are weary of fleeing."

"They have forgotten the dream of a fatherland—"

"They remember the fatherland we lost."

"*No one* remembers the citadel anymore! They cannot even agree on why we left it. Were we driven away by our enemies? Did we flee a war? Was it plague or fire? Where did the 'citadel in the clouds' once stand? In China? In Atlantis? On the moon? Was it ever real, or is it only a story that our poets tell? Not even you know the answer!"

Unruffled, Boris replied, "I presume it wasn't Atlantis or the moon. The China theory has merit."

Aysel snorted and drew her hand away. "You think this dream is madness. Delirium. But you have more reason than I to long for a change in the guard."

"What I long for is of no importance. I remember our poems—"

"The words of the dead! But I will live a life worthy of being remembered, if I must remake the world to do it."

Before Kesha had time to consider what Aysel had said, he felt a hot gust of breath on the back of his neck. That was the only warning he had before the air behind him erupted in an unearthly screech that made him clutch at his ears. Aysel rose onto her haunches, shouting something in response with her long ears flattening against her neck.

Some animal part of Kesha knew that if he froze now, he would be eaten. He couldn't make himself draw breath, but he could at least turn to face the dragon behind him.

The dragon was massive and fog-grey. It had grown almost too thick to fit through the vast circle of the entryway, and from the scars in the scales along its flanks, the lamps on either side of the hall must have scraped its sides when it went in or out. It screeched as though it meant to tear the air open, and at the distant terminus of its mountainous spine, its tail lashed against the pillars and shook loose the dragons entwined there.

That cry must have been speech. It must have been, for all it sounded like a glacier fracturing.

"Go, while you can," said Boris, and at the sound of Russian in his mouth, the other dragon fixed its talons about his throat and shook him until he screamed.

Kesha knew that scream. He'd heard it dozens of times as dying dragons thrashed and seized in the courtyard of the Tarasov keep. He'd never understood, before, that it meant *Dear God, have mercy.*

Aysel turned one rolling brown eye toward him, and he couldn't mistake the meaning in her look. He took to his heels, fleeing over the exiles' poetry that tiled the corridors.

When he reached the round door in the hillside, he battered himself against it until he could squeeze through the gap, and then he ran over the green winter-rye and the hillocks of beets.

I've killed him, thought Kesha as his foot crashed through a thin layer of frost and stuck in the mud beneath. *He's over a hundred years old; he and Aysel were the last ones who gave a damn about their poetry, and I've killed him as though he were only another dumb beast—*

"No," said Kesha, wrenching his foot free and limping over the last untended rows. He flung himself over a stile, startling a nest of yearling pigs, and then he was out of the pen and stumbling into the alley between two back gardens. *No; they wouldn't have killed him for such a small thing. What kind of person kills its own for speaking out of turn?*

Men do, he answered himself. *The dragons did, a hundred years ago. They are no better than men.*

He peered out into the street, surveying the people at their business. With their morning's prayers complete, the Muslims of Täteş had entered the daily commerce of their town, sharing tea in the eateries and tending opticians' and chemists' shops with their Orthodox neighbors. Housewives hung up their laundry and shared gossip at the lines, while their youngest children followed behind with jars of clothespins. It was a peaceful, productive morning, utterly untroubled by draconic violence. They would surely notice a man running as though for his life, even amid the thicker press of pedestrians. Therefore, Kesha paused in the alleyway to catch his breath and considered his next steps.

He had to believe that Söz would permit him to speak with the dragons when he had completed his mission in Moscow.

He had to believe it, because he knew one thing with a nigh-religious certainty: he would never again go back into the dragons' hall uninvited.

END OF BOOK II

DRAKON

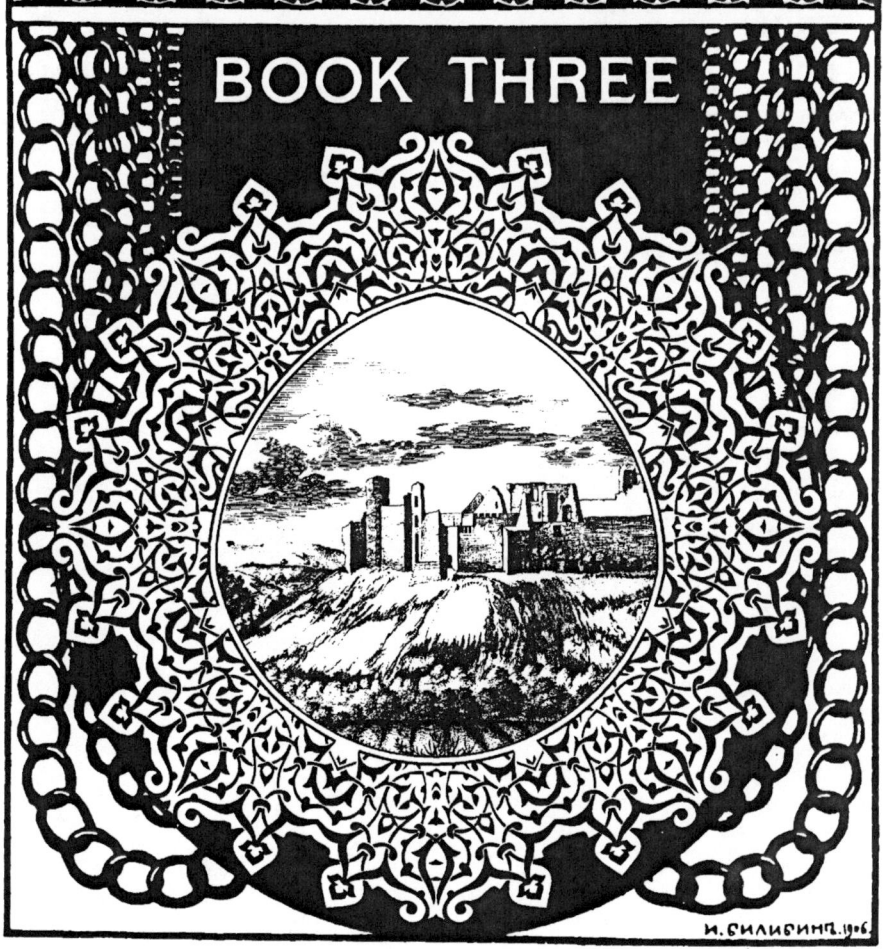

BOOK THREE

CHAPTER ONE

Liza's boot wrinkled along old, well-worn lines where foot joined to ankle. She had spent the last week teaching herself how to make her new foot flex to her liking, just as she'd learned to work the gun mounts atop the towers; she had learned to make it roll from heel to toe as she walked, how to lock it on tiptoe and how to keep it flexed for climbing. The knee joint she'd figured out in the first day, but the ankle joint had required diligent application after six weeks of idleness.

Now, the boot wrinkled across the bridge of her steel foot, and she rolled that foot slightly on the heel until the springs propelled her up to the next rung. Soon she had gained the watchtower, and then the gun tower over that. Behind her, she heard Petya's soles striking the rungs in an even rhythm.

The hills stretched around her, with the town curling over the southwestern valley and the bare orchards tracking the line of the railway to the east. Liza took a deep breath that froze the insides of her nostrils, then breathed out a great cloud of vapor. "You put a tarpaulin over the gun," she told Petya, who had ascended into the sunlight close at her heels.

"Why shouldn't I have put a tarpaulin over the gun? The weather will—"

"Name of God, it wasn't a criticism! We should've been putting tarpaulins over them since we got them. If we can get them off again when we need to, it's only sensible."

At the praise, Petya flushed from the tips of his ears to the point of his nose, and Liza laughed and pushed at his shoulder. The light push very nearly overbalanced her, but she locked the foot and gathered herself against the next stiff breeze. "Are you ready?" he asked, offering a hand to steady her and appearing unsurprised when she declined it.

"If you are," answered Liza. She unclipped the tarpaulin from the gun mount and whisked it away, then slid into the gunner's chair again. It fit her differently than it had when last she'd sat in one of these. She'd gained weight in her six weeks of enforced bed-rest, and she wasn't yet used to her new shape. With a grunt, she fixed her feet against the pedals and looked up at Petya. "What are the settings?"

He knelt on the plate, close enough to adjust her left foot should she need an engineer's hand. "The gun works the same way that it did before. Pump the right pedal to start the spin, and touch the left to halt it. You know that. You'll want to lock the foot at one hundred and twenty degrees so that it aligns with the pedal, then push from the knee instead of from the ankle."

She rolled the ankle joint until her foot caught, feeling the click of the lock reverberate all along the steel bone to the padded leather straps around her stump. "Got it," she said, and as Petya clutched at the loader's handle, she sent the gun into a lazy turn.

The feel of it came back quickly—the roll of the bearings under the mounting plate, the way the gears caught and whined beneath her. "Have to oil these," she said, to which Petya only nodded. The attitude rotor was on the left side, but that was nothing new. She was used to firing the Gatling guns right-handed, and it was only the long absence that made it feel strange today. She adjusted the pitch of the gun, calling down to the courtyard, "Target!"

A plate went spinning up from the courtyard and soared over the fortress wall. The long barrel of Liza's gun tracked it to nearly the apex of its arc, and as her left foot came down hard on the pedal, her right hand clenched at the trigger. The first burst of gunfire nearly deafened her, but the plate fell in shards on the far side of the wall. "Again!" she roared, and far below her, Elliot flung the next plate into the air.

This time, the plate spun high, like a tiny silver coin lobbed at the China blue of the sky. She shattered it into stars and cried, "One more!"

The third just barely crested the wall, soaring northward until it went down in a rain of bullets.

"Good," said Petya, with a little laugh. "Good—what am I saying? You were always the best marksman of all of us. It was beautiful work, Liza."

"It will be harder when I face a dragon again," she said tersely. "They're not like thrown plates. They don't follow predictable paths."

"I've been meaning to speak to you about that," said Petya. "I know you're only just recovering, but I thought that if anyone would want to find a more effective way of pursuing the dragons, it would be you, and I—"

"*Pursuing* them?"

"In the air." Petya released the loader's handle and rose to his feet, dusting off the knees of his trousers.

"I'm listening," said Liza. She unlocked her foot and stood, then took one end of the tarpaulin and drew it over the gun again. Petya took the other, hooking it securely to the edge of the mount. "It doesn't sound very practical to me, but I'm listening."

He squared his shoulders and took a shallow breath to inflate his chest, just as though he'd practiced this speech before a mirror. His professors had taught him elocution at the academy in St. Petersburg, and she couldn't forget that.

"I've been working with Lukin on a design for a machine that overcomes the flaws in our current air transportation. A dirigible or a hot-air balloon simply isn't maneuverable, and in any case, it would be suicide to mount a gun like this on one of them. A single stray bullet, and you'd fall from the sky—"

Liza spat over the side of the tower, flipping open the hatch over the ladder and putting her right foot on the first rung. "And you thought I was the woman to call on, if you wanted to talk about *falling from the damn sky*. Devil take your hot-air balloons, Petya—build me a better gun, and then we won't need to worry about pursuit."

"Leonardo da Vinci thought we could build flying machines," said Petya softly, and something in that softness arrested her.

"Leonardo da Vinci *didn't* build a flying machine," answered Liza. Although she tried to train her voice to gentleness, even she could hear the hard edge to her tone. "We're still paying off Father's debts. Until we've paid them in full, we can't afford to waste our resources on some Italian's toys."

Slowly, Liza lowered herself into the ladder well. Her left foot found purchase on the second rung, and her hands came down to grip the edge of the well. *Slowly does it.*

"You're only being parsimonious to impress Nastya and Misha." Petya looked down at her, neither condemning nor accusing. She tried not to read pity into that look. If she read pity there, she would have to dash it off his face with her fist.

"That's where you're wrong," she said, with a laugh as ironic as Misha's. "I'm doing it to impress *everyone*."

Liza emerged from the lowest hatch and stepped aside to let Petya follow her out. He had returned briefly to St. Petersburg before New Year's and explained his extended absence to his professors, who had no doubt whispered darkly about the barbarian fringe of Russia before granting him leave to return to Liza's side. They knew as well as she did that the first of February probably meant war. They knew Petya was as good as enlisting.

It still surprised her to realize that he had returned to her a second time. They made good partners, she thought. They always had, ever since they'd lost Kesha to the city. Six years ago, when Kesha had fled, Petya had been a gangling thing—hardly able to cross a hallway without tripping over himself, let alone manage the gun. Her father had put him to work cranking and loading her gun until he'd grown into his limbs, and when she heard the familiar beat of his toes on the ladder rungs, Liza could almost imagine they were six years younger.

Then she took a step, and the straps of her new leg pressed against her lower thigh, even through her trousers and long underwear.

Easy enough to imagine the years away, when it meant imagining her leg returned to her.

"Set Hancock on watch," she told Petya, who nodded and peeled off toward the troop quarters. She caught his shoulder before he'd gone far, though, and continued, "Get the rest of them in uniform and line them up by the gates. I want them to look impressive when the men from Moscow come to collect the dragons' heads."

"They're only inspectors," said Petya. "We don't have to impress them."

"What, because we never have before?"

"*No one* has before. They're like coal-sellers or knife-grinders. They're not for *impressing*."

"They're going to carry tales back to Moscow, and I'd rather have someone who's *not* our mother carrying those tales. We've had inspectors out two times in as many months! That in itself is a triumph. What's the harm in having a few inspectors tell the bureaucrats how well we turned ourselves out? It might see more investment in—"

"Are you *listening* to yourself, Liza?"

She let her hand fall to her side, studying Petya in the light of the hall lamp. For the first time since they'd begun to argue, she saw the faint creases of pain between his brows. "I'm listening to you," she said. "Say what you have to say."

"My sister would never put men in uniform and have them line up to impress a couple of inspectors," said Petya. He shook his head slightly, as though he was searching for the joke in what she'd said. "She would laugh at me for suggesting it, because she thinks that men need to be in the towers, where they could do the most good. If you won't let me build what I like because it's impractical, all *right*, but at least be practical about *this*, too."

Bracing one hand on her hip, Liza pressed her lips together and considered the diatribe. A month ago, she would have dismissed it for no better reason than that it contradicted her—and if she chose not to dismiss it now, it was because he spoke sense, and not because she had grown malleable in her convalescence. She had spent the last month dismantling little threats to her power, refusing Oleg Kamensky's half-serious suits and sternly reproaching Cousin Borya for his offers of assistance. She had learned, she thought, to tell when someone wanted her to bend her neck. Petya's reasoning was sound, though, and it cost her nothing to humor him. "All *right*, Petya," Liza said finally. "No parade. We'll dine them well, though. Cheaply, but well."

He breathed out, and with his chest deflated and his shoulders rounded, he looked younger than his twenty-one years. She thought she caught a glimmer of brightness in his eyes, but then he looked down, and the shine was gone. "Good. Good. That's exactly what I'd do, in your place."

Very suddenly, Petya rushed at her, flinging his arms about her ribs and clasping her close against his chest. "You don't know," he said. "You don't know how good it is to see you stand there with your hand on your hip, glaring at me as though I've done something awful—"

She gripped his shoulders in reply, and under the thick

wool of their coats, she felt Petya trembling. If she had been Misha with his sardonic words and his confidential handclasps, she might have known how to soothe his shaking—but she was Liza, and she was Petya's older sister, and she only knew how to squeeze him until every bone in him ached with the squeezing. "Go tell Hancock to take watch," she said, "or by our Savior, I'll do worse than glare at you."

"If you can do worse than glare at me, then I'll be glad," said Petya, and he kissed Liza's cheek before turning once more to go.

Liza gathered herself, resettling her coat and retrieving her cane from where she had let it rest against the wall. Petya had begged her to carry it until she had learned to master the subtle catches and springs of the prosthesis, and although the use of it remained loathsome, Liza had to admit that it was a lovely piece. Solid walnut, with a bronze cap in the shape of a dragon's head. Her grandfather had paid for it, and sent it on the train from Moscow with her mother's jasmine tea. His parcels had arrived in time for New Year's.

Let's pray for absent friends, Misha had said, when Yelena had called for blessings at the New Year's meal. Liza had looked up from the remains of her potatoes and fish, and she had raised her wineglass to reply, *And for absent fathers*.

"Where are you now, Kesha," she muttered as she strode down the hall. It had lost the inflection of a question, in the last month, as the nearby cities had failed to send any report of him. He was dead, she supposed, or in Turkey—and if he was in Turkey, then he was worse than dead. In either case, only prayer could reach him now.

Although Misha professed his atheism to any who would hear him, she caught him now and then before the ikonostasis in the church, lighting candles before the ikons of saints he couldn't name. *Your brother would have said that I made a poor figure of an Orthodox man*, Misha had laughed, *but since he's not here, I shall pretend to know the proper rites.*

She shook off the phantom scent of incense, pacing across the great hall and up the stairs, into the clean, crisp January air.

Kesha was gone, and gone he would remain. Liza's duty was to the living.

CHAPTER TWO

The train arrived in Moscow at precisely 2:37 in the afternoon, by Kesha's watch, which meant that it was fully twenty-three minutes early—and thus, that he had twenty-three minutes to spare to find the nearest telegraph office.

He stepped off of the train with his hands in the generous pockets of his greatcoat, one palm still pressed against the warm metal of his pocketwatch and the other flicking through the bundle of identifying papers that Söz had given him. She had also provided him with a tobacco pipe of Russian make and enough money for coffee and a paper, but not with pen or ink. His task was to deliver her messages, not to send his own.

As he shouldered through the crowd, he kept his eye out for the distinctive blue caftans of cab drivers; they would be waiting at the egress most frequented by businessmen. Common folk—the kind who walked or crowded onto omnibuses rather than hiring cabs—would not require a proximate telegraph for pressing correspondence. They lacked the self-important urgency so common to men of means. If he found the cabs, he would find the telegraph office.

When he looked over the heads of the other passengers, the broad windows of Ryazansky Station showed only grey sky touched with smoke.

Through the door he saw a fellow in a tall hat—beaver fur, judging by the way it shone—being handed into a cab by a portly driver in blue. The driver took his seat on the box and chivvied the horses, who balked at the press of pedestrians in the street.

There. On the far side of the roadway, he saw the respectable storefront of the telegraph office, its windows catching the grey glow of the clouded sky. He ducked out through the door and across the street, past cab drivers hailing him with their arms waving and their hands going up to tip their broad-topped hats. He pushed through the passers-by, feeling a hand slip into his greatcoat pocket and come away with Söz's slip of paper. *So I can't keep it, after all,* he thought, and laughed.

Kesha was still laughing as he stepped into the office, where a very smart-looking young man in livery was taking orders for messages as his companion tapped out the codes. Ahead of Kesha stood two men, also in greatcoats with fur collars, also clearly eager to be gone. "Name, sir?" said the young man, and he took the first man's message and his payment with scarcely a glance.

From his inside pocket, Kesha withdrew a few coins and turned them over lightly in his hand. Old, he registered dimly. They'd been minted in the Forties. Söz kept her news current, but not her currency.

"Name, sir?" The second man offered his name and his messages, all of which went onto the forms and thence onto the telegraph itself. Money changed hands, and then the second man ducked back out onto the street.

"Name, sir?"

Kesha tightened his scarf about his neck. The words sprang almost unbidden to mind; he had said them like a litany of prayers over the past month and a half so as to commit them to memory. *My name is Yefim Yazikovich. I am married. My wife's name is Shura. She is waiting for me in Ryazan, where we live with our little white dog. His name is Sharik—*

"Tarasov," he said. "Take the following message for Mikhail Dmitrievich Orlov in St. Petersburg. If I may?" He took the pen and dipped it in the inkwell, jotting down Misha's address and the brief line over which he had labored in the long hours of his genteel captivity.

Well and pursuing your query among concerned parties to the south. IVT.

"Thank you, Monsieur Tarasov," said the young man, stamping the form and then offering his hand for the coins. After a glance down at the initials, he ventured, "Would you happen to be the same as the—"

"A different Tarasov," said Kesha. "It's been a common misconception lately." He was fishing, he knew—and running very nearly late—but the office was otherwise empty, and he couldn't resist adding, "After the recent business."

The telegraph officer nodded in sympathy. "It was a tragedy, what happened to that poor family. The father murdered, the daughter maimed, the one son dying in the wilderness—"

"The son dying? I hadn't heard *that*," Kesha broke in. His chest felt suddenly tight. He remembered Petya shoving apples at him, frantic and panicked in the ice closet. If he had followed Liza into the hills, and some horrid accident had befallen them…

"The one accused of the murder. Falsely accused, they're saying now. Oh, I know they never found a body, but it stands to reason, doesn't it? If he runs off in the dead of winter and never resurfaces—they'll be finding his bones in spring, mark my words."

"And you say the daughter was maimed? Forgive me; I haven't been following the story."

Settling back on his stool, the young man folded his hands before him. He clearly relished playing the expert, and Kesha scarcely had to feign interest in his tale. Gripping the edge of the counter in both palms, he leaned in to hear the rest. "The story goes that one of the cannon towers cracked under her, and she got crushed in the fall. What else can you expect, when you let a woman manage a cannon like that? I can't think what that family did to deserve such bad luck, but you mark my words, they did *something* awful. Ill luck never follows anyone who doesn't deserve it."

"Careful not to tip yourself back too far on that stool," said Kesha, with a laugh that felt strained at the edges, "or when you fall, we'll have to ask what *you* did to deserve it."

"He's got you there, Vova!" laughed the other officer, while Vova scrambled to straighten his stool. "I've sent your message, Monsieur Tarasov. Thank you for your business."

The bell of the office chimed as he left, and he resettled his hat over his hair. The innkeeper in Täteş had helped him to stain his hair a deep brown; in the reflective windows of the telegraph office, though, he realized that the dye made him look like nothing so much as a younger copy of his grandfather.

He consulted his pocketwatch, which informed him that it was just past three o'clock. He now had slightly less than half an hour to locate the coffee-house where he would be meeting Kent and, on the way, to acquire a current newspaper. "I seldom get papers direct from Moscow," Söz had told him, as solemnly as though she were saying, *I seldom get to visit my dear sister*. "It would be a great service to me if you would bring me a current paper."

Moscow, though, still evidently got news from the borders—and so, too, must Söz. She couldn't have failed to hear of how Liza had fallen and been crushed beneath the tower. And during all those nightly lessons in Draconic, all of the hours she'd spent grilling him on the man he was going to portray…

He looked up, and there were his grandfather's eyes reflected in the window. Yefim Yazikovich's eyes, dark and brown and touched with betrayal.

No, she couldn't have failed to hear. She had only failed to tell Kesha.

The man whom Kesha had been encouraged to call "Kent" was, in his estimation, the most thoroughly British man Kesha had ever seen. He had a weak chin and heavy jowls like a bulldog's, and he had neatly trimmed his white mustache and beard so as to accentuate rather than conceal these features. He wore a jacket in a vaguely military cut, or what must have seemed a military cut to anyone who'd never met a soldier, and he had pinned medals from no fewer than three different national armies to his chest. The one nearest to his buttons appeared to be a Prussian cross. "Peace, Kent," offered Kesha, extending a wary hand.

"'Come not between the dragon and his wrath,' old boy!" replied Kent in a theatrical bellow, seizing Kesha by the hand and pumping vigorously. "You're Yazikovich, yes? Damned shame about Wainwright. Damned shame."

Shame? Was that a cue for the Son of Shame? A moment's thought banished the notion, though. If Kesha was no longer suspected in his father's death, the other man in the ice closet must have shouldered the full weight of the fortress's suspicions. "Accused of murder!" said Kesha, making a *tsk* sound with his tongue as he disengaged his hand. "He'll wriggle his way out soon enough, though. He's far too clever to leave himself in Russian hands for long."

"The better for us, if they lock him up for life!" Here Kent gestured Kesha to a seat across the table from him. The wingback chair was faded where thousands of backsides had worn the fabric thin, and the stuffing had begun to curl out of one arm, but the springs settled into a satisfying configuration beneath his weight.

If Wainwright and Kent served different masters, then it was reasonable to conclude that Wainwright was likewise an agent of some kind. Kesha had not been sent to gather intelligence, but it would have been foolish not to pry when Kent seemed so willing to drop information in his lap. "So you're fairly sure Wainwright is one of *theirs*," Kesha hazarded, without the first idea of who *they* were or why Wainwright might belong to them. He tucked a bit of tobacco into the pipe and lit it. A month's practice had accustomed him to the taste of smoke. "I admit, I've had my doubts."

"Oh, it's quite certain," answered Kent. "A pot of coffee for my good friend Yefim Yazikovich, sir!" The server only peered at Kent as though he were a curiosity, before Kesha repeated the order in Russian. "They don't speak good English in Moscow," confided Kent. "It's damnably difficult to make oneself understood here."

"But elaborate," pressed Kesha. "What makes you so certain that he's one of theirs? And if he's theirs, and not yours, what's the shame?"

Kent took a long swig of his tea and then refilled the cup almost at once. Even for a Moscow coffee-house, the tea was black and vile, nearly viscous even before adding sugar to it. "It's always a shame to lose a worthy opponent," he said, chuckling. "As to the certainty, why, his allegiance is plain in everything he does! He's of the old man's party through and through, whatever else he is. Quite plain in how he's been foxing our communications with the east. Even after they locked him up, he still managed to get a few false messages out with our old Lear cipher. He must have a second in Yureyevsk, someone who's no great shakes at Russian, but damned if I know who."

"You make a fair case. We don't get anything like sufficient news in Ryazan. I've missed a good half of the conversation, with the news moving along the northern line through Nizhny." Here the server placed a pot of coffee before Kesha, filling a cup for him. "It's nothing like St. Petersburg, of course. I got all the news I liked, in St. Petersburg—"

"Aah, St. Petersburg! Here's to her riverside walks and her bosomy women!" Kent raised his cup in a toast, and Kesha could only toast in reply. Kent must have caught the flash of uncertainty in his eyes, because he exclaimed, "Oh, what a cad I am! Am I speaking to a married man?" Kesha nodded, hiding a smile behind his cup. "And to a St. Petersburg woman?" A second nod. "My apologies, Yazikovich. I spoke out of turn."

"Not at all. St. Petersburg is famous for her bosomy women, and my Shura would take the praise as it was meant." He remembered Madame Galiyeva's soft, dowdy figure, and nearly smiled at the unbidden memory. *Bosomy women, indeed.* "I didn't come to speak of women, though. I've come to speak of the old man. I think it will gratify you to hear what I have to tell you."

"Then tell it, man! I'm all aflutter."

Kesha gripped his cup more tightly. This was the moment of proof. This was the moment for which he had been preparing this long month. "I came here to say, *The old man dies in the last act of the play.*"

"The last act, you say." Kent tapped the lip of his cup against his front teeth as he considered. "Hm. That will be hard to manage. It'll require finesse."

"Not your strong suit, I imagine."

"You're damned right it's not. Call on Kent for drama, for fire and show, and he'll deliver in spades, but Kent's not a man for finesse. But I know a few—your type, I mean; Russians—I know a few who are just dour enough to pull it off."

"I believe you'll find that Russians excel at being dour," answered Kesha. "See that you arrange it, though, by whatever channels are necessary. Our party will manage the rest, if you can only get the old man to the stage for the last act."

Finishing his second cup, Kent put the little teacup aside and took a pipe from his coat pocket. He lit it, with a solemnity that was startling after his bluffness and bluster. "We've been preparing this one a damn long time, haven't we? Why, I've been stationed here since before we lost Orlov to Siberia, and you've been sending messages from Ryazan since at least '75...God, you were only a boy then, weren't you. Twenty-odd years old, and already part of the cause...."

"I believe in the cause," said Kesha softly. "I'd hear stories of Orlov and think, *I want to be half the man he was.*"

"I hate to puncture your childhood dreams, old boy, but even he wasn't half the man he was made out to be," answered Kent. "Oh, he could spin a socialist fable as well as anyone, but when it came to making the necessary changes...well, let's say he was always more a newspaperman than a *real* revolutionary." Secure in his English, Kent scarcely even bothered to lower his voice.

"The people loved him, though."

"The people in Russia love newspapermen!" laughed Kent. "Your daily gazettes and your serial novels—why, you've got a newspaper in your coat pocket, and I'll wager you picked it up between the train station and the coffee-house. Russian love of news. You're a walking example of it."

"I had thought that was a passion the English shared," said Kesha, rising to his feet. "But I've discharged my duty here, and I do have a newspaper to read. Thank you for the coffee, Mr. Kent."

At this, Kent rose, too, offering his hand for one last shake. "Thank you for the conversation, Yazikovich. I can't tell you how good it is to meet you at last. I can't tell you how good it is to be *doing something* at last."

This time, Kesha was ready for the force of the handshake. "Nor I, how good it is to meet you. It's been an honor, Kent."

"If this goes off, will you do what you can for my boys at the Ryazan fortress? I know we'd promised...well. We'll take care of yours, and you'll take care of ours. The Crown will remember you fondly when this business is finished." He said it as though it was an article of faith, the mechanism of the Crown's remembrance a sacred mystery—as though he could no longer imagine what the Crown could do for its servants beyond remembering them fondly.

In that moment of parting, he recognized how shabby a figure Kent made, with his borrowed medals and his lofty critiques of journalists. Orlov, at least, had earned the dubious honor of being transported for his political convictions. Kent had only grown old in the company of strangers, waiting for some distant day of glory that he had no power to bring about. "The English will always be the esteemed companions of the new Russia," Kesha assured him, patting his shoulder in what he hoped was a sufficiently comradely gesture. Beneath his hand, Kent's coat was rough and covered in tiny pills of wool. "Your boys won't be left behind. You have my word."

As he departed the coffee-house, though, Kesha's thoughts kept returning to the letter his sister had sent two months ago. *We expect to be beset soon with the English, who have designs on our holdings, and if we are to make a fair showing, we must present them with the full strength of the Tarasov family, which they will have no cause to criticize.*

CHAPTER THREE

"If we can't keep the trains on the rails," Lukin said, as though to himself, "then it won't matter whether we've finished the rails or not."

Petya raised his lamp over his head while the machinists drew aside the cloth that covered the coal car. "Only one or two trains are hit in any given month," he said, although that was difficult to bear in mind with the entrails of one of them before him. "With nearly three hundred successful trips from the Murman coast to Omsk every month, that's less than one percent."

"If the Tsar is in that one percent when he comes to drive a golden spike at Bratsk, though, it'll be on the heads of the border guards," grumbled Lukin. He cast his eyes over the remains of the engine, and the sound of his disgust echoed through the service tunnel.

By the time the load of scrap had reached Petrovsky Station, there was precious little remaining. The thrifty industrialists in Kazan had no doubt rescued the only prize aboard, the Nordenfelt gun. The blast had occurred just east of their territory, and their proximity granted them first right of salvage. The machinists near the Abramovs' territory had almost certainly taken the more delicate parts from the engine, since (as Lukin was wont to remark) they had no talent for detail work. Under the harsh light of the machinists' lamps, the shards that remained in the coal car loomed in forbidding peaks: scorched and twisted metal, sharp-edged where it had broken.

"We can salvage it," said Lukin, lowering his lamp, "but I can't think why you'd want to. At best, we'd get raw metal from it, once we melted down the pieces. There's nothing whole enough to be worth keeping."

"Raw metal will do," Petya answered, and he hung his lamp on a hook over the service track. "Liza absolutely *refuses* to allocate more money for our work, but we have to keep working. You understand, don't you? Even if all we get is enough scrap for a model—"

"I understand as well as anyone can," Lukin replied. "I might not have gone to university in St. Petersburg, but I'm a tinkerer, and I know how hard it is to stop fiddling with a problem." He hung his lamp as well, then signaled his crew to step away from the coal car. When they called the all-clear, he threw the switch that tipped that mountain of scrap out of the car and onto the tracks. Petya joined the machinists in stooping over the pile, sorting out which metal could be melted into something new and which had been too disfigured by rust or fire to survive.

The sharp edge of one piece scored Petya's leather glove; he winced and flexed his hand to be sure that it hadn't sliced all the way through. "You need better gloves," he remarked.

"That's *one* thing we need," Lukin answered, with a wry expression.

"What's the problem you're fiddling with?" asked one of the machinists after they had been sorting the metal for nearly five minutes. "A cannon?"

"If it had been a cannon, Liza would have given me every kopeck I wanted!" The crew shared a low laugh at that, punctuated here and there by the hollow sound of metal striking the coal car or the scrap bin. "She says that she's paying off our father's debts, though, and she can't spare the money for our little puzzles."

"After your father ran out the watchmaker, we all thought we'd be next," the same machinist confided. "Your father kept promising to pay him for maintaining the guns, and did he ever make good on his promises? Not *once*. I told Lukin here, I told him that I wouldn't be a slave to that man. An honest day's pay for an honest day's work, that's all we ask of your family. At least your sister pays us."

"It's more than your father ever did—may he rest in Abraham's bosom, of course," said Lukin, with a faint sound like a cough. "But if she doesn't commission work from us, what's there to do? The machinists' union has always relied on the lord of the fortress, ever since your grandfather's day."

"If you want to talk about Abraham's bosom, talk about Pyotr Alexandrovich," said one of the older machinists, casting aside a rusted piece of metal and knocking his gloves together to clear away the orange residue. "Now *there* was a righteous man."

"May he rest in peace," said Lukin. "But *you* know how important our trade is. You know, just like your grandfather did. Tell them what our project is, Petya."

Petya sucked in a breath. The air tasted of iron. "If you can, imagine a dirigible's gondola, but one that flies with its propellers alone instead of a gasbag—I believe that we'd have an advantage over the dragons at last. Something maneuverable and fast, capable of ducking and wheeling—"

"You could mount a gun on it," quipped the most garrulous of the machinists. "Your sister would be falling over herself to commission it *then*."

"I haven't had any luck with that line of argument," said Petya, but he was laughing now. "She told me to keep making better guns. She's obsessed with making me into the next Dr. Gatling."

"Obsessed with *guns*, I'll bet," the machinist replied, and there was no mistaking either his smirk or his tone. "I bet that fat little lawyer told her *all* about his gun while she was abed—"

Later, Petya would have no clear recollection of what transpired after that remark. He would only remember the beat of his heart echoing in his skull and the way the machinist had drawn in his breath when Petya's hand seized his jaw. The sharp bit of metal was in his other hand, the hand at his side—even in anger, he didn't think he could raise that sharp edge to the man's throat. "Don't say such things about my sister," Petya said. His hand didn't shake at all, although his throat was tight and there was a faint tremor in his voice. "I want you to have work, but she's still my sister, and I won't hear you say those things about her. You're better than that."

He released the man and tossed the bit of metal into the scrap bin. It struck the side like a clapper connecting with the inner curve of a bell. "I'll pay for the scrap and the labor to melt it," he said, stripping off his gloves and casting them aside. "I'm sorry for losing my temper. You deserve better from me."

"Hey," said the machinist, who caught his arm to arrest him. "I'm sorry for what I said about your sister. I just wanted you to know I was on your side. Not hers."

"My side *is* her side," said Petya firmly. With that, he shook himself free and stepped out of the pool of lamplight.

In the tavern, Galya's youngest sisters sat at the counter, tallying jars of preserves and netting bags of onions and beets. They were twins, with the same ethereally pale hair as Nastya; Polinka had tied hers up under a blue silk scarf at some earlier point in the day, but it had since fallen down about her neck. "Is your sister in?" asked Petya, at which Sonya rolled her eyes and Polinka blew out her lips.

"*Which* sister?" asked Polinka, with the condescension particular to girls under ten years of age. "I have *four* sisters."

"I mean Galya—is she in?"

"Galya's in!" cried Galya herself as she emerged from the back room, her apron laden with bulbs of garlic. "Oh, Petya, could you have come at a worse time? I'm all dusty from the cellar, and I smell like garlic, and I have garlic skins all over my dress—"

"And you're still the most beautiful woman in the room," Petya laughed.

"She's the *only* woman in the room," Sonya pointed out, but Galya only clapped a fond hand over her sister's mouth and kissed the top of her head.

"Shush, Sonechka! He's trying to be kind to me when I'm feeling like a horrid troll, and it doesn't matter what he's saying." She spilled out the garlic bulbs over the counter, then brushed the flakes of garlic skin off her apron and her skirt. "Nastya's asked us to do an inventory, but there are so many little piles and boxes and barrels in the cellar that we can hardly walk from one end to the other! So there's nothing to be done but carry everything out of the cellar and count it here, then try to put it back in better order."

"I could build you a set of shelves, if it would help," offered Petya. "If you're piling things and putting them in boxes—"

"Oh, what a dear you are!" Here Galya leaned over the counter to kiss Petya on the cheek, and when she leaned back again she was blushing as though the kiss had startled her. "Of course we have shelves, but we feed half the town. Even with shelves on every wall, even with *rows* of shelves, still the garlic winds up in a pile on the floor."

"Hanging baskets, then? If you show me the cellar, I could—"

"Don't go to any trouble!" Galya insisted, clasping his hand tightly in hers. "It's very kind of you to offer, and you know we appreciate the kindness, but this is a problem for a handyman, not for the lord of the fortress. If you were to demean yourself like that, what would your sister say?"

"She wouldn't thank you for calling me the lord of the fortress. That's the very first thing she'd say."

"Elizaveta Vladimirovna thinks she's a man, but she's *not*," opined Polinka. "But Nastya says we can't be cruel to her because she's started paying her bills."

"You can't be cruel to her whether or not she pays her bills!" cried Galya, and at the sharp note in her voice, Polinka raised her eyes from the ledger. "She's a woman of *good family*. Everyone respected her father and—"

"Everyone did what he told them to do. That's not the same."

Wringing her hands in her apron, Galya shot Petya an anxious look. "You girls keep counting our provisions, and I'll take Monsieur Tarasov up to our parlor. Be good, or I'll be very cross with you—now, you had something to say to me?"

"I did, but it can wait until we get to the parlor," said Petya, taking her arm and guiding her away from the counter. They traversed the narrow stair, past the floor where visitors lodged and up to the sloping attic rooms in which the Vasilevskaya sisters made their home. There were no windows to let in light, but Galya turned up the gaslamp at the top of the staircase, and Petya surveyed the room. It had changed precious little since last he had visited her here, five long years ago.

In Pyotr Alexandrovich's time, before the end of serfdom, the tavern had belonged to a landholder; in those days, these attic rooms might have been servants' quarters. Generations of Vasilevskaya women might have slept under those exposed rafters, shivering as their masters stretched out atop the ceramic stove in what was now the main room of the tavern. Since then, however, some scion of the Vasilevsky family had made the attic into something approaching a home. Uneven wooden paneling spanned the gaps between the rafters to insulate the living space, bits of cherrywood slotted in between boards of pine and fir, and rugs woven from rags and scraps of printed cotton warmed the floors. The room that Galya called the parlor was little more than a closet, but very proudly kept. Someone had tacked magazine pages to the walls here and there, and a little shelf of salvaged books sat beside the single sagging armchair.

It reminded him oddly of his own home—their gnawing debts and the Vasilevskayas' prosperity had brought about an unexpected convergence of circumstances.

"Please, sit," said Galya, gesturing him to the armchair.

"It's customary for the lady to sit first," said Petya, and he pulled up a little wooden stool beside the arm of the chair.

"Oh, *do* sit! I'm not a lady at all, and you'll knock your head on the ceiling." Galya tugged at his arm, and at last, Petya relented and seated himself upon the stool.

"I've been considering," he said, when Galya sank into the armchair beside him. "I know that we've had our differences in the past, and I know that my family and yours have never been exactly on the best of terms—"

"Oh, don't worry about that!" She took his hand and pressed it, and he pressed hers in return. "I can't deny that we've had our troubles, but who remembers those? You and your sister are very good patrons, and we would never think of—"

"I haven't come to criticize you, Galya," said Petya. She must have heard the slight catch in his voice, because she quieted immediately. Her palm was as clammy as his own. "There's no good way to say it, is there? No way but to say it, and be done…I've come to offer to marry you. If you'll have me."

The color drained at once from Galya's face. "No," she said. She let him go and pressed her hand to her mouth. She looked as though she were about to be ill. "No, no—no, Lord Tarasov, I can't even think why you'd say such a thing—"

"We loved each other once, didn't we?" He dropped to his knees, reaching for her hand, but she snatched it away and pressed it with the other over her mouth. Galya rose from her chair in a flurry of skirts, but he had pinned her against it, and she couldn't extract herself without brushing against him—and this, above all else, she seemed loath to do. "Didn't we love each other once?"

"*Once*," she said, and at the plea or the memory, tears came to her eyes. "Oh, Petya—oh, don't say such things to me! I'll take holy orders; I'll have myself transported to Siberia—"

"Then I won't." Petya sat upon the rug of braided scraps, and Galya took the opportunity to extract herself and rush to the door. She stood there, wringing her hands in her skirt until the fabric creased, her eyes white all the way around the irises. He could think of nothing but comforting her in her incomprehensible panic. "I didn't mean to frighten you. We'll be the most chaste, the best of friends—like brother and sister. I promise."

"You say that as though anyone should want to be your sister!" She drew in a long, shuddering breath. "You're kind to me. You've always been kind to me. But to be your sister is to be your father's daughter, and that, I would never want to be. Not when his ghost still hangs over this town like a shroud. No thank you, Petya." Slowly, carefully, she released her skirt and unbent her fingers. "Please, Petya, promise me that I'll never be anything but a friend to you."

"I promise." He drew in a long breath and pushed himself up from the rug, offering his hand. "On our Holy Savior and my hope of salvation, I promise, we'll be friends. Chaste friends."

This time, she took his hand, although her grip was weak and tremulous. "I'll be your friend, if you'll have me," she said, soft and solemn as a vow.

"I will," he said—and at this, she crushed herself against his chest and began to weep in earnest.

He held her for half an hour, stroking her mouse-blonde hair and whispering soothing nonsense against her ear. She didn't answer him when he asked her why she'd flown into such a panic at the offer of marriage, and he didn't answer her when she asked why he'd offered it in the first place.

After their pledges and tears, it would have been the height of cruelty to tell her that he'd thought it politic to reconcile their families.

CHAPTER FOUR

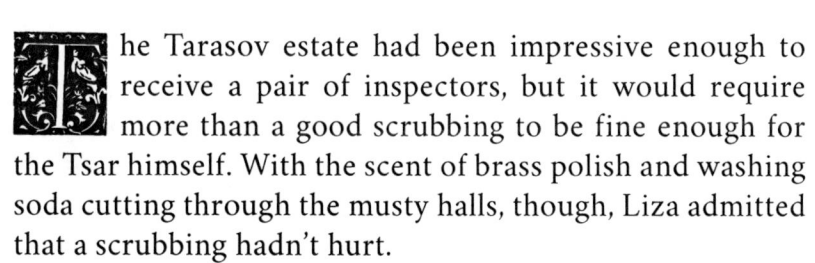

The Tarasov estate had been impressive enough to receive a pair of inspectors, but it would require more than a good scrubbing to be fine enough for the Tsar himself. With the scent of brass polish and washing soda cutting through the musty halls, though, Liza admitted that a scrubbing hadn't hurt.

When Liza had been a child, her Uncle Pasha had insisted upon calling the mess hall the great hall. "This is a lordly estate, not a barracks," he had said gruffly, and at her uncle's direction, banners had been hung between the dragons' heads and ancient weapons had decked the walls. Liza's father had overseen the emplacement of three fine chandeliers, which the servants had brought down and laden with white candles before the neighboring lords came to dine.

The chandeliers had been sold with the dragons' heads; the old gold and black bunting and the banners with the Tarasov family crest had long since been picked apart and sold as partial bolts of silk. Today, though, as Liza surveyed the Russian Imperial flags flanking the head of the table, she found it in her to call that hall great again.

"See if you can find something with our crest on it in the library—or our colors, if you can't find our crest," she instructed the errand boy, who saluted and darted out of the room at once. "Someone get me Jaworski. I need to review our security—"

"The cook wants a word with you," said Petya, who had sprung up from God only knew where. "I told her that the menu was fine as it was, but she insisted that she wouldn't go forward without your approval."

"I don't have time for the cook," Liza replied. "You know better than I do what they eat in St. Petersburg. If you think the menu is fine as it is, then it's fine. Tell her I've reviewed her menu and liked it. Now, someone get me Jaworski. I know he's not on watch—"

"He's right behind you," supplied Jaworski, and Liza pivoted on her good leg to seize him by the shoulders.

"Good," she said, taking in the mild amusement twitching up the corner of his lips. "Good. Can we manage something ceremonial when he gets out of the carriage? Petya won't let me drill the Englishmen to parade in the courtyard, but we ought to have *some* ceremony. I won't have the damn Tsar of Russia thinking we're a bunch of ill-bred country louts."

"Good Cossack stock," Jaworski agreed. "Only the best-bred of country louts. What about this? We'll have a six-gun salute, and the best gunners in the fortress running them."

"That means you'll be in one of those towers," said Liza, with a broad grin. "I can't think of a better man than you for the job."

"It's an honor. I'll prepare the men myself." He clasped one hand over the wrist of the other, squaring his shoulders as though preparing for inspection. "What else? You said you wanted to review security."

"He's most vulnerable when he's getting off the train. We'll want a few men there to prevent the crowd from getting raucous. Coordinate our own men with Utkin's. If he wants to be a constable in this town, he can start earning his keep."

"I'll do that. Only the most reliable men at the station—and he'll be staying at the keep?"

"Is there anywhere else to put up a guest of that caliber? Mother's managing *that*. She'll soon have Father's old rooms ready to receive him. Petya!"

At the doorway, Petya turned, wide-eyed. "Yes?"

"Get me back on the watch rota. This leg is excellent."

Petya only nodded and said, "Right away!" before vanishing from sight.

Liza breathed in, savoring the feeling of adrenaline coursing throughout her body. In the long weeks of recovery, when good sense and her mother's quiet half-threats had kept her pinned within the keep, she had felt an old, familiar longing to be *out* and *doing*. She had bullied Petya into fencing with her in her chair and called for Elliot to wheel her about the courtyard, and with her father's ledgers spread over her bed and a lap desk over her thighs, she had drafted scathing letters to every last one of their creditors.

By New Year's Eve, four years hence, the Tarasov family would finally be out of debt—and still an itch had crept beneath her skin that no fiscal triumph could alleviate.

This eased her. With her own two feet beneath her, men relying upon her to conduct them efficiently and honorably, the promise of a cold watch with a flask of hot tea—*this* gave her purpose.

She fastened the furred collar of her coat about her neck and plucked up her hat from the rack, then swung out of the hall and up the stairs to the servants' door. Hardly anyone used it anymore since Petya had fixed the gates, but she had been confined too long to have learned new habits. She took the gravel drive to the village, teaching herself anew how that shifting stone felt beneath her weight. Too often, she realized almost at once, she rolled her heel to adjust to the uneven surface, and that locked her foot in place and made her stumble. The going was slow for the first part of the journey, and halfway down the hill she paused to sit on a large stone and rest her leg.

Atop the hill, the fortress stood whole and perfect. The

new tower rose proudly toward the clouds, and at the very peak stood their borrowed Gardner gun on an absurd little tripod. It was a poor substitute for the Gatling guns, but until Petya's machinists could repair the innards of the one she'd broken, it would have to do.

She sat in silence, listening to the wind whistling over the low hills and feeling tiny snowflakes melting against her cheeks. At last, refreshed by the interlude, she continued down the hill into the town.

"Mademoiselle Tarasova!" called Kostya the arms dealer, with a genial wave. "You've come down from your tower at last—and on foot!"

"What good is a new leg if you ride in a carriage everywhere?" she said, dropping a hand on his shoulder. "I'm sending the cart down to your shop this afternoon for more ammunition. The usual order. Have it ready to load."

"Ah, so you *are* back! If you'll pardon an old gossip," Kostya confided, "I'd heard rumors that your brother would be taking over tenure of the keep. Due to your injury, of course, and for no other reason—the thought!—but we'd think no less of you if you wanted to retire—"

"Your informants are wrong," Liza replied firmly. "I'm back, and I plan to stay. The fortress is mine by right."

"Well, good health to you, I say!" He clapped her on the back with one meaty hand, and she released him as he released her. "Good health to the Tarasovs, and good health to Tsar Alexander II! Is it true he'll be stopping through on his way to put a golden spike in the rails?"

"I don't know about golden spikes, but he'll stop here for a day. He'll stop at every fortress, if I can trust the Abramovs."

"I never trust the Abramovs," said Kostya, with a delicate shudder. "Such tale-bearers! A good day to you, Mademoiselle Tarasova, and I'll have the ammunition ready just as you ask."

When she had disengaged from Kostya, Liza made her way to the new constabulary that Utkin had established near the telegraph office. *You can't keep sending to Nizhny for officers to inspect every crime,* he'd told her at the end of December, *and someone needs to keep your English suspect in custody.*

"Utkin," she called from the doorway, and he rose like a roused lion from a mountain of paperwork. His hair was askew, as though he'd been raking at it with his fingers, and his cuffs were stained with ink.

"Elizaveta Vladimirovna," he said, with a thin smile. "Have you come about Lieutenant Wainwright's case?"

"I've come about the Tsar's visit, although I'll be happy to hear about the case if you have news."

"It's poor, poor news," said Utkin. "I've tried to wring a confession from him, but he tells the same story no matter what tactics I try. Very irregular. Very disappointing. He insists that he only found the body, and that he carried your father to the keep on his back. This, he claims, accounts for the footprints at the scene and the blood on his shoes. That he stood where the murderer stood, he cannot account for, except to say that it must be a very unfortunate coincidence."

"It's the same story he's been telling since the beginning. I'm not surprised that you can't get anything else from him. He's had time to practice this story until he can repeat it by heart."

"Your lawyer Orlov doesn't think that the charges will stick with a jury. The lieutenant's Russian is good enough to plead well. Our evidence is too circumstantial to convict him. Even the motive...if your brother had asked *what* your father knew, we'd be in a better position now." Utkin drummed his fingers against the desk. "Very poor business. Very poor. Still, we'll see what comes of it, when he's in front of a judge and a good barrister."

"We'll see," Liza agreed, although she felt a sharp, screeching frustration building inside her. "I can't stand the thought that he might go free. Whatever else Petya thinks he is, spy or agitator or God only knows what else—we need only prove that he's a murderer."

"Between the two of us," said Utkin, "it was easier to manage such things in the Sixties. In wartime, the line was thinner between murderers and agitators. Easier to deal with the both of them in a *tidy* fashion, if you take my meaning."

Nothing was clean in that war, Uncle Pasha had told Liza once, but to Utkin she only said, "You served in Poland, then. My uncles both served—I lost my Uncle Sasha in the war. I was only a girl then."

"I didn't know the man, but you can believe me when I say this: your Uncle Sasha died a hero," said Utkin, with a peculiar, muted intensity that Liza had marked in him before. "It was possible to die a hero, once, but not anymore. Now, there are only messy deaths—murder, accident, and death by paperwork, which is the messiest of the three."

The two of them examined one another, Utkin behind his desk and Liza with her weight on her good foot, and as their eyes locked, she felt a common understanding pass between them. *He wants to be my Uncle Sasha*, Liza thought.

Liza turned the conversation toward the Tsar's visit, and for half an hour they held forth on the defensible posts near the railway station, but her thoughts were elsewhere as they spoke. When she left the office for the tavern, she drew her coat more closely about her shoulders.

It had been Uncle Sasha's coat, nearly a generation ago, and after his death, it had become her father's. In the seams, there lingered the scent of gunpowder.

"Your front room looks as though someone's moved a cellar into it."

Nastya smirked, arms folded. She wore a clean white apron over her dark blue gown, and her hair was pinned in neat braids beneath a trim white cap—and yet some regal quality in her bearing made it impossible to mistake her for a servant. "That's because someone *has* moved a cellar into it. I need an inventory, and Yulchik needs to know what to cook for the next month. Sonya and Polinka need something to keep their hands from getting idle. And so the cellar is in the front room—"

"And the gambling in the cellar?" Nastya had the good grace to smile at the interruption, although she didn't laugh. A smile was better, Liza decided. A smile was very nearly sincere.

"Your brother meant to marry my sister," Nastya said, after barely a pause to collect her thoughts. "He bowed down to her in our parlor and begged her to marry him. What do you have to say about that?"

"I say he can marry whoever he likes. Our mother will try to pair him with some dour girl in Moscow, with new money and a common name. If he's going to marry someone with a common name anyway, why shouldn't he marry who he likes?"

"I heard you were paying off your debts," answered Nastya. Her eyes flicked briefly toward her cash box. "The Tarasovs are mercenaries. It wouldn't be so strange, to see you sell your brother to the richest woman."

"I'm not my mother," Liza said, and at once she bit back a curse at her sharpness. "I'm tired of talking about money. You told me to come to you in a month, and here I am." She gestured from her chin to her sternum, as though to present herself for inventory. *Item: teeth (clean), Item: breasts (2)*.

Nastya surveyed her from the top of her hat to the fur collar and lining of her coat, down at last to the tips of Liza's boots. "You look well," she said finally. "Your brother made you that foot?"

Liza raised her chin. "He did. Don't change the subject, Anastasia Ivanovna. You asked me to come to you in a month, and I've come. Were you promising me something, when you asked it?"

"I was offering." Nastya took in a long breath, as though to fortify herself with the scents of home. With the cellar's contents lining the walls of the front room, the air was redolent with cinnamon and radishes and garlic and tea. "I'm still offering, if you want it—but if you bow to me and ask me to marry you, I'll give you the same answer that Galya gave your brother."

"Ask you to marry me!" laughed Liza. "If nothing else, I might do it to see my mother's face. Come to the keep tonight, by the…by the side entrance—" it seemed more than usually unkind, to call it the servants' entrance or the tradesmen's entrance "—and I'll meet you there."

"And then, Liza?"

"And then…" She licked her lips. A shiver traced the nerves that phantom pain had worn raw. "And then, we'll see."

In the heated air of the bedroom, her sheets in disarray beneath her, Liza stretched until her whole body became one glorious ache. "That was good, wasn't it?" she said, and the hoarseness of her own voice surprised her. "Was that good, Nastasya? Nastenka?"

Nastya pushed herself up on one elbow, regarding Liza with cool grey eyes. Liza had never before understood what the French writers meant when they spoke of a woman's dewy white skin, but with sweat collecting across Nastya's breasts and plastering her fine hair to her neck, Liza thought she knew now. "This changes nothing, Tarasova. You don't own me because you've taken me to bed."

"I never *wanted* to own you," said Liza. "I only wanted you to look at me with something other than contempt."

At that Nastya laughed and sat up, adjusting her shift until the sleeves lay nicely over her shoulders. Her laugh was a thin, silvery thing, like the ring of a little bell. "*Contempt!*

What does the contempt of a woman like me mean, to a Tarasov? When your father threw his great gut around in my tavern, in my *father's* tavern, and never expected so much as a peep from us when he refused to pay his bills! When you drank and gambled *in my home*, expecting me to sit with you and laugh and be docile while your father put his hand on my waist—and you want something other than contempt! I have contempt for every last one of you. I could fill barrels with my contempt, but then I'd have no room for brandy!"

"I hate brandy." Snatching up her cane, Liza threw the blankets free and stumped across the floor to where she'd let her trousers fall. Her skin smelled of Nastya's perfume and sweat; she could scrub her flesh until the skin was raw, and she would still smell Nastya on her. "If you have such *contempt* for me, then why did you come to bed with me—to make me fawn over you? You know that I fawn over you. I've made a laughingstock of myself with my fawning over you!"

Nastya didn't answer at once. Instead she wrapped her corset about herself, fixing the clasps in the front and then tightening the laces in the back. She had deft hands, well-suited to the task; she had never had a maidservant to tighten her corset, and so she had learned to be as cunning as a maidservant with her fingers. "I came because I wanted to," answered Nastya, when she had tied off a bow at the bottom of the corset. "And my wanting to changes nothing. You aren't your father. You promised me nothing in exchange. This changes nothing."

For a moment, Liza felt a falling sensation—as though she were falling again from the tower, the earth rising up to break her into pieces. "You fucked my father," she said softly. "You *fucked my father*."

"You make it sound as though I had a choice," said Nastya. Disgust curled her perfect upper lip. Whether it was disgust at herself or disgust at the Tarasovs, Liza didn't care to know.

"Get out," Liza snarled. "Is that what you do to keep your place in this town? You fuck whoever keeps the fortress, and you keep us in your little white palm—well, you're wrong, Anastasia Ivanovna. You're wrong if you think that this changes nothing."

As though unperturbed, Nastya began doing up the buttons at the back of her gown. Her voice shook, though, when she spoke again, and she couldn't meet Liza's eyes. "You're an ignorant bitch, Tarasova, and someday I'll spit on your grave the way I spat on your father's."

"Say another word about my father, and I will not be responsible for what I do to you."

"You never have been," Nastya replied, and with that she plucked up her boots and walked out the door. It fell heavily shut behind her.

Sagging into a chair, trousers still wadded in one hand, Liza groaned and reached for the little bottle of morphine on her bedside table. She couldn't help feeling, in the pit of her stomach, that Nastya had won in a game she'd never wanted to play.

CHAPTER FIVE

To the southeast of Ryazan, in a clearing amid the sparsely wooded land on the banks of the Oka, Boris Baivich lay curled like a cat with his head pillowed on his hindlimbs.

Kesha paused at the edge of the clearing, where the snow lay in an unbroken crust. He quelled the hope welling in him as brutally as he might have quelled an insurrection. *It must be some other dragon*, he told himself. *Some other dragon with a snow-and-coal pattern on his scales.*

The dragon opened one sleepy eye as Kesha's footsteps stilled, then shook the snow from his mane and rose to his feet. "Were you not expecting me?" he asked, in easy Russian that destroyed all doubt. "I can't imagine you were planning to walk all the way back to Turkey."

Kesha recovered himself. He crossed the remaining distance briskly but without undue haste, measuring his steps. Even so, he couldn't keep his voice from trembling. "I'd thought you were dead. That day in the cavern—"

Boris tilted his head, amusement touching the corners of his eyes. "Dead! You really *must* think we're barbarians, if you can believe that any dragon would kill the clan's historian. Our stories would die with me, and that would be a calamity too great to measure. It takes ages to train a historian, you know."

"We tend to shuttle them through universities as quickly as possible and then cellar them in libraries until they've matured," said Kesha, because it was better than saying, *That grey dragon didn't seem to care about your stories when it had you by the throat.* "Three or four years to produce a historian, and then another half-dozen or so before he's generally regarded as any good."

"Your historians sound dreadfully easy to replace," observed Boris.

"That's rather the point, I think. We humans desire only the freshest history."

"Indeed! The Voice wants history so fresh that it hasn't yet been written."

"And Aysel? Is she also well?" Whatever custom protected Boris, Kesha could not imagine its aegis extended to Aysel.

"Aysel is quite well, too, although still discontent with our lot." Boris snorted. "You may as well climb onto my back. The sooner you report, the sooner we can have a proper conversation." He caught a claw in the bag over his shoulder and teased it around until he could fetch out a few flakes of some silvery metal. If the military pamphlets were anything to go by, it was probably zinc.

Kesha heaved himself up on the ledge of Boris's shoulder, settling behind the ridged scapulae and before the fan of his dorsal sail. Boris's back was slick with snowmelt, but the earth beneath where he'd been resting was dry. He might have chosen the spot immediately upon his arrival and then refused to budge from it until Kesha returned. "Are you ready to go?"

"I'm ready to be gone, which amounts to the same thing," Boris said, and with a heave, he pushed himself upright and let his chest expand until he could fling himself into the air.

Weeks of watching them had done little to cool Kesha's wonder at how the dragons rose into the sky—the older ones swift as arrows, the acid glands at the backs of their throats filling their ribs with a light, hot gas; the younger ones, slowly and with care, jetting gusts of fire from their nostrils. "The mix of chemicals is a delicate one," Söz had told him, as they'd watched the dragons take to the air in a shimmering flight. "Even a dram misplaced will ignite the mixture. They release the flame to keep from exploding."

Galen had known it, all those centuries ago, when he had written of the volatile humors. The young dragons, Kesha thought, were like their human counterparts: hot-blooded, their bodies coursing with chemicals that could set them ablaze at any moment. Small wonder they took such care as they ascended from the earth.

For a moment, beneath the thin crusting of ice, Kesha could hear the waters of the Oka gliding past. Then there was only the rush of the west wind and the faint but palpable throb of Boris Baivich's heart. "When we arrive at Täteş," said Kesha, "I hope that you'll tell me more about your poetry."

Boris's ribs swelled beneath his scales, beneath the heavy wool of Kesha's trousers, and he had to grip Boris's mane to prevent himself from being inadvertently shrugged off. "When we arrive at Täteş, I'll let you help me write it."

※

The town of Täteş was by now a welcome sight, and Kesha had taken care to learn its maze of avenues and lanes and frosted gardens. He knew the baker whose white apron he espied from Boris's back, and he knew the children throwing a stick for their spotted dog amid their mother's withered bean plants. When he entered the inn, with its familiar curling ornaments on the molding, Söz was waiting at her usual table with a short stack of papers before her. "You've done well," she said at once, then returned her gaze to her papers. "Word went toward Bratsk within an hour of your arrival in Moscow. I do not doubt that it has made similar haste to St. Petersburg."

"A plate of lentils, please," Kesha told the innkeeper, and he dropped into the seat across from Söz. "I've arranged someone's murder, haven't I."

"You have," agreed Söz, with scarcely an upward glance. "Go on. Tell me what else you believe you have done."

"The English are working with revolutionary factions. That's plain enough. If I've arranged a murder at the hands of revolutionaries, then I must suppose that I'm party to a regicide." He swallowed, then told the innkeeper, "Tea, as well. Honey with it."

"Go on," Söz said. Her voice was as mild as a monk's, but she met his eyes when she said it. He knew that he had her attention.

"The man accused of my father's murder—Lieutenant Wainwright. He was tasked with preventing this, wasn't he? If he's working in opposition to the rest of the English, and in opposition to your aims, then he must be an agent of the Tsar. I can only imagine why he'd be assigned to my family's holdings."

"I have not been privy to the rationale behind that choice, but I suspect that it was because your family's keep is famously understaffed," said Söz idly. "He would have been under little scrutiny, particularly if he could manage to win your father's trust. I do recall that he requested to lodge his men at the keep rather than in the town, although they could have stayed more cheaply there. I can only presume that he wished to gain your family's favor."

"It was a pity he didn't manage it," Kesha replied. "Your man Kent thought him a worthy opponent."

"Kent was not *my* man," answered Söz, smiling faintly. "He was merely a man I used, without his knowledge or consent."

"I understand the principle." A plate of lentils arrived for Kesha, along with tea and a pot of honey, and he began to eat. He was acutely aware, in the moment before he put the spoon to his lips, of the fragile contingency of that cool night at the Vasilevsky tavern. Had his father not come down from the fortress that night, and had he not bled to death in the alleyway...

It was no good imagining what might have been. He remembered how Wainwright had huddled on his bale of straw in the ice closet, the dragons' heads watching with blank and accusing eyes, and in his heart Kesha said a brief prayer for him—a prayer that was equal parts *May he weather his tribulations* and *May he rest in Abraham's bosom*.

When he went to visit the dragons' hall, Kesha wore the uniform of an Ottoman irregular. "The dragons hunt by sight," Söz had told him as she pressed the deep blue coat into his arms. "Such a coat may have saved your life, when you visited them last. They saw that you were dressed as one of us, and they knew that I had marked you as my own."

Atop the bundle had been the tapered woolen cylinder of an Ottoman Cossack cap, and he had wondered idly whether another branch of his family—a branch that had never known the name *Tarasov*—wore such caps to war. "Will you issue me a sword as well?" he had asked.

She had smiled as though she thought he might be joking. "Do you wish me to issue you a sword?"

"I'd prefer a gun. But thank you."

By now, he had worn the uniform long enough that it scarcely felt like a costume anymore. Even the high collar of the undershirt felt nearly natural against his throat. As he crossed the rye fields to the dragons' lair, he wondered if he had ever owned such a comfortable overcoat.

At the door to the round, tiled hall sat an enormous dragon with her claws full of metal rods and lengths of wire. Something about the shape of the dragon's face made Kesha think this was a female, but he couldn't be sure. Even Söz appeared mostly to take dragons at their word when they called themselves male or female. As Kesha watched, she shaped the rods into a rough cross. As she twisted the wire around the rods, he realized that she was weaving a basket.

Säläm came more easily to his lips than *Zdravstvujtye*, for both the Turks and the Tatars knew what it meant. "*Säläm*," he told the dragon, and he tried to calm his anxious heart. He could not forget how the old grey dragon had clutched Boris Baivich by the throat at the sound of Russian, nor could he forget that his *Säläm* was still touched with Slavic accents.

If she could hear Russia in his voice, she took no notice of it. The dragon only inclined her head and replied, "*Säläm*," as easily as though he had been a soldier like Orazbek come to pay call.

"Boris Baivich?" he asked. "*Kayda?*" Where?

The dragon glanced over her shoulder and into the hall. Kesha's Tatar wasn't yet good enough for him to follow what she said, but the cant of her head and her aggrieved tone made her meaning clear enough. *He's inside, and I'm quite comfortable out here in the chill, so don't expect me to take you by the hand and lead you to him.* There was no menace in it. She might have been any old woman taking the air on her porch, irate at having her rest interrupted by an unwelcome visitor.

Only then did Kesha really understand that he had expected the dragons to post a guard against him.

He passed the vast old dragon and stepped into the round hall, onto tiles painted with a history of exile. Somewhere among those unnumbered tiles lay the snatches of story that Boris Baivich had read to him, although he couldn't pick them out amid their fellows. He wondered how many dragons could read the writing there—and indeed, how many needed to. Orazbek had said that the older dragons shared stories of their past. The dragon at the door must have been old enough to remember every incident on the tiles, from the flight across the Himalayas to the splintering of her people in Russia. Had Kesha's Tatar or Draconic been better, or had he been sure she would answer him if he spoke in Russian, he would have turned around to ask her where she had been on the day the dragons defected.

His Tatar was abysmal, his Draconic worse. He kept walking.

After the dry cold of the rye fields, the central cavern's sultry heat made Kesha's skin go clammy with sweat. He wove between knots of dozing dragons, past circles of dragons gathered around some board game played with painted stones, and he paused at every black-flecked white dragon and then moved on. He ought to have been able to recognize Boris Baivich's face; he ought to have been able to distinguish among dragons at a glance, as though they were any other people. Not until he saw a black-and-white dragon hunched over a tray of hexagonal tiles, though, did he feel the faintest spark of recognition.

"I didn't know you glazed the tiles yourself," said Kesha in Russian, once he'd surveyed the room to be sure that the towering grey dragon was absent.

"And mix the glazes, and fire the clay," Boris replied, sighing. "Bai would *weep* at the pigments we use. She had such a deft hand with enamels! She could breathe in the air over a fire and know by the taste of it when it was hot enough to fire ceramics. But of course, none of these barbarians care to learn about pottery."

"Was Bai your mother?" asked Kesha. "Her name is in your patronymic."

"As I understand it, patronymics are meant to identify precisely whose legacy you've failed to uphold. She was my teacher. Our last great poet." Boris yawned and began to brush a batch of tiles with an even coat of glaze. "Humans called her Bai, and she learned this art when the Tianshun Emperor reigned over the Great Ming."

"When, exactly?"

"Do you humans *never* study each other's history? Then there's no hope that you'd understand when it was if I said that it was the year that—" a half-musical scream "—hatched twins with eyes like rubies. *A very long time ago*, that's the best I can do."

"And was she the first dragon to write your poems on tiles? Or do other dragons paint their histories, in other parts of the world? Do you ever speak with other communities of dragons, or are you isolated here?"

Boris laughed. "So many questions! First, these aren't poems; they aren't closed in circles. They're histories, which are an entirely different thing. I understand that there's a tradition of painting poems and histories on tile in this benighted country, which the Turks most probably borrowed—there were dragons living in Turkey before we came under their protection, did you know?"

"Why didn't the Turks use them in their wars against us?"

"That, I couldn't tell you." He tilted his head, considering the glazed tiles. The red clay had vanished beneath a layer of white, which glistened wetly in the lamplight. "Some say that they were philosophers and artists. There are more than a few of us who might have preferred to have been born into such a people. The sort of people who would have to be dragged by their tails into battle."

Kesha thought of his own desertion of the front, and he nodded. He was acutely conscious that he was wearing an Ottoman uniform. "Do you believe that?"

"It's a very good story," said Boris, more quietly. "I am fond of good stories."

He set aside the brush tipped with white glaze and took up a second, more delicate brush. The horsehair had been meticulously cleaned, but Kesha could see faint traces of dark blue staining the handle. "Is there a good story in you?" asked Boris Baivich. "I'll paint it, if you like. After I've rendered it in more elegant words, of course."

Kesha looked from the pot of blue paint to Boris's face.

His eyes were a striking shade of blue, like the sky when the first light of morning touched it. "Is that the price of your stories? One of my own?"

"What a strange thing," Boris remarked, "that I should offer to immortalize you, and be told that I ask too much." He dipped his brush in the blue paint, and Kesha watched him draw a series of signs on the still-wet glaze. At first, the symbols made no sense—they included none of the familiar characters for mountains and dragons and sheep, nor any of the ideograms he knew for *Russia* and *Turkey*.

Then, with a suddenness that stopped his breath, he realized that Boris was writing in Cyrillic.

There came a man, the story read, *who loved poems so much that he could not bear the thought of finding himself in one.*

Kesha laughed despite himself. "Now write, *but then a clever dragon trapped him inside one and cursed him to live forever there.*"

"Immortality must be a curse, of course," complained Boris, but he recorded Kesha's words faithfully until the tile was full.

CHAPTER SIX

At half past eight, the hollow chime of a wooden bell rang out over the dragons' hall. Kesha jerked up from the heat of the kiln at the sound, all of his old training calling him to rise and man the guns—but Boris showed no sign of concern, and although the other dragons roused themselves, they did not appear alarmed. The coiled dragons rose from their knots, and the rest glanced up from their games or projects. The basket-weaver had brought her work inside a bit before sunset, and she made an approving sound and began clamping the wires in place. A tight knot of three dragons continued debating some trivial point (or rather, some point that Boris had declared trivial) in raised voices, their eyes locked and their muscles straining with the effort of holding one another still.

"Not every bell is a warning bell," Boris said, with a significant yawn.

"What's this one, then? A clock striking? A call to prayer?"

"I should tell you that it's both, and see what you make of it. Yes, dragons assign an hour to each god, a god to each hour."

"Nonsense. The bell hasn't rung once since I came, and I've been here since well before sunset. At least four hours."

"Four of *your* hours. How long is a dragon's hour?" Boris rested his elbows on the hearthstone around the kiln, his eartips pricking in amusement. "As long as a thousand, thousand heartbeats, or as long as it takes to forgive a grievance."

For a moment, Kesha wanted to believe in the poetry of those hours, in how they raveled out to infinity when forgiveness would not come, or in their swift passage when hope set the heart aflame. At the end of that moment, he said, "So much for a historian's commitment to truth."

Boris sighed. "Truth is dull. The supper bell is dull. Why *not* gods and grievances?"

"There's a story in the supper bell, too, some would say." He leaned against Boris's flame-warmed scales, nestling into the crook between his forelimb and his ribs. "A good historian could find poetry in that, too—in the story of how the bell was carved, and when, and why."

"In the first years when the Turks began bringing us food, a few of our elders took to meeting them at the entryway and then dividing the food between them, leaving none for the rest of us," said Boris, tossing his head. "One particularly vile specimen said that she was our leader, because the Turks seemed to like leaders, and they believed that she would tell the rest of us about the deliveries. And so the rest of us went hunting, as we always did, and inevitably we hunted from the Turkish farmers' flocks, as we always did. And those farmers brought their grievances to their leaders—"

"As they always did."

One of Boris's ears twitched. "If you think you can tell a better history than I can, you're welcome to try it. As I was saying, most of us had no idea that we were being robbed, although the Turks certainly knew that *they* were. Those who stole from the Turks were punished according to their laws, and those who stole from *us* were honored as our leaders. It seemed an awful lot of unjustly allocated punishment to some of us, and so we asked the Turks to start ringing a bell when the meat came. And that," he pronounced, "is the story of the bell."

"Not dull at all. Are the same dragons still treated as your leaders?"

"The Voice knows better, but her military counterparts are less subtle. More susceptible to force of personality. And it certainly doesn't help that most of these dragons could crumple me like a scrap of cheap paper."

"But still you call one of your elders a 'vile specimen.' Are you a kind of radical? Like Aysel?"

At that, Boris only huffed and nosed Kesha's hair. "Don't be absurd. Radicals have convictions. I have only complaints."

With his back propped against Boris, Kesha had an excellent view of half of the cavern. The dragons went to their supper with the half-starved eagerness of watchmen leaving a long shift, none of the polite simultaneity of a family anticipating the shared prayer before the meal. While a few (and mostly the youngest) went skittering across the floor tiles at the first whiff of roast lamb, the rest moved more warily, watching one another as they went. At the door, a scarred old dragon shoved a pair of youths aside. They let their elder pass without complaint, then gave one another looks of shared resentment before following.

The dragons consider themselves social equals, guided by their elders but not ruled by them, Söz had told him once, but the exchange at the door gave the lie to this claim. If they were all of them slightly starving, they had shaped a kind of social order around this fact, complete with customs for establishing status and precedence.

Were they really a nomadic people not long ago, as Orazbek said? wondered Kesha. *Even Söz couldn't tell me anything about the citadel except that it was a legend, like Eden or Atlantis. Yet Boris and Aysel spoke of a lost fatherland, and even now, they're a people who fire pottery and draw metal into wire for baskets. They're a people with a tradition of building kilns and forges and mines, and making bricks to build them. Nomadic, perhaps, but of necessity rather than inclination. Such a passionate repudiation of a homeland can only come from having one's palaces sacked and burned.*

At last, Boris stretched and straightened, nudging Kesha off of his shoulder. "Shall we have tea?"

Kesha rose to his feet. Over Boris's back, he caught sight of the three debating dragons gathered around an enormous metal and porcelain contraption that looked like nothing so much as a giant samovar. "I didn't know dragons drank tea."

"Tea is the first requirement for civilization," said the nearest of the dragons in Russian, snorting in amusement.

"A *samovar* is the first requirement for civilization, thank you very much," Boris replied. "No country without a samovar can truly be said to have a culture."

"Dragons can't be said to have a culture, either. We have only our ancestors' sad songs, some Russian teapots, and a few cast-off Turkish laws," said the dragon on the far side of the samovar. "The first requirement for civilization is a shared conviction that we *are* a people, and we do not even have that."

The third dragon said something derisive-sounding in their own language, so quickly that Kesha caught only one word: *France.*

"You needn't remind me," the second dragon said. "I have no intention of remaking the calendar. All I mean is that we used to be *a* people. Now, we're only people."

"We have our songs. We have a history," said the first dragon. He (was it he?) poured out a measure of tea into a cup painted with praise for a dragon long-dead.

The second dragon snorted. "*Birds* make music."

"What is your music like?" asked Kesha—but what their music was like, he never learned, for at that moment, the vast grey dragon hauled herself arm over arm out of the entry hall and screamed her triumph until the kettle shook on the samovar.

Kesha shrank against Boris's flank, but the grey dragon seemed uninterested in him or in Boris. She squeezed free of the entrance and immediately seized a haunch of roast lamb in one hand, stripping flesh from bone with her claws and then eating each strip with surprising daintiness. While she was occupied with her meal, two other dragons entered abreast, shouting at each other with the half-dizzy camaraderie of boxers reliving a match.

Kesha's heart lurched. One of those two was Aysel.

Boris raised a cup to his lower lip, resting it against the row of sharp teeth behind it. "You know what they are, I suppose?"

Kesha nodded. "A raiding party."

An irate noise. "I was going to say, 'a device for turning scholars into louts,' but I suppose 'raiding party' will do. Aysel! *Vení!*"

Aysel looked up as sharply as though she had been shot. She said something to her comrade and then crossed the floor to them, her belly dragging along the tiles like a snake's. She settled against Boris's side and took his teacup, drinking it in his stead. Kesha briefly smelled something earthy and sharp, like crushed leaves, and then the cup was empty. *Just like Liza—high-handed, arrogant, not at all concerned with another's inconvenience.*

Boris coughed into the ensuing silence. One of the dragons by the samovar refilled his cup.

At last, Aysel said, "I waited for you to return, after you came to the cavern." She yawned, which Kesha had begun to suspect meant she was uncomfortable, and then scratched behind one pointed ear until gossamer hairs flew from her mane. "I do not enjoy waiting for humans. It is so seldom worth the wait."

Kesha slid his hands in his pockets. With Boris at his side, drinking tea and listening to them talk with an expression of mild interest, the long days of worry felt preposterous. "I thought they'd killed Boris Baivich, or I'd have come back."

Aysel snorted in annoyance. "You speak of how Xia strangled him, do you not? If you let it distress you, you will have no room in your heart for anything but distress. As for Boris Baivich—" she tilted her head, meeting his eyes with one of her own "—he clearly has not learned to stop associating with Russian men or *radicals*." She seemed to savor that Russian word as though she enjoyed its taste.

"Not for want of reminding," Boris replied. "I will eat, if neither of you will." With that, he finished his tea and set the cup down upon the tile, a touch too hard and a touch too fast. It struck with a crack like something breaking. Aysel watched him go.

"I should not have teased him," she said, more softly. "That was not generous. He resents Xia more than he dares to say, for she is to him all of the ugliness of the past without the trappings of poetry."

"Did he have reason to fear for his life?" asked Kesha.

"He is our story-teller! Our writer of poems!" said Aysel at once. "We cannot destroy our story-teller, however we might wish it. Who else would record our histories?"

"The rest of you do not record, then?"

"We *remember*," Aysel replied. "And we teach. Thus, when you ask me why it was that my clan chose to leave your land, I can tell you at once."

"To protest the grant of land to my forebears, and to help the Turks…'make angels'? Can you mean that the dragons have become Muslims?" For that, he thought, the people of Moscow and St. Petersburg would certainly have refused to aid the dragons and burned their histories. For a betrayal not only of Russia, but of God, the priests would have been only too happy to stoke the flames.

She wrote that she saw poor people flinging holy texts into the flames, all because they wanted to burn something. He shuddered, remembering the warmth of Misha's hand beneath his own as he had related Klara Alexandrovna's tale. *Christ and all the saints.*

Aysel tilted her head, though, and a certain solemnity softened her wide brown eyes. "Why should a dragon follow a human prophet?" she asked. "Why should we worship a god with a human shape?"

"Forgive me," he said, to which she nodded acceptance. "My master out of St. Petersburg told me that your people believe the soul is kept in a...an organ, a bladder, at the back of your throats," said Kesha. Under Aysel's steady, surveying gaze, it seemed an unspeakably stupid thing to say.

"*Spiritus*," Aysel said. "Not *anima*. You understand the difference, I hope."

"The spirit of breath, and not the soul." Here she nodded, as though she had been taught to nod the way she'd been taught to speak Latin. "Will you tell me what you mean when you say that your people have joined with the Turks to help them make angels?"

She blew out a steaming breath through her nose. "In Latin, I cannot, but tomorrow I will gather my spirit for a short flight. Come to me at sunrise, Innokentiy Vladimirovich, and I will *show* you what I mean."

When the sun shrugged free of the eastern hills, Aysel was waiting for Kesha in the rye fields. "You came."

"I was curious," Kesha answered. The pale sunlight reflected from every frosted leaf, making the fields gleam cold and white. "And not only about the angels. Twice now, I have heard you complain about the injustices you see. Boris Baivich says that a radical has...how should I say this in the Latin tongue? He says that a radical has not only complaints, but also convictions. And I wished to hear what your convictions were."

"I am convinced that Boris Baivich is an ass," she snorted. "He will tell you that he does not dream of a citadel in the clouds, but he does, and in his dreams he peoples it with poets and philosophers."

"And you?"

Aysel scratched lightly at the frozen earth, as though the question embarrassed her. "I dream of a citadel upon the earth," she said at last. "Perhaps it never existed. Perhaps we lost it long ago. But I would like to learn to build a place, of wood or of stone, to which a clan of dragons could return. Such a place would need poets and philosophers, but it would need hunters and herders and builders, as well. And I would like us to make just laws together, so that my citadel would not be a prison."

"You would be Aeneas, and found a Rome for your people," offered Kesha.

"*I* would not abandon Dido because my destiny lay beyond Carthage," said Aysel primly, but she ducked her head as though the comparison pleased her. "Now, climb onto my back. I have promised to show you the angels."

With Kesha settled between her shoulder blades, Aysel took to the air. She tracked the Volga deeper into Turkish territory, away from the pastoral haven of Täteş and toward the distant shapes of smokestacks and spinning water wheels. Even at three hundred feet, Kesha could taste a tang of metal amid the smoke of the factories. *What kind of angels can they make, in such a place as this?* he wondered, nestling closer against Aysel's neck so that the workers would not mark his shape on her back. *Do they mean to drill down to Hell itself?*

Past the factories, though, lay great, sprawling buildings of glass and steel—like cathedrals, thought Kesha at first, but as Aysel drew nearer, he saw that the windows were all stained with soot and other residues. Chalky deposits of what might have been calcium marked the glass beneath the fixtures. They looked nothing at all like cathedrals, even to the jaded eyes of a man who studied God in St. Petersburg.

"Like train stations," he said to himself, and although Aysel made a high sound of annoyance, he knew that he had guessed it.

They descended beyond the great glass stations, where the Turks had poured cement and scraped it smooth in long tracks. Kesha shifted uneasily atop Aysel's back as she landed, but workers only glanced at him and then returned to their business. He was dressed as one of their soldiers, and so he did not occasion comment. If he had a singularly Slavic nose—well, so did half the men of Täteş. With this in mind, he slid down from Aysel's back and watched a crew of men hurry past with a handcart full of canvas.

He waited for them to pass and then approached the nearest building, his bootheels striking hard upon the cement. A man who might have been Tajik slipped through the door ahead of him, holding it for Kesha as he passed. As Kesha hung back near the door, the man strode into a sheltered corner where a knot of men and white-scarved women stood huddled about a long table. All of them wore the same expression; he knew it well from his landlady's *salons* and his brother's earnest midnight design sessions. It was the expression that scholars wore when they were ready to take the world apart and find the gears within.

Kesha turned away from the engineers, surveying the broad, open space within what he had so precipitously called the station. Through the bustle of workmen and designers, through the maze of scaffolds gleaming dully in the muted sunlight, he could make out vast and towering shapes between ceiling and floor.

From the ceiling hung suspended a latticework of gantries and struts, each one draped over with cables and hooks. At the end of those curving hooks, with workers gathered around them in an attendant swarm, hung a dozen creatures of steel and canvas. Their bellies lay open as though they were hogs in a butcher's shop, but across that empty space, diligent workers had strung a network of leather and canvas straps.

The armatures look nothing like dragons—nothing like the dragons that Kesha had killed in his youth and studied in his manhood—but still he could see that they had been designed to fly.

As the workers strapped a uniformed Turk into the belly of one hulking beast, with its long canvas wings stretching out from either shoulder, Kesha understood why the dragons had called these machines *angels*.

CHAPTER SEVEN

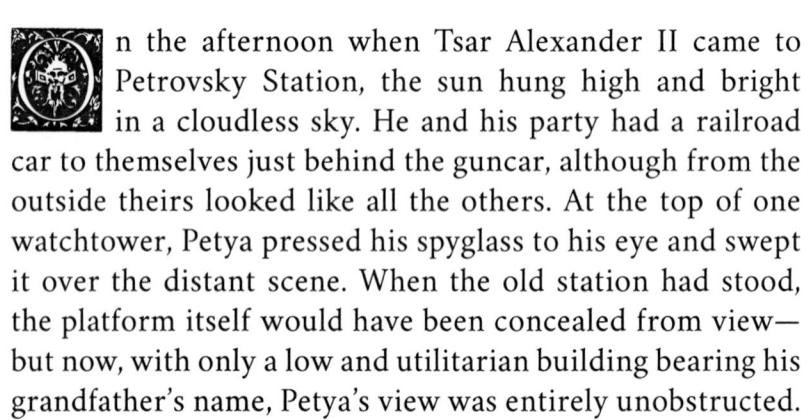

On the afternoon when Tsar Alexander II came to Petrovsky Station, the sun hung high and bright in a cloudless sky. He and his party had a railroad car to themselves just behind the guncar, although from the outside theirs looked like all the others. At the top of one watchtower, Petya pressed his spyglass to his eye and swept it over the distant scene. When the old station had stood, the platform itself would have been concealed from view—but now, with only a low and utilitarian building bearing his grandfather's name, Petya's view was entirely unobstructed.

At the station waited a party of children, the little girls gowned in white and the tousle-haired boys dressed like men in trousers to greet the Tsar's party. First to disembark from the train were two men who must have been the Tsar's younger sons, both of them in military uniform. They looked travel-worn and oddly soft-featured, at this distance, and they leaned in to one another to confer for a moment before putting on genial smiles and greeting the crowd. The Tsar himself was also dressed as a soldier, with his breath steaming the air over the fur lining of his coat and his thin grey whiskers twitching as he smiled. He accepted the salutes of the Tarasov guards, one hand raised toward that distant sun as though it, too, hailed him from afar.

Petya watched as the Tsar and his party squeezed into the Tarasov carriage—Liza had had it reupholstered in velvet for the occasion—and then turned his spyglass to the other men on the towers.

There was Liza, her gown blowing about her legs in the brisk breeze and her hat firmly strapped beneath her chin. There was one of Uncle Sasha's old comrades in arms, who nearly dwarfed the little Gardner gun the Kamenskys had lent them. On the far side were two of the guardsmen who had stayed on despite the slow attrition of their wages and the death of half the men in their family. He knew of no more skilled or loyal gunners than old Osip Moiseyevich and his son Anatoliy Osipovich.

On the other side of the great gate, there was Jaworski, who saw Petya looking and smiled faintly, shaking his head. *Patience*, he mouthed. *Soon*.

The carriage rolled placidly down the main street, through the massed houses and shops to the foot of the hill on which the fortress stood. The horses then began to ascend the gravel drive, their steps slow and stately. The driver knew better than to rattle such precious cargo. He had donned a professional driver's caftan and flat-topped hat for the occasion, and Petya thought that he sat straighter on the box because of it.

He glanced at Jaworski again, who had turned to grip the attitude rotor in one hand. He held up his trigger hand as the gates swung open beneath him. A closed fist—and then, one long breath after, he released his thumb and shook it to be sure that they saw. *One*.

Petya inhaled at that, filling his lungs with chilled air until he saw Jaworski raise his index finger. *Two*.

He had the rhythm, now, and he turned to his own gun and pointed it skyward. Beneath him, he could hear the low conversation of the Tsar's sons as they got down from the carriage. *Three*.

His mother would be raising her hands to greet the Tsar. She had been resplendent this morning in a gown of black silk and a capelet lined with black fur, her dark hair pinned beneath a fetching cap. *Four.*

The next exhale was *five*, and on that exhalation he fired a single, perfect burst into the air.

It was then that the screaming started.

He turned and saw the blood upon the snow. He saw his mother raise her hands to her face, smearing the blood that had sprayed her cheek.

He saw the Tsar's sons kneel beside their father's body, and for a moment he was with Liza in the mess hall, working a thick spray of lead pellets from his father's shredded corpse—but the keep's guns were designed to pierce dragons' hides, and there was precious little left of the Tsar. An awful lassitude stole over Petya then—a stillness like the hare's beneath the hawk's eye.

When he looked up at the gunners ringing the fortress, he saw Liza's post deserted. He saw Jaworski's barrel pointing down into the courtyard, and Jaworski heaving breath after breath as though he were wracked with sobs—and then Liza rose from the hatch at Jaworski's back and pinned him to the ground, grinding his cheek against the mounting plate until he cried out.

His cry sounded like *Adela*.

At the back of the room, Liza sat with her gun trained on Jaworski and her eyes narrowed. Her good leg was crossed over the false one, and her finger tapped impatiently at the trigger guard. "Make him confess, and finish this," she told Petya. "He *used* us. He made us *trust* him, and for what? To get close to the Tsar—"

"I did use you," said Jaworski softly. He raised a hand, at which Liza brought her gun up—but Jaworski only smoothed back his hair and scrubbed his knuckles over his eyes. Around his wrist, Petya saw, Jaworski had wrapped a wooden rosary. Long use had polished its beads to a dull gloss. "But no more than Russia used me."

"Then you confess that you murdered the Tsar," Petya said. His hands were shaking badly. He was glad that Liza held the gun, because he could never have fired it with his hands shaking like this. "You confess that you…that you stayed with us, and earned our trust, so that you could murder him."

"I did," said Jaworski. The hollows about his eyes had grown deeper since yesterday, but from those deep and shadowed recesses shone a crackling fire. "I killed him. I confess that. And if someone else hadn't killed him first, I'd have killed your father, too," he added.

The muzzle of Liza's gun wavered, but she didn't lower it. "You would have killed our father—but you didn't. I don't believe you."

"Why should I lie?" he snapped. "I killed the Tsar. What good would it do to deny killing your father? Whoever pulled the trigger, though, I'd have been happy to shake his hand and call him my brother!"

"Or to plant a carbine in the alley behind the tavern, to screen his escape," said Liza.

"Or that," he agreed.

"Tell us why you killed the Tsar," said Petya. He made his trembling hands lie flat, but still his flesh felt suffused with dreamlike heat. *I must be calm*, he told himself. *I must be calm, or I'll strangle him myself.*

"Why I killed the Tsar—that's a simple enough question." He drew up one knee, resting the heel of his boot against the seat of his chair and lacing his hands together over his shin. "In 1860, his officers drafted me to fight in Poland, and I was a *damn good* soldier even when he asked me to rough up my own people. I almost came to like my comrades, even if they were Russians. They grew on me. Alexander Petrovich

Tarasov in particular."

"Uncle Sasha," said Liza. "He always told us what brave comrades he had. What *loyal* comrades."

Jaworski sucked in a breath and looked as though he would spit. "The bastard did nothing to deserve our loyalty. When the war started, I actually thought he was a good man, even when he got good Polish virgins to fuck him behind the barracks—I even trusted him with my wife's safety. She was a nationalist, an informer, and I told her where I'd be garrisoned and when we'd move. It was the one thing I could do for my country, when I had to murder my countrymen. The one good thing I could do. The resistance held its own while she was reporting on our movements. When your uncle saw what we'd been doing, Adela and I, he promised that Adela would be safe."

Adela. Petya marked the name and asked quietly, carefully, "What happened to her?"

His lips thinned, and his brows drew down. "Your Uncle Sasha burned her alive in 1864, and your Uncle Pasha let him do it—and for that, I killed them both."

In the silence that followed, Petya studied Jaworski's hands. The thin fingers laced over the lower leg of his trousers—uniform trousers from the Russian army, faded over fifteen years of wearing.

Those hands had driven a bayonet into Uncle Sasha's throat.

"Uncle Pasha died in a hunting accident," said Liza. There was a note of pleading in her voice. "In 1871. I was there. You couldn't have murdered him. The war had been over for years by then."

"It had," agreed Jaworski. "And it was some trouble to get work as a gamekeeper, but he didn't know me as well as your Uncle Sasha did—and the pleasure of seeing him fall more than repaid the effort."

Liza's lips skinned back over her teeth. "And my father?"

"Your father's generation was a nest of vipers. I wanted

nothing more than to smoke them out and crush them one by one," said Jaworski coolly. "A man like that didn't deserve life—and clearly I wasn't the only one who thought it. Of all the Tarasovs, Vladimir Petrovich was the worst. He couldn't even *pretend* to be a good man."

"And me?" asked Liza. Her voice was hollow. "I thought we were friends. I thought you believed in me."

Jaworski regarded her with such withering pity that even Petya felt the sting of it. "Liza, you're a tyrant and a bully, just as your father was before you. Just as he trained you to be, with kicks and with praise."

Liza and Petya exchanged a glance. She uncrossed her legs and rose carefully to her feet, keeping the gun trained on Jaworski. "I've heard enough," she said, voice rough.

"I commend the Tsar's death to God," answered Jaworski, with the same faint smile that he'd worn when he'd counseled Petya to patience. "May He put Adela's soul to rest—"

The butt of Liza's gun struck him hard across the face, and when he raised his head again, his nose was bloodied. "I said," she told him, "I *said*, I've heard *enough*."

Petya watched her stump into the hall, her gown rustling with each heavy step.

CHAPTER EIGHT

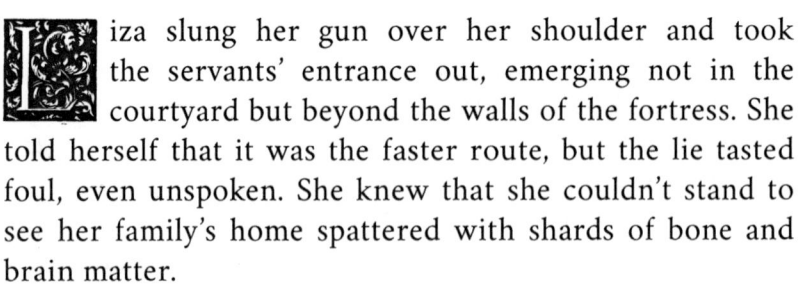

Liza slung her gun over her shoulder and took the servants' entrance out, emerging not in the courtyard but beyond the walls of the fortress. She told herself that it was the faster route, but the lie tasted foul, even unspoken. She knew that she couldn't stand to see her family's home spattered with shards of bone and brain matter.

"Faithful as an old hound," she muttered to herself. Had Petya not been there, had he not been speaking so calmly that one might have suspected him of being insensate, she would have decorated the walls of the keep with Jaworski's innards.

The village rose into view, still decked in streamers and silk flowers. In the tavern, no doubt, men would be drinking to the health of the Tsar and his children. Children dressed as though for church scampered between their parents, utterly unconcerned at the death of their sovereign. Had they not heard the screaming? Did they not *know*?

Liza's foot locked and sent her sprawling, skirts scrubbing the frozen earth. She rose with fragments of stone and grass all over her gown and let loose a single cry of frustration, bird-like and inhuman.

Then she picked herself up, realigned her foot, and continued down the hill to the main road. There, she went at once to the new constabulary station. "Take me to Wainwright," she said, and the young officers straightened in their smart new uniforms. She smelled brandy on the air. They'd been drinking to Alexander II, no doubt, and hadn't expected a wild woman to swing in with half the road on her skirt hem. "Name of God, *take* me to that son of a bitch—"

"Take her," said Utkin, thin lips pressed tightly together. "Go on, Seryozha."

Seryozha gestured her out of the front room, into the back rooms and thence into the shelter beneath the floor. Most houses in this town had only a narrow shelter, a single room big enough for a family with a man-sized hatch atop it, but the officers had carved a new shelter from the frozen earth when they'd taken the plot of land: a prison house of six rooms beneath a single, massive hatch. In one of those honeycomb chambers slouched a drunkard who'd been arrested for exposing himself to churchgoers. In another, Wainwright sat with his cheeks unshaven and his arms draped around his knees.

"Bring him out," said Liza. "I know you have a room for questioning. Take us to it."

"Very well," Seryozha answered, and he lowered himself over the side of the pit to unlock the shackle about Wainwright's right leg. "Madame Tarasova wants to see you," he said, loudly enough to carry. "She wants to ask you a few questions."

"Didn't she have enough time to question me, when she kept me in her ice closet?" Wainwright replied. "As you like. I wait on her least damn whim." He climbed the ladder—poorly, Liza noticed; she couldn't forget that he, too, was an amputee—and then scrambled onto the floor to salute Liza. "Lady," he said, eyes too bright and back too straight. He looked as though he was ready to shatter.

They followed behind Seryozha to the questioning room.

The walls were whitewashed and the floor scrubbed clean. It might have been a sitting room, in another life. "Leave us," she told Seryozha.

"I'm afraid I can't do that, Madame Tarasova. Inspector Utkin says that we have to write down everything the prisoners say in here."

"Everything they say to a *constable*—but I'm no constable."

Seryozha fiddled with one of his buttons. "Utkin would say it was irregular...."

"He says everything's irregular," Liza replied, with a dismissive wave of her hand. "Now *go*, Seryozha—I'm your lord, and constable or no constable, I'm the law here."

Seryozha had been a constable for less than a month. He had been born a serf of Tarasov lords, and he'd been under the Tarasov thumb since he was a boy. He knew better than to argue with a Tarasov who'd pulled rank on him. He bowed to her, touched the brim of his hat, and then wheeled sharply and left the room.

"Something's changed," said Wainwright. He sat on the far side of the plain oak table, letting Liza take the nearer seat. She remained standing near the door, regarding him with her face feeling tight and mask-like. "New evidence?"

"You could call it new evidence," she said. "The Tsar is dead. You're suspected of espionage. Tell me *quickly* what the connection is, or I'll shoot you where you sit."

"In Afghanistan, I was an agent of Her Majesty," he said, without hesitating an instant. His voice was low and rough from disuse, but it never wavered. "I collected intelligence on the Turks and reported it to my superiors. I learned to speak Turkish and Pashto in my liaisons, and I allowed myself to be captured more than once to learn the layout of the Turkish fortifications. When Her Majesty brokered the deal to build the railway to China, I was approached by a few of my acquaintances in the intelligence community, and they explained why we were being sent to garrison Russian fortresses."

"Why." The flatness in her voice reminded her of Petya's, when they had questioned Jaworski. She didn't have him here to stay her hand, and so she had to stay her own. "Why were you sent to garrison our fortresses."

"When the rails were completed, the Tsar was scheduled to begin a celebratory tour. This tour. We were to notify revolutionary elements in each city that his death was the signal to begin a riot. While Russian troops subdued their revolutionaries, English troops would hold the fortresses—and when the revolution was put down, as we were certain it would be, Tsar Alexander III would be only too happy to keep the English in place for their service."

"But you had another plan."

"My allegiance is not to England," said Wainwright simply. He leaned back in his chair, a strange softness touching his features. "I've been imprisoned in a Russian cell, accused of murdering a Russian man, and I have every expectation of being transported to a Russian labor camp—but my allegiance is and has always been to the Tsar of Russia. He was good to my friends in the Duchy of Finland…and I couldn't desert those friends. So I made it my mission to disrupt and intercept what communications I could."

"At first, it went well," Liza ventured. "But then the station was destroyed, and my father camped in the telegraph office—"

"It didn't bother me, that he was camped in the telegraph office. At first, I was concerned that in his drunkenness he'd let them slip through, but later he confronted me privately about a few coded messages addressed to me." Here, Wainwright folded his hands on the table as though trying to recall the scene to mind. "It was a day or two after the station had been destroyed, and nothing had been rebuilt—you remember that he took me aside after supper—"

"I don't remember."

"It was the evening when Jaworski taught us to toast in Polish," said Wainwright. "Whenever he said 'Na zdrowie,' you'd say 'Spasibo' and laugh."

Na zdrowie, thought Liza. She recalled laughing until her sides ached, the heel of her hand coming down hard on the table. "Jaworski killed the Tsar," she said instead.

Wainwright paused for a moment, his lips slightly parted. He pressed them together, though, and then said eloquently, "Damn it all to Hell."

"Then Jaworski wasn't part of your plan," said Liza.

"Not part of the *English* plan," said Wainwright, and he rose to his feet and began to pace the room. For the first time, Liza recognized that telltale shift of weight that wasn't quite a hobble. "Piece of shit—God only knows what will happen now! Even if I failed, at least I had the satisfaction of knowing that I'd prepared my people as well as I could— but he was meant to die in Bratsk, where the rail lines connected. Not here, and not *now*! Let me out, Liza—if my telegraphs are the first to go out, I can at least prevent your people from massacring each other—"

"No," she said, letting her gun fall from her shoulder. "First you're going to tell me what you said to my father when he took you aside. Because he didn't tell me anything, and when it came to running the fortress, my father and I had no secrets."

"He knew that you can't keep a secret when you've been drinking," said Wainwright. "The whole *world* knows that!"

She cocked the gun and raised it to her shoulder. "*What did he tell you?* It's a simple question."

Liza saw the Adam's apple bob in Wainwright's throat. "Very well," he said. His voice was soft as eiderdown, and he raised his hands as he took his seat again. "I told him that I had been intercepting and replacing messages between English spies. I translated them for him and explained the meaning behind the codes, and he agreed to help me."

"That doesn't sound like my father," Liza replied. "My father has never agreed to help anyone in his life."

"He agreed to help me," said Wainwright, "on the condition that he would be recognized publicly, in St.

Petersburg, for his service to the Tsar. I didn't understand why it had to be in St. Petersburg until I met your brother, Innokentiy Vladimirovich."

"I don't believe you," she said. "My father didn't need to prove himself to my brother."

"Didn't he? Then why was he in town, on the night when your brother arrived? Why was he murdered behind the tavern where your brother was staying?"

"Why were you standing over his body as he bled to death?" Liza demanded. "No, what I think happened was this: He discovered your little telegrams, and he threatened to expose you to your superiors unless you sent exactly what he wanted you to send. And on that night, you sent a telegram that he didn't want you to send, and he confronted you about it. He told you that he'd expose you, so you knocked him to the ground and you shot him."

"I did no such—"

"And that's *not all*." She could hear Jaworski's voice echoing in her ears, ringing until her every nerve jangled with the reverberation. *You're a tyrant and a bully, just as your father was before you. Just as he trained you to be.* "You thought you were doing me a *kindness*. You thought that without my father, I might be a better man than he was."

"I've always thought that you could be better than he was," said Wainwright. "But I'm not a Tarasov. I don't destroy things to show my love."

"Don't tell me that you loved me," Liza said. "You can't win me over with your *love*."

"I might have loved you, if you hadn't been trying so hard to be your father!"

Liza resettled her gun on her shoulder. "I'm not my father," she said. "I'll send a message along the telegraph lines to every fortress lord and city garrison, letting them know to expect revolution—and to expect the English to try to push them out of their keeps. That much courtesy, you deserve for your service to the Tsar, and for that I'll ask nothing."

Wainwright's shoulders sagged in something like relief. "Thank you," he said, and he met her eyes. "That's more than I'd expected from you. Thank you."

He looked very frail, this man who'd chosen to take all of Russia on his back. Liza could have snapped him with her two hands, and for a moment the urge to do it made her fingers clench into fists. She worked her hands open and let them fall to her sides. "When they put you on trial for my father's murder," she said, "if what you've said is true, it will be civil war. If they convict you, it won't only be as a murderer—it will be as an enemy agent. They won't transport you, they'll *execute* you."

"I've done nothing but serve Russia. If I can keep that in mind, my conscience is clear."

"Then make your peace with God," said Liza. "For what you've done to my father, I can't forgive you—not even for Russia's sake. Not if it were the only thing standing between me and Heaven."

She left the room, gathering up her skirts as she went, and Seryozha ducked in behind her to take the prisoner back to his cell.

I might have loved you, he'd said, and she knew that she might have loved him, too, as a brother in arms. No other man had respected her so readily, had treated her as a gentleman and fought with her in the courtyard—no other man had been her comrade, and her Uncle Sasha had taught her to value comrades more dearly even than brothers.

Her Uncle Sasha had set his comrade's wife on fire, and his comrade had murdered him in return.

CHAPTER NINE

Kesha was walking with Boris Baivich, as he had done every day since Aysel had shown him the angels—which was to say, he was standing impatiently by as Boris sunned himself on a comfortable stone—when he saw Söz go pelting by with her scarf half-undone and her greying hair glinting in the sun. "Söz!" he cried after her.

"Not now, boy!" she replied, and she put a hand to the stile and leapt it clear.

He had never seen Söz agitated before. He had never seen her outside of the *inn* before, and he craned his neck to follow her fleeing form. She seemed to be sprinting for the hills of winter rye beneath which the dragons lived, pelting straight across the beet fields. For a sedentary woman, she had a remarkable turn of speed.

"Something's clearly gone wrong," said Boris Baivich with a yawn. When Kesha gave him a curious look, he only snorted in a defensive fashion and added, "What? You were thinking it, too."

"She's had a message," said Kesha. "She does nothing but get and send messages—and she's learned something that threw her into a panic. If we're lucky, she'll have left it at her table, with the rest of her papers. How are you at reading Turkish?"

Boris snorted once more. "I can read Latin, Greek, Mandarin, Russian, Arabic, and Turkish regardless of its script, in addition to my own language—bring me her papers, and we'll see what her bad news is. We'll commence our lesson another time."

At this, Kesha set off in the direction from which Söz had come, jogging carefully so as not to twist his ankle. The people in the outlying farmhouses knew him well, and the old women only laughed as he hurried past their front porches. An unaccustomed warm spell had struck Täteş, and on every hopeful garden plant there were new shoots and buds straining skyward.

The innkeeper scarcely batted an eye when Kesha burst in. "Söz forgot a paper," he said, breathless and frantic. "Sent me to fetch it—"

"On the table," he said, gesturing with his dishrag. "You'll have to hurry to catch her, though. She was running at a fair clip when she left here—"

"I'll just take them all," Kesha answered, and he scooped up the topmost papers and clutched them to his chest.

With the innkeeper waving him off, he sped into the streets again, past the laughing grandmothers and the children digging up bean sprouts to bring indoors. At the very edge of the village, Boris Baivich was waiting with his forelimbs braced on a fence and the pigs behind it all crowding into the far side of their pen. The warm air bore a fetid aroma of pig shit and a perennial buzzing of flies.

"I've been waiting for *ages*," he said, scratching idly at his ruff. "It's not polite to eat them, is it? The pigs, I mean. It would be barbaric to eat the *humans—*"

"Look at this," said Kesha, taking out his sheaf of papers and passing over the top sheet. Boris Baivich took it carefully in a taloned hand, perusing the neat rows of letters. "What does it say?"

"This is just a report on mayoral politics in Kazan," said Boris Baivich. "And in Russian, no less. For the love of all things holy, did you not even *read* the papers? Hand me only the papers in languages you don't understand, and we'll stop dallying unnecessarily."

"I was more concerned with haste."

"Be concerned with *clarity*."

The next two pages were in Arabic script, and Kesha passed them over. The one beneath that was a report on Polish rye production, which he shuffled to the bottom of the stack. A newspaper from the town around the Abramov fortress had been divided into quarters and tucked beneath it, but nothing of note was ever published in that paper—

"*Wait*, you ridiculous boy. *Read* the headline before you toss it away."

MURDER

> *13 January, 1881. In a brutal act that has shaken all of Russia to its core, Tsar Alexander II was murdered by a Polish separatist agent inside the fortress at Yureyevsk. Captain Ludwik Jaworski, veteran of the Russian Army and distinguished serviceman during the Polish Uprising of 1863, made his full confession before the Tsar's stricken sons, Grand Dukes Paul Alexandrovich and Sergei Alexandrovich. The people, too, grieve for their beloved Tsar, and several Polish businesses in St. Petersburg have been put to the torch while the traitor approaches the capital. Riots have broken out in Kazan, Yekaterinburg, and Bratsk, reportedly led by students and radicals. Amid the turmoil, Pyotr Vladimirovich Tarasov, de facto commander of the fortress at Yureyevsk, claimed that he could not comment on how the traitor had posed as a loyal member of the Tarasov household for so long—*

"The Tsar," said Kesha. His breath came short. He had known since departing Kent's company that the man would die, but he had never imagined that he would die within Kesha's family home. He heard the flies drone over the pigs' trough, and he remembered the way the flies settled on neglected hunks of dragonflesh in the courtyard in summer. The Tsar must have been shot down just like that—exploded. "Söz told me that she meant no harm to them."

"No harm to whom?"

"To my family—the Tsar was murdered in my family's fortress."

"If the Voice told you that," Boris Baivich said carefully, "I would believe she meant them no harm. She's an inveterate liar, of course, but even a liar knows not to make enemies among those who aren't expendable. The Voice isn't *stupid*."

"And I'm not expendable? I don't doubt for a moment that she'd kill me the second she thought she'd squeezed every drop of use from me."

"Oh, she might," said Boris Baivich, yawning. "Probably *will*, really. But she hasn't yet, and until then, she can't afford to lie to you. Not about something as important as clan."

Kesha studied the paper, searching for sign of what had startled Söz into running. *The Tsar will be succeeded by his son Alexander Alexandrovich, hereafter known as Alexander III*—no. *His celebratory tour of the new trans-continental rail line was to have ended on the 28th of January in Bratsk, where the two lines joined—*

The flies droned on, and in the moment of realization, their humming seemed to comprise his entire world. *The old man dies in the last act of the play.* "He wasn't supposed to die at my family's fortress," guessed Kesha, after the moment had passed. "He wasn't supposed to die yet. Söz was counting on a murder in Bratsk, a little over two weeks from now, when the moratorium on changing the borders was about to end. But Jaworski saw his chance and took it, and now her whole timetable is ruined. You wanted to know what had gone wrong...well, perhaps this is what's gone wrong."

Boris wasn't listening, though. His blunt white muzzle was pointed south, his eyes raised skyward. The droning sound filled the heated air.

From the south came a droning swarm—not dragons, for all their bulk, and not birds, for all they flew like geese headed north for summer. "The angels," said Kesha as their shadows passed over the streets of Täteş. If he strained his eyes, he could see men huddled in the bellies of those mechanical beasts, held in with leather straps and grim determination.

"*Homines volans*," Boris Baivich said in return. "It was always a better term than *angeli*, but Aysel must be *symbolic* about such things."

"What would I call them, in Russian?"

"Call them flying engines, if you like," said Boris Baivich. "It's what they are. Or call them angels and let Aysel have her way. What does it matter what you call them? They're going somewhere else."

"Where are they going?" Kesha asked, but he knew that the answer was *north*—and that in the occupied land south of the border, *north* could only mean Russia. "What are they—"

"You humans ask such *stupid* questions," Boris snorted. "Next you'll ask me how we can get ahead of them, and the simple answer is that we can't. They're faster than even the fastest dragon. So you might as well put the Voice's papers back where you found them, because when she and Xia return from the factories, you might find you've become 'expendable.' Xia has somewhat old-fashioned notions about eating people who speak, and dragons don't scruple to kill their criminals."

"No."

"Don't be ridiculous, man. You'll learn nothing further about our poetry if you've been torn to—"

"I told you *no*." A cold, crackling tension had arisen between them, and Boris Baivich cocked his head as though he had somehow misunderstood. "Fetch me Aysel. If you and I can't get ahead of them, then perhaps Aysel and I can get behind them. She's part of the air corps, isn't she? They'll know her. We can reach Yureyevsk while they're still spread thin, and then..."

In Boris Baivich's wide, liquid eyes, Kesha finally saw what might have been compassion. "Then what, Innokentiy Vladimirovich? You and Aysel will gather up a few foolish radicals, and we'll start building a philosophers' citadel on the ashes of your family keep? What good does it do to arrive too late for a warning, too weak for a rescue?"

And what then? asked his father, whose voice would never entirely leave Kesha be.

As the two of them stood regarding one another, the drone of the angels faded into the distance. *I haven't the spirit for heroism,* Kesha thought. *I was bred to be a coward, and a coward I've remained. A liar and a thief—one who flees into the night with guns at his back, and who tells himself that he can never return.* He felt his resolve bleed out of him like heat through an open door, and in his smallness, he wished to tear the world to pieces and be torn apart in his turn.

He remembered Misha's warm hands on his, and how he had whispered in a dreaming voice all those weeks ago in a little coffee-house, *I needn't tell you that he failed, and all of his books and papers were destroyed. His daughter, though, was a prodigiously brave woman, and in the dead of the night, she slipped into the very offices of the Collegia and prised free a panel....* He remembered the smallness of that space behind the panel, and the lightness of Misha's little collection of salvaged books. Only so many as a brave young woman could have carried in her two hands, in the dead of night, into one of the best-guarded spaces in St. Petersburg.

He remembered how much hope those few books had kindled in him, for all they had come too little and too late.

And what then? asked his father's ghost, across the gap between the living and the dead—and Kesha answered him, "Then we accept the risk of failure, and do what we can.

What else can anyone do?"

"Die ridiculously," said Boris Baivich, with a sound like a sigh. "I'll fetch Aysel. She always did have a taste for lost causes."

CHAPTER TEN

All along the towers, the watchmen looked up and to the south. In Osip Moiseyevich's tower, Petya screwed the steel plate back down over the gears of the gun mount and straightened to scan the sky.

"Dragons?" said Anatoliy Osipovich. "Can't be," answered his father. "Dragons don't move like that. More a swarm of locusts, by the looks of them, but I've never seen locusts in winter."

"Should we ring the warning bell?" Petya asked. At that, Osip Moiseyevich put the spyglass to his eye and leaned over the edge of the low wall. His puckered old lips drew together like the mouth of a purse.

"Best ring it," he said finally. "Better to have put the town into a panic for nothing than to be caught unprepared."

"Should I send someone down to wire the Abramovs and the Kamenskys?"

"Boy, how long have you been running this fortress? Go. Have the telegraph master put it through." With a light push, Osip urged Petya toward the hatch and all but stuffed him down the ladder shaft. Feeling thoroughly vexed, he clambered down the ladder and turned on the warning bell. The frantic ringing sent men scrambling to their stations, and no doubt Liza would be raising her head and dashing down the corridors to a watchtower. The watch bell had been quiet since Liza had got her new leg. She'd be relishing the opportunity to put herself to use, even if she didn't get a chance to shoot anything.

Petya, though, hurried out of the fortress by the servants' door, hearing the great gates swing shut to brace the walls against an assault. "A waste of effort, if it's nothing but locusts," he said to himself, but he jammed his hat more tightly over his ears and hastened down the hillside to the town. The blackout cloths were up over the windows and the streets had emptied quickly. People were huddling in the shelters beneath the floorboards, no doubt, waiting for the watchmen at the train station to turn off their bell.

He wrenched open the door of the telegraph office and knocked on the hatch. "I need to send a telegram!" he cried, but the telegraph master only shouted, "*Go* away!" through the insulated metal.

"It's Pyotr Vladimirovich Tarasov," Petya tried again. "I need to wire the Abramovs and the Kamenskys about what we've seen—"

"Oh, very *well*," came the telegraph master's tinny snarl, and then he swung the hatch back and emerged from the shelter. In the moment before the hatch swung shut again, Petya saw that the shelter was surprisingly well-appointed and well-stocked. He thought he saw glass jars of pickled beets and a cot with a quilt strewn over it. The shadowy, amorphous shape in one corner might have been a settee. "What's the message? Let's be quick about it."

"Tell them—" Petya hesitated. "Tarasov to Kamensky. Relay to Zaytsev. Unidentified flight detected. Number unknown. Northbound, and approaching at speed." The telegraph master tapped out the message with barely a pause, his old fingers sure on the key.

Tap, tap, taptap, went the telegraph, and the telegraph master paused before approaching the eastbound line to duplicate the message. "We're receiving a message," he said. "'Abramov to Tarasov. Flight inbound. Not dragons. Advise caution.'"

Then, only moments after, another message. The telegraph master recited it over the unending clamor of the warning bell: "'Abramov to Tarasov. Relay to Kamensky. Flight is armed. Train down.'"

"We have to warn Liza," said Petya, but the telegraph master shook his head.

"If a train has been hit, she's seen it—we'll warn the Kamenskys, and then we'll go to ground like sensible men. Shut the hatch on your way down. I'll join you when I'm finished." Much as it wrenched at him, Petya saw the sense in his argument. While the telegraph master tapped out the message on the westbound line, Petya ducked into the shelter and clambered down the ladder, closing the hatch behind him. His hobnailed boots struck hard on the metal floor, and for a moment he stood in the darkness with a sick feeling in the pit of his stomach—then, with a start, he realized that he could feel a faint breeze.

In a metal-sheathed shelter beneath the earth, with the only entrance closed off and no other occupants to speak of, he had felt a cool breath of air.

He felt about for the knob of the gaslamp, then twitched it until it glowed only faintly. In the dim light, he examined the telegraph master's bolthole. To one side lay the cot he'd seen earlier, and to the other, a well-worn chaise longue. A cabinet of pickled vegetables stood along one wall, and ropes of sausages hung from the ceiling, out of reach of rats and mice.

Beside the cabinet was a grating, tall enough to permit a child to pass through upright or a man to pass through at a crouch.

The telegraph master swung the hatch open and shimmied down the ladder only a moment later, screwing the hatch shut and agitating his upper arms. "Brr!" he said. "The news from the east is dire. No, Pyotr Vladimirovich, we're going to stay put until this passes, and then we'll take stock—"

"Where does this vent go?" asked Petya.

"The station and the machinists' shop, if you follow it to the end," said the telegraph master. "But you could reach nearly anywhere, if you liked. The tavern, the armory, the bakery—even the old smithy, although that's a private residence now. We had these built during your grandfather's day, in case anyone should become trapped after a fire or a collapse. A way of getting air, food, drink, and tools to citizens in the shelters."

The vent sprang open at a touch. Its hinges were well-oiled, and the passage behind it dusty but clear of debris. The floor was lined with smooth grey stone, unpolished by trouser knees or children's feet. "It's hardly ever used, is it?"

"Not to reach the telegraph office. Only the men at the station ever use it to come here—a few of them came out through here when the station was destroyed. They wanted me to tell the rail company about the delay." His long fingers tapped elegantly at his elbow, and his smile turned wry. "I can't say they aren't devoted to the company."

Above, the sound muffled by the insulated hatch, the first burst of gunfire rang out.

Petya fell to his knees, crawling into the ventilation shaft as though into a tomb. Within the dark enclosure, he could scarcely hear the bells.

Beneath the town's main street, Petya discovered a central shaft tall enough to permit him to stand. All along the walls were piled years of refuse, fragments of chicken bones and tangles of hair and thread. A shoe lay half-unsoled atop the corpse of a child's rag doll. Through the smaller shafts that branched off to either side, he could hear mothers singing to their anxious children and old men speculating about what would be blown to bits when they emerged. Those shafts were the only source of light, and even those faint rays came only intermittently in the gloom.

At the end of one passage, someone sat huddled against the grate with a red checked blanket about her shoulders. She rocked and shivered as though she was cold.

In the dimness, he could only barely make out the white-painted letters on the wall: *Bakery*, it said, and even through the fetid smell of the shaft, he thought he could catch a faint whiff of yeast. He pressed his hand to the cool stone and moved on, picking his way carefully over a collection of nut hulls that crunched like fingerbones beneath his boots.

Tavern, said another sign, with a shaded gaslamp over it—Nastya's was the best-stocked cellar in town, and of course the tavern would be a logical gathering place in times of struggle. He remembered Sonya and Polinka carefully tabulating onions at the counter and Galya with garlic skins on her skirt.

The first blast rocked the ground and sent a noise like thunder echoing through the shaft. Petya startled, pressing his back to the shuddering wall. Sonya and Polinka faded at once from his mind. He closed his hands at his sides and hastened onward, past the sign that Kostya the arms-trader had pegged to the wall and past a bundle of blankets not big enough to wrap a babe. The passage met the station's shelter, the way barred by a grate and an iron door beyond it—*But of course*, thought Petya, as the bombardment began in earnest above him. *The men at the station know they're a target. If their shelter should be blown open, they couldn't risk filling the shaft with smoke.*

A right turning took him around the shelter and then into darkness. He groped through open space, sliding his feet along the ground, until the toe of his boot struck metal. He knelt and felt the telltale shape of an iron rail, with ties set at intervals along the ground. He was in a service tunnel in the machinists' shop, and if he followed the track's slope downhill, he would find himself in the shop itself.

The rolling crash of the shelling sounded louder in the service tunnel. His heart throbbed beneath his breastbone, and his throat seized and clenched at the taste of smoke on the air.

Petya put his right hand to the wall and tracked the tunnel uphill, following the tracks out of the ground to the railway line. The bombardment shook the earth and made the railroad spikes whine in the ties.

As he drew closer to the mouth of the tunnel, his eyes starving for afternoon light, he recognized instead the red glint of fire.

From the mouth of the tunnel, it seemed the whole world had been set ablaze.

"A *sky-train*."

Petya clasped his ash-roughened hands behind his back. His left thumb kneaded the veins at the right wrist, kneaded and pressed until he could feel the tendons squeaking against bone. "A sky-boat is a better thing to call it, I think. Like a hot-air balloon, but more maneuverable—"

"You've already explained it to me a dozen times. What in God's name does your sky-boat have to do with anything?" With a snarl of disgust, Liza wadded up the design. Her eyes flicked to the fireplace, and for a second that stopped his heart, Petya thought she was going to cast it into the flames—but she seemed to stay herself, and smoothed the paper out again. "*Today*, of all days, you come to me again with this shit. Have you no respect for the dead?"

As her callused fingers splayed over those careful pencil lines—those rows of calculations over which he had slaved for days, the corrections that his professor had drawn in chalk—his heart gave a little start and began to beat again. "This will win us the war," he said. He could scarcely raise his voice enough to be heard.

Liza caught his chin and steered him around to look her in the eye. Her grip was surprisingly gentle. He turned as though of his own volition. "Name of God, Petya," she said, no more than a soft and familiar blasphemy. The hollows of her eyes were dark and finely lined. He couldn't remember whether they'd looked so old, in October. There was ash smearing her cheeks. "Don't think I'm not grateful for what you've done for me, but this isn't a game. The whole *shape* of the war is changing, and I don't have the time or the resources to let you build toys."

"You've always thought of me as a child, Liza!" Even he could hear the plaintive note in his voice, and he hated it.

"You *are* a child!" She released him with an incoherent sound and paced away. Each time her left foot fell, the heel struck heavily on the floor.

"I'm a child who built you a new leg," he said, "and if you trust me, I'll be a child who builds a ship to take on the dragons."

For a long moment, Liza stood silhouetted against the flames. The glow picked out the reddish strands of her hair and spun them to gold. She could have been a saint in an ikon, haloed and hollow with purpose.

He knew that she was thinking of those winged monstrosities from the south, spiraling and diving like vultures over the ruins of their little town. *How many hours until they return?* she must have been wondering. *How many more until the fortress falls?*

"Use the scrap, then," she said at last. "Go to the next fortress and use the salvage from the train the dragons blew. If you need a gun, use the gun we lost. The gun I lost—the machinists still have it in the shop. We don't have time to bring in new metal."

"I'll need men," said Petya.

"You can have the English," said Liza. "Half of them are children, too."

CHAPTER ELEVEN

The fires had died by evening. In every house that had survived, the blackout curtains had gone up, and light shone from the windows. "What good is it to pretend the houses are empty?" Nastya had demanded when Liza protested. "They've burnt the empty houses, too."

The station had been destroyed again; the rail lines westward were blown. The church was still standing, but the bakery and the optician's shop had gone up in flames. Two dozen souls were huddled on the floor of Nastya's tavern, their houses lying in heaps of ash atop the scorched metal of the shelters. Those denizens of the flophouses who'd survived the bombing run were taking shelter across the rails in the machinists' shop.

It wasn't as bad as it had looked, when everything had seemed to be aflame. The people whose families had been born in Yureyevsk knew better than to build their houses close enough to spread fire quickly—because they knew they'd be hiding in holes like rabbits when the fires began to blaze in earnest—but the flophouses had gone up like so much kindling. They had lain like a wall of fire at the edge of her vision, crackling and sagging to the ground.

"I need a drink, Nastya," said Liza thickly. "I promised

you that I wouldn't—but sweet *Christ*, I need a drink."

Nastya didn't even raise her eyes as she seized a bottle and poured out a generous measure of liquor. She slid the glass across the counter. "You have ash on your face," she said, and that gave Liza some hope. If she'd seen the ash, she must have been stealing glances.

Liza downed the liquor and passed the glass back for a refill. "Then give me a handkerchief with the drink."

"You'll only get more ash on your face when you go outside." Nonetheless, she took out her pocket-handkerchief and licked one corner, dabbing the damp cloth over Liza's cheek.

"They'll be back," said Liza softly. "We're not ready to fight anything like this. As long as I've lived, it's been a flight of three to seven dragons, too high in the air for precision bombing—we're not *trained* for this."

"Don't let them hear that in town," said Nastya. "You're the lord of the fortress. You're the closest thing we have to an object of faith, and I will not permit you to destroy that, too."

"Too?"

Nastya said nothing. She filled Liza's glass, then tucked her handkerchief into her apron pocket and went to serve the baker.

When she had finished her drink, Liza lowered her left foot to the ground and then her right. There were chafing marks ringing her left thigh—Petya had told her not to run on this new leg of hers, but hadn't she been foolish enough to run?—and now she winced at the fresh, shallow pain of them. It was a newer pain than the old, deep ache below her knee, and it made the latter wound feel all the deeper.

She walked slowly, carefully across the tavern floor, only giving in to the urge to hobble when she had stepped out into the evening gloom. Across the northern horizon, she could see smoke rising in gouts and gobbets from the smokestacks of the machinists' shop.

If Petya could make his sky-boat fly, that was all to the good. If he couldn't, she only had five proper guns, the Gardner gun on its tripod, and the popguns of the English—and after what Wainwright had told her, she couldn't even be sure *they* weren't trying to steal the fortress out from under her.

She remembered sitting in her father's unused wheelchair, a bundle of guns across her lap. *No*, she realized, with a slow-dawning sense of hope. *No, I have a whole damn town full of gunners. Poachers and veterans of the war in Poland—and if their guns wouldn't have scratched a dragon's hide, these new monsters have soft, human bellies.*

She wheeled on her good leg, flinging the door of the tavern open again. "Have every hunter and soldier meet me at the fortress at eight," she called. Nastya's head snapped up, and for a moment her dark eyes locked with Liza's. "Every last one of them. Have them bring their guns—and if they don't have guns, make Kostya *give* them guns. The best he has."

Nastya's eyes softened, and she nodded once. "Yulchik!" she called into the back. "Yulchik, you heard what she said—Galya, get old Konstantin Bogdanovich out of bed—"

"I served in Poland," said the baker. "Let me fetch my gun, and I'll follow you."

I'll follow you. Liza felt her heart swelling. Try as she might, she couldn't blame the stinging in her eyes on the lingering smoke. "I have an errand to run first," she said, clasping his forearm the way her Uncle Pasha had clasped the arms of his hunting party. "Be there at eight, and be ready to serve Russia."

She limped across the street to the constabulary, where a man slid the barrel of his rifle out the door on the first knock. "Name of God, Seryozha, the Turks wouldn't *knock*!" shouted Utkin from the back, and then Seryozha put up the rifle and swung the door open.

"Madame Tarasova!" he said, with evident surprise.

"What brings you to—"

"I need your prisoner," she said. "Wainwright. Bring him out. I need him at the fortress *now*."

"This is highly irregular—"

"I don't *care*," she snapped. "I don't care if he's killed the Tsar himself—if I still had Jaworski, I'd use him, but they've taken him west, and I need a man who knows how to drill soldiers. Lieutenant Wainwright is the only commissioned officer in this town. He can pay for his crimes when I've finished with him."

"On your head be it."

"It *will* be on my head if I let the Turks blow my town to bits." She drew herself up to her full height, although it strained at her bad leg and sent shooting pains up her thigh. Standing upright, she towered over Seryozha and stood almost a hand's breadth taller than Utkin—let him look down his nose at her *then*!

Utkin studied her for a long moment, during which she dared not blink. At the end of that moment, he glanced away. "Fetch the prisoner," he said, and Seryozha sprang to obey. "Keep him in leg irons. Do I have your word that he'll still stand for his trial, the day after tomorrow?"

"You have my word," said Liza, offering her hand to shake.

Utkin refused the hand—but then over his shoulder, she caught sight of Wainwright's haggard, pale face. "Elizaveta Vladimirovna," he said, with a wry little smile. "Have you come to kill me?"

"Better than that," she answered. "I've come to *use* you."

As Liza and Wainwright hastened to the gravel drive, arms around one another's shoulders for support, she plied him with questions. "The Turks have a new machine," she said. "A flying machine made of steel and canvas, big enough to hold a man inside. We've shot down a few of them over the fields, but Petya says they're too burnt to study. Tell me—did you know they'd be building these?"

"I didn't," he said. "I had no idea the Turks were planning *anything*."

"Then they're *not* in league with the English?"

"Much as you want me to know absolutely everything about Her Majesty's plots and alliances," said Wainwright through gritted teeth, "you've shut me in prison for two months. My intelligence is out of date."

This, Liza had to admit, was true. "Do you remember how to drill soldiers? Or is that, too, out of date?"

"*That*, I can do. Where are your soldiers?"

"They're *coming*," she said. "Some have served. Some are poachers. You'll make them into soldiers."

"What, before my trial?"

"Before your trial," Liza agreed. "Two days—make good use of them." They began to ascend the uneven stone, Wainwright's legs unsteady from disuse and shackled closely together, Liza's false leg locking and chafing. She blew out an impatient gust of air, and Wainwright shifted to take more of her weight on his shoulder.

"Will you slow down, for my sake?" he asked—if she knew he meant *for your own sake*, she chose to ignore it.

"All right."

Slowly, shoulder to shoulder, they climbed the hill. They passed a scrap of burnt canvas, skewered through with a steel spine, and Wainwright bent to pick it up and pocket it. "For your brother to study," he said, when Liza looked at him askance.

At the servants' entrance, the errand boy was waiting. He twisted his hat in his hands and then appeared to catch himself doing it, at which he tucked the hat behind his back. "Lady Tarasova," he said. "We've—that is to say—"

"He means to say," broke in Misha, who stood at the foot of the stair, "that we've sent for more ammunition, but your munitions dealer says there's not much more to be had."

"Have the machinists make molds for bullets, then, and have them melt down whatever scrap Petya hasn't seized. No—have them tear apart the train cars for more scrap. Get the Nordenfelt guns off the guncars. Mount them where they'll be useful. We'll take the Imperial Rail Company's bills once we've turned the Turks away."

"A word, Lord Tarasov," called a familiar voice from just over Liza's shoulder. "I've come a long way."

"I don't have time for a word," she said—and then the voice registered, and she looked back and down the hill.

Upon the slope stood Kesha, scarcely more than a frost-touched silhouette while her eyes adjusted to the dimness. As he stepped into the light, she saw that his cheeks were shadowed with a beard and that he wore an Ottoman uniform under his heavy Russian coat, but even so she would have known her brother anywhere. In the clear night air, he seemed almost too sharply drawn, like a dream or a memory. He held both hands before him, palms out. "Please don't shoot me until I've had a chance to speak. And if it's not too much trouble, please refrain from shooting the dragon in the plum orchard."

"The—" began Liza, but she got no farther before Misha pushed past her and sped across the snow-crusted stones to crush Kesha in an embrace.

"You *miserable fool*," he said, shaking Kesha by the shoulders. "Sending me a telegram in *St. Petersburg*, as though you could doubt that I'd be right here in this horrid, backward little town waiting for you—my aunt had to redirect the wire—"

"You *wired* him," demanded Liza, while Wainwright stood back from the entire tableau with a look of incredulity. "From *where*?"

"From Moscow," said Misha, releasing Kesha and tugging him to the door. "Now, let's all get inside, before we catch a chill."

"Your watchmen need to be more on guard against

approaches from the ground," said Kesha, and Liza gave in to the urge to crack him hard across the face.

"My *watchmen* just fought three dozen Turkish machines, and we're out of shot," she said, and slapped him once more for good measure. "And now I hear that all this time you've been in *Moscow* and consorting with *dragons*, while the people in your town were dying—I'll *disown* you for this, Innokentiy Vladimirovich, see if I don't—"

He was grinning, though, and grinning all the harder for the way his lip was bleeding where she'd struck him—and through that blood she recognized the little boy she'd fought with and stolen her father's liquor with and chased the trains with when they'd been too young to know better. "Kesha," she said, and threw her arms about him. "Kesha, your hair is *brown*—"

"Like yours," he said, laughing as he held her back. She breathed in the scent of tobacco on his Turkish uniform. "Like Petya's, like Mother's—"

"I'll slap you again," she said, and laughed against his cheek. "Is the dragon in the orchard yours, then? Why did you bring a dragon here?"

"Because she knows about the angels," he said. "The Turkish machines—and because she thinks that she can broker a deal for her people."

"What kind of godless bastard calls a flying machine an *angel*?" Liza kissed her brother's cheek and said softly, "That's not a real question. Name of God, why didn't you tell us you were alive? If you could wire Misha—"

"I thought you wanted me dead."

"I *did* want you dead," Liza admitted. "And now I need you, whether or not I want you dead. Misha's right; we'll freeze. Go inside and warm yourself. I'll send someone to fetch your *dragon*. We're out of shot. We couldn't fire on her if we wanted to. Misha, go to the machinists' shop with a sample bullet and have them start making us spares. Wainwright—"

"Yes, sir." He straightened, standing at attention as though she were his commander. Only the faint expression of delight on his face belied his attentive obedience.

"See if someone can get you out of those leg irons. You need to teach our men to *move*."

The dragon wheeled over the plum and cherry orchards, through the powder-light snow. Although Osip Moiseyevich had been warned of what to expect, Liza knew well how his hands must itch for a rifle. "Dragon approaching from the east," he called down from his tower.

"Let her land," answered Liza. She stood with Petya in the center of the courtyard, hands folded neatly at her back, chin lifted parallel to the ground. The two of them watched in uneasy silence as the dragon circled the fortress once, as though assessing it for weaknesses.

Slowly, the dragon came to rest in a heavy coil between Liza and the gates. She was a massive creature of sharp talons and rolling eyes, her body long but sleek with muscle. Even in the darkness, her scales gleamed dimly with reflected light from the snow. As Liza watched, a jet of steam issued from the dragon's nostrils.

There came an air-shattering, sibilant shriek—and yet Petya's brow wrinkled as though he understood something in it. "Is that...did the dragon just say *Salve, viri Sarmatae?*"

Liza knew not a word of Latin, but even she could recognize that she had been hailed.

CHAPTER TWELVE

Almost the moment Kesha had descended the stairs, he crossed paths with his mother in her gown of mourning black. She froze at the sight of him, one hand still half-raised to seize the rail and her mouth drawn into a grim line. He might have said that she looked as though she had seen a ghost, but the courtyard had been full of that look when he'd tumbled through the gates. Even in Liza's eyes, there had been at least as much hope as fear or anger.

Yelena Sergeyevna Tarasova looked him over as a woman on an icy bank might scan for a crossing.

She lifted her gloved hands to cup his face. "Oh, my son, my boy," she breathed. "Your sister swore you were dead. *And may he find a warmer hearth in Hell*, she said…but I couldn't believe it."

"Mother," he said, his hands coming up to fix on her arms. "Mother, I'm very much alive. But I've had a very long journey, and I could use nothing so much as a proper meal and a cup of tea."

"Tea, of course," she said. "I've had some of my own tea sent from Moscow. The jasmine-scented tea. It was your favorite, when you were a boy."

Before he'd met Söz, he wouldn't have noticed the way bait followed switch. Now, he could see little else. *She wants something from me, too, and that hasn't changed since my father's death. Perhaps she's always wanted something from me.*

When he didn't offer his arm, she took it anyway, threading her hand through and pulling him close. "So much has changed, since that night," she said. "And not only the new Tsar, or the Turks in their flying machines."

"Liza seems to have the defense of the fortress well in hand. She's gathering the townsfolk. She'll teach them to fight as an army—"

"So she says," said Yelena distantly. "I believe she's sent the errand boy into town for more bullets. We'll have to drink our tea in the kitchen." She guided Kesha to the little table in the kitchen and sat while he topped up the tea in the samovar. The cook kept it exactly where she had when Kesha had been a boy, and he returned to the tins with a familiarity that he'd thought long-forgotten. He left his mother's jasmine-scented tea untouched. "I wonder how she will pay her new soldiers, when the first panic has passed? Your father could teach men and children to be soldiers, too, in his day, but he couldn't pay them when he'd taught them. He never had a head for accounts."

"Liza is a better soldier than either Petya or I will ever be. That much I know, whether or not she can manage her accounts." To that, she said nothing. When the tea had finished brewing, he took down the pot and filled a little china cup for each of them. He searched the cupboard for honey, then paused. *Jam*, he reminded himself. The marmalade lay close to hand, the last shining remnants clinging to the sides of the jar. These, he scooped into his teacup and stirred. "You want me to say that she's unfit to hold the fortress, I take it."

His mother placed her cup upon a saucer and smoothed her skirts to sit, as gracefully as though she were taking tea with a tsarina. "This is a new era, Keshechka. Your father's ghost must not claw it back into the past."

"In Turkey, I met another woman who saw a new era bearing down on her," he said, with a neutral smile that Söz might have admired. "She thought she could take control of it, too, by replacing one Tsar with another."

He drank, and so did she.

"You, I raised well," Yelena said at last. She smoothed back his hair, now as brown as her own. "Too well, perhaps."

She took a long swallow of tea, as if she meant to curb further questioning with it. "I see you've put on a Turkish uniform."

"When the Turks took me in, I was wearing what I'd worn when I ran from the fortress. The uniform was warmer—and you always taught me to make myself amenable to the foibles of new acquaintances."

"Your sister might have shot you for that. She may yet."

"Then she'd only be doing what she'd promised to on the night I ran. I'm still not entirely sure she won't, but when I saw the angels—"

"The angels?"

"That's what the dragons call the Turkish machines. Not what the Turks call them." He drummed his fingertips on the table. "I'm not making much sense. Such a lot has happened since I left St. Petersburg—it's hard to catch you up at a reasonable pace."

"Then tell me," said Yelena, at which she caught his hand in both of hers and pressed it still. "Are you well enough to go on?"

A lump rose in his throat. "Yes, Mother," he said softly. "I'm well. I've never been better—I've never been more convinced that I'm doing work that matters. And as for what's passed in the last months...we've lost nothing irrecoverable. I really believe that."

"Nothing except the Tsar," she said.

"Nothing except my father."

"Nothing except your father," she agreed, but it was only the kind of rote pronouncement that widows were expected to make. No suggestion of grief colored her voice, and her eyes remained clear and dry. "Even if I could, I would not recover him."

"I think I agree," said Kesha, "but I still grieve for him. Or for the reconciliation that we could have had. For the man he could have been."

She pressed his hand again, her fingers dry as paper and unyielding as iron. "Then grieve for that man. Grieve for him as you would for a character in one of Goethe's stories. When you've spent your sorrows, though, remember that such a man never existed—and then stand up, and return to your business."

With the tea cooling slowly in his cup, he remembered his father's bloodied face, and his own shame at thinking *They will suspect me* before *I never had a chance to make things right*. For the first time since that hideous night when Jaworski had walked him up to the fortress with a gun at his back, Kesha gave himself permission to mourn.

When he had finished his tea, he rose from his chair and left his mother still seated like Patience at the table.

"This is what the machines look like," said Kesha, unrolling a sketch before Liza, Petya, and Lukin. The lines were childish and wavering, and he saw Petya's fingers twitching as though he meant to take a charcoal stick to the sketch to correct it. He put a lantern down on one end to keep it unrolled, and he laid a volume of Schiller on the other. "The men are strapped in here. There are two engines, one at either side, and they work in tandem."

"They must be very light," said Petya.

"I couldn't tell you," said Kesha, but Lukin was already speaking over him.

"Their wingspans are wide—curved, too, by the look of it. Light engines would do to keep them flying, if the steel frames were strong enough. What would happen if one of the engines gave out, do you think?"

"Were there—" Petya plucked up the charcoal and drew a sort of double-bladed apparatus beside the ill-drawn engines, with lines behind each to show them spinning. "Was there anything that looked like this, in the engines? At the backs? Propellers, like on a dirigible."

"Yes!" said Kesha. "That's what made the awful buzzing sound."

"Ah," said Petya, glancing over at Lukin. "Probably nothing, then, but the pilot might flinch. What about the man inside?"

"There are more canvas and leather straps to keep him in place," Kesha affirmed.

"What are you saying to them?" said Aysel, leaning over Kesha's shoulder and examining the plans, first with one eye and then the other. "I cannot understand what you are saying. I did not take you all the way to Russia to be left out of your important negotiations."

"We are describing the...what is the word? The way in which the angels function. The...the mechanism of the angels," he said. "The wings, the...the swords—"

"*Falces*, not *gladii*," she huffed. "Yes, the curved blades that propel them through the air. Did you tell them of the gas?"

"Of the...what?"

Leaning back to scratch behind her ruff, she said delicately, "The gas that permits dragons to fly. The Turks fill bottles with our fluids and use the gas to raise themselves into the air. They could not rise without it. The design is not yet sufficiently advanced."

"That's very helpful," he said, then turned again to Liza and Petya, whose pupils had gone to pinpricks. "Aysel tells me that the dragons use a...a kind of combination of fluids to generate a gas, and that gas allows them to rise into the air. These fluids are what the Turks use to lift their machines. They're especially flammable when they're not combined in a very particular proportion—"

"No wonder the machines burned so badly when they fell," said Liza. "I'd thought they were still loaded with bombs."

Lukin bent over the diagram. From the tracks his fingers traced on the paper, Kesha thought he was searching for viable fluid and gas reservoirs. "Foolish, to make the wings of canvas and then go into the air with such dangerous chemicals aboard."

"No more foolish than flying in a dirigible, and people in Bohemia and Switzerland do it for a lark," replied Petya. "I've seen photographs in the engineering department—"

"No one's *shooting* at them in Bohemia or Switzerland," said Lukin. "And where do they keep their bombs? They carry a damn lot more than any dragon ever did."

"That's a mechanical problem," Petya guessed. "Payload versus altitude. Dragons have only so much room in them for hydrogen gas, and they can only carry so much before they can't climb out of the reach of the guns. But once these machines are in the air, they can use their engines to gain altitude."

As Kesha pointed to the reservoir at the rear of the machine, with a chute like an ovipositor, he turned to relay the observation to Aysel. "Why did the dragons carry on their attacks, even after the borders closed?" he asked, and he tried to bear in mind as he spoke that many of the dragons he'd watched twitching and seizing in this very courtyard might have been Aysel's friends. For all he knew, she could smell their blood painting the walls. For all he knew, this place was a hallowed battleground to her people. "You couldn't take and hold territory. You could only destroy so much on any one raid. So many have died, and for negligible gain—"

"Not so many," she answered. "Only as many as we could not feed."

Kesha remembered the too-thin dragons jostling for position at the ring of the dinner bell, and his stomach lurched. "No," he said softly. "No, that can't be true."

Aysel's voice was hard. "Can it not? But even so, I escorted many criminals and sick dragons to their deaths at your guns, so that Russian men could crow over their corpses and think themselves strong enough for the coming war."

"It was a spectacle." Kesha felt as though he was going to be sick.

She snorted in irritation. "And you wonder why I call myself a radical! My kin executed their weakest to make yours believe that we were the strongest weapon in the hands of the Turks."

Lukin, who had been listening to their conversation with an expression of concentration, ventured, "To seem... to me to seem, you are strongest." He spoke the Latin of a man who had never been classically educated, consonants still Russian and sentence half-conjugated, but there was something earnest in his expression that bid Kesha to urge him on. In Russian, he continued, "These machines can be manufactured in nearly infinite quantity, but they're more vulnerable than the dragons. We were caught by surprise this time, but next time, we'll know better where they can be hit."

"I've never killed a man before," said Petya, his face made hollow by the lantern light radiating up from the table.

"You've killed dozens of dragons," said Kesha in reply. He was painfully aware of the radiating heat of Aysel at his back. "In what way is it different?"

Petya glanced up at Aysel, and in his expression was the dread of a man facing down uncertain damnation. "I suppose it's not," he said at last. "I suppose it's no different."

CHAPTER THIRTEEN

In the ever-burning fires of the machine shop's forge, Petya watched metal fuse and run. The smiths poured it into long sheets, and when it had cooled enough to work, the English conscripts helped to hammer it over a frame—a frame that Petya had cobbled together from an old steam engine's frame, bent until the blunt, snub lines became something resembling falcon-sleek.

There were lumps and odd angles everywhere that the old frame had resisted his efforts. *It will rust at the weak places*, he thought to himself. *It's the very poorest steel.*

There was no time for better. There was hardly time for this. The forge swarmed with machinists drafted to melt train cars into bullets, with miners and mothers packing bullets into magazines. Toy soldiers and printers' letters melted together in crucibles, and the machinists lamented the lack of lead. Women had brought their grandmothers' pans to be melted, and those, too, went into the forge.

At his own worktable, which he shared with a man retooling bullet molds, he had torn apart an old clock and put the gears to work in turning a bevy of tiny, spinning hands.

"Call them the Hands of God," Lukin had told him. "Since the Turks call their monsters 'angels.'"

"I'm not a political enough man to say such things," Petya had answered. "*Falces*—that's what the dragon called the propellers. Not *gladii*—swords—but sickles, like any farmer has."

"Sickles, then, if 'propellers' won't do," said Lukin. "Call them that."

He hadn't needed to say that to identify with the farmers, too, was to be political. It was a position that he found palatable, and so it might pass unremarked.

Petya screwed the thin steel shell about his scale model and wound the little key on the underside. He knew, in a way that soaked him with cold sweat, that he would never have another chance to test his and Lukin's design before the machinists had built it in full. In his room in St. Petersburg, no doubt his wire armatures were gathering dust just as the clockwork creatures did in the Kunstkamera.

The Turks were fascinated with clockwork monsters—he had known this for *years*, had even viewed their creations with the professional boredom of a St. Petersburg student used to marvels, and he had never imagined what a such a machine might do with a man to pilot it.

He set the model down on the table, feeling the key strain against his fingers as he steadied the little steel sky-boat. *Sky-train*, Liza would have said, without masking her contempt.

He released the key, and the rows of propellers began to spin. They built momentum slowly, until they were spinning too quickly for him to make out individual hands—for a breath, and no more, the model rose from the table.

By this time, the spring had wound down, and the gears abruptly stopped turning. The model crashed onto its side, propellers still spinning feebly.

He fought down the urge to panic. It had indisputably raised itself into the air, without explosive gases or hot air to buoy it. If he'd only had a longer spring, it would have continued to rise. The engine of the sky-boat would run on coal, like a proper steam engine—the problem of the spring wouldn't arise. He couldn't permit himself to panic because he had to refine the design *before his men finished building it*, and if he panicked he would be no use to anyone.

With shaking hands, he unscrewed the thin little propellers from the sky-boat's wings, then tipped them into a scrap bin bound for the forge. "Delay work on the propellers," Petya told one of machinists. "Delay work on the propellers," he said again in English, to which a boy in borrowed gloves nodded assent and put up his hammer.

Petya took out the sheet of steel that he had been allotted for his model and began to punch free longer hands. These new propellers, he would curve carefully, like the wings of birds.

He had as much time as he needed. Not even his mistakes were unsalvageable. The scrap would go into the bin and be melted down for bullets.

Nothing was beyond repair.

He braced his first propeller on the edge of the work table, gently hammering the leading edge around the curve of the well-worn wood. The sharp rear edge scored his palm—he would have to remember to file them smooth, when he had time to file them smooth—but he turned the blade around to beat a curve into the second propeller in turn.

"You're bleeding," observed the workman beside him. "That metal's rusted. You'll get lockjaw."

"This needs to be done," said Petya. "Until someone else can do it, I'll just have to bleed."

"Suit yourself, but you won't do us any good if you lose your hands," the workman replied.

"They need me," Petya said. *I've never been needed as they need me tonight*, he thought, and in the back of his mind, his father laughed, *Name of God, Vladimirovich, what bad habits he's picked up in the city!* His sister crowed, *It demeans your heritage to say you want to be as noble as a laborer.*

He screwed the new propeller into place, then began to punch out a second set.

Falces, not *gladii*. He would earn his sister's respect as a laborer while she earned his as a soldier, and neither of them would be accounted noble for it. He reached for the cup of tea one of the young mothers had brought him and found it grown cool. He drained it anyway and swiped at his aching eyes. The dry heat of the shop stung them.

This time, the model boat rose nearly to the ceiling before the key gave out, and those machinists who noticed sent up a ragged cheer.

Dawn came cloud-shrouded, cold in a wet way that promised thick snowfall. Petya raised his face into the wind and let it beat over his cheeks until they stung. It woke him as the increasingly weak tea had not, to breathe in through his muffler and taste the chill even through the aroma of breath-damp wool.

"They'll attack in daylight, if they attack again," Kesha had said. "They don't have lights to guide them, and they have a long way to fly."

"If the Tsar had died to their schedule, in Bratsk," Wainwright had agreed, "they would've come on a nearly full moon. It's too dim now to steer by."

"They didn't get the revolution they were expecting, either," added Kesha. "A Polish separatist seeking revenge doesn't inspire Russians to revolt."

"Not without a full moon—or plenty to drink," Wainwright answered wryly, and he'd looked up at the sky with his breath filming the air.

The clouds had obscured the evening's waning sickle moon, and now Petya could scarcely see the butter-gold disc of the sun behind them.

He strained his ears, but he heard only the muffled

sounds of the machinists' shop and the squeak of the handcart returning from its journey down the westbound line. Elliot returned with one of the miners from the town, both of them worn and grim. A blanket-wrapped bundle lay strapped to the cart between them. "What does it look like, down the line?" he asked them. "Did you get as far as the Kamensky holdings—"

"Gone," said the miner. He smelled as though he had recently been sick. "Wiped out. I've asked the survivors to bring whatever salvage metal they could, but they're afraid to come out of their shelters. The Kamenskys are gone, or near enough to gone. We were bringing this one back," he said, gesturing to the bundle, "but I'll be surprised if he survived the journey."

"It looked like Hell on Earth," said Elliot in English, as though he had read the subject of their conversation not in the miner's words but in his quavering voice. "Even in Afghanistan, I never…I've never seen anything so bad as that. There were still fires…."

"Tell me," said Petya, "Tell me—how many survivors were there?" He repeated the question in English, but Elliot only shook his head.

"Seven or eight who came when we knocked at their shelters," the miner replied. "Maybe more, in the deep parts of the fortress. But the Kamensky territory is mostly farmland. Most of the farmers couldn't afford to have shelters put in. And the Kamenskys were all up on the towers. The one we brought looked like he'd taken a bad fall. Worse than your sister's."

"The wire has been destroyed," put in Elliot, as though he had only just remembered. "The telegraph line—that's the one that follows the rails, in a ceramic pipe. Yes?"

"Yes." Petya's heart sank. "It was destroyed, then?" In Russian, he added, "The telegraph line was destroyed?"

"The man at the telegraph office had been sending distress calls since last night," said the miner gruffly. "Nothing got through. God help the poor man."

"Have the telegraph master send a message to the Abramovs. See if the eastern line is still intact," Petya told him. "Then go up to the fortress—both of you, go to the fortress—and let my sister and the lieutenant prepare you to fight. I'll take him."

"I want to sleep," said the miner. "Can't a man sleep, after he's had his house burned over him and then taken a handcart six verst in each direction?"

"Sleep, then—but sleep quickly. There are quarters in the fortress…only go. We have to be ready when the Turks return."

"You think they'll return." The miner rubbed his gloved hands together, blowing on the thumbs. "Well, I can't think what they'd come back for, after what they did to the people on the Kamensky lands—"

"They'd come back for *us*," said Petya. "We've survived. The fortress is standing. We're bringing scrap back and forth along the eastbound line. God only knows who else has survived, but they'll come back for them, too—and we have to be ready when they do."

"*You* haven't slept, either," the miner said shrewdly. "All right. I'll take your quarters and carry your gun. But why should I trust my safety to a man who doesn't care about his own?"

He turned, then, catching Elliot by the arm and dragging him across the tracks to the main street. Their trousers, Petya saw, were smeared with soot and what might have been blood.

It looked like Hell on Earth. He folded that thought away and placed it in a neat little box, then closed the box and sealed it. The miner was right. Petya *hadn't* slept, and he couldn't permit the image of the Kamensky fortress to haunt his dreams. He stooped to free the man strapped to the handcart, undoing the canvas straps one by one. As he worked, he rounded his shoulders against the ash-laden wind.

The man on the cart groaned softly and tried to raise his arm. Even under the rough blanket, Petya could see that his arm ended only a little past the shoulder. Whether shrapnel had sheared it or Elliot had cut it off to save the stump, Petya couldn't have said. It would probably send him into shock to carry him all the way to the fortress, although he would be safer there. Petya would have to roll the handcart down into the machinists' shop instead.

He pushed back the blankets, tilting the man's face up. He studied the dark hair and eyes, the prominent nose. Through the crusted blood, he recognized Oleg Romanovich Kamensky. "You're safe here," he said softly, tucking the blanket back around him. Oleg was only a year older than he was. They had never been friends, but they had been children together, and last year he had dared to imagine that they might be brothers by marriage. "We'll get you warm, and…"

Oleg's eyes stayed fixed on the sky as Petya spoke, though, and eventually he recognized that he would have to close them with his fingertips. The earth would be too cold to bury Oleg properly, and so Petya wrapped him in the blanket again and left him beside the rails.

By now, his cheeks had ceased to sting. He felt the skin draw tight when he suppressed a sob. How cold was it, today? How would his new-forged flying machine handle such deep, aching cold? He descended once more into the service tunnel, into the lamplit space that smelled of salt and steel, and immediately the heat of that space bled into his chilled skin.

He couldn't permit himself to dwell on Oleg's death. His sister needed him, and she trusted him to make her the weapon that would win her her war.

Only a few hours more of work, and then he would let himself sleep. A few more hours, and he would be able to tell her that he had put her modest, contemptuous dreams to shame.

CHAPTER FOURTEEN

"We want to fight."

Liza studied Yulchik, Nastya's next-oldest sister—a fleshy girl with heavy shoulders, mouse-blonde like half of the Vasilevskaya girls. "You and who else?" she said, when Yulchik didn't blink.

"There are six of us," she answered. "My sister Galya—four of the women from the mines—"

"And you want to fight."

"Galya and I can shoot a gun," said Yulchik. "The others are stronger than some of your men. *Use* us, Elizaveta Vladimirovna. You can't afford to be short-handed."

You're women, Liza wanted to tell her. With Yulchik standing before her, a velvet ribbon closing the lace lining of her collar, Liza wanted to order her away and make her take shelter. "Six of you, are there?" she said instead, folding her arms. "Put on some trousers. Go to the armory. Have Konstantin Bogdanovich give you each a gun—a *new* gun. Then get in line with the rest of them, and Lieutenant Wainwright will drill you."

"You won't regret this," Yulchik said, bowing low to her. She squared her shoulders when she rose, gathering up her skirts in one hand as she made ready to dash down the hill.

Liza couldn't help smiling, although she felt her stomach churning as though she were walking on a new-frozen river. At any moment, she might plunge through the surface and into darkness. "See that I don't."

───

At half past nine, the distant thrumming began—or perhaps it only grew loud enough to be audible. Liza had the uncomfortable suspicion that it had been lingering on the edge of her consciousness for long minutes before she had been able to identify the sound. "Ring the bells!" she cried to the watchmen, who dutifully obliged her. She waved to Wainwright, who gave her a tired salute as she turned to descend into the fortress. He and his soldiers, newly emerged from the earth, had concealed their bright red uniform jackets beneath the weathered brown coats of Russian men.

The men and women in the courtyard had been drilling all morning, learning to disguise their shapes against the broken stones of the hillside. Wainwright had taught them to curl in the shadows, guns concealed beneath the flaps of their coats, until the target came into range. "And—UP!" he'd cried, swinging his arm skyward; up the poachers had come, rising to their feet. "JUST the Christ-fucking gun, soldier!" Wainwright had bawled. "Stand up and make yourself a goddamn target. What do you think this is, a bottle-shooting party? Cling to those rocks like you'd cling to your mother's skirts, you pissants—"

It had been, Liza had realized just past dawn, a long time since she'd heard Wainwright swearing as though he *enjoyed* it. She'd forgotten what a joy it was to hear.

She could use some joy, after Kamensky's death. She could not forget that, if she had married him as their fathers had hoped, she would have died with the rest of the Kamenskys.

In the doorway to the keep, she stole a glance back at the girls of her town. Yulchik had spoken truly; the Vasilevskayas were better marksmen than half of their comrades, and the women from the mines learned quickly to wheel, to crouch, to fire on command. If their shots were still flying wide of the mark, so were everyone else's.

Galya was gripping her gun, face very pale as she scanned the sky. Timid little Galya, who flew into a panic at a marriage proposal from a handsome young man, now stood straight-backed and ready to defend the land of her birth.

They were what she had, and she'd use them. She couldn't afford to be short-handed.

Liza climbed the ladder to her tower, relishing the way her foot caught and released each rung. Beneath her trousers, she'd soothed the chafed skin with lotion and then bandaged it, and now the ache was no worse than the ache of anticipation in her chest. She passed by the watchman, who bowed to her in that brief but deep fashion typical of the older class of veterans. "I'll be loading your gun," he said, raising his voice to make himself heard over the clangor of the bells.

"Have they brought the new magazines?" The watchman gestured to the boxes that littered the round room, and Liza grinned. "Good. Help me haul them up."

From the top of the tower, she could see Kesha settling into the gunner's chair on the far side of the fortress. At this distance, with his hood drawn close over his brow and his jaw grimly set, his face might have been their father's. She waved to him once, and he raised his hand in recognition before turning to study the attitude rotor.

The last time he'd been in one of the gunner's chairs, they'd had to crank the guns to keep them firing. Then, Liza had been only twenty-two, huddling in the keep and raging at being forbidden to join him.

The watchman below her handed up a box of magazines,

and she took it and heaved it into easy reach of the mounting plate. Six years ago, she would have struggled under the weight of it. Now, she put her hand down for another.

By now the buzz of the approaching machines had grown to an all-pervading whine that raised the fine hairs on the back of Liza's arms. "Faster," she said under her breath. "They're nearly on top of us—and I'll need you to load me when they come."

"If I die today," the watchman told her, passing her another box, "then tell my family it was an honor to die loading your gun."

Perhaps it was only a pretty story to ease their hearts—but as she bent to take the final box of magazines from his waiting hands, she said with equal solemnity, "If I die, shoot a few dozen of those bastards who killed me."

The first bombs fell into the open mouths of the mines, and Liza gritted her teeth against the percussive tremor that made the very air vibrate. "Hold steady!" she called down. "Don't waste your first shot!"

"Hold steady!" Wainwright echoed from the watch room of the westernmost tower, in a carrying voice that must have been audible on the far side of the silent town. "Wait for them to come into range!"

The world entire seemed to hold its breath. The clouds issued forth a few, moist snowflakes, which the wind caught and sent skidding eastward. *The Turks will be fighting that wind*, Liza told herself. *And so will I.* "Come on, you bastards," she growled, squeezing the attitude rotor in one hand and settling the other on the trigger. "Come close enough for my gun."

She drew in a single, deep breath—and at the end of it, she fired.

An angel exploded into flame as her burst struck the

oil reservoirs, canvas wings going up almost at once. The pilot screamed until he hit the earth, but by then the other gunners were firing, and Liza couldn't be bothered with whether he was screaming or not. "Where in *God's* name is the dragon?" she shouted, but no one could hear her, and soon she'd forgotten there had been a dragon at all.

The world all around her was burning. Her men were burning, and she could do nothing but squeeze off round after round until she'd emptied her magazine. She pivoted right, following a spiraling angel as it fell skidding to the ground. Her loader clung to the handles on the mounting plate as she whirled, nearly flying clear when she crashed to a stop. He slid a new magazine into place the moment he'd steadied himself, though, and she unloaded it into the grounded angel. When she brought her gun up again, she fired more carefully, because by now the angels were over the town.

The angels were over the town, and it would burn with them if she sent them down in flame. *"Aim for the engines!"* she shouted, and she heard Wainwright echoing every word. By now their soldiers were firing from the ground, faint pops against the merciless thunder of the Gatling guns. She could hear screams through the whine of the engines and didn't know whether her men or the Turks were screaming.

Nothing to be done but to keep firing. Nothing else to be done.

The snow had begun to fall in earnest now, fat flakes concealing the angels from view. She shot at shadows as the wind drove her collar hard against her cheeks, blowing her hat back from her head until the strap tugged at her throat. A flake blew into her eye at the very last moment, sending her final shot wild.

"That's all the magazines we had," her loader said. His voice sounded raw, as though he'd been screaming. Still the crackle of rifles sounded from the ground, but every Gatling gun except Kesha's had gone silent.

Her ears were ringing. Her ears were ringing so badly that she could hear her pulse in them, because otherwise, there was no way to account for that deep, rumbling, throbbing sound in the background of her hearing—like the buzz of the angels' engines, their spinning propellers, turned low and menacing.

"Do you hear that?" Liza asked.

Her loader only nodded and said, "I feel it. In my bones, I feel it."

Through the white curtain came something that sent the wind into whorls and eddies—something that blasted the gathered crust of snow from the rooftops, that made the soldiers beneath it shudder and cross themselves. This shape was vast and black and slow, turning as though to regard the fortress before shuddering and approaching Liza's tower. She rose from the gunner's chair, reaching for the pistol at her waist even as the thing's spinning blades tore her hair from its pins and sent it whipping wildly. The beast's broad raven-black hull shadowed her as it halted in the air, hovering over her.

A hatch in the underside swung open, revealing an iron stair with a rail welded to one side—a rail for women whose legs could not be relied upon. "Come inside," called Petya, over the heart-deep throb of the propellers. "We need a gunner."

Rolling her heel to unlock the ankle joint, Liza climbed into the belly of her brother's sky-boat, where Lukin winched up the stair and bolted it in place. "He wouldn't have any gunner but you," he said, and Liza gave not a single damn for the disapproval in his voice.

The gun that had shorn her leg had been stripped of its heaviest parts and mounted to the underside of the hull, and the gunner's chair was waiting for her. "Name of God," she said, prayer-soft, sliding into the seat that her brother had prepared for her. "Name of God, I should never have doubted you."

To Petya, she shouted, "Take us up!"

"More coal!" he cried in reply, at which Lukin threw another shovel's worth into the boiler.

They rose into the air, into the white blindness above the highest towers, and Liza laughed with wonder as she rose. The sky-boat cut through the whirling snow and sent the angels scattering, their canvas wings shuddering with the breeze of their passage.

The Turks carried no guns. They couldn't have imagined they had reason to carry them. They fell one by one as Liza raked them with shot, either diving to ground for safety or falling with their wings punctured.

It was, she knew, a long way home for them—a long way to walk, in the worst storm of the season.

Good, she thought, as she slotted another magazine into place. *They should never have come to my home, if they wanted to go back to theirs.*

CHAPTER FIFTEEN

Kesha scrambled down from the tower as soon as the shooting stopped. "Tell them not to shoot the prisoners," he told the first person he happened across, one of the innumerable Vasilevskaya sisters. She gave him a tremulous nod as he released her.

"I might have *shot* you!" she cried with an expression of anguish, clutching the long barrel of her rifle to her chest.

"Don't shoot *me*, either," he told her, and then he sprinted across the new-fallen snow to the first angel he'd brought down. He'd been careful to clip its wing, and it had fallen without burning. Those his sister had hit had been less lucky. As he'd watched the angels burst into flame, he'd realized with a sickening certainty what accident had befallen Selim's commander.

Levering up the hull of the angel, Kesha found the man inside unconscious, his straps only half-undone. "Here," he said, more to himself than to the soldier, unbuckling the rest of the straps and then hauling him free. "Here, let's see how badly you've been hurt." The bone of his shin had torn through his trousers; the fall had snapped it. His clothes were stiff with freezing blood.

The man's eyes fell open, unfocused and hazy with pain.

"Traitor," he said in the Tatar language, and then Kesha placed his face. One of the soldiers from Täteş—the one who had greeted him when he'd first arrived. The one with the Slavic nose. Ibragimov.

"Traitor," he agreed in the same tongue, turning his attention to the man's leg and slicing the trousers free before fixing his hand at ankle and knee. "This will hurt. Count of three."

He nodded. "One," said Kesha—and then he cracked the bones back into alignment before Ibragimov could resist him. He screamed and beat at Kesha with his fists, but by now Kesha was cutting free the straps of the angel and tightening them tourniquet-like around that broken leg.

"Liar," said Ibragimov, with a choked, sobbing sound.

"I'll carry you to the fortress," Kesha replied, "but then I have to see who else I can save. Arm around my shoulders."

"Söz should've had you killed," said Ibragimov, although he put his arm around Kesha's shoulders as instructed. His other leg was sound, and he braced it on the ground as Kesha stood. "I should've shot you the moment you landed in the beet fields—"

"I'm here to save your life," said Kesha as they hobbled uphill. "No one will torture you. I *promise* it. My friend will take care of you and your comrades. I made him promise."

"Promises, from a traitor and a liar." With every step, the soldier's face crunched up in agony. "I'll never go home again—"

"First, we'll have to treat your wounds so that you *can* get home."

They stumbled together through the servants' entrance, where Misha was waiting to take the soldier on his own shoulders. "How many more of these do you plan to bring me?" Misha demanded.

"As many as I find," answered Kesha. "I knew these men. I won't let them die."

"You seemed happy enough to shoot us down—" Ibragimov

cut himself off with a hiss as his heel struck the edge of a stair.

"He speaks Russian," said Misha, eyes widening. "That was rude. You speak Russian!"

"I'm Tatar," Ibragimov said as Misha led him off. He left a trail of blood behind him, despite the straps around his leg, and Kesha realized with a sinking heart that he would most probably lose it. "From Täteş. Your people would call it Tetyushi."

He could delay no longer. Tightening his muffler against his neck, Kesha sped once more into the fast-falling snow.

The wounded were scattered throughout the town, healing at their own hearths. The dead lay wrapped in winding-sheets in the courtyard, where they could be counted. Liza stood at the feet of one young English soldier with wide grey eyes and fair hair, examining his visage with a stony expression. Kesha couldn't tell what she saw in those eyes, but it made her go hard and cold and still. "Cover his face," she said at last. "Close his eyes. Wainwright, how do your people bury the dead?"

"It's different on the battlefield," he replied. "We say a prayer and bury them quickly. Too quickly. We're used to warring in hot climes, where the bodies go bad. Sometimes, there's no time to do anything but burn them."

"We'll bury them in the churchyard, then." decided Liza. "Like civilized people. Kesha—there you are."

Kesha tightened his coat around himself, raising his gaze so that she might inspect him. "Yes?"

"Misha says you've brought him Turks."

"I've brought him wounded soldiers."

"He says they speak Russian."

"Most of the Turks I met did speak Russian, yes. The ones who didn't spoke a Tatar dialect."

Liza folded her arms. "Are they Christians?"

"Some of them," hazarded Kesha. "Some are Muslims—we'd say Mohammedans. But their word for it is *Muslimun*."

"Muslims, then." Liza blew out a breath through her lips. "I don't know how to bury a Muslim."

"Then ask them."

"And what am I supposed to do with the ones who are still alive?"

"You've got an expert on jurisprudence here. Maybe he'll know how you should treat prisoners of war."

"And where in God's name was your dragon?" demanded Liza. "We could have used her in the air. That was certainly the plan last night—but now you've brought a bunch of Turks into my keep, and I don't have the first damn idea what your plan is anymore—"

"When we saw the clouds this morning, we agreed that she should go south today, before the storm ended. She can navigate through the snow. We have to hope that the Turks can't yet. The storm was a gift, Liza—"

"Some damn *gift*," she snarled, looking down her nose at him. The effect was only slightly marred by the thick mats of snow in her loose hair. "The only gift we've had so far today was Petya's sky-boat, and even that nearly crashed as he was setting it down—"

"It's been a miserable night," said Kesha gently. "And a more miserable morning. Come inside, and we'll eat a proper meal and get warm. That's the best thing we can do for the dead." He offered Liza his hand, and to his great surprise, she folded her hand over his.

"He pushed me around the courtyard when I was in Father's old chair," she said as they made their way into the hall. "I wanted to be *out* and *doing*, and he didn't scold me and tell me to go back to bed like I was a silly girl. He helped me up the stairs, and then he pushed me around the courtyard...."

"The English boy?"

"Elliot," she agreed. "Your Turks killed him. He was learning to speak Russian, and they killed him before he could do more than count to ten." For a moment he thought she might say more, but then she pressed her lips together, released his hand, and flung open the door to the keep. The wind wrenched it out of her hands and sent it clattering against the wall, and she stumped down the stair and let Kesha wrestle the door shut again.

Wainwright met Kesha's eyes as they forced the door against the jamb. He remembered the man's cold hands and hollow cheeks in the ice closet, and their tacit understanding that one of them must stand trial. "You're surprised to see me alive," Wainwright said. "I credit the inefficiency of the Russian court systems."

"When is your trial?" asked Kesha.

"Tomorrow."

Kesha hesitated, glancing down at Wainwright's hands. "Do you want to talk about—"

"I don't, actually." With that, Wainwright strode after Liza, and Kesha followed after in a stunned, contemplative silence.

Not a reprieve, then. No more than a respite.

Kesha woke with his head pillowed against Misha's shoulder and an uncomfortable crick in his neck. He straightened, rolling his head about, then arched his back to clear out the remaining kinks. "It's been *ages* since you did that," Misha observed. "Fell asleep on my shoulder, I mean. I've no idea how often you break your back."

"Less than one might expect, given Aysel's complaints that I use her like a horse. Dragons refuse to wear harnesses—she says it demeans them—and so there's little to do but hang onto her mane."

"You have something of a rapport with her," said Misha,

carefully neutral in the way that meant he was probing.

"You've been wondering if I've learned the reason for the Defection," Kesha guessed, to which Misha nodded. "As the dragons tell it, there were several small and haphazard defections, rather than a single grand gesture. When Russia sold its conquered land to human soldiers, rather than granting it to the dragons as we'd promised, the dragons were divided over how to respond. As Aysel tells it, some turned on both humans and dragons, and Russia did nothing to protect the dragons from their own. The Turks bought the loyalty of some of them. At least one clan. I'm not entirely sure of whether it was only one clan, or whether they still consider themselves a clan. They promised the dragons protection and the use of a bit of land."

"At some more material cost to them, I imagine. Loyalty is all very well, but one can't eat it, spend it, or win a war with it."

"And the Turks are practical people. The dragons have a sort of air corps, not quite attached to the Turkish military. Because if they were, then the Turks would be violating their treaty. But so long as the dragons aren't Ottoman citizens, the Turks have plausible deniability for the raids."

"Very tidy," said Misha appreciatively. "I can only imagine that we had a similar sort of arrangement. Little wonder Empress Yekaterina balked at granting them land. She'd have had to sign away the land as an independent nation or give them citizenship. Perhaps even titles. Your friend might have been Lady Aysel, if things had gone another way."

"As to Aysel herself, she was the one who rescued me when I was wandering the rails east of here. She and her companions are dissatisfied with the way their elders manage things, and they want land to build a state and a culture of their own. I don't think they actually expect Russia to grant it to them, but they're willing to revive the old negotiations and see whether the angels make Russia any more amenable to their terms."

"So you've sent for a lawyer—"

"You *would* say I sent for a lawyer! I sent for an *historian*, and that's better. His name is Boris Baivich, and he's the... the poet, I suppose, of his clan. Something like a skald."

Kesha rose to his feet, offering his hand to pull Misha up in turn. Misha took it, but he made no move to rise even when Kesha tugged at him.

"Before we continue," he said, "I want you to tell me the truth. Should you be tried, I'll have to build a case in full understanding of the facts—and you know that I find criminal law utterly distasteful. It will be quite difficult enough to put an argument together under the very best of circumstances." He released Kesha's hand to remove his spectacles, polished them with his handkerchief, and replaced them, before fixing Kesha with a bland and solemn look that made him feel twelve years old. "Did you kill your father?"

"I didn't," said Kesha. "I wished him dead, as so many boys wish their fathers dead...I never grew out of wishing him dead, or I didn't until I saw him lying in his blood on the floor of the keep. But I didn't kill him."

"It's a surprisingly common thing to hear," said Misha mildly. "Not that boys wish their fathers dead; that other men wished *your* father dead, and stayed their hands. He must have been a difficult man, to have inspired so much helplessness and fear."

"He was a necessary man," answered Kesha. This time, when he offered his hand, Misha rose easily to his feet and fell into step at his side. "He made the world revolve around him. Without him...without him, we have nothing to center us, and so we go drifting in our orbits like lost planets."

"Thus, the struggle for the keep. Your mother wishes to install you as the rightful heir—have you any interest in the position?"

"None at all," said Kesha, pressing Misha's hand as they reached the door of the study. "I've told you a dozen times before, I want nothing more than to live in your library and speak to you about Spinoza at your fireside. I left this place because *that* was the sort of life I wanted to lead—and if I despised my father, it was because he forbade me to lead it."

"I shall hold you to that," laughed Misha.

In the hall outside, Kesha smelled meat roasting. Mutton, he supposed. The Muslim Turks would have refused pork and bacon, although their Orthodox counterparts had never shown any aversion to it. In Täteş, he had learned to recognize an Orthodox household at a glance by what animals they kept in their yards—those little yards like the ones the housewives still kept on the outskirts of Moscow, washing strung up out of reach of curious swine. "Do you know," he said as they walked, "I learned a few things about your father, in Moscow. Do you want to hear them?"

Misha made a *tch* sound, considering. "Is it likely to make me think better or worse of him than I did before? Unlike you, I've never had any particular inclination to kill my father."

Kesha remembered, with a faint start, that the heroic Dmitri Orlov had been sent to the labor camps when his son was only a child. "I didn't mean to be unkind, when I spoke of boys wishing their fathers dead."

"It's beyond my power to change," said Misha softly. "But go on. What did you learn about my father?"

They emerged into the mess hall, half of which had been curtained off to preserve the modesty of the wounded, and took a seat at the nearest table. There, one of the English soldiers gave Misha a knowing smile and pointed him to a coffee pot amid the massed teapots. Misha poured for them both, and Kesha took a fortifying sip before speaking. "When I was in Moscow, I met a fellow whom I knew as Kent—an English intelligencer who had been stationed there for many years, and who spoke of your father as part of his network. He claimed that he had been planning the assassination of the Tsar for many years. Since a fellow named Orlov ran a socialist newspaper, before his untimely transportation to Siberia."

"And my father was involved in the plot?" Misha stirred a sugar cube into his coffee, watching the spoon click against the sides of the cup. He had never taken sugar in St. Petersburg. The coffee was better there.

"Based solely on Kent's intelligence—and I stress that he spoke of Orlov in the least flattering terms possible—I believe that your father wished to bring about a socialist revolution without bloodshed. Not even shed by people whose politics he couldn't bear."

Although he had placed his spoon neatly alongside his cup, Misha didn't raise the cup to his lips. He only watched the ripples on the surface go still. "It's the most heartening defamation I could have expected," he said, when the table rocked and set the surface of his coffee to rippling again. "Thank you for telling me."

"Here's to fathers," said Kesha, although he raised his cup no higher than his chin.

"Here's to sons," answered Misha. His eyes were on Liza, who sat at the head of the table with deep shadows under her eyes.

CHAPTER SIXTEEN

Liza took a long drink of coffee and studied the inventory sheets before her until the numbers swam. Plenty of meat, potatoes, and grain for the next few weeks, but precious little fruit if the trains couldn't come to bring more. Few enough bullets for the Gatling guns, but perhaps enough for the rifles. The mines had been blown out in the last attack, which meant they'd have no more ore until they could get the shafts clear again. She'd had Hancock make her a roster of troops, and looking at their numbers, she wished she hadn't. Better not to know how many were dead, and how few remained to hold the line.

When she looked up again, she saw one of Kesha's Turks standing before her—a grave-looking man with grey in his hair and beard, wearing a fur cap singed from the flames of his descent. "Yes?" she said, and hoped to God he knew enough Russian to answer.

The man doffed his cap and gave a stiff, respectful bow. "You are the commander here?" he asked, and when she nodded, he straightened as though for inspection. "My name is Selim Kaya. In my army, I hold the 'chorbadzhi' rank," he said. "In Russia, you would say 'colonel.' I command these men." He looked over to where his Turks sat, stern-faced under the watchful eyes of Liza's own troops. "You have my formal surrender. I place myself and my men into your care as prisoners of war."

Liza narrowed her eyes at that speech. *He slaved over those words like a playwright,* she thought, *and now he delivers them like an actor.* In his place, Liza knew that she would have raged against her captivity. She would have demanded her freedom, demanded the rights to which her birth entitled her. If some ember of rage burned beneath this Colonel Kaya's cool features, though, he hid it well. But for a little lingering pain tightening the skin around his eyes, he appeared quite calm, as though it was a matter of no consequence to him whether she accepted his surrender. Nonetheless, Liza knew better than to imagine that he was making no demands of her.

Colonel Kaya was asking her, in full view of the forces of three nations, to declare them both bound by the laws of civilized warfare. He was declaring himself a valuable prisoner to be exchanged or ransomed, rather than an irregular combatant to be executed. To accept his surrender was to accept responsibility for his life and the lives of his men, even if her own men demanded those lives in recompense for their own losses.

She met his eyes. "I can't be responsible for your men if they start anything. If they hurt my people, or try to escape, or aid the enemy in any way, I will not help you."

"I would do no less, in your place," said Kaya.

"Then you have my word. As lord of this fortress, I accept your surrender and pledge to treat your men with honor." Liza stood and offered her hand, which Kaya shook. He had a strong grip, callused where a sword hilt would rest against his palm. "What can you tell me about the angels?"

"Is that what your people call them?" Kaya looked momentarily dumbfounded, but then recovered himself. "I regret to say that I can tell you nothing. The method of their construction is a military secret that I am forbidden to share. But this much I can say: they will return to finish what they began, and they will level both the fortress and the town."

"They can try," said Liza grimly. "If they manage it, they'll flatten you with us."

"This had occurred to me. May I sit?"

"Go ahead." Liza swept her papers to one side, then gestured Kaya into the empty seat at her left. "I don't envy you. Would you take up arms against your own people to save your men?"

"I would rather you surrendered to them, madame."

"What—and let them occupy the town? Bend our knee to invaders?"

"Täteş was once an occupied town," said Kaya. "Now, its children grow up never thinking that they might be anything but Turks."

"Yureyevsk isn't Tetyushi." The Russian name rang like iron. "No surrender. Not now, not ever."

"Then I fear that this fortress will be our grave. Your people don't deserve such an ignoble death."

Liza poured out some coffee for him, then slid it across the table so hard that a little spilled over the lip of the cup. "If you thought that, then you shouldn't have come over the border to kill us. Now drink your damn coffee."

Kaya did drink, slowly but steadily, until the cup was empty. "May I make one request, madame?"

"Apart from your lives? Name it, and we'll see," said Liza.

"A little pocketwatch," said Kaya. "So that we might know when it is time for prayers."

Liza's jaw clenched. *No*, she wanted to say, for no other reason than that he had asked for it. She was so damnably tired, and the only pocketwatch she had with her was the one she'd swapped so many times with her father—and it seemed too much to give Kaya even such a small thing, after his people had blasted her keep to Hell. Far too much, after she'd laid out Elliot under a winding-sheet.

But she had given her word to treat Kaya's Turks with honor, and it would have been dishonorable to deny them their prayers because she was too heartsore to part with a pocketwatch.

She reached into her pocket and unhooked the watch chain, then laid the watch on the table. "When you're exchanged or ransomed, I'll want this back," she warned.

"Thank you." Kaya folded his hand carefully over the watch, as though he knew what giving it had cost her. "And thank you for saying that we'll survive to be ransomed."

CHAPTER SEVENTEEN

In the belly of the keep, under Yulchik's watchful eye and ever-ready gun, the wounded Turks began to recover and the whole ones protested their treatment. Many, Petya thought, were Tatars rather than ethnic Turks—several spoke Russian easily, paid their compliments to the cook, and muttered in low tones about what game the Tarasovs were playing. Petya longed to ask them what they knew about the angels, about the admixture of chemicals in the fuel and the queer combination of propulsions that allowed them to fly, but he suspected that it would be far easier to pry those secrets from the machines than from their pilots.

Petya sat to one side with his mess of kasha, watching a pair of gunners help Anatoliy Osipovich out of their makeshift hospital and onto a bench. An explosion had knocked him against the wall of one of the towers, and from the glazed look in his eyes, Petya thought the blast had concussed him. He kept slurring, "You see, I'm fine, I'm perfectly fine," even as he brought his fork down just to the right of his sausages again and again.

"Yes, yes," said Osip Moiseyevich calmly, guiding his son's hand from plate to mouth. "You'll be fine once you've eaten."

"I'm perfectly fine," Anatoliy repeated, and then he leaned over and was sick on the floor.

Petya watched as Osip's hand tightened on the fork until his knuckles went white. There was something dire in his eyes, something fell and cold as an ice storm. Petya had last seen that expression upon him before his oldest sons' funeral, when everyone had feared that he would carve the cost from Petya's father's skin. Now, Osip Moiseyevich rose to his feet with great dignity and stepped away from the bench, then strode across the room to where the Turks sat eating their kasha.

Petya was scarcely conscious of standing, but when Osip raised his fork like a blade over a young Kazakh soldier, Petya was there to catch his wrist. "Stop," he said, even as Osip's free hand reached out to seize the man by the hair. "Name of God, Osya—"

"They came for a war, damn it all!" snarled Osip, and then Liza had his other hand and forced it behind his back until Petya thought he heard the bones creaking. "They came for a war! It isn't fair that they should take the last of my sons and sit here eating our kasha—"

"Stand *down*," said Liza, and her voice was steel and fire. "It *isn't* fair. It isn't right. But I just swore on my honor that I would see no harm come to these men, and you will not make a liar of me, Osip Moiseyevich."

"Your son is right here," said Petya softly. "He needs you. Go to him."

The three of them stood for a moment, each straining against the others. The pressure on Petya's cut made tears spring to his eyes; the ache of it seared from palm to elbow, dull and diffuse and hot. Then, just when the pain was almost too great to bear, Osip Moiseyevich shuddered as though a silent sob had shaken him. Slowly, one muscle at a time, he relaxed in their grip. When Petya prised the fork free, he did not resist.

Petya and Liza shared a look. She nodded once and guided

Osip Moiseyevich back to his seat, then sat at his side as Anatoliy Osipovich insisted that he was fine, perfectly fine.

During the commotion, the young Kazakh soldier had taken cover beneath the table. Now, he emerged with a startled laugh. "That was close," he said. "My name is Orazbek Musa. And to whom do I owe my life?"

"Pyotr Vladimirovich Tarasov," said Petya. "But you don't owe me anything. The Tsar might decide to ship you off to Siberia rather than exchange you, so I can't say I've improved your lot."

"Alive in Siberia is better than dead and in the ground," replied Orazbek. "Pyotr Vladimirovich Tarasov, you say? Give my regards to your brother. Tell him to practice his conjugations."

The sheer, casual cheer in Orazbek's voice felt like a slap. "Did you know it was us you were attacking?" Petya demanded. "If you had any regard for him, how could you come to kill his brother and sister?"

"How could I?" Orazbek sat again, clasping his hands together. *Trying to show me that he isn't a threat*, thought Petya. "I could tell you a thousand things. For one, I could remind you that you aren't keeping British troops in your fortress for the pleasure of their company. I could explain the strategic importance of the southern rail. I could probably even tell you why this attack makes sense, given the current composition of Parliament. I could tell you that a man with no other prospects for advancement must distinguish himself in war to show that he has Allah's favor. But you're asking me whether I have a reason why you in particular had to die, and why I in particular had to kill you. And I don't have an answer for that, Pyotr Vladimirovich. I don't think any of us does. I don't think war allows us to speak in particularities, because if we did, then we might be forced to recognize that every particular thing is worth preserving."

"That isn't an answer."

"It isn't. I am sorry I tried to kill you, though. And that isn't an answer, either."

Petya longed to say, *I'm sorry I tried to kill you, too*, but he couldn't bring himself to form the words. "I should go," he said instead, and made for the door.

In the entryway of the mess hall, Liza flung an arm about Petya's shoulders and began to shepherd him toward the stair. "Let's check for telegrams," she said as she marched him down the hall. "The Abramovs might have sent something. The line to the west is blown, but God only knows how the east has been faring."

"We could," Petya offered, standing obediently still as Liza fastened the catches of her coat and tugged her stocking up over her false leg. "You really don't want to get that wet. You shouldn't take it into the snow—"

"I'll be *perfectly all right*," she said tightly, and thrust both of her hands into her muff. Neither of them remarked on how much she sounded like Anatoliy Osipovich, stabbing at his sausages with a spoon as vomit cooled on his shirt.

They were almost to the stairs when Petya heard a soft susurrus of bombazine behind them. "Mother," he said as he turned. At the name, Liza paused with her false foot on the first stair.

Yelena stood with Liza's cane clasped before her in both hands, both shield and offering. "You left this in the hall," she said. "The ice will be treacherous. You may want it."

"I don't," said Liza shortly. "If I'd wanted it, I would have brought it with me."

When he'd been a child, Petya hadn't recognized how his mother's face hardened when she fought with someone— but now he marked it well as her expression stilled and her eyes grew cold and vacant. "Then I'll keep it until you want it again," she replied. Even her voice had a dim, far-away quality, as though she was speaking to people long-dead in a distant land.

"So that when I do want it again, I'll have to ask you for

it." Liza laughed once, sharp as the sound of a gavel. "Have it run to my rooms, if you want me to have it when I need it. I won't beg you for my cane."

The accusation broke over Yelena like an infantry charge against a fortress wall, and she turned away without the least sign of perturbation. "You will believe what pleases you," she said coolly, and glided back down the passage with the dragon-headed cane still clutched in one hand.

Petya wondered how many times he had seen her walk away like that in his childhood, before he'd seen her board a train for Moscow at last.

When their mother turned a corner and vanished from view, Liza appeared to shake herself. "Come on, Petya. We still have time to check for telegrams before the trial."

"You oughtn't to have been so cruel to her," he said as they mounted the stairs together. "She only wanted to give you your cane, and you as good as told her she was only doing it to control you—"

"She *was*," said Liza shortly. "She's a political creature. Misha will tell me that she tries to manipulate me to flatter me, but you and I both know that she only likes having me in her power."

"Little wonder, when our father always had her in his!"

Liza halted at the head of the stairs, hand raised to the latch on the door. Her nostrils flared with suppressed emotion, but she only said, "Say what you think, then."

Petya drew in a long breath and flexed his aching hand. "Can you imagine what our father would've done, if she'd let him see that she cared enough about us that he could've used us against her? Don't you remember how cruel he was to Kesha, just because he was her favorite?"

"Kesha was his heir."

"Kesha hated him so much that he stole four thousand rubles and ran away to St. Petersburg. He couldn't bear to live in our father's house another day." The more Petya spoke, the more his conviction grew, until it blazed in him like a righteous flame. "And what sign did our mother ever give that she loved him? A name. A fond look. A new book from Moscow. But even these scraps were enough to put our father onto their scent, and he found a thousand little ways to punish our brother for it."

"I won't have you speak of our father that way—"

"You know that I'm telling the truth!"

Liza's lips drew back over her teeth as though he'd spat upon an ikon, but she did not deny his charge. "I won't plead for Mother's scraps. I won't take her politicking and her plots and her 'believe what pleases you' for tokens of affection, the way you and Kesha do. I once begged at her knee, but never again."

Petya fastened the flaps of his hat under his chin. "But you will need the cane. Next time she offers, you could take it."

Liza looked thoughtful for a moment, fingertips stroking the latch. "Next time, I might." Then she opened the door on a swirling spill of snow.

When Petya looked up from the latch, all thoughts of their mother went out of his head. His breath caught. He raised a single, shaking hand to direct her attention to the courtyard.

All about the inner wall, a bevy of dragons huddled, scales dull beneath the unremitting grey of the sky. They twisted around one another in whorls and knots, thick dozens pressing tight together against the wind that licked along the grey stone. As one, their eyes snapped open when Petya and Liza stepped out of the shadow of the doorway. "We have come, as we promised," said one in low, whistling Latin. Through the screen of snow, Petya thought he recognized the copper dragon who'd called herself Aysel.

Liza sucked in a sharp breath. There was fury in her eyes, her cheeks hollow with the effort of biting her tongue. "He didn't even *ask*," she said under her breath. "He simply *assumed* I'd put them up."

"They're our guests," said Petya, taking her arm. "We knew that the dragons might come north—"

"I didn't agree to keep them all in my damn courtyard," snapped Liza. "First Turks, and now dragons, and he expects me to bow down and *thank* him for the privilege of letting me play his *steward*—oh, I could spit in his eye!"

"I bring Boris Baivich to translate on my behalf," said Aysel, with a yawn that showed all of her long teeth. She gestured to a black-dappled white dragon who lay curled not far from her side.

"I don't think much of your Russian hospitality," sighed the white dragon, stretching out his taloned hands and flexing them pointedly. "Are there no sheep in Russia? No self-satisfied young pedants? I'd been given the impression that Russia was a land of pedantry and sheep. Don't disappoint me."

What did one say to such a demand? Petya trudged past their long, sinuous shapes, feeling very small beneath their naked regard. He kept his gaze trained upon his boots as though it might persuade them to ignore him. Liza tilted her face up when they reached the gate, calling up to the watchmen, "Tell Kesha that his dragon's come back—and brought every damn dragon in Turkey with her. And tell the bastard I'll have words with him when I get back."

This barest courtesy complete, Liza began to stride ahead through the snow. "Let me go ahead and pack the snow down for you," Petya offered, circling her like an anxious herding dog. "It's the least I can do."

"You've built me a flying machine. What more could anyone do? I lost my leg, and you let me take to the air. Our brother fills up my fortress with enemies, but *you* gave me the sky."

"I did it for our town, too," said Petya, but she said nothing to that, and so he continued tracking a path to the telegraph office. *Perhaps she doesn't care what happens to the town, as Lukin has always suspected,* thought Petya. *Or perhaps she thinks it goes without saying, that her good and the good of the town are commensurate.*

The first two times she stumbled, Liza waved away his offers of assistance. The third time, she hooked one arm through his and slogged grimly on.

"Ah, Pyotr Vladimirovich!" declared the telegraph master, when at last they tumbled through his door. "Elizaveta Vladimirovna! Warm yourselves by my stove. It's been a miserable storm, and I have terrible news."

"Tell us," said Liza, drawing up the stool on which their father had once stationed himself and pulling back her coat over her false leg. With great care, she checked the stocking that she had stretched over the joint of the leg, frowning as she prised free the woolen fibers that had caught in the hinge. "The terrible news. What is it?"

"We've got a telegram from the east," said the telegraph master, seating himself again on the ceramic stove and rubbing his hands together.

Petya brought the other stool close to the stove and perched at the edge of it. "From the Abramovs?"

The telegraph master passed him a slip of paper, one side printed with a pattern of long and short marks. Beneath them, the telegraph master had translated the message out of Schilling code and into Cyrillic.

ALL STATIONS EAST HAVE BEEN DISMANTLED AND DEPOPULATED. COMMENCE EVACUATION OF YUREYEVSK UNDER THE AUTHORITY OF VOX POPULI.

"*Vox populi?*" asked Petya, passing the message to Liza. "Has the revolution come after all?"

"The Turks are playing tricks on us," she said, once she had passed her eyes over the paper. "They want us to surrender, so they pretend they've already won."

"But if they *have*—"

"If they've won, then we're what remains. Are your men building me another flying machine? With two of those, I could reap the Turkish angels like wheat," she said, the same way she had said *Let's check for telegrams*. There was a brittle brightness to her expression, a flickering but clear light in her eyes that made Petya ache from his palms to his ribs.

"If we could stop them from making more angels," he said. "If we could destroy the factories—Kesha knows the place, and if there are more factories, the dragons will know them—if we could destroy *those*, then it would actually matter to reap them like wheat."

Liza turned to him, dark brows shadowing her eyes and the hollows to either side of her hawk nose. "You could do that," she said. "You could prevent them from making more."

"I could make it more *difficult* for them to make more. If we can't make the Turks forget how to make them, it still takes time to build the infrastructure for machines such as these. With enough explosives, we could set them back a decade."

"Says the man who built a flying machine in two days!" she scoffed.

"Two *months*—Lukin and I have been working on it since your fall. Or three years. It's better to say three years," said Petya. "Almost as long as I've been in St. Petersburg, I've been designing this machine. I've built models and armatures, and I've *tested* my theories, although never on this scale. Kesha brought my designs when he came, and he left them for me when he fled. I built this flying machine because I was equipped to build it, not because of some genius on my part."

She studied the floor for a long moment. Whatever she saw there, she stiffened her spine and turned to meet his eyes again. "I'm sorry I crumpled your plans. I see now what they meant to you. All those years of planning, put on paper—and I wadded them up as though they were rubbish."

"It had been a trying day for all of us. I forgive you," he said, and put a hand on her shoulder. In the thin gap between glove and sleeve, his skin was an angry red that he could not blame on the cold. Thin, dark lines tracked like pencil marks over his veins. *I should see the druggist soon, before this gets any worse.* "May I take the tunnels to the machinists' shop?" he asked the telegraph master, who had been listening intently to their conversation and who straightened at being addressed.

"The tunnels?" interrupted Liza. "What tunnels?"

"They connect the raid shelters," Petya told her. He knelt and drew back the hatch; the reverberation rattled his bones when the handle struck the floorboards. With his uninjured hand, he turned on the lamp inside the shelter. "See the grate? You can creep through the vents in case of fire or collapse. There are signs for the armory and the station—and at the far end is the machinists' shop."

"Hmm." For a moment, she looked as though she might speak again, but then she returned to prying free her stocking from her knee. "I'll see you in the courtroom in an hour. Be ready to tell me that you can cripple the Turks."

"I will," promised Petya. He put his injured hand to the first rung of the ladder, barely suppressing a hiss at the unexpected pain of pressure.

"And be careful of cripples," she told him when he winced. "We're dangerous men."

CHAPTER EIGHTEEN

One of the Turks had died between the mess hall and the water closet, and if Selim Kaya himself hadn't been with him when he died, Kesha didn't like to think what sort of Hell would have broken loose. While Selim's men prepared their comrade's body, Kesha looked over his sister's men and wondered how many of them would have liked to help the Turk on his way.

"They'll test you," said Misha in an undertone, once they'd put a door between them and the rest of the men. "There's no utility in preserving your Turks—I don't like thinking of murdering them any better than you do, but they make the men uneasy. Now that one of their men is dead, they make *me* uneasy."

"Then you think I should kill them all. You've been reading too much Machiavelli," Kesha said shortly.

"I think you've won yourself no friends by saving them, and made yourself at least one enemy," Misha answered, pressing his spectacles up his nose. "Your sister sees the Turks as your men, and as threats to her own. Their colonel has pricked her honor, but I shouldn't like to think what she'll do if it comes down to honor or mutiny."

"She'll have to enforce some sort of discipline on them,

or they'll never fear her. That's in your Machiavelli, too. Now, if you want to talk with the dragons, spare me your lectures on expendable Turks."

Kesha was nearly to the top of the stairs when the warning bell began to sound. Over a decade of training had taught him only one response to that din, and even now he felt compelled to put aside all he was doing and go to the gun turret. "The storm is too bad for the angels," he said, arrested, his hand on the banister and his body poised to spring for the nearest ladder well. "I should—"

Misha, who had half-lifted the latch, now opened the door and peered into the sky. "Stay," he said, so softly that Kesha almost missed it beneath the frantic ringing of the bell—and then, in a voice that brooked no disobedience, "Stay. Look."

Surmounting the last of the stairs, Kesha peered out through the doorway. The first explosive fell only moments later, sending a percussive vibration through the air that made his ears ring. The wind drove tiny, stinging snowflakes against his brows, against his eyelids, and he tilted his face up to the high, grey sky.

The air was roiling with dragons.

Three of them sailed in formation to defend the south gun tower against Xia, vast and mist-silver and writhing with fury. Her thick talons tore a gash into the hide of one of her kin, sending a shower of scales and blood tumbling to earth. The next one, she caught in one massive hindlimb and ripped from chin to mid-chest—a fire poured out of the dragon's gaping ribs, impossibly bright against the dim sky. Kesha turned his face away, shielding his eyes, but that red burn still stained the blackness behind his eyelids when he blinked. "Aysel!" he cried, but then he heard a curtailed human scream that made his head snap up.

A hulking, midnight-black dragon perched atop the southern tower, with Osip Moiseyevich's body clutched in his forelimb. Kesha knew that it was his body, because he could see the head lying at the foot of the tower.

He must have gone up into the tower to cool his blood, after the mess hall. He must have gone up to man the gun, and he was there when the dragons came.

The dragon cast the body aside—*when he was sure I was looking,* thought Kesha wildly—and fixed its hand and its hindlimb over the barrel of the gun that Osip had been manning. He seemed to concentrate for a long moment, and then he snapped the gun free of the tower, mounting-plate and all.

Kesha watched the black dragon's chest expand as he gathered himself to rise. When he ascended, he carried the gun with him, clutched against his shoulder like a child's popgun.

The red smear over Kesha's gaze pulsed like a heartbeat. He felt a straining agony within him that was half grief and half utter despair.

When the sky cleared and the explosions died down at last, Kesha counted the dragons who went soaring east. *Twelve*, he thought, all of them those vast, thick-trunked beasts that Aysel had identified as her elders.

A moment later, two of the young dragons picked themselves up from the courtyard and followed after, one of them still trailing blood from a torn flank. Her leg dangled limply, as though the muscle had been severed.

Kesha fled the entryway, wading knee-deep in the thickly drifted snow. Bits of gore clung to his shins, and he couldn't have said whether they were human or dragon. "Aysel!" he shouted, but none of the answering screams was hers. "Aysel, where are you—" In some distant part of him, he realized that he was speaking Russian, and she could no more understand him than she could understand the whine of the wind, but the Latin wouldn't come. He could think of nothing but that dragon trailing blood, and the fire pouring out of a dragon's chest until it washed the landscape red.

"Aysel!" he called, voice raw with screaming, and only then did the shadow descend from the clouds overhead.

"Here," she answered, raw-voiced, and he burrowed against her shoulder the moment her feet touched the ground. He carded his hands through her mane, registering how singed it was in patches and how it smelled of burnt hair. *Of course it smells of burnt hair*, he told himself. *Someone has burnt it.*

"What happened here?" he asked, when she had begun grooming his hair in return with the blunt edge of a protruding tooth. Behind him, he heard Misha render his words into Latin, but his voice was distant and detached. *He's seen a man's head torn off in front of him*, thought Kesha. *Has Misha ever seen someone die before?*

For a few long seconds, he felt Aysel's chin rubbing insistently over his temple, and then she spoke. "What did you suppose would happen?" she asked, and there was something of a scream lingering in it. "I told you that I would bring you only the youngest—"

"I didn't think the older dragons would *kill* you!"

"You have *read* our poetry," she snapped. "You have spoken with our poet. Tell me what the poems say, man. Tell me what *feeling* they express."

Kesha remembered the poem that he had drawn in the condensation of the ice closet, the old trope that the Yekaterinburg translator had said was so common. *I feel akin to the sheep on the run, who is harried over the low hills until death overtakes it.* In that line of poetry was the whole substance of that mythic sublimity that had made Kesha's blood quicken and his breath catch. "The feeling of being hunted," he answered, low and wretched.

"And who do you suppose *hunts* dragons?" she demanded.

"Other dragons," said Kesha. He felt as though he were made of light and ether. *Who do you suppose hunts men?* said a voice like Starikovich's, deep in his breast. *Other men—*

"We came to you to sue for land," replied Aysel. Only then did he see the way her nostrils and her mouth had grown red and swollen, the skin cracked along the tender places. Her wide brown eyes were tear-wet with the strain of not bursting into flame. "Our poet spoke flattering words to the strongest, that they might join us. We came to Russia in our dozens on the hope of what your ancestors promised us. But *do not imagine* we will not be hunted for this choice. Our grandparents hounded our parents out of the east, and so shall our elders hound us out of the south. We have come on the hope of a better life, not a new one."

"Where is Boris Baivich?" asked Kesha. "I need to speak with him. I need to ask him what he remembers about—"

"He is dead," said Aysel. There was an unmistakable tremor in her voice.

Panic gripped him, compressing his lungs until he could scarcely breathe through the urge to scream. It was unimaginable that Boris Baivich should be dead. It was impossible that all he knew should be dead with him. Across the span of centuries, Kesha seemed to see books burning in the thousands. "He can't be dead. You told me that the dragons would never kill their poet."

"He was no longer *their* poet," she said, then drew back from Kesha's shoulder to scratch at her singed ruff. That gesture meant consternation. It meant that she could find nothing to say. He felt Misha's gloved knuckles brushing his wrist, and he clutched that offered hand as though it were life itself.

"Then who will be your poet?" he asked. "Who will remember your history?"

"I suppose it must be you or I," she said. "Now let me go. I must remove my dead."

She rose slowly into the air, jetting steam and fire from between her lips and giving a little, nasal cry of pain at each breath. Kesha watched her go, and Osip Moiseyevich's head watched him watching.

CHAPTER NINETEEN

The courtroom in Yureyevsk saw little use, for although there was a sitting judge in the town, civil disputes vastly outnumbered criminal cases, and these were often settled in the solicitors' offices. The townspeople were at once very private persons and deeply interested in one another's business. Accordingly, they sought to conduct their most vital affairs outside of court.

When last Liza had been to the courtroom, she had watched the trial of a murderer. He had come to Yureyevsk from the west, seeking work as a miner, and he had struck another man with his hammer and shattered his skull. The trial had been brief but fierce, and women had attended in their best gowns and hats. It had been summer, then, and even the poorest women had wielded little fans of folded paper against the smothering heat. Never had Yureyevsk had so clear a villain. Even the Turks were only an abstract figure of menace, when compared with the slim, greasy-haired stranger who had come by train.

The man had been hanged for his crime, although his lawyer had pleaded to have his sentence reduced to transportation. It had not, the judge felt, been prudent to let such a murderer live.

Today, by contrast, the courtroom was very nearly empty. The jury box was full, of course, and a barrister stood stationed on each side of the room like a sentinel. Nastya, Utkin, Liza, and Petya sat waiting their turn to speak as witnesses, and Wainwright sat in the defendant's stall with his cheeks new-shaven and a fresh shrapnel cut stitched unevenly over his cheekbone. It made him look thoroughly disreputable.

Beside the jury box, Seryozha stood in his constable's uniform, clenching and unclenching his fingers as though he was thinking of wringing someone's neck.

"How did the last raid go?" asked Utkin, while the defense made its opening argument. "I heard blasts—"

"I was in town, and I wasn't about to run through the snow with this leg," said Liza in reply. "My brother will have handled it."

"You place a great deal of trust in the man you once accused of murdering your father."

"I've trusted two murderers already to help me run my fortress," she said, forcing her tone to lightness. "What's one more?"

"The business with Jaworski was a bad one," Utkin admitted. "A bad business—"

Before he could continue, however, the prosecution called him to the stand, and Liza was left to exchange glances with Nastya. "Do you believe he's guilty?" Liza asked in an undertone.

"I believe it's a waste of our time and our resources to be trying him now—the bells were ringing at the keep. I heard explosions in the town. The druggist's shop was blown out, and the optician's is still burning. You told us," said Nastya, "the Turks wouldn't come while the storm held."

"Then I was *wrong*," said Liza, low, fierce. Her face felt hot with blood and shame. "Name of God, Nastya, let me be wrong just once!"

"You can't *afford* to be wrong. We rely on you to keep

us safe. As you said, you've trusted two murderers already. There are dragons at your keep now, Tarasova. How long must we trust your next batch of murderers before you unmask them as villains? How long must we wait for the scales to fall from your eyes?"

"Be quiet, Nastya. Let me think—can a woman not *think* around you?"

"Think, then. It would be the first time I'd seen you do it."

"Excuse me," said Petya, "but did you say the druggist's was hit?"

"Blown to flinders," said Nastya. "I don't know if the druggist made it out."

"That's terrible news," he said, and he seemed to mean it. He circled a fingertip over his gloved palm, his eyes fixed on the ceiling. His brow was damp with sweat.

Liza closed her eyes, closing out the drone of the prosecutor's questions and the deeper rumble of Utkin's replies. It still jarred at her, to hear Utkin speak without Polzin to echo him—but Polzin had a career and a wife in Nizhny Novgorod, and so he had stayed behind.

He had been meant to testify today, but of course the trains weren't running from Nizhny after the Turks had blown the rails.

She had to think. There was something tugging at the edge of her consciousness, or there had been, just before the warning bells had begun to ring. She had pulled her hat back on and made for the door of the telegraph office, but the telegraph master had caught her by the wrist. "You can't run out during an attack any longer, Elizaveta Vladimirovna," he'd said sharply. Not unkindly, she realized now, but at the time she'd wanted to drag her fingernails over his eyes. They had sheltered beneath his floorboards, and Liza had paced from one end of the room to the other and lamented that she couldn't climb out and shoot something.

There. She'd almost had it.

"No further questions," said the prosecution, and then

she heard his chair creak as he sat again.

She had so little to say that it felt foolish to be in town to say it. "You are here to avow that you tested each one of the guns in the village, and that not one of them matched your father's wounds. That's no small thing. It points to an outsider," Utkin had told her nearly a week ago. "It's pertinent."

Liza had accepted a cup of tea from him and answered, "It proves nothing. It only proves that we *haven't* found the weapon yet, and God only knows where it is."

It proved something else, though, and something that she had often considered during her long confinement. It proved that she and Jaworski had not been sufficiently thorough in their investigation of the town. Of course, he *wouldn't* have been. He'd come here to murder her father. If any man deserved her suspicion, it was the man whom she had trusted with the success of the investigation.

But Petya had been in the watchtower with him on the night of the murder, and Petya wouldn't have lied to her about that. If she could trust no one and nothing else, she could trust Petya.

There was that nagging sensation again, returning like the taste of a spider swallowed while she slept.

"Elizaveta Vladimirovna Tarasova, please rise and approach the bench."

Liza smoothed down her skirts and put aside her muff. *I have nothing to say but that I know nothing. I have nothing to add but that I haven't found the gun that killed my father. I might as well not testify at all.*

Her eyes locked with Wainwright's, and he offered her an encouraging smile. It wasn't comforting in the least, to be reassured by a man who'd soon be condemned to death.

In the end, the jury deliberated for only half an hour.

"Guilty," pronounced Seryozha, with a carefully neutral expression that Liza thought meant he was smirking on the inside. At Liza's side, Petya drew in a quick little breath, too soft for a gasp. When he reached for her hand, she gripped his palm until her knuckles ached. She squeezed until he told her in an undertone, "Liza, you're hurting me."

"He was useful," she said in an undertone. "He could still be useful—"

"I don't think so," said Petya. "He was a spy for the English. Even Kesha said it."

"Kesha said he was *our* spy—"

"If he was our spy, why do the Turks keep coming here?"

"First you said he was a spy for the English. Now you say that he was a spy for the Turks!" Liza let go of his hand, gritting her teeth for fear that she would shout at him. She folded her arms tightly, squeezing until the wet wool of her jacket squeaked. In a carrying whisper, she continued, "He's helped to drill our men, and who knows what we'd have done without his help? For all you know, we'd have fallen just like the Kamenskys and the Abramovs—"

"Order," called the judge, and Liza stilled and silenced herself. At his bench, the judge seemed to regather his aplomb. He had presided over burglaries and a single tradesman's murder during his time in Yureyevsk, but of course he had never judged in such a case as this. A foreigner, a soldier and a spy, found guilty of murdering the lord of a fortress should've been tried before a military tribunal. If he were quivering on his elevated seat, Liza would scarcely have been surprised.

Utkin gave the judge a long, meaningful look, and at this the judge coughed and shuffled his papers. "It is the finding of this court that Lieutenant Peter Wainwright, of the army of Her Majesty Queen Victoria of Great Britain and Ireland, is guilty of premeditated murder—and, further, that in committing this murder, he permitted the enemies of the Russian Empire to gain a tactical advantage—"

"Avoiding the question of his allegiance," said Liza.

"—thus making him a *de facto* enemy of the state. This court therefore sentences him to execution at the nearest convenience of the, ah—"

He had been doing so well, thought Liza.

"—the nearest convenience of Lord Innokentiy Vladimirovich Tarasov."

Liza hissed, clamping down on a protest.

"The court admits his conflict of interest regarding the victim, but, ah…" The judge polished his spectacles. "The, ah, precedent is to permit a neighboring lord to execute the sentence, but recent intelligence suggests that this is no longer an option."

At the far end of the witness's bench, Nastya heaved a sigh. "That's done, then," she said. "Perhaps now we'll be able to do some *real* work."

The court adjourned shortly thereafter, and Liza and Petya slipped into place on either side of Wainwright to escort him back to the keep. He had heretofore borne himself upright, straight-backed and clear-eyed as a nutcracker in soldier's paint, but in their departure from the courtroom, he moved as though he might fall to his knees and crawl at any moment. "I would humbly request," he said as they walked, "that you forestall my execution until we've driven the Turks back."

"That's for *Lord Tarasov* to decide," said Liza. "He'll execute you *at his convenience—*"

"Everyone knows that he'll defer to you in this," Wainwright replied. "You're the master of the fortress. He obeys you in all things. If you tell him that I'm useful, he'll listen to you."

"You're wrong, if you think he obeys me in all things—but I'll see what I can do to convince him."

"I don't ask that you forestall my execution indefinitely. I'll protest my innocence until I die—but if I've been sentenced to die, I won't beg for my life."

"Because you want to die for Russia," said Liza, dangerously light.

"Because if I must die, then I want to die for Russia," he agreed, and something in his matter-of-fact tone, his absolute calm, made Liza admire him as she never had before. "I was a loyal servant of the Tsar, and I failed him. I failed all of you, and I've watched the land I love best fall to pieces because of my failure. If I have to die, I want to die with hope in my heart and a free Russia before my eyes."

"Then you will," Liza promised. She linked her hand with Wainwright's, clasping it to seal their agreement as much as to reassure him. She pressed her palm to his, gloved fingers folding over the edge rather than interlacing. They held one another tightly for only a moment, then let go. Petya was watching, and she met his gaze. *He never suggested that I marry Wainwright*, she thought, and then on the heels of that, *I could have loved him—not as a wife, but I could have loved him all the same.*

At the gate, Galina Ivanovna gave them a tired salute. She was bundled up until only her eyes showed over her thick muffler, and she bore a rifle against her shoulder with a slow-growing ease. "I was afraid you'd been caught in the raid—I'm glad you're well! How did the trial...oh! Lieutenant." At first she seemed about to curtsy, but then she remembered her gun. Instead, she only saluted again.

"I've been found guilty," said Wainwright, raising his brows. "Stand straight, Private Vasilevskaya. Salute, because if you bow or curtsy, you'll have a hell of a time getting into a firing position."

"Yes, sir," she replied.

"Good work, soldier." He clapped her on her free shoulder, then strode past her and into the courtyard.

There were new bodies being laid out on the fresh snow, the wind catching at the edges of the winding-sheets and ripping them free. "It looks bad," said Petya cautiously. "It looks like an awful lot of—"

"Six bodies," said Liza, and then she looked up to the towers ringing the courtyard. She caught sight of the southern tower in the fading sunlight and a low rage boiled in her breast.

The gun was gone. The gun was gone, and a thick smear of red-black tracked down the tower.

"Dragons," pronounced Liza. "So they turned on us after all—"

"They turned on their own," said Kesha, who rose from winding a body with his skin rubbed raw from the wind. He looked as though he had been weeping. "They came and destroyed their children for joining us. They destroyed us for helping their children to run from them. They came out of the storm, and killed their own poets—"

He cut himself off, slipping his hands into his pockets. His face closed off as though someone had shut the blinds behind his eyes. At length, he continued, "Aysel told us that the dragons have been serving for years as decoys. I think we're meant to understand, now, how dragons really fight." His voice was hollow. "That's all there is to report. Tell me your news."

"We received a telegram from the east," said Petya. "It told us to surrender. It said the other fortresses were all gone. It was signed *Vox Populi*—"

"Söz," said Kesha. "The Voice. If she's styling herself the Voice of the People, though, she must want us to think this a revolution—"

"And for all the rest of the world knows, it *is* a revolution," said Wainwright slowly. "Because I had Liza send telegrams to tell them to expect one. If the Turks have destroyed the telegraph lines, the cities to the north still probably think this is revolutionary activity."

"Wainwright has been sentenced to die," Liza broke in, and all of them turned to her at once. "The judge has put his life in your hands, since you—" and she scarcely paused, although she wanted to fling the title at her brother like a weapon, "—are the lord of the fortress. He wants to survive to see us win. Grant him that."

A quizzical look flitted over Kesha's face, swift and faint as a fish darting beneath thick ice. He exchanged a glance with Wainwright that Liza couldn't read. "I can't pardon him?"

"I don't think you can."

"He's in your hands, then. Sweet Christ, Liza—you know I never wanted any of this. I never wanted to play the headsman."

"You certainly did all you could to spare the Turks from the axe." She couldn't make herself answer him rationally. Her whole body felt taut, suspended between the urge to flee and the necessity of remaining.

"Yes, the Turks," said Petya, before either of them could speak. "We can discuss our inheritance later. For now, we have to deal with the Turks." For a moment Liza thought he meant the Turks in the fortress, but Petya continued: "We have to accept that we can't do anything *new* against their dragons right now. Another flying machine might do some good later, but for the moment—"

"Yes, let's concentrate on the angels," Liza agreed. "You wanted to destroy their factories."

"I do. It does no good to let them *keep* constructing them. We can tackle the angels and the dragons alone, but if they come together, if they keep coming, then we'll be overwhelmed."

They stood together in the fading light, each of them considering the prospect. Six new bodies lay between them, and even under the winding-sheets, Liza could see that they had been mangled until they had ceased to be shaped like men. She scarcely doubted that, had she been on the wall, she would be wrapped in one of those sheets.

"Let me do it," said Wainwright into the silence. In his faded red pelisse and his too-large hat, he looked utterly ridiculous. There was a gravity to his expression, though, that made it impossible to laugh at him. "Let me do this one, last thing."

Liza looked to Kesha, and Kesha looked back at her. "All right," she said at last. "One last thing."

"Tomorrow morning," said Petya. "I've arranged it. By then, the machinists will have prepared dynamite enough to destroy a small town."

"Let's hope it's not our own," said Liza. "Tomorrow morning, then, we'll make ready to fly."

CHAPTER TWENTY

In the wing that had been theirs since their birth, the wing that they had shared in their childhood with their mother, Kesha caught up to his sister at last. She was shedding her coat, the fur lining of which had grown damp with snowmelt. Her hands shook and she leaned heavily on her good leg, but still she stumped down the hall at an appreciable rate that made him dash to keep up. "Liza," he said, a moment before he closed his hand on her newly bare wrist. "Listen to me, Liza—"

"Leave me be," she said, shaking him loose with a single jerk of her arm. There should have been venom in her voice, and that absence of vitriol frightened him more than he cared to admit. "I have nothing to say to you. Go spend time with your Turks. Go to your dragons and learn their *poems*, or whatever damn thing you do with dragons nowadays."

"This isn't about dragons or Turks. It's about us—about our family. I know it must look to you as though I've come back to claim the estate, and that couldn't—"

"That's *exactly* what it looks like. You come here after the Turks have blown us to Hell, when everyone is spoiling for a fight, and you tell us that we're not allowed to kill them. And what could I do? If I backed you, I was as good as showing them I'd let you take command. If I challenged you, I'd have to declare you a traitor for aiding our enemies. You had no *right* to put me in that position," she replied, unlocking her door and shoving it open.

"You would have done the same, in my place."

"In your place, I would have beheaded every last one of your Turks and saved my bullets for the next wave of them," she said. "And if I agreed that they were worth saving, if I agreed that the peace was worth a few deaths on our side, then *I* had the right to say so. It's bad enough that they think they can kill your Turks. If they think they don't have to listen to *me*, then we're all as good as damned."

It was closer to absolution than he had ever hoped to get. He could not press her for more. "I never meant to usurp your place. Please believe that."

She sat at the edge of her bed, gesturing him to a narrow little chair that had been pulled flush with the corner. "Sit."

He did as she bid him, watching as she peeled free her boots and then the stocking over her false leg. The leg itself, she unlatched next, drawing out the stump and flexing what remained of her leg at the knee. Kesha hadn't seen her without the prosthetic since he'd returned to the keep, and in that first moment, he could see nothing but the vast expanse of pink skin and puckered flesh. "They cut it cleanly," he said, after a moment of staring. It was no good to pretend that he had been doing anything else. "And Petya did good work on the new leg."

"I know he did," she said, with a hollow little laugh. "When I've been walking around all day, when the leg is cooperating, I sometimes forget it's not real. Then the pains come shooting through my foot—my *real* foot—and there's not a damn thing I can do to stop them. Nothing but drink morphine and turn over in bed."

"I'm sorry," said Kesha. He hesitated, then rose from his chair to sit beside her on the bed. "I know that it was my fault that you lost your leg. In Moscow...in Moscow I heard that you'd been maimed, and I couldn't help thinking that I owed you whatever I'd taken. An eye for an eye."

"And a foot for a foot?" Liza tilted her head at that, as though considering the merits of the proposition. "No," she decided at last. "We were all in the wrong, that night. I shouldn't have been drinking and making threats. Petya shouldn't have taken me seriously. You shouldn't have run. Old Tarasov hot-bloodedness and Tarasov suspicion. It was everyone's fault and no one's."

"Still, I owe you." He offered her his hand, and she eyed it and turned her face away. Instead, Kesha folded his hands in his lap, thumb tracing circles over one heavy knuckle. "Misha told me that he made a bargain with you. In exchange for my safety, I'd cede my right to the keep."

"And pay back every kopeck you stole," she agreed. "With interest."

"You said once that our family wasn't a pack of usurers—"

"I changed my mind." She folded her arms.

"The money is..." His face grew hot, and he clenched his hands together, raising his eyes to meet hers. "Don't you see, Liza, I never *wanted* the keep! I never wanted to be the lord of a fortress. I never *wanted* this inheritance, and now it's hanging around my neck like a millstone. I simply can't make this place *work* the way you can, or the way you could, if you had the men and the money to pay them. If Söz was telling the truth, and if this really is the last fortress standing on the border, it's because *you* were the master of it. If I had been the master, it would have fallen long ago."

"You wouldn't say that, if you'd been here." Liza looked down. "I tried to run it the way my father ran it. Like a tyrant. A bully. And the fortress nearly fell, under me. Everything was *burning*, Kesha. I watched my town burning. Until I saw it in flames, it had never been *mine*. But then I went down to the town, and there were children whose houses had burned drinking soup in Nastya's tavern, and Nastya told me that I was the closest thing they had to an object of faith. That's just how she said it: the closest thing they had to an object of faith, and she wouldn't permit me to destroy it. And that's what it means to be the lord of the fortress, I think. Our father never understood it, but Nastya did." This time, when Kesha offered his hand, Liza took it and gripped it in her own. "It's my town. It's my town the way my hand is mine, the way my leg is mine. Separate it from me, and it will still be mine. And if it's mine, I have to take care of it."

"When this is finished," said Kesha, "I will have Misha draw up a deed signing over the entire family estate to you. It rightly belongs to you. I was only the custodian of it by an accident of birth, and a poor custodian I made."

"Absent landlord," she told him, solemn and accusatory. "Thief. If I'd been born with a cock, we wouldn't be *in* this mess."

"I can't contest it," Kesha replied. "I wanted to be out among men, to *know* them the way only scholars of divinity knew them.... I wanted anything but to be here, where no one cared for knowledge or for men's souls. I wanted to be away from our father, and so I left in a way that I thought would mean he'd never follow me."

"You abandoned me," Liza said, low. "You abandoned Petya. He could forgive you that, but I haven't. I never will."

"I abandoned everything I loved," agreed Kesha, and when he leaned against her shoulder, she draped her arm about his waist and kept him close. "And I don't regret it. If I could choose, I would be in St. Petersburg right this moment, studying the soul and forgetting that I'd ever known anything about Turks or dragons or flying machines. If I don't regret what I did, how dare I hope for forgiveness?"

"Then go back to St. Petersburg," said Liza. "Go back and write about the soul. It will be the first book on the soul that a soulless man ever wrote."

"You know that I can't," said Kesha. He let his head fall to her lap, and she threaded her fingers through his darkened hair. All along the scalp, it was growing back red. "Not until this is finished. This place needs you—"

"And I need you." She tugged lightly at his hair, the long strands wrapped about her fingertips. "Do you remember when we hopped the train and rode all the way to Arzamas? You wanted to see the cathedral, so we packed a hunk of cheese and bread in a cloth and climbed on the back of the timber train—"

"You said it was how people hopped trains," replied Kesha. "You said you'd seen them do it a dozen times."

"You would have been hungry and lost if I hadn't gone with you. Someone would have stolen you."

"And then we were hungry and lost together, when we'd finished our bread and cheese."

"We were *together*," said Liza, lips quirking. "Will you hold the fortress for me, tomorrow morning?"

"Only for tomorrow morning," agreed Kesha. "I'll go back to St. Petersburg when this business is finished, and then you'll never see me again."

"I'll see your money once a month, or I'll have your head," Liza warned him. "You won't leave without making a contract. And I'll expect Petya back, too. I need a brother to help me run the fortress, and the people like him."

"Petya will come back if he *wants* to come back, and none of your bargaining or your contract-making will change that."

"It's a shame," said Liza, with a sigh.

"A shame?"

She nudged Kesha off of her lap, reaching over to the table beside her bed and picking up a little jar of salve. He couldn't miss that it sat beside her bottle of morphine. When he had removed himself, she rolled up the leg of her trousers and began to apply the salve where her false leg's straps had chafed rings around her thigh. "A shame that I'll never see you again. We had a few good times, before you abandoned me. And you're a better shot than Petya. A better drinker, when I could convince you to drink."

"A worse brother."

"A worse brother," she agreed readily. "But a better friend. When I think of the wrongs you did me, I'll always remember that one first of all: you took my best friend from me."

Kesha averted his eyes as she applied her balm, looking instead to the pattern of the bedspread, the drape of the sheets. She must have spent over a month in this room, recovering from the loss of that leg. She must have grown to despise that green calico quilt and those linen sheets. "Was I really your best friend?" he asked, when he realized that she had finished speaking.

At that, Liza laughed. "Name of God, Kesha," she said, turning to him with a wondering look. "Didn't you realize? You were my *only* friend."

"Then I'm doubly sorry," he said. "I couldn't have known. No, I *could* have known, but I never cared to know. I'm so sorry."

"Don't be so glum, Vladimirovich," she said, smiling faintly and offering him a salve-slick hand. "It's my fortress now. You're not allowed to be glum in it."

"I'll be glum wherever I like," he replied, but he was laughing too hard to be glum anywhere at all.

CHAPTER TWENTY-ONE

"We have time enough for a sweep over the Abramovs' lands, don't we? I want to see how bad it is," said Liza.

"We really shouldn't delay in the air," said Petya, casting a long glance at the dynamite nestled in the belly of his flying machine. "The boiler might throw off a spark any second. The longer we linger, the more likely it is we'll blow ourselves to bits—"

"There's an entire sheet of metal between the boiler and the dynamite. Hell, we could probably go as far as Kazan. Easy as riding a train." Petya swallowed down whatever irritation he felt at her disregard, only nodding once, tightly. "Kazan, then?"

"Why not go as far as Kazan? There's an entire sheet of metal between the boiler and the dynamite," muttered Petya, settling into the conductor's seat and fixing his hands on the controls. The skin over his palm felt too tight, which meant swelling, which meant the infection was worse. A part of him longed to tear off his gloves and see what lay beneath, but he knew very well what he would find. The cut, red-rimmed and suppurating, smelling of decay. His veins dark and sluggish from wrist to elbow.

Better not to look at his hands.

Behind him, Wainwright sat with his hands on his knees, his hat tied firmly beneath his chin. Petya wondered that he had ever thought Wainwright imposing. He was a little man with missing toes, in borrowed clothing and a borrowed language. He was the shabbiest figure of insufficiency that Petya could imagine, and he inspired no feeling but pity.

This pitiable little man had murdered Petya's father. Petya couldn't permit himself to forget that.

Liza climbed in at last, seating herself beside Petya. She had a good view of the interior of the sky-boat from that position, her back to the broad window and her eyes fixed on the crates of dynamite. "You ought to take the gunner's chair," he told her over the ever-louder whirr of the propellers, but she shook her head and grinned.

"In a moment," she said. "I want to talk to you first—and while Wainwright is with us, someone has to keep an eye on him."

By now, the propellers were mere blurs on either wing. In the pit of his belly, Petya felt the moment when they left the ground. Dizziness nearly overtook him in a cold, shimmering wave, but he rode that wave until he felt lucid again. He mopped sweat from his brow. "What did you want to say to me?"

She brought the ankle of her good leg to rest against her other knee. "I wanted to apologize," she said at last, as though it pained her. "You know this machine better than I do. You know *boilers* better than I do, and there's dynamite enough aboard to blow us all to pieces. I shouldn't have treated you like a panicking child."

"You've always treated me like a child when I take anything seriously," Petya replied. As he hovered over the fortress, the dragon called Aysel climbed slowly into the air ahead of him. Kesha had promised that she would be their guide, and when she began to track the rails eastward, Petya followed her shining copper curves through the cloudless sky. "I've learned to expect it."

"Well, when you're wrong to take things seriously, you *should* expect it." She leaned back in the gunner's chair, settling a pistol over her lap where Wainwright could see it.

"I'm wrong less often than you think I am," said Petya. From the low hills before them, he saw a faint thread of smoke rising. The pain in his hand was almost unbearable; his blood seemed to run thick and slow in his veins. He shivered. "You and Kesha and Father and Mother were always so caught up in your politicking. Nothing *could* be serious with you, because if it were serious, then you would have to recognize that you hated each other—"

"I never hated them," said Liza at once, but there was no conviction in it.

"—and I was only a *child*, Liza. I was only a child, and to me, everything was serious. I grew up knowing that my family was at war, and wanting to *fix* it. You kept treating me like a child because if I was a grown man, if I was old enough to know better, you'd have to see that I was *right* to take everything seriously—and none of you could bear that. Not one of you."

She said nothing in reply. Perhaps there was nothing she could have said.

"We're coming up on the Abramovs' town," said Petya, at which Wainwright rose from his seat by the boiler and came to stand behind them. Liza turned, leaning forward in her seat. Together, through the uneven glass of the window, the three of them surveyed the ruins.

The fortress had been shattered at the base, each tower knocked sprawling over the ground. It must have been some time ago, for snow had already gathered on the pieces. A carriage lay upturned on one side of the road to the fortress, its sides splintered and burnt and its wheels turning lightly in the breeze. The station had been blown out from the inside, and amid the snow, fragments of glass shone ice-bright. Smoke still rose from it, although the houses had long since ceased to burn.

There were human shapes beneath the snow, safely blanketed away where their dismemberment would disturb no one.

"I'm sorry, Petya," said Liza, but she was scarcely audible over the incessant roar of the spinning blades.

"I forgive you," he answered. In the face of such absolute destruction, he could do no less.

CHAPTER TWENTY-TWO

On the western shore of the Volga lay banks of tall buildings, their glass dully gleaming in the morning light. No smoke rose from the factories, which surprised Liza somewhat; the smokestacks over her machinists' shop had issued forth black pillars of smoke since the Turks had crossed the border, and she had grown nearly used to the smoke rising against the pale clouds behind.

This looked *clean*. It looked utterly untouched. "Where are they?" she muttered to Petya, but he shook his head.

"They're winning. Little surprise the factories are empty."

"Little surprise."

"But all the same, I'd expected some resistance," said Wainwright. "These are the most valuable resources in the Ottoman Empire, and they were scarcely even guarded. Why is that?"

"Because they don't *know* that we know," said Liza. "Oh, they will soon enough. Kesha has flooded our courtyard with dragons, after all. It was like a big, stupid sign pointing to him. But I think he's the only man in Russia who knows where the angels came from, and certainly the only man in Russia who knew where they were made. Why should they guard the place? For all they knew, it was under no threat."

"And they pretend that the attacks on our towns were the work of revolutionaries, and they leave no one to tell a different story. *Vox Populi*," agreed Petya. "The train station of the Abramovs was blown out from the inside, and not from above. As though it had been done by insurrectionists."

"There were riots in Kazan after the Tsar died, just as you'd said there would be," said Liza to Wainwright. "Only students and workers looking for an excuse to smash things, but enough to put teeth in the lie."

Ahead of them, Aysel gave a screech and seemed to seize and jerk in mid-air. *Distress*, that meant, or so she'd taught Liza last night. "Set us down," said Liza. "She's seen dragons."

"Then they've seen us. We don't have much time." Wainwright swallowed, offering Liza a faint smile. "Are you ready?"

"Always trying to reassure me," she scoffed. "Set us down *faster*, Petya."

"It's difficult to settle us without toppling over," he said. "If I overbalance, God only knows what the dynamite will do—"

"As fast as you safely can, then." The long, sledge-like runners of the sky-boat settled on the snow-dusted earth of the riverbank, and at once Liza took to her feet and began to haul the crates free. *Careful, careful*, she thought she heard Petya saying, but his spinning blades made it impossible to tell whether she was hearing him or only anticipating what he'd say. *Careful, or we'll be blown to pieces—*

"There," huffed Wainwright, setting down the last of the dynamite. He caught her hand and squeezed it. "Go," he said, eyes lit with that madness that she remembered from their fight in the courtyard. When he grinned at her, she grinned back, and for the space of a heartbeat she felt that they understood one another completely.

As she sprinted for the sky-boat, the world seemed to snap into focus around her. Wainwright had not killed her father on that night, and so he didn't deserve to die. She had believed in his guilt so firmly, so irrationally, because it allowed her to ignore the simple truth of what had happened on that cold night at the tavern. Once she accepted this, her choices became very simple.

She remembered the tunnels beneath Yureyevsk, and she knew what she had to do.

Liza shut the hatch behind her, sliding easily into the gunner's chair. "Make us fly again," she told Petya, smiling until her teeth ached. "I want to show the dragons what *I* can do in the air."

They rose slow and ponderous, swaying to one side or the other as Petya brought the wings into line with one another. All around the gunner's chair, the magazines slid and clattered against the walls. Sighting along the barrel of her gun, Liza caught a glimpse of Wainwright's faded red pelisse vanishing between the glass buildings. Then Petya brought them soaring over the station houses, prow pointed up, and Liza saw for the first time the dragons that had made Aysel sign *Distress*.

Two of them came tearing out of the high blue sky, their mouths open like the mouths of panting dogs and their eyes glinting diamond-bright in the cold sunlight. Just as Liza brought her gun to bear, though, they banked hard and began to climb, rising until she couldn't angle her gun enough to catch them. "Take us *up!*" she cried. "Take us up; I can't shoot the damn things from here!"

"I'm *trying!*" Five years ago, Petya had cranked her gun for her, clinging to the loader's handles and trying not to go spinning off the tower. Now, Liza clung to her gun as Petya brought them around again. In the uncontrolled terror of the spin, she squeezed off a burst of gunfire that struck nothing but empty air—and there, suddenly, was Aysel, screaming something incoherent as she dove beneath the whirring blades of the machine.

"Bring us *up!* Bring us—" but then a silver-grey dragon

was staring down the barrel of her gun from thirty sazhen away, and she fired before she had a chance to second-guess the shot. The shot caught the grey dragon through the eye, tearing out the back of its skull and making it seize and curl up in mid-air. *Distress*, that gesture said, and now Liza knew why.

The corpse seemed to hang suspended a moment, then fell to earth like a mountain collapsing.

Her breath clouded the air before her, and she scanned the narrow aperture for any sign of scale or flashing eye. She could hear the dragons screaming, but whether they were screaming at each other or screaming for her, she couldn't guess. *When this is over*, she vowed to herself, *I'll get Petya to make this thing wider. I can't see through a window this small.*

"There, Liza!" Swinging about, Petya brought her into line with a vast black dragon, its taloned legs locked on Aysel's back and its teeth in her neck. With each kick and each wrench of its powerful neck, it sent a shower of copper scales and deep red blood spiraling to the ground below.

Liza's hand stilled on the trigger. It would be so easy to let the dragons destroy each other—so easy to abandon Aysel to her brethren, and damn the consequences if she failed. In the tight space of the gunner's alcove, with scarcely two arshin of space through which to view the world, it would be *easy* to draw in on herself and become omnipotent and cold.

She squeezed down on the trigger, clipping the black dragon on the ear and making it scream and loosen its hold. Aysel writhed and tore herself free, ascending as Liza emptied a magazine into the black dragon's neck. It went down in a long rain of fire.

For the first time in a minute, Liza drew in a breath through her nose. "Good steering," she said, with a smile that doubtless looked as faint as it felt. "For a loader."

"Good shooting," said Petya hoarsely. "I'll—"

The blast from the glass buildings cut him off. Liza felt the percussion of it in her teeth, felt it in the hollows beneath her cheeks and in the pit of her stomach. She felt it as though the whole world had been blown loose. The glass buildings crumpled, fire reflecting from every surface.

From the carnage strode Lieutenant Wainwright, a wisp of a man in a red pelisse.

"Take us *up*," said Liza. For a moment, Petya seemed not to hear or heed. "Take us up," she repeated, and this time, Petya shook himself and took the controls.

They rose slowly, and Aysel rose with them. She was bleeding. Her blood steamed in the cold air. For the first time, Liza wished she had the words to ask after a dragon's well-being.

"What about Wainwright?" Petya asked as they climbed. "What happened to him? Is he still down there? Did he explode himself?"

Far below, Wainwright tore his hat off and waved it at the departing sky-boat. Liza watched him as he grew small beneath them and then slipped from view. When she caught Petya's eye, she knew that he'd seen. "That's what happened. And if anyone asks, you saw it, too."

CHAPTER TWENTY-THREE

There was, thought Kesha, something of the condemned man's last meal in this morning's breakfast. The tables of the mess hall were laden with bowls of beet soup and fresh, black bread, butter in tubs and plates of bacon and sausage, and even platters of mutton for their Turkish guests. There were a few bottles of wine and brandy amid the coffee and the tea; the cook had brought out the last of the apples and laid them in bowls about the table.

Liza had said that the Turks would throw everything they had at the fortress today, and Liza was seldom wrong in matters of war. The old guards and the townsmen broke bread together with their former enemies, all of them well aware that this might be the last meal that they shared.

"You should say something," murmured Misha. "Look at them. They're all waiting for death. You should say something, or they'll forget to fight for their lives."

"What should I say? 'Once more unto the breach, dear friends, once more—'"

"We've closed up enough walls with the English dead," Misha replied, glancing over to the table where the last of the English soldiers huddled. They had borne the worst of the casualties, for they had done the fiercest fighting. Those who remained were hollow-looking, guns hanging at their backs while they dined.

"Then what? 'But Thou said to Thy disciples, "Whatsoever you shall ask in prayer believing, you shall receive," and "Whatsoever you shall ask in my name, that will I do," wherefore I dare to invoke Thee'—"

"Or perhaps only, 'Better to die a thousand times than pay court to Philip!' The right words come from and for their time. *Kairos*," said Misha, squeezing Kesha's hand. "Surely you're rhetorician enough to remember that."

"I was teaching a boy to read Aristotle when I left St. Petersburg," answered Kesha. Recognizing the gap between there and here made him feel heavy and distant. "It feels so long ago."

He rose then from his seat, crossing the floor as though wading through a shallow sea. The conversations around him echoed strangely in the windowless enclosure of the mess hall. They resonated in his ears like the buzz of innumerable insects, each voice redoubling the others.

Those voices quieted when he took his place at the head of the room. *They expect a speech*, he thought. *That's how it's done, isn't it? Men see death on the horizon, and they want a speech to teach them to die nobly. It doesn't save them from death, but it absolves them of their terror.*

The room was a sea of faces, Russian townsfolk with long beards and soft brown coats sitting alongside neatly kept Turks still in their uniforms. When he looked to the English, their faces ran together over the searing red of their jackets. "We came to this place, by accident or by design," he began, and even those closest to him leaned in to hear him.

Kesha swallowed and raised his voice. "We came to this place," he said, loudly enough that he could feel his throat straining, "by accident or by design, with the intention of passing on. We did not come to give our lives—"

The men at the nearest table shifted uneasily. Kesha swallowed again and licked his lips. He was no Demosthenes, to lay out for them why they should go to war.

"We didn't come to give our lives, but when the enemy comes, we'll be ready." He had no idea what readiness entailed; he knew only that he would soon be seated in the gunner's chair, watching the wave of dragons and angels break over him and hoping to bring down enough of them that he'd have some hope of surviving.

At the base of his skull, in the small bones of his fingers, he felt a twitching urge to flee. Even if he could have permitted himself to run, though, there was no place to go.

He had been standing before the assembled throng in silence for several long seconds. Their stares were politely incurious. He had spoken, and failed to move them, and now they wished only to see him sit again and stop making a fool of himself.

"When the Turks come, *we will be ready*," came a voice from the back of the room, and every head turned at the sound of it. The man spoke Russian with scarcely a trace of an accent, although he wore a Turkish officer's uniform, and his sonorous statesman's voice carried easily to every corner of the hall.

From across the room, Kesha met Orazbek's eyes, and wondered if at last he had found that impossible thing that would show the hand of Allah guiding him.

"I am Orazbek Musa, and yesterday, you would have called me an enemy. Perhaps today, in your hearts, many of you still call me an enemy, although you break bread with me and help me to honor my dead. I say to you that when the Turks come, we will be ready. From the air, all men look small, and all men look the same. From the air, I couldn't tell my own brother from one of the Tarasovs. When my comrades come, they will not distinguish between us. They'll destroy Russian and Turk, Englishman and Kazakh, dragon and Tatar alike."

Kesha sank into a chair as Orazbek spoke. In some dim and distant part of him, he recognized that it was his father's chair. His sister's chair.

"When the Turks come, we will be ready—because when they come, we will need each other to survive. I never expected that I would survive, when my vessel fell to earth. If the fall didn't kill me, I thought, the Russians would, and I pledged to sell my life dearly. Imagine my surprise, when Innokentiy Vladimirovich Tarasov himself came to my side and asked if I could walk! Imagine my surprise, when his own brother and sister saved my life a second time! Even the Englishmen, whom every Turkish citizen learns to hate as he reads his morning paper, have helped to bandage my soldiers and to bury my dead! Therefore, when Tarasov says that when the enemy comes, we will be ready, I believe him—but to this I add, *and we ourselves will not be enemies.* Whatever harms they can do to us, in this little fortress and this little town, we are ready to take care and to take charge of each other. We will survive so that we can remember this day, so that one day our grandchildren will tell stories of where the peace began. So long as *we* are not enemies, we will be ready to face all the world."

At that last declaration, the Turks rose as one to applaud. The Russians took next to their feet, striving to outdo their messmates for sheer volume. The English, many of whom knew only Russian enough to recognize *Englishmen* in the speech, rose last of all, but there was something achingly hopeful in their faces. They knew, without having to be told, that they had been included and found worthy.

Something swelled and burst in Kesha's heart at the sight of his countrymen applauding a Turk as a comrade. *I couldn't move them,* he thought, *but if I could help this to happen, if I could bring these people into one place, then my life has been worthwhile.*

Over that vast and resonant applause, though, came the ring of the warning bell, and the men left off their cheering and fled the room to take their stations. For a moment—a long moment; a moment so long that it might have been an age—Kesha caught the eye of a woman with mouse-blonde hair and a long rifle clutched to her breast. *Galya*, he thought. *Galina Ivanovna.*

Her knuckles closed whitely over the barrel of the gun, and then she, too, ran to her position.

Kesha fled to the western tower, where the gunner's chair was waiting for him.

CHAPTER TWENTY-FOUR

"Do you think he'll be all right?" Petya asked, as the sky-boat sailed north on a wind of its own making. His face was very white—whiter than Liza might have expected, even after the shock of the blast. Earlier, he had been sweating despite the cold; now, his skin was dry as chalk. "I know you were close to him. I...I wouldn't have been able to kill him, either, in your place."

"It wasn't a matter of being *able* to kill him. He didn't deserve to die." She looked away, across the snow-capped hills that bordered the Volga. Wainwright might yet manage to cross them, if his luck turned.

"Do you believe he was guilty?" Petya asked.

"No, I don't," she answered, and hugged her good knee to her chest.

Together, they watched the wind send the snow dancing into whorls, the ice on the Volga flowing and cracking. In the long silence, Liza listened to Petya's breath coming shallow and quick, and she realized that she hadn't heard him take a deep breath since Yureyevsk. "You don't sound well."

"I'm not," he admitted.

She remembered yesterday in the courtroom with sudden clarity. *That's terrible news*, Petya had said when

Nastya told him that the druggist's shop had been hit, and she'd never thought to ask *why* he'd sounded so upset. "How long haven't you been feeling well?"

He glanced down at his hands. "Three days? But it was only bad these last two."

"Three days? Name of God, Petya!"

"Yelling at the problem won't help—"

"Neither has ignoring it. God! There must be someone in town who knows a little medicine. Some Turk, some dragon, *someone*." Perhaps old Olya knew some ancient remedy that would help him, but she wouldn't bet his life on it. Liza realized, with a sick feeling, that her brother looked nearer to death than life.

She drew in a deep breath and shook herself. "We'll get to the keep, and we'll find someone who can help you. You'll be all right, Petya. You'll be all right." With that, Liza rose from the gunner's chair and began shoveling coal from the scuttle into the boiler, arms working like pistons. It might not have helped to speed them on, but at least it felt like *doing* something rather than sitting idle. At least the scrape of shovel on coal helped to drown out the part of her that wanted to shriek, *I should have seen it.*

When she looked back, Petya's hands had fallen from the controls.

In a moment she was at his side, shaking his shoulders and lightly slapping his cheeks. His skin was fever-hot and slack under her fingers. "Petya," she said. "Petya, listen to me." He trembled, and Liza caught his hands. They clutched at hers, closing on her palms until blood and pus leaked from the wrist of his glove. When she wrenched the glove free, she saw a ragged slice across his palm, the edges livid with infection and black tracks marking the veins.

"No," she said. "No, Petya, I'll take us to the ground. Please, just tell me what to do, and I'll put us down." He slumped in her hands, though, and God damn it all, she knew *nothing* about how to care for him. She eased him out of the chair and laid him on his side as though he were drunk.

Someone had to take them to the ground, or they would crash. They would crash like the angels crashed, spewing fire and machinery—someone had to take them to the ground, and there was no one else but Liza to do it.

She took the controls in her hands, the way she had seen Petya do less than an hour ago. Her hands were shaking. The machine was shaking, and she had no idea how to make the thing obey her. For all her life, she had let herself be steered. She had been raised to know nothing of helms.

"I need you, Petya," she whispered. "Tell me how to get us to the ground."

His eyes flickered open at his name. Although his chest scarcely rose or fell, still there was accession in that look. With one failing hand, he reached forward—and with her own left hand, she eased a lever to the fore.

The propellers slowed, and as they slowed, the sky-boat began to fall.

With her left hand still on the lever, her eyes on the river's sinuous curves, she reached for her brother's hand and took it.

They ploughed into the frozen earth on the eastern bank, the impact dashing Liza against the panels at the front. They were upright, though, mercifully upright, and the boiler hadn't spilled. She shook herself and began to crank open the hatch. With both hands, she pulled Petya down the stairs and out into the open air.

He had stopped breathing by then, but still she massaged at his throat and his cheeks as though it might help. She tore open his sleeve and saw the black veins creeping from wrist to elbow, indelible as a tattoo. "You fool," she cried. "You fool, you *fool*, why didn't you tell me—"

Because you told him he was a child for wanting to build you a sky-boat, she realized as Aysel alighted behind her. *Because he had no time for anything but making you proud.*

She turned to Aysel, who pressed her hot, scaly chin against Liza's hair as though that solved a single damn thing. "I don't know how to fly," she said, throat tightening. "I don't know how to speak Latin—why in God's name am *I* the one who's left—"

Aysel said something that Liza couldn't understand, but it was *something*, and it sounded kind.

"Take my brother home," said Liza. Her voice shook. "Take him home. I'll make my own way."

She had no right to ask this boon. She had murdered Aysel's people by the dozen, and she had gloried in their murder. She had made a life of murdering them. "Take my brother home," she said. With one hand, she indicated Petya—whether he was alive or dead, she was too distraught to say—and with the other, she pointed north.

"Take my brother home," she said. She pressed one hand to her chest, and with the other hand, she indicated the sky-boat. "I'll figure this out."

Aysel padded over the earth, her belly trailing heat as she went. In her fragile hands, she caught up Petya and cradled him to her chest.

The dragon rose, bearing Liza's brother away. She watched until they became a dark speck against the perfectly blue sky.

When they had gone, she returned to the sky-boat. She climbed up the stair and slid into the conductor's seat, and there she wept with her face cradled in her hands. For long minutes, she could do nothing but let the sobs wrack her.

Then, her weeping over, Liza scrubbed a hand over her eyes and reached for the levers once more.

Her brother was gone, and she remained. She had to teach herself to steer.

CHAPTER TWENTY-FIVE

By the time Aysel returned, the fortress had been reduced to two standing towers, each one buttressing the other over the gate between. Kesha prised one hand free from the attitude rotor and hailed her. His arm felt leaden, his shoulders aching with the strain of holding his position.

He didn't realize until she drew nearer that she held something against her chest, in those delicate arms that seemed too small for her massive frame. The thing she held was smaller, and it hung from her like a broken doll. Until she was almost upon him, wheezing and blowing steam in her descent, Kesha could not force himself to identify that limp thing as his brother.

For only a second—an infinite second, a second that threatened to become the remainder of his life—he considered flinging himself from the tower in his grief. When that second ended, though, Kesha crawled carefully down from the topmost platform of the tower and into the ladder well. He paced through the halls of the keep as though he were haunting them. The ceiling had been blown out in places, shattered by bombardments that had pierced the stone and steel, and at times he found himself blinking at sudden streams of sunlight or reeling from twisted pipes. Every hallway was strewn with broken stones.

The library had been demolished. So had his mother's rooms. From his tower, he had peered through the cracked earth of the courtyard and seen her next-best gown lying out over her bed, coated with a fine layer of dust.

The servants' entrance had been blown in. There had been a new handle on it, when he'd arrived. Now, only a few fragments of timber clung to the hinges. He took the door to the courtyard instead, which had survived mercifully intact.

Petya lay upon the trampled earth, his lips blue-tinged. "What happened to him?" asked Kesha softly. He knelt at his brother's side, registering as he did the condition of Petya's clothes, the condition of his skin. No bloodstains, and no shattered bones. One glove missing; an older cut across his palm. His veins tracking dark from wrist to elbow. "What happened?"

"I do not know," said Aysel wearily. "I am half-burst with pain. I cannot fly. Give me some food and a place to lay down my head. When I have rested, I will return for your sister." She permitted Kesha to scratch briefly along her brow-ridge, but then tossed her head after a moment and drew clear of his searching hand. "Now, let me rest and eat, or I will expire."

She crawled away on her stomach, like a snake. No doubt the other dragons would take her in at their little camp by the ruins of the station.

Kesha knew that he should go back to the tower in case the Turks returned, but with Petya's staring eyes upon him, he could not bring himself to care. Left alone with his brother's body, Kesha could do little but lift it into his arms and carry it through the gates. His chest was still warm where it had lain pressed against Aysel's, but his face and hands had hung free and cold.

Petya would never again steal the blankets and complain at Kesha's cold feet in the shared darkness. He would never swaddle himself again like an infant just-born. It was now Kesha's task to wrap him one last time in a soft sheet, to kiss his cold cheek once more and bid him sleep well.

Parts of the town still stood. The church had been left untouched, and the armory and the tavern seemed mostly intact. People would be gathering there, now that the bells had gone quiet. There would be food and warmth for all there, and new-made soldiers sharing drinks to toast their survival.

Kesha wanted neither food nor warmth. He wanted peace, and so he turned his steps toward the churchyard.

The copper-sheathed onion domes rose over the neat rows of gravestones, only some of which had been shattered by the bombardment. The English had made a last stand there, firing from the shelter of the headstones, and he could still see their bootprints impressed upon the gathered snow.

His father's grave lay somewhere amid those old, smooth stones, within the family plot where his own father and brothers had been put to rest. Since he had come back to Yureyevsk, Kesha hadn't yet brought himself to face their accusatory monuments. This time, too, he passed them by.

He pushed through the door of the church and laid his brother down before the ikonostasis, where the angels and the saints looked on grave-faced. As he had done since his boyhood, Kesha picked out the faces of their namesakes among the painted throng: Saint Elisabeth. Saint Innokentiy.

Saint Peter.

"Forgive me," he said. He could not touch his brother's face or close those staring eyes, and so he touched the saint's face instead. The paint was achingly bright, ochre and gold leaf touched with Prussian blue. "Forgive me. I've failed them all."

No one gainsaid him, and no one absolved him. He curled up on the floor beside Petya's body and drew his coat over them both, and there he lay in silence until the world went blank.

Kesha woke to the sound of the door closing, and he opened his eyes on faint lantern-light. A cane fell and fell again on the wooden floor. "Misha said I'd find you here," said Liza, who set the lantern down in the aisle and came to sit at Kesha's side. She looked as worn as he felt, eyes bright within deeply shadowed circles, and she was wearing the same clothes she'd worn the day before.

"Did Aysel bring you back?"

She shook her head. "I couldn't leave the sky-boat where the Turks could find it. I figured out enough to bring it back. Petya would have wanted me to bring it back."

Liza bent to close their brother's eyes.

"What now?" asked Kesha. He gathered his coat around himself and sat upright. He couldn't bring himself to look at his brother's body. "What's left?"

"Now, we rebuild. The machinists have been sealing up the pipes in the keep, and the sappers are reinforcing the ceilings. The survivors are gathering in the machinists' shop, in the tavern, in the tunnel beneath the town—"

"What tunnel?"

"I asked the same thing." Liza's face grew hard—or perhaps it had been hard from the beginning. "So much for that. We'll worry about it in the morning. I've been sent to be sure that you don't freeze to death on the church floor." She offered her hand, and he took it.

"How did he die?" asked Kesha, letting Liza pull him to his feet. He fastened his coat at the front and picked up the lantern, holding it aloft to light their way.

She didn't answer at first. She only leaned on her cane, with a furrow between her brows that might have been pain or worry. "Infection," she said, when the two of them had stood poised to go for some time. "I think he cut open his hand while he was working, and that was that."

And that was that. When Kesha turned to trudge to the keep, Liza took him by the elbow and guided him to the tavern instead. As he approached, he saw that part of one wall had been blown out. The Vasilevskayas had covered the gap with a quilt, which billowed and bellied like a sail in the faint breeze.

Nastya lay in a nest of blankets on the floor, with her sister Yulchik curled within the curve between her shoulder and her knee. She put her finger to her lips when Liza and Kesha came in, then gestured them to take a place by the stove. Sonya and Polinka were curled atop it like kittens, and the lantern caught golden on their hair.

Kesha and Liza settled in the gap between an English soldier and a Turkish airman, huddling against one another to preserve their warmth in the pervasive chill. "Your coat smells of him," said Liza, soft as a breath.

"I'm sorry," Kesha replied, but she only gave him a blade-thin smile and buried her cheek against the collar.

"Don't be."

This time, when sleep came to claim him, it drew down like a warm blanket. If he dreamed, he didn't remember his dreams.

"There are men coming from the west on horses and with carts. I do not think they are Turks. They wear the uniforms of men of Russia." Aysel gave a faint yawn that exposed her swollen palate and gums. She had been snapping at clean snow since she came to ground, but now Kesha recognized that it was to soothe the inflamed skin and not a gesture of dismay.

"How near are they?" he asked.

"Two *fersah*. What is *fersah* in Latin?" She twitched her tail in agitation. "*Fersah*. They will be here in less than two hours. They are very close, and their carts slow them very little. Why would men come from the west? Who are they?"

"I do not know," said Kesha. "We have lost the message lines. We have lost the trains. Perhaps they have come from the city to see what has become of us. From Nizhny."

"Such a lot of men, to see what has become of a little town!"

"God only knows what they think has happened to us, in the rest of the country. We will make ready to greet them."

"All of us?" The question was pointed. Kesha looked up at her, and she turned her head in reply, meeting his gaze with first one eye and then the other. "Will *all* of us greet them?"

"All of us," he said softly. She leaned in to press her jaw—her jaw which no doubt ached with new burns—against his hair, and he stroked her ruff in turn. He registered for the first time that her eyes were the same shade of brown as Petya's had been. "Yes. All of us who remain."

Over the remains of Petrovsky Station, the imperial flag flew high. There had been no proper flagpole on which to mount it, and so the machinists and the miners had bolted together a series of struts to raise the flag far above the ruins.

By now, Kesha could see the thick line of soldiers approaching along the tracks; the hills funneled them close together in the valleys. As Aysel had said, they wore what appeared to be Russian uniforms, but then so had Jaworski. It meant nothing that they dressed as Russian soldiers.

"If they're *not* Russians," said Lukin, "we've as good as damned ourselves with that flag."

"If they're not Russians, we're damned anyway," Liza replied tightly. She hadn't yet changed out of yesterday's clothes. Perhaps she had forgotten that she was still wearing them. She had slept in her false leg and awakened complaining of phantom pains. "The last damn thing I need is a Polish invasion."

When the wind unfurled the flag, though, emblazoning the gold and black against the thin, high clouds, the people of Yureyevsk could hear the little army put up a ragged cheer. "Thank God for small mercies," said Liza. She didn't have to say, *We couldn't have handled another thing gone wrong.*

The town assembled slowly at the old platform, housewives with their heads bound in scarves and farmers tired of chasing their runaway pigs over the hills. A small flock of sheep settled in the lee of the station's last standing wall, drifting there like snow. Three Englishmen passed a cigarette between them, smoking against the early-morning chill. Misha had taken up a seat on an old rain-barrel, gathering grammar-school children about him to conduct an impromptu lesson on Latin conjugation. Kesha could hear the rhythmic cadence of *amo, amas, amat* still droning in the background as the column drew up short at the platform.

At the head of the column rode a man whom Kesha recognized faintly from the papers—a tall man, fresh-faced and gaunt at once. Whether he had grown his beard to hide his youth or his gauntness, Kesha couldn't have said, but the soft under-hairs hadn't yet grown in to fill it out, and so it lay sparse and frazzled over his smooth cheeks. He sat very straight on his horse, with a posture particular to Prussian officers in well-boned supportive gear.

This was Grand Duke Sergei Alexandrovich, the second-youngest son of the Tsar. *The former Tsar*, thought Kesha. *His brother is the Tsar, now.* The man couldn't have been older than Petya, and in his eyes there was that same, flat hoping after hope.

"We've held the town, Your Grace," Kesha managed.

The horses were nickering nervously. They could smell that dragons had been here, Kesha imagined, and perhaps they even knew that the dragons remained. Sergei

Alexandrovich reined in his dancing horse, though, and answered, "So I see. What have you done with the rebels?"

Kesha and Liza exchanged a glance. Her eyes narrowed, and then she raised her chin to their guest. "You took the only rebel in Yureyevsk to be tried in Moscow. This wasn't the work of rebels. This was enemy action."

"The Turks crossed the border," put in Misha, "using flying machines. They destroyed the towns immediately to the east and west of us, and if we are to believe them, they've done substantially worse than that. We've lost the rails and the telegraph lines, and that makes ascertaining what's happened elsewhere rather difficult."

"'Rather difficult.'" The duke gave a faint, weary sigh. "Shall I tell you what's happened elsewhere? The fortress towns are blown to pieces. The larger towns are all but untouched. Nizhny put down a small radical uprising, and Ryazan has been utterly peaceful. The survivors of Kamensk could tell us nothing but that God had rained fire down on them. They spoke of avenging angels. As we've approached the town where my father was murdered, I've been half-inclined to think they were right."

"Allow me to introduce you to the angels," said Kesha, gesturing Orazbek and Chorbadzhi Selim Kaya to the fore. They came willingly enough, Kaya offering a salute and Orazbek making a formal bow.

A little light quickened and flared in Sergei Alexandrovich's eyes. Yesterday, it would have looked like the flicker of ambition. Today, though, Kesha could recognize a hunger for success—*any* success, no matter how trivial. Something to report back to his brother in St. Petersburg so that he might hear, *You've done well.* "You've taken prisoners. We'll take custody of them, of course."

"Not without your word they'll be well treated," said Liza. "These men are my prisoners, and I won't turn them over until you guarantee me their safety. If they help us to rebuild, I have half a mind to give each of them a verst of land and a few sheep to encourage them to stay."

Whatever Sergei Alexandrovich might have said at that, he was cut off by a cry of dismay from one of his men. Tracking the soldier's pointing finger, the soldiers caught the silhouettes of three dragons coming in to land at the station. Before Kesha could shout for them to halt, the duke raised his pistol and rapped off a single shot.

It glanced harmlessly off of the thick scales at one dragon's cheek, and she shook her head in irritation and ascended. The soldiers brought up their guns and unloaded them into her comrades' bellies, but they only shivered and screamed and then took to the sky. Kesha's Draconic was still weak, but he thought he knew obscenities when he heard them.

"Is this a trap, Tarasova?" asked Sergei Alexandrovich, his eyes still on the dragons departing. "Since my father's death, I have often wondered if your town was a trap—"

"I can tell you everything you want to know regarding your father's death," said Kesha, "if you'll only put down your weapons and have your men do the same."

"You're the other Tarasov, aren't you. Innokentiy Vladimirovich. The papers wanted you for a patricide."

Kesha felt the accusation in those words like a blow, but he didn't falter beneath it. "I am Tarasov."

"If we're to deal with one another, I insist that you exterminate the dragons. I can't trust that my men will be safe under constant assault from—"

"No."

Kesha turned to his sister, who folded her arms across her chest. She was haggard, her loose, dark hair wind-blown and her coat whipping back about her legs. In one hand, she held the dragon-headed cane that their grandfather had had made for her in Moscow. "No," she said again. "No, we're not going to exterminate the dragons. We're going to put them to *work*. The Turks may have their angels, but an angel is nothing to a dragon, and they *know* that." Beside her,

Lukin and Selim Kaya were nodding.

"In only a few days, the borders will open again," said Misha, whose glasses were frost-fogged. "But the Turks have destroyed our border guard, and I doubt we'll have it rebuilt in a few days. Your forefathers promised the dragons this land, and then reneged. Here is your chance to right that breach of contract and to defend your borders in one stroke."

"I'm being maneuvered," said Sergei Alexandrovich in an undertone. Admitting it was an admission of weakness, and before his men, he couldn't afford to be weak. "It's too convenient. The border guard has been all but destroyed, leaving no claimants to the land. It's a scheme."

"*I'm* a claimant to the land," said Liza. "This is the land of my father, the land of my grandfather. This is the land where I'll bury my brother, and I won't turn away anyone willing to help me defend it. Not Russian, Englishman, Turk, or dragon."

"You were wrong to trust, before. *I* paid the price for your misplaced trust." In his eyes, Kesha could see written an unspeakable grief. *He's another boy who's lost his father*, he thought. *He wants to break something so that he can heal himself. So long as there are traitors, so long as there's a revolution, he isn't powerless before death.*

"Let your men rest and eat," said Kesha. It wasn't in him to be gentle, but at least he could be kind to a fellow-sufferer. "You can choose to burn Yureyevsk to the ground, if it suits you. But choose it later, once we've given your men kasha and tea. I have something to show you."

Slowly, his eyes locked to Kesha's, Sergei Alexandrovich dismounted. He passed his reins to a soldier younger than he was and gestured his second down for a low conversation. "Very well," he said, when he had finished. He stood rapier-straight, bayonet-thin. His face betrayed nothing at all. "Show me what it is you want me to see, Innokentiy Vladimirovich Tarasov."

Kesha reached out and took the grand duke's arm, leading him away from the massed men.

It was time, at last, to visit his father's grave.

The earth was frost-hard, and it yielded only grudgingly between Kesha's shovel and the Grand Duke's. Beside them stood Vladimir Petrovich's headstone, every ridge of it capped with snow. Between them lay a shallow pit, not yet deep enough to bury a man.

"This isn't the first man I've buried," said Sergei Alexandrovich. He leaned on his shovel for a moment and wiped his jacket sleeve over his brow, for despite the biting wind, the exertion had made him sweat. The hair at his brow had frozen in spikes beneath his cap. "If you mean to show me death—"

"I don't mean to show you death," said Kesha. "You watched your father shot down in what ought to have been his moment of triumph. You probably touched his face, when he fell, and begged God to give him back."

"He didn't have a face after the gun caught him," Sergei Alexandrovich replied. His voice was level, empty of all but the mere fact of what he had seen and done. "But yes, I begged God to give him back. I still pray every day for it."

"Then his death taught you all that death can teach you."

Sergei Alexandrovich regarded him in silence for a moment. "Then you mean to show me how you bury your brother. What will that teach me?"

In the face of that flat regard, Kesha found he could not say what Petya's death had taught him. He wanted to speak of nothing but how Petya's kvass had tasted, and how he had built model trains of twisted wire, and how he had loved to visit museums crammed with the wealth of the ancients. It was a foolish thing to want to tell a prince, that Petya had liked lemon ice in summer and hot chocolate in winter. "The dragons have poems," said Kesha instead, "and I don't imagine you've ever read them, because their poetry was burned more than a century ago. Their poetry, and their philosophy, and their art—everything burned in the city squares of Moscow and St. Petersburg, and we burned our Bibles and our own poetry with them."

The Grand Duke said nothing, but his shovel carved ever deeper into the cold ground.

"I had a friend. If he'd survived, I think he would have been my teacher. His name was Boris Baivich, and he was one of the last dragons born in Russia—"

"A *dragon*," said Sergei Alexandrovich, frowning as though he meant to stop the conversation.

"Hear me out," said Kesha. "He was his people's poet, tasked with recalling their history and recording it for those who would come after him. He was..." Kesha groped for words. *Contemptuous*, he thought. *Kind, and brave. He knew that in joining me, he forfeited his safety, and I'll never know why he did it.* "He was my friend," said Kesha at last. He felt unbearably small.

His shovel struck the earth and turned over a few shards of dirt, and still the Grand Duke said nothing at all. Kesha was glad of it. He had half-expected a lordling used to heedless command, rather than the solemn shadow of a man who turned over the earth with him. When he had recovered himself, Kesha licked his dry lips and tasted blood where they had cracked open.

"Boris Baivich told me the stories of his people, and I was too blind to understand them. He told me of Xia, a great grey dragon who came west with her companions when their citadel fell. He told me of Vasil Liuvich, who was driven to the far north by his clan when he refused to join the Turks. He told me that there were no poems about how the Defection splintered his people, because if he spoke for a thousand years, I couldn't imagine what he'd seen. The history of the dragons is one of being driven from place to place, of being cast out by those upon whom they relied for love and sustenance…for every abandonment, they grieve, and their language makes every word sound like a cry of pain. A dragon once told me that her people had no culture but the sad songs of their ancestors, and what she meant was that theirs had become a culture of grief. The poetry of the dragons is a poetry of leavetaking and of being hunted. It chronicles how they destroy one another."

"As does our poetry," said Sergei Alexandrovich, but his brows drew close together. A shiver seemed to run through him, although that might only have been the chill wind. "If you were to read Dostoevsky—"

"Or *King Lear*?" asked Kesha. "We destroy one another; this I cannot and will not dispute. We destroy one another, and then we write tragedies and tell one another that it's our nature to destroy and then to avenge what we've destroyed. We and the dragons are much alike in this respect. If I were a nihilist, I could say that the destruction matters little…but I've always been a poor nihilist. It matters that my brother is dead, and it matters that your father is dead, and it matters most of all that Boris Baivich is dead, because he might have known what to say to a grief that could swallow me up."

"And without him to say it, what remains, beyond digging graves?" asked Sergei Alexandrovich. He surveyed their grave as though measuring it with his eyes, jaw flexing with suppressed emotion. "Tell me what remains, Tarasov. You've brought me here to sue for something. Sue for it."

In the snow on his father's headstone, Kesha sketched a stanza of poetry, looking up when he had finished it. "'Here rest we exiles of the world,'" he recited softly, "'By thunder driven o'er the hills. / We lie beneath the stranger stars / And know not how to plot a course.' In our language, the confusion is plain enough, but in his language, you can hear the fear as well. There's nothing so terrifying as a world that we can't navigate. We want to break it apart and put it together again in shapes that we understand."

"You'd plot me a course, then. That's what you brought me here to show me." His voice was as cold, as unyielding as the winter wind.

"I brought you here because the world we know has changed, and you and your brothers have the power to break it or to map it. So I want to show you how to tend the dead without being hunted by them," said Kesha. "To remind you that we are more than our grief. To tell you, at my brother's grave and my father's, that we have a capacity to love at least as powerful as our capacity to destroy—and to beg for your mercy for a few exiles under strange stars."

CHAPTER TWENTY-SIX

As the troops began to disperse, seeking hearths or making their own, Liza's eyes fixed on Konstantin Bogdanovich idling near a group of gossiping soldiers. He plied them with tobacco and a flask, encouraging them to share the news after their long and difficult march. As he did, Liza turned and crossed the street to the armory. It was still intact, or so it had looked from the air, and there was little enough comfort there to keep anyone from sheltering in it. All to the good.

With her last remaining hairpin, she picked the lock and swung inside, surveying the guns along the walls. *Short barrel*, she told herself. *Flared muzzle. Somewhere between a blunderbuss and a carbine.*

Her eyes lit on the musketoon displayed on the counter, and she plucked it up from the frame. She made a distracted sound, a *hmm* of confirmation, and then pushed aside the card table to get to the shelter underneath. The light at the mouth of the hatch kindled when she turned the knob, and at that she smiled.

Just as Petya had said: there was a grate in the bottom of the shelter like the one at the base of the telegraph master's. She climbed down the ladder with the musketoon thrust into her belt, shutting the hatch behind her.

The grate came free at a touch. She had to get down on her knees to crawl through it, and for that, she had to remove her false leg. She set it upon the spread of her coat and dragged it behind her as she climbed three-limbed into the tunnel beyond.

There was little enough light to be had there. A few people were using their shelters as living spaces while they rebuilt, but even these were mostly out and about in the daylight. *She wouldn't have had light, either, though, unless she carried a lantern.* Liza fixed the geography of the town in her mind as she fastened her leg anew and straightened in the tunnel.

She shuffled forward, her feet striking piles of blankets and clothes and what sounded like books in the darkness. The tunnel had become a living space for the displaced. It was warmer than the shelters, certainly. Warmer than the tents that had been rigged in the ruins of the keep.

Liza's searching hand found the expected passage, a narrow gap in the darkness with no end that she could feel, and she stooped to enter it. Her shoulders scraped either side. Only a very slim person could pass comfortably through the space.

The next grate was well-oiled. She pushed through without resistance and felt about for the light, but in the end, she settled for climbing the ladder in full darkness.

This aperture was larger than the one in the armory, and the hatch more difficult to lift clear. She slid out on her belly into the tavern and let the hatch clang shut behind her, then pushed herself onto her hands and her knee and rose from the floor.

By then, a few of the Russian soldiers had entered to share tea and a meal, and they studied her as though she were a madwoman whom they might have to restrain. "Keep your eyes on your drinks," she growled, then turned to where Nastya stood filling the samovar. As Nastya straightened, Liza forced her voice to an ill-practiced gentleness. "I need to speak to you in the back. Come with me."

Nastya frowned, and for a moment she looked ready to protest, but then Liza twitched her coat aside from the musketoon in her belt. "As you like," said Nastya, lips drawing tight as though she'd sucked on something sour.

They left Yulchik to serve the soldiers their tea and stepped into the back, where a cooking stove and oven shared space with a few barrels of brandy. "I'd wondered, while I was recovering," said Liza. "I'd wondered how it was, that I hadn't found a single gun that matched the wounds in my father. I'd wondered how it was that, when I and Jaworski went to the armory to confiscate the guns, there was no evidence that Kostya had done anything but host a card game that night. No tracks from the door but the ones we'd been led to expect. Identical stories from all of the men who played that night, and what's more, from their wives as well. It occurred to me that they might be concealing something, but with seven different stories, all of them agreeing, all of them equally confident…and you know Kostya can't keep a secret to save his soul. If the rest of them could lie that well, *Kostya* couldn't, no matter how he hated my father."

"Don't say this," said Nastya. Her face was hard as flint. "You don't want to say this."

"There was *one* way that it was possible, though. If, after Kostya and his friends had gone to bed, someone crept through the tunnels under the town and placed the gun in plain sight. And perhaps he would even have thought it was strange, that he should have one musketoon too many. Perhaps he would have wondered, for only a moment, whether this was the gun that all of the fuss was about." Liza pulled out the musketoon from her belt and offered it for Nastya's inspection, but when Nastya raised a hand to take it, Liza withdrew it again. "This was the gun, wasn't it? If I loaded it with shot and fired it, I'd recognize the report—"

"What do you want me to *say?*" snapped Nastya. "With

your long stories and your possibilities—what do that you want to hear from me? Say it and be done!"

"We arrested a man who had dedicated himself to keeping our Tsar safe," Liza answered. She felt as though she were standing a handspan to one side of her body, listening as her voice grew tight. "We arrested him, and we tried him, and we *convicted* him, all because his *boots* were bloody. Because he couldn't explain why he hadn't seen the woman who'd killed my father."

"I killed him, then," she hissed. "I killed Vladimir Petrovich Tarasov, and I'm not sorry."

At that, Liza flowed back into her body as though she were filling a bowl with blood. She laughed, softly, not unkindly. "You didn't kill him," she said. "But I know who did, and so do you—and I want you to tell me *why*."

Nastya seemed to take the measure of Liza, with her loose hair and her officer's coat over rumpled clothes and a false leg. Like the soldiers had before her, she seemed on the verge of declaring Liza a madwoman and having done with her. "Why," she said finally. "Well. Here's why."

She leaned against the cooking stove, careful to keep her apron strings clear of the hot part. "When I was fifteen," said Nastya, "my father began to get sick. That was ten years ago. My mother was pregnant with Sonya and Polinka. My father had been taking jobs around town while my mother kept the tavern, and that was how he paid it off. The tavern, that is. Galya and I sold flowers in summer and served in the tavern in the winter, and Yulchik even did a turn in the mines. She was strong and small. They needed girls like her to pull carts through the smallest passages. She came back every day after dark, with dirt under her nails and bits of stone embedded under her skin, and she never had a bath that got her truly clean…we saved every kopeck we earned, and all of it went to paying off our lease."

Liza made an affirmative sound. She had been eighteen then, and her father had been trying to wed her to an

Abramov or the elder Kamensky. She had dined at their keeps, under the staring eyes of preserved dragons' heads, and she had longed to be their comrade rather than their bride. *They're all dead now*, she thought. *The Kamensky boys and the Abramovs and their sister. All gone.*

"Well." Nastya wrung her hands in her apron. "When he first began to get sick, he couldn't work the way he used to, and we began to miss payments. Your father was our leaseholder, and in those days he was *rich*. You remember it. You remember how your family used to ride around in your sledge, with bells on the horses and fine velvet caps on your heads—"

"I remember."

"Rich men are cruel," said Nastya, and in those four words were a decade of suppressed hatred. "I went to the fortress to ask that he forgive the missed payments, and he told me that there was no force on Earth that would make him forgive them. He told me that he was preparing to speak with the solicitor to see about seizing the tavern from us, and then he would turn us out into the streets." She sucked in a long breath through her teeth, then released it again. She glanced through the open door to the tavern's main room, and then she lowered her voice. "I offered him my body as recompense. He *haggled* with me, Liza. Do you have any idea what that kind of shame feels like? To offer a part of yourself that you've been taught to treasure, to sign it over like a deed of property, and to have a hateful old man tell you what that part is worth—"

"So that was what you meant." Liza had to sit, or she would be sick. She propped herself on a barrel of brandy and tugged her coat more tightly about herself. "When you told me how he'd promised you things, in exchange for your body…I was cruel. You would be right not to forgive me that."

"You were cruel," agreed Nastya. "It's done now. We have title to the tavern. We fought him in the solicitor's office to keep it, when we'd paid him every last ruble we owed and still he refused to give us the title. 'The price has changed,' he said. But by then, he didn't have the money to pay his lawyer, and I did. I made sure that I did. This much, I owe to your brother: he stole your father's lawyer away, and gave us our tavern. Not many thieves can say that."

"But it wasn't settled, or there wouldn't have been a murder."

"I'm coming to the murder." Slowly, carefully, Nastya undid her apron and draped it over her arm. "I taught my oldest sisters to shoot because I couldn't stand the thought that they'd fall prey to a man who only wanted to shame them. I used to take them out in the early morning to shoot bottles beyond the mines, after our mother died. We only had my grandfather's musketoon at first, but they learned to shoot well with it, and in time, I bought us a blunderbuss to keep under the counter. A gun beneath the counter and a gun in our rooms. That seemed sensible. It seemed *safe*."

"And what happened, on the night my father died?"

"He came down to the tavern after you had gone." Nastya's fingers twitched on the apron strings. "Very late. After most of the others had cleared out, and soon enough he'd cleared out the rest of them with his theatrics. He kept sighing that his son had finally come back to him, and begging me and Yulchik to tell him whether he should go up to speak with him." Her voice went high and mocking, a sneer pricking up the corner of her lips. "'Tell me, pretty Nastyusha, will he look me in the eye if I knock on his door with my hat in my hand? Will a son respect his father if he comes hat in hand? What then, Nastya?'"

Once, Liza would have snapped, *Don't mock him!* Today, she only nodded and let Nastya go on.

Nastya compressed her lips, breathing through her nose. "He finally decided that he was going home without seeing his son, and he told Yulchik to go upstairs and fetch our sister. 'Which sister?' she asked him. 'The pretty one,' he said. 'I want to talk to her. Only to talk to her.' *Only to talk to her!* What could we do if he kicked up a fuss? He was bigger than we were, and too drunk to see reason. Nothing less than a kitchen knife would have brought him around, if he turned violent."

Here, she looked to her musketoon in Liza's hands. Whether her expression was one of fondness or resignation, Liza couldn't have said. "Galya came down. She must have had the gun under her coat—I would have told her to carry it openly, if I'd seen it. A man respects a gun he can see. But she went out to the alley to speak with him. After that, I heard a shot, and she came running in with her coat open and the gun in her hand. 'I've hurt him,' she said. Her voice was so small. 'He tried to touch me, and I've hurt him.' I told her to hide under the floorboards, and if she heard anyone come in, she should go into the tunnels and hide there. I told her that I would keep her safe, and then I dried the mud she'd tracked in and pretended I'd seen nothing at all."

In the ensuing silence, the rattle of teacups on tables seemed particularly loud. Liza could hear her mother's Moscow accent, the voices of the soldiers, the flap of the quilt tacked over the hole in the wall. She could hear the beating of her own heart, and the tap of her thumb against the stock of the musketoon. "And you were willing to let another man die for that. A man who'd never wronged you," she whispered.

"I was protecting my sister," said Nastya. "What else could I have done?"

In that question, there lay the memory of Kesha and Petya curled up on the church floor under one coat. In that question was the scent of Petya's hair on Kesha's collar, and the way Petya had stretched one failing hand out to help Liza steer. "What else?" asked Liza wearily. "She was afraid. She was right to be afraid. I would have done the same, in your place."

"But you'll make someone atone for his death all the same."

Nastya pushed off from the stove and sat at Liza's side. She offered her hand—her work-rough hand, reddened from the washing—and threaded her fingers through Liza's. "Let me be the one to atone, then. I'll confess, and let them transport me for it."

"After all you've suffered—"

"It's my place to suffer for my sisters," said Nastya. "At least I won't leave them in poverty. That's something. I can make a new life for myself, even in a labor camp."

"Can there be labor camps anymore? It seems ridiculous for there to be labor camps, with so many towns in ruins."

"Then I'll make a new life for myself on the ruins of a town. Believe me, I *will* make a life."

Liza looked down at their linked hands. She remembered how Nastya had called her an object of faith and vowed, in that queer insulting way of hers, to protect her. When Liza spoke at last, it felt like an enchantment breaking. "My father's legacy isn't worth defending."

Nastya let her head fall to Liza's shoulder, and Liza pressed her lips to Nastya's brow. The two sat together in mutual quiet, watching through the door as Yulchik poured out tea and the soldiers toasted their ragged Mother Russia.

EPILOGUE

Easter, 1881

Kesha alighted from the train with his suitcase under one arm. In the end, there had been little that he cared to take with him. A few books, a draft of his thesis, two suits of clothes. A few of Petya's wire models, salvaged from the rafters of their shared room. Some mementos that his mother had pressed on him while he had stayed with her in Moscow, waiting for the connecting train: photographs from his childhood, the Tarasovs preserved for the historical record as stern children in wool and lace. A tin of jasmine tea. The memory of her hands clasping his at the station, and the warmth in her slender fingers.

He had burnt the letter notifying him of his failure to pass his thesis defense, and then he and Starikovich had shared a glass of cognac. "You wrote something *true*," he had said, rapping his cane once against the floorboards and downing the dregs of his drink. "And I don't care what those stuffed-shirts at the academy say, your sources were impeccable."

"They're not ready for philology and folklore in their theology," Kesha had replied. "It's just as well. I won't be able to write anything of merit until I can hear the stories in their original language."

On the morning of his departure, the papers had announced martial law in Poland, painting demonstrators as rioters and rebels to justify their summary execution. They had done the same for Jaworski when he'd reached St. Petersburg, and spoken not a word of the wrongs that had been done to him. In their latter pages, the papers had reported Turkish victories over the English in India. Somewhere to the east, he imagined, Söz was gathering stories in English and Hindi. He wondered whether he should wish her well.

The main street of Yureyevsk was crowded with men and women dressed for Pascha services. At the top of the hill, the two remaining gun turrets still stood, now buttressed on all sides. The gate between them led to nowhere.

"We haven't got the gate to work properly, since we lost Petya," said Liza, and he turned at the sound of her voice. She wore her hair up in a neat, practical bun, and she leaned with both hands on her dragon-headed cane. Her gloves were light summer gloves, her trousers finely cut without ostentation. She seemed to have been standing on the platform for some time, waiting for him to disembark. "I could see you looking," she said, when he tilted his head at her. "I couldn't bear to tear it down. He was obsessed with getting that gate to work."

"Engineers and their projects," said Kesha. He offered his free hand to Misha, who took it and descended the step onto the platform. "How is the first nest? I'd had a telegram from Aysel, of course, but…"

"Latin doesn't code well, I know. I've heard *every* complaint. She keeps harrying the telegraph master to use Morse code, but he won't have it. No one else in Russia uses Morse code, he says. Not even the Turks use it."

"The English use it," Misha put in, which only earned him a withering look.

"The English have no right to be teaching her Morse code, when she doesn't speak good Russian yet," said Liza. "They have no priorities at all. It's not my business to watch them; that's why I need a second in command—"

"Well, you have one now," said Kesha.

"And he's brought his lawyer, too. We're all of us damned." She hooked one arm over Kesha's elbow, forcing him to shift the suitcase to his other arm. Misha, far from taking Kesha's part, only laughed at his plight.

"I shall wait for my luggage," he said. "Go on, the both of you."

"Misha has contrived to bring an entire library to Yureyevsk," said Kesha, when Liza gave him a questioning look. "He insists that he'll open a proper school here, but I know that he only wants to keep his finger upon the pulse of international relations."

"I don't blame him."

The quiet that came after made Kesha swallow hard. For a moment, he had dared to think that things would be easy between them, as they had been easy in their youth. Now, though, he recognized that these silences would always arise, without Petya to fill them and to smooth them over. "I'm not ready for this work," he said softly, and she turned to offer him her full attention. "I've thought of myself as a scholar for so many years.... I don't remember what it is to be second in command. I was never born to be your right-hand man, the way Petya was."

"That's all right," said Liza. There was a new gentleness in her eyes when Kesha brought himself to meet them. Something had changed in her when she'd gone south with Petya and Wainwright and returned alone, and now he could feel her straining to shield him from that yawning gulf of grief within her. "I could use a right-hand man, I won't deny it. But you know that I'm left-handed." This time, when he laughed, the laugh rocked him until the deep places in his chest ached. When he met his sister's eyes again, his own were wet.

"And what then?" asked Liza. In her voice was a wry and hollow echo of their father, but no more. Soon, perhaps, he would stop hearing echoes everywhere. "What *now*?"

"Now we go on," Kesha answered. "What else can be done? We go on, together."

He folded his palm against hers, and she gripped it as though her fingers were a vise. Together, they looked to the west, both shivering slightly in coats too thin for the brisk breeze. On the horizon, they could see the faint figures of dragons in flight.

THE END

ACKNOWLEDGEMENTS

In many ways, Drakon's path to publication resembled the treacherous West Virginia roads that I traveled in my youth: steep and crooked, kinked with switchbacks and hairpin turns. I could not have made it to the end of this journey without the help of my friends and colleagues, who encouraged me when the way ahead seemed impassable.

As I wrote and edited this book, I went through several major life changes: three moves, four different jobs, and a battle with depression that's left lingering scars on my psyche. Before anyone else, I have to thank Kate Sullivan and Athena Andreadis of Candlemark & Gleam, whose patience, compassion, and practicality helped guide Drakon through that rough terrain.

For their help with military history research and building a plausible alternate history, I thank Christopher Pipinou and Amber Baughman. Pip's tireless zeal for naval vessels and early military aircraft helped inspire me to research the fascinating history of anti-aircraft guns and the Turkish air force (both well worth a look even in our timeline). Amber raised excellent tactical questions about the practicalities of fighting against a draconic air corps, some of which the Russians manage to solve and some of which remain urgent and unsolved at the conclusion of the novel. Pip and Amber were also good enough to point out flaws in my military tactics, inconsistencies in my technology, and exploitable loopholes in my treaty law. Any errors that remain are my own.

For his help in working out the biology of dragons, I thank my father. He patiently listened as I chatted for hours about monotremes and catalysts, and he used his background in animal anatomy and physiology to help me think through the logic of these wondrous bodies. With my father's help, my dragons were able to take to the air. (Again, any errors are my own.)

I would never have finished this book without the thoughtful critiques and commentary of my writing circle on LiveJournal. They offered encouragement when I was snagged, suggestions when a character acted illogically, and frank honesty when a scene didn't work for them. They also told me when a moment or a line had moved them, and more than anything else, the desire to move them again sustained me. I will never forget the kindness and honesty of the people who took the time to read and respond to a very early draft. Thank you all.

Finally, I owe an incalculable debt of gratitude to my family and my local friends, who helped steer me through the hard days. Writing a book is difficult work, but sometimes, even the daily minutiae of being a person is difficult work. My thanks to them for offering a table and dice, a pot of soup, a coffee, or a listening ear when I needed them most.

ABOUT THE AUTHOR

A.M. Tuomala lives in western New York, somewhere between Niagara Gorge and the Eternal Flame. In addition to hiking those sublime landscapes, Tuomala enjoys researching Gothic fiction, collecting rocks, and building new worlds. *Drakon* is Tuomala's second book.

You can follow the author online at:
www.amtuomala.com
Twitter: @amtuomala

The ADVENTURE CONTINUES ONLINE

VISIT THE CANDLEMARK & GLEAM WEBSITE TO

Find out about new releases

Read free sample chapters

Catch up on the latest news and author events

Buy books! All purchases on the Candlemark & Gleam site are DRM-free and paperbacks come with a free digital version!

Meet flying monkey-creatures from beyond the stars!*

WWW.CANDLEMARKANDGLEAM.COM

*Space monkeys may not be available in your area. Some restrictions may apply. This offer is only available for a limited time and is in fact a complete lie.